EMPIRE
HIGH
Homecoming

IVY SMOAK

φ

To Ryan.
These books almost broke me.
Thank you for holding me while I cried.

CHAPTER 1

Saturday

Matt

I took a deep breath as I put my foot down on the gas. I thought any second now I'd start panicking. But I felt eerily calm with my decision.

There was a reason I'd proposed to Brooklyn when we were so young. Because I'd always known what I wanted.

A wife.

Children.

A family.

A home.

I'd wanted all of it with Brooklyn. When I first saw her step into Empire High, it was like I could see it. There was a piece of her missing. And I wanted to fill it. I wanted to be enough for her.

I'd pictured saying "I do" in front of all our friends. I'd pictured a house full of kids. I'd pictured painting our kitchen yellow to remind her of her mother. And drinking hot chocolate on snow days. I'd desperately wanted all of it.

But when she passed away, I told myself I couldn't have those things. I'd promised her forever.

And I'd been drowning ever since.

I'd let myself miss Brooklyn so much that I'd forgotten I needed to live my life. But I knew what I wanted now. I knew what I needed. And I didn't think

Brooklyn would be upset about it. If anything, she'd be furious that I'd been taking time on this earth for granted. Because if there was one thing we both knew, it was that you were never promised another day.

Mourning her for the past 16 years was torture. I was destructive in everything I did. And if I kept going the way I was…my time would be cut short.

I took another deep breath as I turned down the street toward Kennedy's apartment. I was still waiting for the panic to set in.

But…it didn't. This was right. I was allowed to move on. I had to move on.

I pulled into an empty spot outside Kennedy's apartment, cut the engine, and took a few more deep breaths. Kennedy was Brooklyn's best friend. My head told me this was all wrong. But my heart? I was falling in love with her.

I reached into my pocket and pulled out Brooklyn's engagement ring. At the time I'd given it to her, it had meant everything to me. Passing on a family heirloom to her in hopes of creating our own family.

I'd dug it up from the spot by her grave because I thought it would feel like an end. Like giving me my heart back. And it did.

The mud and grime caked on it didn't take away from its beauty. I'd get it cleaned later this week. And once it was all clean…I'd put it in the room with all the paintings of Brooklyn. Or I'd pack it all up in storage. Tucked away somewhere I couldn't look. To give me the space I needed to find myself again. This ring would always belong to her. But I needed my heart back.

HOMECOMING

I opened up the glove compartment and placed the ring inside of it. I closed it and took another deep breath.

I'd always love Brooklyn. She'd always have a piece of my heart. But she couldn't have the whole thing anymore. I still wanted the same things I'd always wanted. And I couldn't have them with her.

And honestly, the way I was feeling had nothing to do with her. Because I was lying to myself. I wasn't just falling for Kennedy. I'd already fallen. I'd already made my decision. I was ready to fucking live my life.

I was going to propose to Kennedy. Tonight. I had no ring. Just a bag of to-go fries and some tulips. And I knew that Kennedy wanted to go slow. But I could no longer afford to do things slowly. I'd wasted too much time. And for the first time in 16 years, I felt free. I was happy. I was excited about my future instead of drowning in my past. And it was all because of her.

I'd propose tonight. She wouldn't care that I didn't have a ring. Kennedy never cared about stuff like that. She understood that actions were more important than material things. But I'd still find her the perfect ring tomorrow. Something that made me think of her instead of the past. Neither of us needed any more reminders of Brooklyn. We'd always love her. But it was too painful to be reminded of her every single day.

I took another deep breath, waiting for the guilt to seep in. But it didn't. I felt at peace. I picked up the fries and the tulips and climbed out of my car.

Sixteen years ago, Brooklyn had found her engagement ring. My proposal to her hadn't been grand. And this time I didn't even have a ring. You'd think I would have gotten better at this the second time around.

I hit the call button and waited. And waited. I hit it again and there was still no response. I balanced the flowers and bag in one hand and pulled out my phone. Kennedy knew I was coming. I'd just texted her about it when I left the graveyard. I pressed on her name on my phone to call her.

But it went straight to voicemail.

I took a step back on the sidewalk and looked up to the window of her apartment. It was pitch black. Had she fallen asleep? I tried calling her again, but it went straight to voicemail for a second time.

It had been thirty minutes tops since I'd texted her. She'd seemed excited for me to come over. I scrolled through our texts to see if I'd said anything stupid. Sure, that was probably one too many eggplant emojis. But I'd only been joking around. Kind of. Had that scared her off?

Fuck.

What was I doing?

She told me she wanted to take things slowly and I'd basically propositioned her for sex. And I was about to propose. I'd probably lost my mind. But it didn't feel like I had, and that was somehow even more worrisome.

I hit the call button again, but she still didn't buzz me up.

A chill ran down my spine and I turned around, but there was no one on the sidewalk behind me. I knew that Jefferson's mom wasn't a hitwoman now. And Mr. Pruitt said that he wasn't having me followed. No one was watching me. But...I still felt uneasy. I couldn't quite explain it. Like something about the fall air was off. Like something had suddenly shifted. And I had the strongest sense of déjà vu. Like I was here to see Brooklyn instead of Kennedy.

My phone buzzed and I quickly looked down. But it was just a text from Tanner asking me when I'd be home. I sighed and looked back up at Kennedy's window. I was here to see Kennedy. Not Brooklyn. And I wasn't against climbing up there. I'd gotten pretty good at it in my teens.

Before I could jump up to grab the bottom of the fire escape ladder, an old man walked out of the building. I ducked inside just as the door was closing. I took the steps two at a time. My heart was hammering against my chest when I reached her floor. But my excitement for the proposal was gone. I was worried something was wrong. Because even if Kennedy hadn't answered her phone, Mrs. Alcaraz surely would have answered the buzzer. It was almost 11 o'clock. They had to both be home. Just like I was supposed to be home by now, thanks to Tanner's stupid house guest rules.

I didn't even glance at Brooklyn's old apartment door. Something definitely felt off. And now my heart was beating even faster. I hurried over to the Alcaraz's and knocked.

No response.

I knocked louder.

No response.

"Kennedy!"

No response.

"Mrs. Alcaraz!" I yelled louder and pounded on the door with my fist.

"Shh," said Kennedy with a sniffle from behind the door.

Not just behind the door. But low. Like she was sitting on the floor. And judging from the sniffle she was definitely crying.

"Kennedy?" I said and pressed my hand against the wooden door.

"Please, lower your voice," she said with a sob.

She was definitely sitting on the ground by the door. I knelt down. "Kennedy, open the door," I said a little quieter.

"I made a mistake, Matt," she whispered through her sobs. "I knew I should have never kissed you. I don't know what I was thinking. I'm so sorry. I'm so so sorry."

Sorry? Why was she sorry about that? Kissing her was the best thing I'd done in years. "Kennedy, let me in."

"I...I can't. Please just go." Her voice shook with each word.

"I'm not going anywhere."

"I can't let you in."

"Okay. Then come out."

"No," she said through her sob. "You have to go." There was so much pain in her voice.

"Kennedy, I'm not going anywhere until I see you." I needed to pull her into my arms. I needed to tell her than no matter what was wrong, she had me now. We were an us. I wanted to take away her pain.

"Matt, please, I can't do this. Please just go."

"I don't know what's going on, but I know what'll make you feel better. I have fries."

There was a muffled sob. "You can leave those by the door."

"Kennedy, you're being ridiculous. Let me in right now, or…I'll knock down the door."

"No you won't."

"Yes I will. I'm dead serious." This door looked pretty flimsy, honestly. I made a mental note to get the Alcarazes a more secure door.

My threat was greeted by silence.

"Okay. I'm doing it," I said. I set down the fries and flowers and stood up.

But before I could ram my shoulder into the side of the door, Kennedy opened the door the tiniest crack and squeezed through. She gently closed it behind her. Her eyes were red and the tears weren't even dry on her cheeks. She looked like she might be sick. But I didn't even care if it was contagious. I needed her in my arms.

I pulled her close, but felt her hand against my chest, pushing me back.

"Kennedy…"

"Please don't touch me," she said through another sniffle.

I took a step back, even though it pained me. I'd always listen to her telling me no. I knew what she'd been through. And I wouldn't put her in that position again.

She folded her arms across her chest, but it wasn't in anger. It was more like she was hugging herself. Holding herself together. She was looking down at the ground, like she couldn't even look at me.

"Kennedy." What the hell was going on? What happened to the flirtatious texts? We were on the same page here. I knew that we were. What the hell had happened in the last half hour? "Kennedy?" I said a little softer.

"We're done, Matt," she said.

"What?"

She finally looked up at me. And her eyes didn't match her words. She looked like she wanted to be back in my arms. Like she wanted me to kiss away the tears on her cheeks.

"Baby…"

"Don't," she said more firmly. "I'm so sorry. About all of it. I wish I could just undo the last few days. I just want to undo them." The tears started streaming down her cheeks again.

"How can you say that?"

She just shook her head.

"Whatever you think is wrong with us…we can work it out."

"Matt, we were always meant to be friends. Nothing more."

Every word out of her mouth was a complete lie. I needed to pull her into my arms. I needed to show her that she was wrong. But she'd told me not to touch her. And I couldn't. I couldn't cross that line when she'd told me no.

I felt paralyzed. I needed to make her understand how wrong she was. So I said the first words that popped into my head: "I love you."

She shook her head. And her bottom lip trembled as she tried to hold it together.

"I'm in love with you," I said again.

"No. You're not."

"Yes I am."

"Matt," she said. "No. Take it back. Take it back," she sobbed.

I couldn't bear it. I knew she'd told me no. But she was breaking right in front of me. And I wanted her to know that I'd be there to catch her when she fell. I put my arms around her again.

For a second she tried to push me away, but then she melted into me. She sobbed into my shirt. Her back shook with her breaths and I just held her tighter.

She was crazy if she thought I'd ever walk away from her like this. She needed me. And God, I needed her too.

CHAPTER 2

Saturday

Brooklyn

Sixteen years ago, my father ruined my life. I never should have given him a chance to ruin it again.

And I definitely wasn't going to give him a third chance.

The gun started shaking in my hand when I heard footsteps on the other side of the door.

I knew I was doing the right thing.

My father was a monster.

And for half my life, he'd convinced me that I was too. That everyone was better off with me dead. It didn't matter whether it was true or not. What kind of father did that? What kind of father tore his daughter down instead of building her up? He'd known how broken I was after my fight with Matt. He'd known I was vulnerable. And he'd taken advantage of me. He'd never loved me.

He'd told my mother to get rid of me.

He'd stolen my kidney.

And I forgave him. I let it go. But I couldn't ever forgive him for what he'd done to Miller.

No.

Never.

Nunca.

My father was a monster. And he deserved to die. Miller deserved justice. Jacob deserved that for his father. I had to do this. For Jacob. For Miller. For myself.

I took a deep breath to steady my hand. And then I cocked the gun as the door slowly opened.

My father was standing there in some weird little nightcap and nightgown. I would have laughed if I wasn't so fucking angry with him. He'd just ruined my life for the second time. I'd been happy back in high school before he kidnapped me. And I'd been happy now in my life with Miller.

Why did he have to do this to me? Why was he always trying to break me? Why couldn't he just let me live my life? I clenched my jaw to try to stop the looming tears.

"Angel," he said with a sad smile.

My hand started shaking again. He looked ridiculous. And the sad smile on his face just made the whole thing even more ridiculous. Why was he sad? I was the one that was sad. He'd taken everything from me. For a second time. I was barely holding on.

"You're okay." He put his hand to his chest. "Thank goodness you're alright."

Thank goodness? I couldn't tell whether he seemed surprised or confused. But tears started forming in his eyes. And I had the oddest sense that he was…*relieved.* It wasn't the reaction I was expecting. He wasn't supposed to be relieved that I was okay. He'd been trying to kill me. He was probably just trying to throw me off because I had a gun pointed in his face.

I tried to steady my shaking hand. "Yeah, I'm okay. No thanks to you."

The sad smile turned into a frown. "What?"

God, I wanted to pull the trigger. There would be something really satisfying about seeing his blood splatter on the oriental rug behind him. I thought hitting a target in a shooting range felt good. This would be a million times better. My father deserved to die.

But...he wasn't supposed to be acting this way. He was supposed to be begging me for his life. Not dressed in a nightgown looking relieved to see me. He wasn't even reacting to the gun at all. Which just made me angrier. Did he not think I was going to pull the trigger? Because I was. I lifted the gun higher.

"You're not thinking clearly." Miller's words echoed around in my head. Clear as day. The memory of his voice a whisper in my ear. He'd told me that when I wanted to shoot the deer that was eating my Henry tomatoes. He knew I didn't really want to shoot an animal. But then he'd convinced me to learn how to use a gun just in case there was a real threat. My father wasn't an innocent animal. He was a real, living, breathing threat. And maybe if I'd come back sooner...maybe if I'd confronted him after all these years...none of this would have happened. Miller would still be alive. I'd still be dancing with him in our kitchen right now.

I couldn't stop my bottom lip from trembling. I couldn't afford to think like that. I'd lived a life full of regret and heartache until I met Miller. He'd healed me. He'd reminded me what living felt like. And he deserved so much more than the end he'd gotten. *I'm thinking clearly, Miller. I promise I've thought it through. I'm doing this for our family. I'm doing it for you.*

"Is my grandson alive?" my dad asked. He took a step forward like he wanted to hug me.

I immediately took a step back. Did he not see my gun? Did he not realize that I was about to blow his fucking head off?

"Did my grandson make it?"

I finally registered his words. And it felt like he'd slapped me. He knew he had a grandson. He knew it. I wasn't sure how he'd found out about Jacob. But he was definitely only pretending to care about Jacob's safety. If he cared about his grandson, he wouldn't have blown up my fucking car and tried to kill all of us. Jacob could have been in there. I could have lost him too. If Jacob had put on his shirt right away like I always nagged him to do...I could have lost him.

The gun shook in my hand again. I almost lost everything. Every single piece of me. Because of my father.

"Please tell me that my grandson made it," he said. "And did Miller?"

Like he didn't fucking know. "Don't say another word." He was just trying to throw me off. I wanted to tell my dad to get on his knees. To put his hands behind his head. And repent for his sins. To me. And my family. To Miller. But my damn hand wouldn't stop shaking. I couldn't shoot him like this. When he looked sad and ridiculous. And when his actions made a million questions run through my head. "Could you...change? Or put something over that?" It would be easier to kill him when he looked more composed. I'd been envisioning him how he used to be in my head. That's how I would get this done. One of his freshly pressed suits would be more fitting.

He looked down at his nightgown. "My goodness, yes, come in, come in." He pushed the door ajar and stepped to the side. "I can't believe I opened the door in just my nightshirt again. My robe is in my office." He started walking toward the closed doors, without a care in the world, not at all concerned by the gun pointed to the back of his head.

"Stop," I said. I wasn't going to let him go in there and grab his own gun. Or alert his staff with the press of a button. Wait, where was his staff? The foyer was empty. And everything was eerily silent. I looked up the stairs. I expected to feel something being back in this haunted apartment. But I just felt numb. Like I knew I'd be paralyzed if I let my past seep in. Because the last time I was in this foyer Matt had called me a liar.

Just the thought of Matt standing here made me feel claustrophobic. My chest started to feel like it was tightening. I shook away the thought of Matt. I was not going to have a panic attack right now. I needed to be in control. And I needed to get the hell out of this foyer. "I'll get your robe," I said.

"It's just on my chair in there."

Seriously, why wasn't he reacting to having a gun pointed in his face? The idea that he wasn't taking me seriously pissed me off. I opened up the office door. There was a robe draped over the back of his desk chair. I grabbed it and my hand froze.

There were pictures of me on his desk. And not just of me. Pictures of me with Miller out on the dock. Pictures of me with Jacob in the garden. Pictures of all three of us playing in the grass. How did my father get these?

They didn't look like they were far away. But they were all from the same angle of the back of our house. An angle that could easily be captured from across the lake with an expensive lens. Hidden in the trees. Where

HOMECOMING

I'd kept thinking I saw someone. I hadn't been imagining it. Someone had been watching us. My dad had been watching us. Or someone he'd hired. Had he known where I was the whole time? Plotting how to ruin my life again? For how long?

These pictures didn't look like they were taken for nefarious reasons though. They'd captured moments of joy from my life over the past several years. Tears ran down my cheeks as I stared at Miller smiling. I loved his smile. Especially when it was directed at me. I loved him so much. And I was never going to get to see him or his smile again. I was never going to hear his laugh. Or dance around the kitchen with him. I quickly wiped the tears off my cheeks.

God, I couldn't be weak right now. I had to hold it together for just a few more minutes. For Miller. And for Jacob. I was doing this for them. I clenched my jaw. I could do this. I knew I could.

But I froze again when my eyes landed on a picture of Miller and me in the backyard. I remembered that day. I'd just gotten back from a run and he'd finished building my planters. I was in his arms and he was twirling me around.

That was really early on. Years before Jacob was born. And it kind of answered my question of how long my father had been watching me. I was pretty sure it was the whole freaking time. Another picture caught my eye. Miller was holding baby Jacob in one arm and his other arm was slung around me out on the dock. Our feet were bare, dangling in the water. The picture embodied our life there.

I'd left everything behind after the explosion. All my pictures. Every single one except for the few on my phone. I needed this one. Miller's smiling face tucked against my chest would somehow help. Right? I was willing to try anything at this point. I pulled the picture out of the frame and tucked it into my coat. I would have taken all of them, but I heard a noise in the foyer.

I rushed out of my father's office. He was just standing there calmly, still not a care in the world about my gun.

Had he already alerted someone? Was that why he was so calm?

"Where's your phone?" I asked.

"On my bedside table."

I didn't know whether or not to believe him. But it didn't matter. This was all about to be over. "Put this on." I threw his robe at him.

He pulled it on, but it didn't help. If anything it made him look more ridiculous. The silk robe was shorter than his nightshirt. So it just looked like he was wearing a double-layered dress. And his stupid little hat made the whole thing more humorous. How was I supposed to shoot him when he looked like that?

I moved my gun to my left hand, hoping it would stop shaking.

I tried to focus on his face. There were only a few new lines around his eyes and mouth. He didn't deserve to look as good as he did. He was the one that should have died. Not my husband. I'd lost so many people. I wanted to make a trade. Hell could have my father. I just wanted Miller back. And my mom. And my uncle. I blinked fast so the tears wouldn't fall. "You've been watching me this whole time."

"Well, of course. I love you. I had to make sure you were safe."

"Safe?" Did he really think I was an idiot? That I was still that easy to manipulate? "You tried to kill me!"

"You think *I* tried to kill you?"

"The bomb was in my car."

He nodded. "Ah, that explains your theatrics," he said and waved at my gun, finally acknowledging it.

Theatrics? This wasn't theatrics. I was going to kill him. Was he really that confident that I wouldn't?

"Maybe we should retire into the sitting room so we can talk, princess."

Princess? Seriously, how many times did I have to tell him not to call me the same thing he called Isabella? I wasn't Isabella. I was nothing like her. *Screw him.* I didn't pull the trigger like I'd planned. But I did the next best thing. I punched him square in the nose.

I heard a cracking noise.

Fuck. Did I just break my hand? I shook it out, but my knuckles ached. No one told me how much punching someone was going to hurt me. But the look on my dad's face made the pain worth it.

"What on earth possessed you to do that?" my dad asked, grabbing at his nose. Blood spilled between his fingers. He pulled off his night cap and put it against the blood.

"I'm not your princess. And I don't need to talk." God, my hand hurt. I shook it out again.

"Well, now that we're done with whatever that was, we can have an actual discussion. First let's get some ice." He turned around and started walking toward the kitchen.

He left me standing in the foyer with a throbbing hand and a gun pointed to the back of his head. Seriously, why wasn't he scared of me? I was very scary right now. I could easily shoot him.

But I wasn't as good of a shot with my left hand. And he was pretty far away.

I tried to shake out my hand again. *Ow.* Honestly, some ice sounded nice. I followed him even though I knew nothing good would come from a conversation. He'd try to weasel his way back into my heart. He'd try to manipulate me. Control me. Just the way he always did.

But I was older now. It wasn't as easy to play games with my heart. My father was a monster. And nothing he could say would change my mind. I followed him through the dining room and into the kitchen. He pushed through another set of doors to the staff kitchen.

I'd never seen my father step foot in the staff kitchen.

He opened up the freezer and pulled out two ice packs. Then he went to a drawer and found a couple of tea towels to wrap them in. "Here you are."

I took the ice pack from him. The coolness instantly made my hand feel better. "Where is all your staff?"

"Oh, they're in the Hamptons with Patricia."

Why was his wife in the Hamptons? "Isn't it a little late in the season?" I was pretty sure the Hamptons were a rich people summer thing. And it was well into fall. The crisp air outside made me feel claustrophobic. Threatening me with memories of Matt. I needed to get this over with and get as far away from this city as possible.

"She lives there full-time. And I live here full-time. I only ever really needed bodyguards anyway."

"You're divorced?" I wasn't sure why I was asking him these questions. None of them mattered.

"Isabella was the only thing we had in common. Well, that and the business of course. So when Isabella passed…we drifted apart even more. Oh, you did know that your sister passed, yes? I'm not sure what you stayed up to date on."

"Half-sister." I thought that was a very important distinction to make.

"Right. Your half-sister has passed. Were you aware?"

I'd tried my best not to stay up to date on any of it. My father's words had twisted around my heart, making me believe everyone was better off without me. And I did believe it. I had to. But there were creeping thoughts. Like how happy could James be if he'd married Isabella? He hated her. We all hated her. I pushed the thought aside. "Yes, I knew she was dead."

"I thought you might come home if you'd known."

"I had my own life." What on earth would make him possibly think I'd come back here? He'd successfully ruined my life in this city. There was nothing left for me here.

He nodded.

"You didn't answer my question," I said. "Are you divorced?"

"I've told you before. I'm stuck in this relationship. But we are no longer living together."

"Okay." So they were separated?

"I've been making arrangements for this day. I knew you would come home to me eventually. To take over what's rightfully yours."

"What's rightfully mine?"

"The family business."

He was delusional. I wasn't a mobster. And I wasn't here to take over something I despised from a person I despised even more. "I didn't come home to you."

"Then why did you come?"

I swallowed hard. It was a ridiculous question. Didn't the gun I'd put to his head make my intentions obvious?

But I'd punched him instead. And now he had an icepack pressed to his bloody nose. I hated that I felt bad about it. I wasn't a monster like him. But I needed to be a monster for just a few minutes. I owed it to Miller. I had to do it.

I gripped the handle of the gun tighter. "I came back to kill you, dad."

CHAPTER 3

Saturday

Matt

I held her until she finally stopped shaking. Until her breaths evened out. I was scared to say anything. I just wanted to freeze time with my arms around her. Because I was worried that as soon as I spoke, the spell would be broken. That she'd push me away again. Tell me to go. Tell me we were done.

And she was wrong. About all of it. We weren't done. This was only the beginning. I could picture it all with her now. The house I'd been renovating was a home. I didn't want to sell it. I wanted to fill it with our children. I wanted Mrs. Alcaraz to teach our kids Spanish. And our home to smell like empanadas for Sunday dinners. I wanted to start our family.

But I needed to know what was going on. Why she'd suddenly decided to push me away. I needed to help her see what I saw. How great we could be. She had to see it. I couldn't be the only one.

I lifted my hand from her back and let my fingers run through her hair, tilting her head up to mine. "What happened tonight?" I whispered.

She opened her mouth and then closed it again. "I can't tell you. I wish I could, Matt. But I can't."

"You can tell me anything."

She shook her head. "It's not…it's really complicated."

I wanted to kiss away her frowns. Instead, I just dropped my forehead to hers. "I can handle complicated. Just tell me. Let me in." Kennedy had seen every side of me. The good, the bad, and the really bad. I remembered how much I'd relied on her after Brooklyn's death. How much she helped me keep going. But I didn't just want her smiling face at a high school lunch table. I wanted her. All of her.

She took one deep breath, like she was breathing in my exhales. And then she took a step back from me. "I can't tell you. Not this." Her voice was so firm. "I've made so many mistakes in my life. And I'm done making them. I'm done."

I knew my face fell. She was talking about us. Dating *me* was the mistake. *We* were done. I wasn't sure how something that felt so right could possibly be wrong. We'd had this conversation already. We were on the same page. Brooklyn would have wanted us to be happy.

"I'm going to go back in there, Matt. And you're going to go home." She hugged herself again. "And we're going to go back to being friends."

I shook my head. "No we're not."

She picked the tulips up off the ground. She started blinking fast like she was about to cry again. "These are beautiful. Thank you." She grabbed the French fries too. "And I need these. So I'm keeping them."

The corner of my mouth ticked up, even though it felt like there was a knife in my chest. We used to be just friends. I pictured her laughing at Empire High and always stealing my fries in the cafeteria. I hadn't noticed her back then. Not really. I hadn't thanked her for holding me together after Brooklyn passed away. She'd been there for me in more ways than I ever realized. She was the only one that understood my pain. She just got me.

And she needed to let me in. Because I wanted to be there for her too. I wanted her to count on me. Her acts of kindness were innocent back then. Taking care of her best friend's grieving fiancé. But I wasn't standing here innocently. I wanted everything with her. If this was a guilt thing, she was crazy. She'd always been a good friend to Brooklyn, even if she didn't see it.

"I have an idea," I said. "Those fries are probably cold. How about I take you out for some warm ones and you can tell me what happened after I sent you all those eggplant emojis in that text."

"That sounds…" She closed her eyes. "…Perfect. Which is why I'm declining the offer."

She wasn't making any sense.

She slowly opened her eyes again. "Goodnight, Matt."

"I'll see you tomorrow?"

She shook her head.

"Kennedy. I'm not giving up on us."

"There is no us, Matt." A stray tear trailed down her cheek. She wiped it away like she was angry with herself.

"Yes there is. I've said it before and I'll say it again. Brooklyn would have wanted both of us to be happy. I'm sure of it."

She pressed her lips together. "I'm not sure of anything anymore."

That wasn't very encouraging. She hadn't confirmed it exactly, but by the expression on her face it did seem like the Brooklyn thing was at least partially to blame for her sudden shift of perspective. Why wouldn't she believe me when I told her that Brooklyn would be happy for us? I truly did believe that. She'd be horrified that I'd been stuck at 16 for my whole adult life.

"Please, just go home," Kennedy said.

God, didn't she realize that I didn't have a fucking home? Not since Brooklyn died. For 16 years I'd barely been holding on. And I was done living that way. "The past is in the past, Kennedy. Can't we just agree to keep it there?" I took a step forward but she put her hand up to stop me.

"No."

I wasn't sure if she was saying 'no' in response to my question. Or telling me not to get near her. Either way, what the hell was I supposed to do? She wasn't going to let me in tonight. "We'll talk in the morning then, okay?" I hated how desperate I sounded. But I was. Desperate for her. My eyes dropped to her lips.

She didn't respond. But I swore I heard a sharp inhale. Her body betraying every single one of her words.

It took every ounce of my restraint to not step toward her again. "I'll call you in the morning," I said.

"No," she said in a rush. "Don't. I'll...I'll call you, okay?"

"Okay." I could wait for her to call. I could handle that. She'd talk to me when she was ready. And hopefully she'd be ready really early in the morning, because I had a feeling I wouldn't be sleeping tonight.

She nodded. "Goodnight, Matt."

Her goodnight sounded an awful lot like a goodbye.

There was a light wailing noise behind the door. Had they gotten a cat? "What was that?" I asked.

"Nothing. I have to go," Kennedy said. She opened the door and quickly closed it behind her.

There were a few more wailing noises and then silence.

I wanted to bang on the door. I wanted to kick it to the fucking ground and tell her I didn't care about the past. That I was finally ready to embrace the future. I could at least tell her that I wasn't allergic to cats.

Instead, I turned around and walked down the dingy hallway. I passed by Brooklyn's old door and again didn't look at it. I was finally ready to be happy. How could the memory of Brooklyn still be torturing me after all these years? Why couldn't the past just stay in the past?

**

I honestly wasn't sure how I ended up in the bar down the street from Tanner's place. I didn't remember driving or parking or anything. It was like I was in a trance. I downed my glass and shot Tanner a text letting him know I'd be late.

And exactly one minute later, which was at least five minutes too quickly to get here from his penthouse apartment, he slid into the stool beside mine at the bar.

"Bad night?" he asked.

I just stared at him. "How did you know I was here?"

He shrugged. "Just a feeling."

"You had a feeling I was at this bar and got here in exactly one minute?"

"One minute? Nonsense. Pretty sure it took me a while to get here. It's late. You must be sleep deprived or something. That can really mess with your head."

I didn't think that was it. Did he have my phone tracked or something? Honestly it didn't even matter. I downed my second glass of scotch. "I had a crazy night."

"Do tell."

"Remember how I told you Penny had a surprise for me tonight? Well, the surprise was that she thought I was gay."

Tanner laughed. And then he must have seen the serious look on my face. "Oh, wait. You're serious? She's friends with Justin, right? Like she's met a gay man in real life?"

"That's who my surprise blind date was with."

"Wow."

"Yeah." I took another sip of my drink. "She saw you mouth kiss me at that restaurant and for some reason assumed that I was in love with you. And that you didn't love me back. I have no idea why that was her assumption though, because *you* clearly kissed *me*."

Tanner laughed. "What is with people mistaking celebration kisses as something homosexual? This era just doesn't understand proper affection between male friends."

This era?

"But Penny was right about one thing. I'm way out of your league," he said with a laugh. He waved down the bartender for a drink.

"I think you have it backward," I said.

"Nah." He lifted up his glass that the bartender just dropped off. "I don't think so."

"It really doesn't matter in this fake scenario who had unrequited love for who."

"If you say so. Since yours was unrequited. Even Penny agreed and she knows you very well."

"I'm done with this conversation," I said.

"Fair. Since I won. On a related note, are you going to tell her you aren't gay?"

"I didn't have to. I kind of yelled it to the whole restaurant. And she showed up. And I may have been talking about Brooklyn too and it all just kind of came out."

He raised his eyebrows. "No more secrets."

I nodded. "I told her everything. I even showed her the paintings of Brooklyn."

"You took her to your serial killer room?"

"It's not a serial killer room."

Tanner gave me a weird look. "It's a little like a serial killer room. Or at least a stalker's lair."

Honestly, he had a good point. "Penny may have mentioned that it wasn't healthy to spend time in there."

"Agreed."

"I had a great conversation with her, though. She's a really good friend."

"I know. I've been trying to tell you not to put your dick in her for years."

"What? If anything you've told me the opposite."

"Have I? I don't recall. She's one of your best friends' wives. That would have been highly inappropriate."

"Yeah. It would have been." Seriously, he didn't remember telling me to hit that on numerous occasions?

"Especially now that you're even from the whole Blue Parrot Resort fiasco."

"What you did to me was worse," I said. "Especially because of Nigel." I'd never forget the way Nigel had stared at me when Tanner had slipped me boner pills as a joke.

"I don't understand why you don't just ignore him," Tanner said.

"I don't understand how you think he's ignorable?"

"Eh, I've been stuck with him for so long. He blends into the walls. If you let him."

What did that even mean? Whatever, it didn't matter. "Penny really helped me though. I finally said goodbye to Brooklyn tonight. I'm ready to move on. For real this time."

Tanner nodded. "That's good. At least it didn't take you a few hundred years."

"What?"

"That old saying…" He tapped the top of the wooden bar as he thought. "That heartache takes two lifetimes to get over."

I didn't know if that saying actually sounded familiar or if maybe I was a little sleep deprived. But I found myself nodding my head. "It feels like two lifetimes."

"Exactly." Tanner slapped me on the back. "So you're ready to finally embrace the present." He waved down the bartender and ordered another round for both of us.

"Yes." More than I even realized. I was ready to embrace it with Kennedy. I felt really good about coming clean to Penny today. For taking that step of saying goodbye to Brooklyn. I didn't want to talk about what happened with Kennedy right now. Hopefully she'd calm down in the morning. And we could just keep getting stronger.

The bartender slid us our glasses.

Tanner caught his in one hand and lifted it in the air. "To new beginnings!"

I tapped my glass against his.

"Hear, hear! It's late though, and you really do look unwell. We should probably get home before Nigel starts to worry." He downed his glass and then patted the front of his suit jacket. "Shoot, do you have two pence I can borrow?"

"Two pence?"

He cleared his throat. "I meant a twenty."

"I'll pay for the drinks, you cheap ass."

He laughed. "I'll get it next time."

But we both knew he wouldn't.

CHAPTER 4

Saturday

Brooklyn

My father smiled. And for the first time I saw some of his old cruelty there. He was staring at me like I was a little girl with little thoughts. That anything I said was insignificant.

"Angel, you're not going to shoot me. Blood is a stronger bond than anything else. We both know that. You're here for answers. And probably for some help. I can offer you both."

Blood meant nothing to me. And I didn't need his help. I already knew where Jacob and I were going. I had a plan.

Just like I'd had a plan for Miller and me to get away from my dad all those years ago. I swallowed hard. That plan...it hadn't worked. My dad had known where I was. Why had he waited so long to act? He'd told Miller that he'd kill him if he ever laid a hand on me again. But he had pictures of Miller doing just that. Over a dozen years of images of Miller touching me. Holding me close. Kissing me. Miller and I were rarely not touching.

"I see your mind swirling with those questions. Go ahead and ask. I'll give you an honest answer." He lowered the icepack from his face and dabbed at the blood under his nose with the tea towel.

"You don't know what an honest answer is."

"I've always been honest with you."

God, he was so full of shit. "I don't have any questions for you. You told Miller right to his face that you'd kill him if he ever touched me again. I saw all the pictures on your desk. You knew what was going on. Nothing you can say will make me believe it wasn't you."

"So Miller is dead?" He shook his head like the news saddened him. "I'm so sorry, angel."

"You're sorry?" My voice cracked. I was going to punch him in the face again if he wasn't careful. "You're the one who killed him!"

"It wasn't me."

"That's the best you've got?" He wasn't even trying. He didn't have an alibi. 'It wasn't me' wasn't good enough. I needed witnesses. I needed proof or his brains were going to end up on the cabinets behind him.

"You know it wasn't me, Brooklyn. If you thought it was me you would have shot me as soon as I opened the door. Of course it wasn't me. I know that you loved him. I would never."

I laughed. "Why? Because it would hurt me? Look around, Dad. Bringing me here after my uncle's funeral *hurt* me. Making me live with Isabella *hurt* me. Trying to tell me Matt wasn't a good choice *hurt* me. Stealing my kidney *hurt* me. Kidnapping me *hurt* me. Letting my mom die when your money could have helped save her *hurt* me. You've done nothing but hurt me my whole life. Even before you knew I existed. Hell, you even tried to make my mom get rid of me."

"Well, I have a few things to say about those horrific accusations. I never knew your mother was sick. If I had, I would have done something. She was the love of my life."

I used to believe him when he said that. But he didn't know what love was.

He steepled his fingers as he stared at me. "And as we've previously discussed, I invited you into my home so you'd be safe."

Invited me? He'd dragged me kicking and screaming.

"I thought I had Isabella under control. And this next bit is really starting to weight on me. I did not steal your kidney. You signed it away to me. I'd really appreciate it if you stopped saying I stole it. That sounds terrible."

I was clenching my jaw so tight that it hurt.

"And you asked to leave after your surgery. I was worried about Isabella's threats and I was trying to keep you safe. You even asked me to take you away. You begged me to get you out of this house…"

"You kidnapped me!"

"I disagree."

"You put me in the middle of nowhere and said I couldn't leave!"

"For you own safety, angel. And I'd hardly call a beautiful beachfront property the middle of nowhere. You were happy there. With Miller. And when you ran off, I let you. Because Isabella was at the treatment center and I knew for the time being you'd be safe in California. I gave you the taste of freedom you wanted."

"You…you knew I was in California?"

"Of course. I could see it in your eyes. That you were going to betray me."

"*Me* betray *you*?" *What the fuck?*

"Indeed. So I gave you an 'untraceable card' to make purchases with. He put 'untraceable card' in air quotes.

My stomach sank. I'd believed him. I thought it was untraceable. But God, I was so naïve. Of course it wasn't untraceable to him.

"And you took the bait," he said. "You bought a cute little place by a lake for you and Miller. And then you took a little solo vacation to California."

It wasn't a vacation. I'd been so fucked up. I'd been so broken. He acted like he knew everything, but he knew nothing. If he was having me followed, couldn't he see from the pictures how I was feeling in California? How badly I'd needed someone to love me. For *him* to love me. Instead of him wanting to just keep me in a cage.

"I will admit, I was impressed when my bank alerted me that millions of dollars had been drained out of my account right before you took off. And the lake house you picked out with a piece of it was quite lovely."

Wait…he knows about all that?

"The money movement was clever. It's all yours too. You've earned it. Why have you not touched the rest of it, by the way? It was almost like you knew I could see it afterward. Like you knew I was watching you. Did you? Know I was watching?"

I just stared at him. He knew everything I'd done. He knew all of it. I was honestly a little surprised he wasn't the one holding a gun to my head. "If I knew you were watching I would have left."

He nodded. "Interesting. So why didn't you use the money?"

"Because we didn't need it. I never needed anything from you. I never asked you for anything. I just wanted to be left alone."

"In a lake house that my money bought? With a bodyguard I was paying for?"

I heard the ownership in my father's statement about Miller. He was trying so hard to twist everything. But he couldn't. I wouldn't let him. "The bodyguard you *used* to pay for. The only person that despised you more than I did was my husband."

"Miller didn't despise me."

"Yes he did."

"Well that wounds me." He put his hand to his chest. "I take great pride in keeping my staff happy."

"By keeping them happy, do you mean beating them senseless when they wrong you?"

My father shrugged. "If you're referring to your homecoming when Miller lost eyes on you, then yes. You could have been gravely hurt. You *were* hurt."

"Because of Isabella, not Miller!"

"If Miller hadn't let you out of his sight, that never would have happened."

"Fuck you."

"Language," he said and dabbed at his bloody nose again.

I just gaped at him. He couldn't be serious right now. He was never a father to me and now he was telling me not to swear? *Seriously. Fuck. You.* "Fine. So when you say you take great pride in keeping your staff happy, you actually mean you kill them when they wrong you?"

"On the rare occasion. But like I said before, I didn't kill Miller. I didn't blow up your car. Yes, I knew where you were. But I was letting you live your life. Just like you requested in that eloquent letter you left me at the beach house."

"I remember the letter. I specifically told you to not do anything to Miller."

"And I didn't. I let the both of you run off. I wasn't blind. I knew what was happening. And I was relieved when you went to the lake house to be with him. Because even though he was technically no longer my employee, he still had years of training and experience working for me. I knew he'd keep you safe. And I also knew how much he loved you."

My heart felt like it was burning. Like it was stuck in the flames with Miller. And now there was also a knife in my chest, slowly twisting. Miller *loved* me. Past tense. I tried to blink away the tears. He was gone. He was really gone. I was here to avenge him. And I was letting my dad get in my head with his old tricks. But he couldn't talk his way out of this. He'd killed my husband. I knew he did.

"Miller pretended to die all those years ago in order to leave with you. He gave up everything for you. He was like a puppy following you around."

"Don't." The tears in my eyes were threatening to spill. "Don't talk about him that way."

"It's the truth. And you being with him was a win-win scenario for both you and me."

My love life shouldn't have had anything to do with my father. My stomach churned.

"I got the comfort of knowing you were safe with one of my bodyguards. And you got to be happy thinking you made the decision to be with him all by yourself."

My stomach churned again. "What do you mean by that? That I'd be happy thinking I made the choice to be with him?"

"Well, I'd hoped it would happen. Forcing you two to live together at the beach house for several months went just according to plan. A great bodyguard with very weak willpower." He smiled to himself. "I remember making a big show of being upset that he touched you too, remember? I was trying my best to be a good father and I'd recently read that teenagers love doing the opposite of what they're told. I figured you'd want him more than ever after that. I was correct."

"You're pure evil." He was discounting my love for my husband. Telling me it was an elaborately orchestrated plan. He was wrong. I fell in love with Miller slowly, with a broken heart. And Miller healed it. He fixed me.

"You're welcome for the past 16 years of happiness. How could someone evil have given you such a wonderful gift?"

"You didn't give me that gift. Miller did. Jacob did."

"Is that my grandson's name? Jacob?" He smiled. "When can I meet him?"

"You must be joking."

My father slowly shook his head.

"Never. You can never meet my son."

"You can't keep me from him."

"Damn right I can."

"Language."

Okay. I'd had enough. I lifted my gun back up, my knuckles aching as I gripped the handle. I shouldn't have punched him. I should have just shot him. He was doing what I'd feared. Twisting everything. Making my memories hazy.

He held up his hands like he was finally scared of the gun. "Angel, I'm truly sorry if the last 16 years weren't wonderful. You looked happy. I was happy that you were happy. I would have interfered if I thought you needed it."

"If you knew I was happy then why'd you take it away from me? Why did you kill Miller?" *Why?*

"I didn't. The bomb was in *your* car, Brooklyn. And I'd never to do anything to hurt you. Yes, I've made mistakes in my past. And I can't undo them. But I would never do anything to hurt you now. You're my angel. You saved me. You know I wouldn't hurt you."

He was entirely full of shit. But the bomb was in *my* car. Not Miller's. And that had been bothering me for weeks. Why had it been in my car? Why? I only needed one answer from him. "So if you didn't put the bomb in my car, who did?"

"There's been a little unrest with the families. We can get into more details about that when you start working with me. Soon this whole empire will be in your hands."

He was delusional.

"But there was a disagreement. A pretty big one. The Locatellis want me out."

None of that meant anything to me. "Okay…"

"I was being careful when I sent the photographer to your house. I swear it. But…maybe I got a little greedy with wanting pictures of my grandchild. He's growing so fast. And…someone must have followed the photographer. I didn't know it until the explosion. But it had the Locatelli signature all over the bomb. They were trying to hurt me by hurting you. They knew you were my one and only weakness. And they wanted me to know they were behind it."

Hurt him by hurting me? They hadn't just hurt me. They'd taken Miller away from me. They'd stolen the love of my life.

"I'm sorry," my father said. "Truly I am."

He was sorry? He'd led the murderer right to my doorstep.

"I had my guy over there right away," my dad said. "He took care of everything. Worked with local law enforcement to smooth it all over so that the public would think it was just a car issue. Forensics was taking forever to identify who was in the car though. When I heard that all three of you were missing, I was worried sick that I'd lost you." There were tears in his eyes.

I didn't know what to say. It was all lies…right? But my dad sounded sincerely upset about the idea of losing me. I took a deep breath. I'd come here for a reason. And now he was messing with my head.

"I'm so glad you and Jacob are okay. And I'm sorry about Miller. I could tell how much you loved him."

I opened my mouth and then closed it again.

"And as for revenge…" he looked down at the gun. "There's no need for that. It's already been taken care of."

"What?"

"Remember Poppy? Your cousin? You met her at Thanksgiving."

"I remember." I remembered Rob and James saying she was the worst. I remembered her looking a hell of a lot like Isabella. And a chill ran down my spine at the thought of someone that looked like Isabella running around town.

"Well, Poppy took care of it for you. A little tit for tat. Poppy loves car bombs. The Locatelli family just lost its one and only heir."

"You…you…killed Locatelli's son?"

"For you."

"I didn't ask you to do that! I don't want anyone else to die!" I knew the irony of my words when I was holding a gun, ready to kill him.

"I thought they'd killed you. Or my grandson. Or my son-in-law. Honestly they're lucky I only responded with one car bomb. I had half a mind to wipe their entire family off the map."

He was insane. "Are you sure it wasn't Poppy who put the bomb in my car? You just said she loves car bombs."

"She does. But she's on our side."

"There is no *our* side."

"Of course there is. Poppy is your dear cousin. And now that you're back in town, the two of you will be quite close, I'm certain of it. Speaking of Poppy…we really should discuss Matthew.

I had no idea what Poppy had to do with Matt, but I didn't care. I was about to tell him that I wasn't staying in the city for long, but he cut me off.

"And I hate to say I told you so. But…I told you so," he said with a smile. "In that huge list of reasons of ways I hurt you, you mentioned Matt. But I was clearly right about the two of you. Since you chose Miller over him."

"That doesn't make you right. If you'd never forced me to leave town then Matt and I…" I pressed my lips together. Matt and I…what? Would have lived happily ever after? I wasn't going to go there. Because I didn't regret any part of my life with Miller. I'd had everything I'd ever wanted with him and wouldn't change a second of the time we'd had together. Matt and I were never supposed to be. I was done believing in fairytales and happily ever afters.

"It does make me right. Matthew Caldwell is a notorious playboy. He was never the right choice for you. I've been trying to tell him for over 15 years that you were alive. Ever since I promised you at the beach house. And he never answered a single one of my texts to come speak with me. He never cared about you and…"

"Stop." Each year we were apart stung less and less. If my father was trying to get under my skin it wasn't going to work. Matthew Caldwell was dead to me. And he had been for years. I'd never forget waking up and my engagement ring being missing. He'd asked for it back. He hadn't said a word at my funeral. He'd forgotten about me so quickly. And he'd moved on even faster. "I definitely didn't come here to ask questions about Matt."

"Right. You came here to kill me."

I just stared at him.

"Well, what else do I need to explain to you, angel? It was the Locatellis. And I made sure we got even with them. There's nothing else to discuss really."

"A life for a life."

He nodded.

"That's not even. Miller was my whole world."

"Do you want me to kill Locatelli's niece too? Or maybe his wife?"

"No!" I didn't want that. I just wanted Miller back. I wanted to rewind time. I wanted to go home.

"You're going to be just fine, angel. Time heals all wounds."

I shook my head. Not this. Not this time. I wasn't going to get over this.

"Here's what we're going to do. You're going to go get Jacob. And the two of you can live here with me. We can be a family."

He truly was delusional. "I'm not staying. Jacob and I have to get out of town."

"Why?"

"Because the cops…" my voice trailed off. I still felt like I was on the run even though my father said I wasn't a suspect. Probably because I planned on running after I shot him. But now everything was turned upside down.

"Like I told you, my guy took care of everything. Local law enforcement has been paid off. No one suspects you in the case. Your name is in the clear. The two of you will stay here with me. End of discussion."

No. My father couldn't control me anymore. I wasn't a scared 16-year-old girl. I stood up, holding the gun steadier than ever. "No," I said firmly. "I will never stay here again. And if you want me to believe your story, I need to…talk to Poppy." Honestly I didn't want to talk to her. I didn't want anything to do with this family. But Poppy was the car bomb enthusiast. Maybe I'd be able to tell if she was telling the truth.

"Yes, the two of you will be good friends, I'm sure of it. But it's awfully late. Let's arrange a meeting tomorrow, yes?"

I nodded. I needed sleep. Desperately. My head was at war with my heart. My head was telling me that my father was a liar. I knew that for a fact. He'd lied to me ever since I'd met him.

But my heart? It was a lot stupider than my head. Standing here after all these years staring at my father, I didn't want to have to kill him. A part of me still just wanted for him to actually care about me. My heart always had a way of getting me in trouble.

CHAPTER 5

Sunday

Matt

The chorus of bells made me groan. "Nigel, cut it out."

"Master Tanner said you'd extra enjoy them this morning. And I've been practicing."

I groaned again. "Tanner's being a dick."

"Dick," Nigel said as more bells chimed.

What? I opened my eyes and I was ass naked in bed. *Not again.* "What the hell?" I pulled the sheets over me. "I didn't go to bed naked, Nigel."

"No you did not."

"Then why am I naked?"

"You looked uncomfortable, so I helped."

I needed to get out of this fucking apartment. I sat up and ran my hand down my face. "Do you have any news from Poppy's house manager?" As soon as Nigel dug up some dirt on Poppy, I could get out of this mess I was in. I was really hoping he'd find something about murders the Pruitts or Cannavaros committed. Or money they laundered. Or any laws they'd broken would be fine.

It was possible it wasn't just guilt about Brooklyn holding Kennedy back from embracing us. Maybe it was this crazy thing I'd agreed to with Poppy. Being her fake boyfriend definitely put a damper on being Kennedy's real boyfriend. I had to fix it as fast as possible.

"It hasn't been 48 hours yet, Mr. Caldwell. The time will expire tonight. And I will not let you down. It's our secret mission. Just you and me. We'll meet in private and everything."

Right.

"I'll go draw your bath in the meantime."

Shouldn't he be talking to Poppy's staff in the meantime? "I'm fine, Nigel. I'm just hungry."

"One second then." He ran out of the room and returned literally right away pushing in a cart of food. "All your favorites."

"I can just eat in the dining room with Tanner."

"Oh, he's not here this morning. He's at…worship." He nodded his head, like he was pleased with what he'd said.

Tanner had almost as much to drink as I did last night. How was he not nursing a hangover? And wait…at worship? "Is Tanner a religious man?" I knew a lot about him, but I hadn't known that. But it was Sunday and he had already left. It made sense.

"Lots of religions, yes."

"What does that mean?"

"He's been through most of them. Not any time recently though."

I just stared at him.

"Fine, you caught me in a lie! He's not at worship. I don't know why I did it. I've been bad. Maybe I need to be punished." He turned a little like he wanted me to smack his butt and smiled up at me.

"No, you're good, Nigel."

He sighed. "Very well. Anything else you need this morning?"

"Yeah…where is Tanner?"

"Didn't I say?" He grabbed his bells. "I think I already said. Bye!" He scurried off without answering my question, his bells jingling along with him.

Well, that was weird. But everything Nigel did was weird. So it was actually normal. Seriously, I needed to move back to my place. Hopefully Nigel's schedule would open up sooner than next year. I really couldn't imagine staying here through Thanksgiving. And Christmas. And New Year's. And definitely not Valentine's Day. I could not, *would not*, see Nigel on Valentine's Day.

I grabbed my phone off the nightstand and texted Tanner. I hadn't told him about Kennedy last night, but I needed his advice now. Before I did something stupid and called her ten times when she'd specifically told me not to.

I stood up and looked around for my clothes. It looked like Nigel had taken them. Hopefully to clean and not to do something weird with. I opened the closet doors.

"Oh, and Mr. Caldwell?" Nigel said and walked back into the room.

Jesus. I jumped behind the closet door so he couldn't stare at me naked anymore. "What, Nigel?"

"This arrived for you late yesterday evening." He walked into the room, not caring at all that I was trying to hide from him in the closet, and handed me the manila envelope.

"What is it?" I asked.

"I don't know. But I can open it for you." He pulled out a letter opener from his lederhosen.

Wait, why was he wearing lederhosen again? I decided it was better not to ask. Nigel could do whatever he wanted in his free time. "That won't be necessary," I said and grabbed the envelope, holding it in front of my junk.

"Anything else you need? I can spoon-feed you some of the oatmeal."

"I'm seriously good."

Nigel nodded. "Very well, Master. I mean, Mr. Caldwell. See you for our secret rendezvous tonight at 9 pm. I'll fax you the details. I mean text. Because I'm a modern day boy. Good day." He ran out of the room.

Nigel had to be the strangest person I'd ever met. And that was saying something. Since Tanner was one of my best friends.

I opened up the manila envelope and pulled out the contents. *Jesus.* It was me and Poppy's relationship contract. Mr. Pruitt had said he'd send it over immediately. I'd been hoping immediately meant like…in a week. I needed time to figure out what to do with the information Nigel brought me tonight. I'd just have to plan everything out quickly. Because there was no way in hell I was signing this thing. I tossed it onto my bed and picked up my phone when I saw it was blinking.

There was an unread text from Rob. I clicked on it.

"I heard Penny thought you liked that D. I'm totally cool with it if you're gay. Probably cooler than Tanner is. I bet he's homophobic, don't you think? He seems like the type. Loser."

"I'm not gay," I texted back.

"It's cool if you are."

"I'm not." I hit send and then quickly texted again. "Want to grab brunch?" I went back in my closet to look for something to wear.

"Honestly, man, that sounded really gay. I love that for you."

"Do you want to grab brunch or not?" I was going to talk to Tanner about this, but since he was at worship or something, Rob could help me out. Besides, Rob was happily married. He probably had better advice anyway. Because as much as Tanner talked about true love, he wasn't in a relationship.

"Of course I want to grab brunch," he texted. "As long as we can go to that place with eclairs."

If I was gay, then so was Rob. "See you there in thirty minutes."

"Plenty of time to get your makeup on."

"Go to hell," I texted back with a laugh.

"Love you too."

I sighed and turned back to my closet. Which I was still standing in. And yes, I could see the irony in having that whole conversation while I literally stood in my closet because I was hiding from Nigel. I grabbed an outfit and hopped out of the closet. *Damn it, that didn't make it any better.*

***

Rob slid into the booth across from me. "You look like shit."

"Yeah, I know." I took a sip of coffee and then looked down at my phone again. There was still no text or call from Kennedy. "I need some advice."

"Okay…" Rob just stared at me. "You're freaking me out, what's going on? Hold that thought, I need pancakes." He waved over the waitress and ordered way too much food for one person. "Now you have my full attention," he said when the waitress walked off.

"Why did you order so much food?"

"Because it's brunch. And all you had was coffee. We'll share."

Honestly, sharing plates with him didn't bother me. I couldn't even remember the last time I'd gone out to eat when someone didn't think I was gay. Oh wait. No, I remembered. It was when that crazy redhead had set my dick on fire. I'd much rather do this.

"So what's up?" Rob asked. "No wait, let me guess. Nigel did something weird to you in your sleep."

Actually yes. He stripped me again. But that wasn't what I needed to talk about. I had Nigel under control. *I think.* "It's about Kennedy."

"Nigel did something to Kennedy in her sleep?" He looked oddly excited by the thought of that.

"No. I mean…I hope not." I wouldn't put sabotage past Nigel. He seemed to want my full attention. But I doubted he had anything to do with why Kennedy had a change of heart last night.

"Wait, does that mean Kennedy slept over last night?" He wiggled his eyebrows.

"Rob, just let me get this out, okay?"

He held up his hands. "Sorry. You go."

How should I put this exactly? I leaned forward so I could lower my voice. "What do you think is the best way to propose to someone who isn't currently speaking to you?"

"Who isn't speaking to you?" Rob whispered back.

"Kennedy."

"You're going to propose to Kennedy?!" Rob practically yelled.

"Would you lower your voice!"

"I don't understand why we're whispering. This is very exciting stuff. I'm gonna call James."

"No."

"I already hit the button. He's on speed dial."

"What's up, Rob?" said James.

"Matt is going to propose to Kennedy!"

Oh God. I leaned my head back on the booth and stared up at the ceiling.

"Wow. That was fast," James said.

It wasn't just the words, but the way he said them that made my head snap back up. "You think it's a bad idea?" I asked.

"I just think...well, it doesn't matter what I think," James said.

I grabbed the phone out of Rob's hand. "I care what you think, man."

James sighed. "Matt, you were a mess last night. With everything about Brooklyn being out in the open... Don't you think you need to take some time to let the dust settle and not rush into something? We all love Kennedy. But...it just seems a little sudden."

"Oh, no!" Rob said. "We're going under a tunnel and the call is breaking up." He made a bunch of weird noises and then ended the call. "Sorry about that. I thought he'd be more enthusiastic. Let's call Mason instead!"

"No, stop..." but Rob had already hit Mason on speed dial.

Mason answered in three rings. "What do you want, Rob?" Mason asked with a yawn. "It's freaking early."

"Nice to talk to you too. Your brother has big news that he wanted to share with you. He's going to propose to Kennedy."

There was a shuffling noise and Mason cleared his throat. "Are you serious? Why are you telling me? Matt, are you there?!"

"I'm here," I said.

"What the hell? Why did you tell Rob before you told me?"

Okay, this is ridiculous. "I was just asking Rob for advice."

"Rob gives shit advice. Forget everything he said. Here's what you do. Date her for a couple years and take things slow like I did with Bee. It's the best way. Stretch that honeymoon phase out for as long as possible."

"Matt?" It was Bee now. "Don't listen to anything Mason says. There is nothing wrong with going fast instead of at a tortoises' pace. Your brother has commitment issues."

"I do not," Mason said.

"Okay, thanks guys!" I said. "Gotta go!" I hung up on them.

Rob started whistling and put his phone in his pocket. "Oh, our food is here. Perfect timing." He cut the stack of pancakes down the middle and piled syrup on his before dropping a dollop of butter on mine, just the way I liked them. "Dig in."

"Dude, what the hell?"

"Oh, you want syrup today? I guess you are celebrating." He lifted up the syrup bottle.

"No." I pushed the syrup back onto the table. "I'm trying to get your advice here. Not loop everyone in so that Kennedy will probably find out before I pop the question."

"Hmmm. Have you already told Tanner?"

"No."

"Well good. Now all your actual best friends know before that imposter."

"You seriously just called all of them to make sure they knew before Tanner?" I took a bite of pancakes. "You're ridiculous."

"You're ridiculous," he said over a mouthful of food. "Your best friends should know first." He swallowed his bite. "And now I can focus. Why isn't Kennedy speaking to you?"

"I don't know. I had such clarity last night. I'm ready to move on from everything in the past, you know? I want to do that with her. And I thought we were on the same page. I texted her last night telling her I was coming over. And she seemed excited to see me. But when I got there, she didn't buzz me up. She didn't answer her phone. I was able to get into the building when someone walked out. And even then it took a lot of convincing to make her come out to talk to me. She was crying…I…I don't know what happened."

"Did you ask her what was wrong?"

"Of course I asked her. She kept saying she couldn't tell me."

"Hmm. Interesting. What else?"

"She told me what we did was a mistake. She was trying to push me away."

"And then what?"

"Eventually I calmed her down enough to at least let me hold her while she cried. But as soon as she calmed down she pushed me away again."

"And then…"

"She told me not to reach out to her. But that she'd reach out to me. And then she slammed the door in my face."

Rob pressed his lips together and nodded.

"So...what do you think the best approach is here? All that keeps going through my head is the boombox outside her window thing. Do they still sell boomboxes somewhere?"

Rob just kept nodding.

"Do you have another idea?"

Rob sighed. "So...here's the thing." He took another bite of pancake and chewed it really freaking slowly. "I have good news and bad news."

"Okay..."

"The good news is you're about to save a lot of money."

I just stared at him.

"Because there's no reason to buy a ring. Since the bad news is that Kennedy dumped your ass."

"It was just a disagreement."

"Eh. No, you've been dumped."

"She said she'd call me."

"And how many girls have you said you'd *call?*" He put call in air quotes and stared at me. "She's probably long gone by now. Back to Chicago to avoid you. What did you do to screw that up so badly so quickly?"

"Nothing."

"Did you talk about Brooklyn a lot?"

"No...I...I mean...maybe a little."

Rob shook his head. "You probably talked about her *a lot*. And it was already a delicate situation with the two of them having been best friends and all."

"I don't think that's what happened."

"Well, was there anything else weird about last night?"

I tried to think. "Actually, yeah. She refused to let me in to talk. And kept telling me I had to go. And there was this weird wailing noise inside her apartment before she slammed the door in my face."

Rob gasped. "Secret. Baby. Romance."

"What?"

"I don't know. Daphne reads some romance books sometimes and she loves those secret baby ones."

"I have no idea what you're talking about."

"I'm not exactly sure either. She reads a lot and the stories blur together in my head. But I think the gist is that there's always a surprise baby in the mix that someone doesn't know about. So did you sleep with Kennedy 16 years ago? Maybe you have a surprise baby together. That kind of thing. Ooooh Daphne is going to be so excited about this! I can't wait to tell her." He grabbed his phone again.

I pulled it away from him. "It wouldn't be a baby then. It would be like 15. And no, I didn't sleep with her back in high school."

"Well, that doesn't mean there's not a secret baby. Maybe she has a secret baby with your worst enemy!"

"Mr. Pruitt?"

"Oooh! An age-gap romance too!"

I laughed. "The wailing noise didn't sound like a baby. I think it was a cat."

"Well then you're either looking at a cozy mystery or a furry romance, I think. I'll have to ask Daphne to be sure. Either way, that's not nearly as fun." Rob sighed. "What a bummer. A double bummer really. Because now there's no baby and your ass is still dumped."

CHAPTER 6

Sunday

Brooklyn

The sun streaming through the blinds lit up my son's peaceful face. He rarely looked this peaceful when he was awake these days. His cute little smiles had turned to frowns over the past couple weeks.

We were both broken.

But it was my job to be strong for him. I lightly ran my fingers through his hair. *My sweet boy. What are we going to do now?*

I'd been so focused on growing my family. I never in a million years thought it would shrink. I'd taken time for granted. And I hated myself for it. Every morning I woke up since Miller died, my heart was filled with regret. I just wanted to go back. Hold Miller tighter. Kiss him longer. Tell him how much I loved him more often.

A tear trailed down the side of my face and onto my pillow.

"Don't cry, Mommy."

I hadn't realized Jacob had opened his sleepy eyes.

He reached up and touch the tear on my cheek. "Daddy doesn't like when you cry."

Present tense. Present tense was slowly killing me. "I know. I'll stop, okay?"

He nodded and snuggled into my chest. I held him tight and kissed the top of his head. I would never take a second for granted with my son. "I love you."

"I love you too, Mommy."

I'd come to New York for one reason and one reason only. And I'd failed. Jacob and I should have already been over the border by now. Far away from this hellish city.

I didn't trust my dad. I couldn't possibly.

But…what if…

The words floated around in my head.

But what if he hadn't killed Miller?

What if he really had been waiting for me to come home to him?

What if he really did care that he had a grandchild?

What if he did love me in his own twisted way?

What if he was actually telling me the truth about all of it?

He said he'd already gotten justice. Not that murdering someone was justice for Miller's life. I pressed my lips together. I'd thought killing my father would be justice though.

I kissed the top of Jacob's head again and yawned. I hadn't slept a wink, even though I was exhausted. I just kept reliving that conversation with my dad. Over and over on an endless loop. I wish he had a tell when he was lying. If there was just a way for me to know. But I wasn't sure I'd ever be able to know if he was telling the truth.

And I doubted Poppy would actually help. I didn't know her. And I definitely didn't know any of her tells. I was supposed to meet up with her and my father in a couple hours. My father had texted me about it. Which made me feel sick to my stomach. He'd had my number this whole time. He'd known everything this whole freaking time. He'd been watching. Waiting.

I felt…exposed. Miller and I had been living in this happy little bubble. I had no idea it was more of a snow globe. Someone controlling everything from the outside. Just waiting to throw it on the ground and shatter it into a million tiny pieces.

Jacob's breath evened out as he fell back asleep, snuggled against me. And I couldn't help but think about all the previous times he'd snuggled up to me just like this. The only difference was that Miller had always been across from me in bed. If I closed my eyes it was almost like I could reach out and touch him. *Almost*. My fingers came up empty and the knife in my chest twist-ed.

If my dad had just stayed away…

If I hadn't used that "untraceable" card he'd given me…

If I'd been brave enough to ask someone else for help. Someone with resources that could actually make me disappear. I pictured that day when I drove back to NYC 15 years ago. I'd gone to Matt. I thought he'd be happy to see me. That he'd keep me safe. Because he loved me. Because he promised me forever.

Thinking about it made me feel sick to my stomach. I knew the kind of guy Matthew freaking Caldwell was. I knew better than to give him my heart. I knew better than to ever believe he was waiting for me.

I should have gone to James and Rob's house. They would have helped me. Their father seemed almost as bad as mine. And he certainly had the resources to make someone disappear for good.

Instead, I did it on my own. We'd been sitting ducks, just waiting for my father to come ruin us.

I'd felt it. The first time I'd seen someone in the woods. I'd felt it and Miller hadn't listened… I made myself stop my train of thought. There was no way in hell I'd put any blame on my husband. He'd tried to keep us safe. He'd kept us safe for so many years. There was no way for us to know.

But if I'd convinced him to move…

I wanted to scream. And throw things.

Miller had promised me I wasn't bad luck. He'd promised me.

So why did everyone I love die? My mom. My uncle. Matt might as well have died. I looked down at my son and saw Miller's nose. If Jacob was awake, I'd see Miller's eyes staring back at me too. I was bad luck. It was my fault that Miller was dead.

Mine.

I should have never gone to that lake house. I should have stayed on the west coast and drowned. Miller would still be alive if I'd stayed away.

I was selfish.

I'd put him in danger.

It's all my fault.

It felt like the whole world was caving in on me. I couldn't breathe.

Fuck.

It felt like someone was standing on my chest. *I can't breathe.*

I closed my eyes and tried to picture something happy. But all I could see was Miller's face. I untangled myself from Jacob's embrace as I gasped for breath. I fell forward off the couch, my hands landing hard on the threadbare carpet.

"Hey," Kennedy said and grabbed my shoulders.

"No," I gasped. "I can't…"

Kennedy held my hand. "Breathe, okay? Look at me."

I stared into her eyes.

"You're safe here. Breathe in and out."

She said the words again, slower this time. I tried to listen. She said them even slower. I exhaled slowly, a sob escaping my throat.

I started crying harder as my breath caught up to me. I put my head on her shoulder. "I can't live without him."

"Without who?" She ran her hand up and down my back.

"You didn't read the letter?" Kennedy had never been great at following rules. I kind of just figured she would have read it immediately.

"No."

I lifted my head from her shoulder. I didn't have the strength to tell her everything. But it was in the letter. "You can read it now."

"Are you sure?"

I nodded.

She stood up and pulled me to my feet. She guided me over to the little table in the kitchen and put a kettle on the stove. "It's going to be okay, you know." She grabbed my hand and squeezed it. "Whatever's going on…we're going to fix it together."

God I'd missed her. I nodded, even though it wasn't possible to fix all of it.

She let go of my hand and picked up the unopened envelope on the table. I just stared at her as she slowly opened it and unfolded the paper inside.

Her eyes started going back and forth. But she paused almost immediately and closed her eyes. "If I had any idea you were still out there…" She squeezed her eyes tighter and then opened them. "Matt didn't believe it, you know. He hired several PI's to track you down. But every one of them came up empty. Until there was no other option but what we thought was the truth…"

"Don't," I said, cutting her off. Why did everyone keep bringing up Matt? I wasn't here for him. I could so easily picture Matt sitting right here at this table with us. His face permanently frozen in my mind at 16. I swallowed hard.

"But I feel like you should know that," Kennedy said. "That Matt really tried."

I didn't know what to say. Why would a man who asked for the engagement ring back and said nothing at my funeral try to track me down? Just to make sure I wouldn't show up again and ruin his life? "Okay," I said. Her words made me feel sick to my stomach. But they didn't change anything. Matt and I had been done for years. I hadn't mentioned anything about Matt in my letter to her and Mrs. Alcaraz. There was a reason for that. I just wanted the past to stay in the past. Matt breaking my heart all those years ago wasn't important. It was done. I knew stepping foot in this city would bring the memories pouring back. That was why I didn't plan on staying long.

"I'm sorry," she said. "I'm not trying to push you. But…why didn't you come back?"

I took a deep breath. "Keep reading."

"I should have known your father would do something like this. Kidnap you and keep you hostage." She shook her head and started reading again.

After a couple minutes she looked up at me. "You got married." It didn't really come out as a question, but there was no judgement in her voice.

I thought there might be. She knew everything I'd promised Matt. And yet...she didn't make me feel guilty. I nodded as my eyes filled with tears too.

"I remember him. That nice bodyguard. He always made you feel safe." She smiled. "I could tell how much he loved you, even back then. You could see it in his eyes."

God, she was going to make me cry. "Keep reading."

She smiled harder as she read about Jacob. I'd left a few instructions in the note. About not making him wear a shirt all the time. And letting him watch football on Sundays. I needed to make sure Jacob never forgot his father. Football would keep them close. It would make him remember.

But Kennedy's smile quickly fell. And a tear ran down her cheek. "Oh, Brooklyn." Her eyes kept scanning the page. "No." She kept shaking her head and more tears fell.

I wished it wasn't true. God, I'd do anything to change it.

"Your father did this to Miller?"

I'd wanted to make sure I explained why I did what I did last night. There was just one problem...I hadn't done it. "I don't even know anymore."

The tea kettle started whistling. Kennedy wiped her eyes and ran to the stove before the noise could wake

Jacob. Her hand shook as she poured us each a cup of tea.

But she didn't turn back around. She pressed her hands onto the counter, like she was trying to hold herself upright.

I stood up and put my arm around her back.

"No one deserves as much pain as you've been through. No one. Especially someone as kindhearted as you. You don't deserve this." She grabbed a paper towel and blew her nose. She choked out a laugh. "And you're not supposed to be comforting me. I should be the one comforting you." She grabbed the two teacups. "Come on. Sit down. You need to fill in some blanks for me."

I sat back down and took a sip of tea.

"Do you want to tell me about Miller and your life with him? Or…is it…"

I shook my head. "I can't talk about him right now."

"Okay." She leaned forward and lowered her voice. "How much does Jacob know? I mean…does he know about what happened to his father?"

"He saw the car explode." I wished he hadn't. I desperately wished he hadn't witnessed all of it.

"Puta mierda," Kennedy said and looked up at the ceiling, blinking fast. "I feel like my heart is breaking."

"Jacob was so brave." I puffed up my cheeks and exhaled slowly, trying to make myself not cry. "I'm so proud of him. If it wasn't for him, I'm sure I'd be sitting in jail right now."

"Are…are you sure Miller's dead?"

I nodded. I was positive. But I knew why she asked. Because I was sitting here very much alive and she'd thought I was dead too.

"He's not going to come back in 16 years with a crazy story like this?"

I laughed, even though it was forced. "No. He...he's gone." The words made the knife in my chest twist again.

She lifted up the letter again and scanned the last few lines a second time. "So...did you do it? Did you kill your father like the letter said you were going to?"

I felt like a coward. A failure. "I couldn't."

"Because you're not a killer, Brooklyn. Do you really think the cops are after you? You really think they would believe you did this to your own husband?"

"My dad said he paid off local law enforcement. That I'm in the clear. But I don't believe anything he says. He also swore he didn't do it. And I don't know what to believe."

"Well, where was he when it happened?"

"He didn't say. He just said he'd never hurt me because he loved me."

"Yeah, but he didn't hurt you." She waved the letter in the air. "He killed your husband."

"The bomb was in *my* car though."

"What?" She scanned the letter again.

"I didn't put that in there. I know how confusing it all is. I'd parked behind Miller the night before. He was moving my car so he could drive his. I was supposed to die. Not him." My voice cracked.

"Oh my God."

"My father said it was some rival family or something. The Locatellis. That their signature was on the bomb."

"Their signature?" She exhaled slowly. "And suddenly we're in a crime show."

"Yeah I know."

"I know I'm missing a lot of details, but you don't believe your father, do you? He locked you up for almost a year before you escaped. He's a psychopath."

"I don't...I don't know. He swore he'd never hurt me..."

"He stole your fucking kidney!" Her eyes grew round and she clapped her hand over her mouth. "Shoot," she whispered and looked over at Jacob who had started to stir. "Sorry."

"It's okay. He'll be a little more alert this morning and I can't wait for you to really meet him." I turned back to her. "I have to step out in a couple hours though. I'm meeting up with my dad for lunch to try to get more answers. I don't think I'll be long." I just wanted to get this over with. Hear whatever lame alibi Poppy had. And then I'd figure out my next move.

"No. No way are you going to meet up with him again alone. I'm coming with you."

"But Jacob..."

"My mom will watch Jacob."

"Kennedy, I don't want to pull you into this mess. I shouldn't have even come here. I don't want to put you in danger too..."

"Brooklyn," she said, very sternly. "You are not doing this alone. Because you don't have to. You have me."

Tears pulled in my eyes. My uncle had said something similar to me all those years ago. A few doors down the hall from this very spot. *You have me.* "Thanks, Kennedy. But I'm not going to put anyone else at risk." I was so tired of losing everyone I loved. I was just so damned tired.

"I'm making the choice myself. I'm coming with you to this evil luncheon with daddy dearest," she said and put her pinky in the air as she took a sip of tea.

I couldn't help but laugh. That was the Kennedy I knew and loved. I wiped the remaining tears out of my eyes. "You look really happy by the way," I said. "I'm so glad you're good."

The smile fell from her face, but only for a second. "Yeah." She cleared her throat. "I have a lot to catch you up on."

"Sixteen years' worth of stuff."

"Mhm."

"And I want to hear all of it. What college was like, what you're up to now. All of it."

But it would have to wait because Jacob was up. He shoved the worn blanket off of him. He looked a little bewildered as he looked around. But then his eyes spotted mine and a smile spread across his face. He jumped off the couch and ran over to me.

I lifted him onto my lap. "Good morning, sweet boy." I kissed his cheek. "Do you remember Mommy's friend from last night? Kennedy."

He shook his head and tried to tuck his head under my arm.

"He's a little shy," I said. "Jacob, look at me."

He stopped squirming and looked up. I peppered his face in kisses until he was laughing. "This is my best friend. You're going to love her too, I promise."

"Noooo."

"Jacob," I said with a laugh.

He ducked under my arm again.

"It's okay," Kennedy said. "I have stranger danger too." She scooted her chair back. "Don't you dare get close to me, Stranger Jacob."

He giggled when she pushed her chair back again.

"Does the little stranger want some breakfast?" she asked.

He smiled from his hiding spot. "Cuppycakes."

I bit my lip. I'd been giving him whatever he wanted to eat. I'd really dropped the ball on the healthy eating because we both needed comfort food. "Is that okay if I whip up some cupcakes real quick?" I asked. "He loves them."

"For breakfast?" Kennedy asked.

"Just…for now."

She nodded. "Well, we probably have everything you need for normal cupcakes. But not granola flax seed cupcakes or whatever weird healthy thing you do to them."

"I actually just make normal cupcakes."

"No way," Kennedy said with a smile. "With sugar and white flour and everything? That's so unlike you."

I laughed. "I know. Jacob gives me and his father plenty of exercise." I pressed my lips together at the mention of Miller.

"I bet." Kennedy smiled down at Jacob. "So…cuppycakes for breakfast?"

"Cuppycakes!" Jacob yelled and ducked out from under my arm. He seemed significantly less scared now that cuppycakes were going to be made.

"Jacob is my little helper in the kitchen," I said. I stood up and plopped him back down in my seat. I started humming as I pulled ingredients out of the fridge and pantry. It only took me a few minutes to whip up some vanilla cupcakes with homemade cream cheese icing. I felt more like myself than I had in weeks as I poured the batter into the cupcake tin. I was even humming. I touched my throat after I closed the oven door. For just a second, after everything that happened, I felt a slice of normalcy.

I turned around to see Kennedy's chair pulled up to Jacob's. He was drawing something for her, pointing at it and describing what it was.

I was humming and baking. And my son was smiling and laughing.

Guilt wrapped around my chest. I remembered feeling this way before. All those years ago whenever I'd been happy after my mom's death. And my uncle's. And when Matt broke my heart. I felt guilty for being happy all those times.

I exhaled slowly. I'd never be as happy as when Miller was here. But I'd never feel guilty for my son's smiles or laughter. Never. And I never wanted him to feel that same pain I did. I never wanted him to feel guilty for living. I wanted him to keep smiling just like this forever.

He gave me hope that we could get through this. Together. It still felt like my heart was shattered. But I was wrong when I thought I'd never have a home again. Because Kennedy's place had always felt like home to me.

I had planned on running after speaking to my dad. But now I was rethinking all of it.

CHAPTER 7

Sunday

Matt

"Can you clean this for me?" I asked and pulled Brooklyn's ring out of my pocket. This was the third jewelry store I'd been to this afternoon. And each store clerk told me the same thing after looking at the ring with disgust…that I should just put the diamonds on a new band. They immediately gave me the ring back and started showing me their newest inventory. But that wasn't what I wanted. I needed *this* ring back. It was like it held a piece of my heart. I just wanted someone to fix it.

The old man adjusted his glasses. "Oh my," he said in a thick accent. He lifted it out of my hand and put it up close to his face. "What happened to this?"

"It's a family heirloom. We found it in the backyard when we were doing construction. Buried in some dirt." It was the same lie I'd told the other two jewelers. I didn't want to go into my sordid past with a stranger. And digging it up from beside Brooklyn's grave sounded bad. Really bad. If he knew the truth, he'd probably call the cops and have me arrested for grave robbery.

"Hmm." He turned the ring around in his fingers and looked up to me. "Buried, you say?"

I nodded.

"How long in dirt?"

I shrugged like I didn't know for sure. "Maybe like…16 years or so."

He pointed to the band. "Oxidized."

"Is that why it's black?"

"Yes, yes. But I can fix that. I'll need time."

"Yeah, of course." I breathed a sigh of relief.

"Such a beautiful piece," he said. He pulled out a cushioned box and placed it inside like it was a prized item instead of trash like the other jewelers thought.

I should have come straight here. Those new jewelry stores didn't appreciate stuff like this. But this place had been around for ages.

"I'll need your paperwork."

My paperwork?

He grabbed a clipboard with a sheet of paper for my information.

Oh. Yup, this was definitely an old-fashioned place. The last jewelry store I tried had made me look at diamonds on an iPad after I specifically said I wasn't interested.

I quickly filled out the information and handed the clipboard back to him.

"Come Tuesday or Wednesday. I have fixed this."

"Thank you so much."

"You have good day now."

No upsell. Or cross-sale. Or anything. He lifted up the cushioned box and turned to go into his backroom again.

"Wait," I said.

He paused in his tracks and turned around. "Yes?"

"I'm actually looking for a new ring too." I was too annoyed at the other stores to really bother looking. But now that I knew Brooklyn's ring was in good hands, I was ready to get back to what I needed to do.

"A new one?"

"An engagement ring, yes."

He looked down at the cushioned box in his hand. "But this piece...I fix. I make beautiful."

"I know. I just...I need a new one too."

He shook his head and chuckled. "New is not better."

His words hit me in the gut. I knew that. And that wasn't what I was doing. I wasn't replacing Brooklyn. I was just...choosing myself first for the first time in a long time. Kennedy wasn't better than Brooklyn. She was different. She was good for me in different ways.

"That one's for a friend," I said, lies coming easy to me these days. "Now I need one for my girlfriend."

He frowned. "You give this one to girlfriend." He lifted up the box.

I shook my head. "I need a new one for my girlfriend."

"No. This one better. You give this to girlfriend."

"I can't do that. I..." my voice trailed off. "Help me find a new one."

"No."

"What?"

"You give this to girlfriend. I fix. You have good day now." He turned around and disappeared into his back room.

Well, that wasn't very helpful. And now I was wondering if I should have entrusted him with Brooklyn's ring. Maybe he hadn't even understood what I wanted.

Or maybe he had. And he just didn't understand why I'd give a family heirloom to a friend and a new ring to my girlfriend. I sighed and ran my hand down my face.

And what did any of it matter anyway? Buying a ring wasn't going to make Kennedy suddenly text me and say everything was fine. Rob was right…she'd dumped my ass. I pulled out my phone. There were still no messages from her. Every ounce of me wanted to go back to her apartment and demand answers. But that hadn't worked out so well for me last night.

I had to respect what she wanted and wait.

After all these years with my life on pause, I thought I'd be good at waiting. But I never meant to be 32 and still stuck in the past. On some of my worst days I still woke up and reached out for Brooklyn in my bed. It had been 16 years. I'd spent half my life missing her. And I was done being stuck.

I'd go to a different jewelry store. Another older one without pushy store clerks. But one that was hopefully more helpful than this guy. Fourth time was a charm, right?

I pushed out the front door and was almost blinded by camera flashes. "Shit," I said under my breath as I backed up into the store again, covering my face. The cameras kept flashing, taking shots through the window. My stomach sank. *Son of a bitch.* One of the last jewelry stores I was in must have tipped them off. And I knew exactly what the paparazzi was trying to capture.

I could already see it clear as day in tomorrow's gossip magazines. That I was here buying a ring for Poppy. The cameras kept flashing and I turned around. This was the last thing I needed right now. Kennedy seeing me coming out of a ring shop with Poppy's face plastered next to mine in a dumb magazine? She was already freaked out.

Fuck. I pushed back outside. "I'll pay you for those photos. Double what you're being offered by anyone else."

One of the photographers stuck out their hand and I pulled out my wallet. *Shit.* I'd spent my last cash at the bar last night with Tanner. That cheap ass. I needed to get to an ATM. But I already saw one of the photographers climbing into a taxi and driving off.

I flipped the bird at the paparazzi. Not that ruining one shot was going to get me out of this mess. I hurried over to my car. Just because I didn't have any cash on me didn't mean I couldn't fix this. One of the many perks of having a tech genius friend.

***

Scarlett opened the door with a huge smile on her face.

"Scar," I said and gave her a stern look, wiping the smile from her face. "We just talked about this. No opening the door." I walked into the apartment and closed the door behind me.

"For strangers. You're not a stranger. You're Uncle Matt."

This little girl was terrible at following instructions. She was going to be a handful when she was older.

"So I can't be in trouble." She smiled again. "Let's go play."

"I'm actually here for your dad, kiddo."

She stuck her lip out. "But I want to play Barbies."

"Maybe after I talk to him." I loved playing with her. But Barbies was not my favorite. For some reason she never let me be Ken. I always had to be her sidekick. She was used to playing with her cousin, Sophie. I couldn't wait till she was old enough for me to teach her poker. And pool. I wanted her to be able to put any guy in their place.

"Daddy's with Mommy."

"Where?"

Scarlett shrugged.

That was not at all helpful. "Are they in his study?"

"I don't think so."

"Are they in the library?"

"No."

I peered into the kitchen but didn't see them. I walked past the kitchen and into the huge great room. They weren't there either. But Scarlett had all her Barbie stuff out. "Are they even home?"

"Yes. We'll wait for them and play." She slipped her hand into mine and pulled me toward her toys.

I sighed as she sat down on the carpet.

"Kiddo, tell me where your parents are."

"They're busy doing grownup things."

"Where?"

"Upstairs."

Oh fuck. Were they having sex right now? Who was watching Scarlett? "Where is your brother?"

"Liam's sleeping. He's been real bad. He didn't sleep at all last night."

"Who's watching you?"

Scarlett pointed to one of the cameras. "Secru...secur...secrutitty?"

I tried not to laugh. "Security?"

She nodded. "Mr. Briggs is in there. Or Mr. Porter." She pointed to the camera again. "One of them is always in there."

I wasn't sure she understood that Briggs wasn't actually inside that camera. And I knew they had security watching them at all times. But this was a little inappropriate to leave Scarlett all alone unsupervised in person.

A part of me wanted to go up there and yell at them for being bad parents. And the other part of me thought it was probably not wise to see Penny naked. Yes, I'd had a little crush on her for years. But I'd finally squashed it. We were better off as friends. I hesitated. Nope, it was still better if I didn't see her naked. And I certainly didn't need to see James' ass.

I sat down Indian style on the rug with Scarlett. "Okay, let's play for a few minutes." I reached for the Ken doll.

But she slid a blonde Barbie into my hand. "You be my best friend. We're going shopping for dresses before the ball tonight."

"How about I be Ken and tell Barbie what she looks good in?"

"Uncle Matt, Ken can't see me in my dress before the ball. And his name is Axel, not Ken."

"Axel, huh?" Axel was our friend Tyler's son. It drove James crazy that Scarlett had a crush on Axel. But I actually found it quite entertaining. The two of them were adorable together.

"Yes. Axel is my boyfriend."

"Whatever you say, kiddo."

"I do say. We're going to get married and have ten babies and live happily ever after."

"I bet you will."

She nodded with a smile. "You try this dress on." She handed me a big, poofy dress in a hideous pink color. While she started changing her redheaded Barbie into a tight-fitting blue dress.

"This is the one you want your friend to wear?" I asked.

"Yes."

"It's a lot of material."

"Yeah, it's my least favorite."

"Then why did you give it to your friend?"

Scarlett looked up at me. "So she looks terrible."

"You want me to look terrible?"

She giggled. "You're not wearing the dress, Uncle Matt."

I know that. "Why would you want your friend to look bad though? Shouldn't she look good at the ball too?"

"No."

I stared at her.

"I have to look the best so Axel loves me."

"Scarlett, why do you think that?"

She pressed her lips together.

"Last time Axel was here he said my pigtails were silly. And Sophie didn't have pigtails. So I think he likes her better now."

I tried not to smile. I'd seen Scarlett put pigtails in her own hair. And they did look silly. Because she always did them quite lopsided. I wasn't sure why she didn't want her mother's help with her hair. But whenever she did pigtails she insisted on doing them all by herself.

"You know what I think?" I asked.

She shook her head.

"That you don't have to change a single thing about yourself for a boy to like you, okay? Never."

She scrunched her mouth to the side. "I still want to wear the blue dress. And you wear the ugly one. Please, Uncle Matt?"

I smiled. How could I say no to her when she said please? "Okay. I'll wear the ugly dress." I quickly changed my Barbie into the poofy number.

Scarlett hopped her Barbie over to mine. "You look great in that," she said to my Barbie.

Wow, she'd already mastered an artful lie. "You don't think it's too much?" I asked in a high squeaky voice.

Scarlett giggled. "No. It's the perfect amount. Wait!" She grabbed a winter hat that didn't match the dress at all. "This'll make it better." She pushed it down on my Barbie's head.

"Thank you!" I squealed. "You look amazing too."

Scarlett twirled her Barbie around. "Yes I do. Let's go to the ball."

We drove around in a pink convertible. Posed for pictures on a red carpet. Scarlett finally handed me the Ken doll. "You be Axel."

Score. I shook my head. I wasn't sure why I was so excited to finally be a man. And then I immediately hated every word I'd just said in my head.

"Wait," Scarlett said. She stole Ken back and put the other Barbie in my hand. "Bathroom emergency."

Oh no. I hated when she did this. Why did she never give more notice? "Okay, let's go." I started to stand up. I went to grab her but she laughed.

"Not me. I don't need to poo right now."

Good to know.

"I need to talk to Sophie in the bathroom."

"Okay." I sat back down and we hopped over to an empty spot on the carpet.

"I'm sorry I made you wear that dress, Sophie. You look awful in it."

"What?" I said in a shrill voice. "I look bad?"

Scarlett smile. "Terrible. Switch with me. I'll wear it for you."

"That's really sweet," I said in my normal voice and ruffled Scarlett's hair.

"Axel should like me even when I look silly. Right, Uncle Matt?"

Scarlett rarely ever listened to me. Hence her opening the front door for me again. But she was actually taking this to heart. "Right, kiddo."

We swapped dresses. And she even pulled the ugly winter hat over her Barbie's head. "Ready, Sophie?" she asked.

"Ready!" I shrieked.

We walked back into the ballroom and started dancing again.

I grabbed the Ken doll. "I love your dress and your hat," I said in a deep voice.

"Axel doesn't sound like that," she said with a laugh.

His voice was still a little high-pitched. But he'd grow out of that soon. I glanced at the clock on the wall. I'd been playing with Scarlett for over 30 minutes. What the hell were James and Penny doing up there?

"Dance party!" Scarlett yelled. She tossed her Barbie to the side and started shaking her hips.

Apparently the ball had come to us. I stood up and mimicked her moves.

She laughed as I spun her around in a circle.

We kept dancing for another ten minutes before she plopped back down. She started humming to herself as she made Barbie and Ken dance.

I looked over toward the stairs. It had been a really long time. Surely they were at least under the covers by now, right? "I'm gonna go check on your parents. Stay right there, okay?"

Scarlett nodded.

I went up the stairs. The door to the master bedroom was wide open. Interesting choice. What if Scarlett had wandered up here? She would have been scarred for life.

I put my hand in front of my face, hoping to block them going at it, and peered into the room. "What the hell are you guys doing up here?" I asked.

There was no response.

I lowered my hand. The bed was empty and perfectly made.

I walked into the room and checked in the master bathroom too.

Empty.

Huh. They hadn't actually left Scarlett alone here, had they? I wandered out of the bedroom and heard Liam cooing from his room.

I hurried down the hallway. If they left their baby alone…my thoughts trailed off as I entered the nursery.

James' head was resting on the slats of the crib. His eyes were closed and he was snoring lightly. Penny's head was in his lap and she was out cold too. A children's book was on the floor beside them. They must have fallen asleep reading to Liam. Scarlett had said he hadn't slept last night. They all must be exhausted.

Liam cooed again and started kicking his little legs. His parents were sleeping, but Liam didn't seem keen on a nap right now.

I stepped over Penny's body and leaned over the railing of the crib to lift Liam. He quieted down when I pulled him to my chest. I smiled down at my friends. Of course they hadn't left Scarlett all alone. They were great parents.

"Let's give them a break, okay?" I whispered to Liam.

He looked up at me with big watery eyes.

I went back out in the hall and closed the door gently behind me. "Shh," I whispered to him.

He didn't respond. Because of course he didn't. He was a baby.

"Liam is going to play with us for a bit while your parents take a nap." I set Liam down on the carpet next to us.

"Hi, Liam." Scarlett leaned over and kissed his little forehead. "You can be Axel now," she said and gave Liam the Ken doll.

What the hell? Seriously, why did she always make me play a female part? "I can keep being Axel," I said.

"No."

"Why?"

"Because his hair is plastic. And it's okay if Liam gets slobber on it. He's slobbery right now."

Oh. Well, that was a very practical reason.

Liam put Ken's head in his mouth and bit it.

Scarlett scrunched up her nose, but didn't pull the doll away from her brother. "He's a bad Axel," she said.

"He's trying his best."

Scarlett shrugged. "Dance party?"

HOMECOMING

"Dance party," I said with a nod. I pulled the Ken doll out of Liam's mouth and lifted Liam into my arms. And then all three of us started dancing around the room.

CHAPTER 8

Sunday

Brooklyn

"You really don't have to come in," I said to Kennedy. I was standing outside the diner my dad had taken me to years ago. The one he said my mom and him used to frequent. And I knew exactly why he'd chosen this place. He was playing games with my head. This was emotional warfare.

There was just one problem with his sneaky plan…didn't he see that this made him look more guilty? There was absolutely no reason to mess with my head if he was telling the truth. "I'm serious," I said. "I can handle him myself."

"Too late," Kennedy said and opened up the door.

I was glad she had come along. But I really hoped this didn't put her on my father's radar.

The diner hadn't changed one bit. There were still black and white checkered floors and cute little red booths. The smell of French fries hung in the air, making my stomach growl.

"Table for two?" the hostess said.

"No, we're meeting someone…" Kennedy looked around.

"Two someone's actually," I said.

"What?" Kennedy asked.

"Yeah, sorry, I forgot to mention that Poppy was tagging along. She's supposed to be his alibi or something."

"Poppy? Poppy Cannavaro?" Her face looked really pale.

And I had a feeling I knew why. Because if she'd ever run into Poppy in the city, she knew Poppy looked a hell of a lot like Isabella. Enough to creep anyone out. "She looks a lot like Isabella, doesn't she?" I looked around the restaurant. It didn't look like they'd arrived yet.

"Um…" Kennedy's voice trailed off. "Right. Yeah, they look really similar. You know what?" She grabbed my arm. "There isn't really anything they could say that you'd believe anyway, right? So what's the point in even talking to them? I think we should just go get lunch and catch up. Because we really have a lot to catch up on."

"Maybe we can stop by Central Park on the way back and go for a walk to chat afterwards? But I really need to get this over with. I need my head to stop spinning."

"Right. Of course."

"Table for four please," I said to the hostess.

"Right this way."

We followed her to an empty booth. I slid in right next to Kennedy so I'd have a good view of my father and Poppy's faces during our lunch. I needed to know that they were lying. And my head was clearer today. I'd be able to tell. I had to.

Kennedy fidgeted with the menu. But it didn't really look like she was perusing the options. "So…besides for the fact that Poppy looks like Isabella…what else do you know about her?"

"Nothing. I mean…not nothing. I met her once. At Thanksgiving." I pressed my lips together. I remembered the pudding flying onto her face and her screaming. I'd found it funny for a minute. Until Matt didn't. Until everything broke. I pushed away the thought. "And it seems like she's working for my father. My dad said that she got vengeance against the Locatellis already. Apparently she's fond of car bombs, which I find highly suspicious."

Kennedy nodded. "Okay, cool."

I gave her a weird look.

She quickly shook her head. "I mean not cool. What kind of psycho is fond of car bombs?"

"Yeah. And if she's that fond of them, who's to say she wasn't the one behind the bomb in my car?"

"Good point." Kennedy started fidgeting with the menu again.

"Is everything okay?" I asked.

She put the menu down. "Are you planning on seeing Matt while you're in town?"

I hadn't expected the question. And I honestly hadn't even let myself consider the possibility. I immediately shook my head. "No. I'm not." There was no point. I hadn't come here for him. And I really wanted everyone to stop mentioning him. I wasn't here to relive my past. I was here to move forward.

"I really feel like you should see him," Kennedy said.

"Why? What's the point of re-hashing old wounds?" Just thinking about facing him after all these years made my stomach twist into knots. What was there to say? I'm so happy that you're so happy without me? Silence said that enough.

"It's not about re-hashing old wounds. It's about...healing. You two were so in love."

I was already healed. *From that.* I'd moved on. I was happy with Miller. "It was a long time ago."

"Does it feel like that long when you're here in New York? Because it all feels rather recent to me. And you two were so in love," she said again like I hadn't heard it the first time.

I shook my head. I didn't want to talk about this. Everything she said made my stomach twist even more. Because Kennedy was wrong. Matt and I hadn't been in love. Yes, I'd been madly in love with *him*. But he hadn't loved me back. I think a part of me always knew that. That I didn't belong in his world. That I never would.

"You're really not going to see him?"

"No."

She exhaled slowly. "Okay. Well then." She pressed her lips together. "I really need to tell you something. Actually a lot of somethings. But... Shit," she said under her breath, and looked over at the door.

I followed her gaze. Poppy had just arrived. I was hoping her similarities to Isabella wouldn't affect me. But...her dark hair and sharp features made my heart beat a little faster.

She pulled off her sunglasses and looked around the little diner in disgust. And then her eyes fell on me. Her lips curved into a smile, and it reminded me so much of Isabella that I actually stopped breathing. That same fear washing over me whenever Isabella turned my way. Just waiting in horror to see how she'd torture me next.

Poppy dismissed the hostess with a flick of her wrist and walked toward us. Her heels clicking on the linoleum floor made me wince. It was like being back at

Empire High all over again. Isabella's heels echoing in the hall as she approached me to torment me. I couldn't believe I was in my thirties and still haunted by those memories.

"Brooklyn, darling," Poppy said. She leaned down and air kissed both my cheeks.

I stayed perfectly still, thinking one wrong move might set her off.

"So good to see you again after all these years." She grabbed a napkin off the table and wiped off the booth before sitting down. "Interesting choice for dining."

"My father chose it."

Poppy laughed. "Uncle Richard would never." She turned her attention to Kennedy. "And you are?"

Kennedy cleared her throat as she stared at Poppy. "I'm Kennedy."

Poppy just stared at her.

"I'm Brooklyn's friend."

Kennedy was always outspoken. But she seemed suddenly reserved in front of Poppy. Almost like she was scared of her.

"Well, Kennedy, this is a family meeting," Poppy said. "We need a little privacy."

"She's staying," I said.

Poppy smiled and it stretched her skin awkwardly around her mouth. "If you say so, cousy."

I gagged a little in my mouth. It was like how Isabella always called me sissy. Just because I was Poppy's cousin didn't mean I wanted to be called that.

"So where is Uncle Richard?" she asked. "It's so rare for him to be late." She pulled her phone out of her purse and started texting.

I glanced over at Kennedy.

She shrugged.

"So…how have you been?" I asked. *Killed anyone's husband recently?*

"I've been fantastic." She smiled again and put her phone away. "How about you?"

I winced. Was she serious? She knew what this meeting was about, right? "I'm…not great," I said.

"Oh. Right." She put her hand to her chest. "I'm so sorry for your loss, cousy."

Are you?

"Speaking of relationships. I'm dating this really great guy."

That was a really insensitive segue. I'd known Poppy and I wouldn't be friends when I met her 16 years ago. As soon as my friend James had said she was the worst. If James didn't like her, I kind of figured I wouldn't either. And her looking like Isabella's just-as-evil twin didn't help. But now I knew for sure that we would never be close. What kind of person would talk about their amazing relationship in front of someone who just lost the love of their life?

"And it's definitely getting serious," she added.

"Really?" Kennedy said, deadpan.

"Yes, really," Poppy said. "Super serious."

"I'm so happy for you," I said. I just didn't want to hear about it right this second. I just wanted to get this meeting over with. I had a bunch of decisions to make, and her current relationship status had nothing to do with any of it.

Poppy smiled again, her lips curling evilly. "Wait, I think you might know him actually."

"Oh yeah?" I'd been out of town for 16 years. I doubted I knew whatever tool she was currently dating.

IVY SMOAK

He was probably some douchey hot-shot CEO of a company that was inadvertently ruining the world somehow.

"Mhm. He went to Empire High at the same time as you."

"Awesome." I hoped it was Cupcake. That guy was still on my shitlist for what he'd done to Kennedy. Poppy and him deserved each other.

"Aren't you dying to know who it is?" Poppy asked.

No. Not really.

Kennedy grabbed my hand under the table and squeezed it. I looked over at her. She looked like she was going to be sick. Wait...was it actually Cupcake? I'd never bring him up. I didn't want Kennedy to ever have to think about that creep. But from the way she was holding on to me for dear life, I was pretty sure my guess was correct.

"Wait," Poppy said. "Oh my gosh, silly me. I almost completely forgot. You two…"

"Angel," my father said, cutting Poppy off mid-sentence. "You came."

Kennedy exhaled slowly and let her hand fall from mine.

"Of course I came." I needed answers. Real ones. Not orchestrated lies.

Poppy gasped. "Uncle Richard, what on earth happened to your face?" She put her hand on her nose.

My father had two black eyes. And his nose was red and swollen. Honestly, my hand didn't feel much better than his face looked.

"My daughter has a mean right hook," he said, with a hint of pride in his voice.

I was pretty sure he was the only father in existence that would be thrilled that he'd gotten punched in the face by his own daughter.

Poppy gasped again. "You hit him?"

"At least I didn't shoot him," I said. For someone who loved car bombs I didn't know why she couldn't wipe the shocked expression off her face. Maybe it was stuck that way from all the Botox.

"Let's order," my father said.

Poppy shook her head and pushed her menu aside. "I'm good."

"Are you sure?" my father asked. "They have a delicious sandwich here made with real homemade turkey. And the chocolate milkshakes are the best in town."

Poppy just gaped at him.

He waved the waitress down. "Four of the usual," he said, without asking anyone what they wanted.

But I didn't even care. I remembered how delicious the turkey sandwiches and milkshakes were and I was actually craving them now.

Poppy was stunned to silence.

"You'll like their sandwiches, I promise," my father said without looking at her. "Okay, angel. Where did we leave off in our discussion last night?"

He'd been trying to convince me to move back in with him. Which was clearly never going to happen.

"All that matters is one thing. Did one of you or someone who works for you kill my husband?"

"What?" Poppy said, like she was truly offended by the accusation. "It was the Locatellis. Their signature was all over the bomb."

That's exactly what my father had said. Almost word for word. I shouldn't have given them so much time to make their stories match.

I stared at her, trying to see if she was lying. But…I couldn't tell. Or maybe I just didn't want to believe what I was seeing. Poppy looked calm. Composed. And…not guilty. "But you love car bombs," I said.

"Of course I do. They're so fun to set up. And the anticipation of waiting for your target to get into their car… Absolutely thrilling." Her eyes twinkled as she said it. Not even the Botox could keep her from looking happy talking about her car bombs. "I have a video of one of my car bombs taking out the Locatelli heir. Would you like to see it? It'll make you feel so much better. It was the perfect retaliation."

Again, it was the same thing my father said. But the look of pure happiness on Poppy's face was hard not to believe. She'd gotten a thrill from murder. I swallowed hard. What was I doing sitting here with these people? This wasn't me. I wasn't one of them.

My mind had been clouded last night. I'd been acting like a Pruitt instead of like myself. I wasn't a monster. Miller had made sure I knew that. And I was pretty sure he'd be disappointed with my plan for revenge. He'd be disappointed that I was even in the city. Exposing our son to this toxic environment.

"Seeing one of your car bombs was quite enough," I said. I just needed to get out of here.

Poppy frowned and leaned forward. "You can't possibly think that bomb was mine. It was in *your* car. Not your husband's. And neither of us would ever hurt you. We're family. Blood doesn't hurt blood. And honestly, the car bomb being in your car is a moot point anyway. Because Miller was family too. We wouldn't have hurt him either. Right, Uncle Richard?"

My father nodded. His eyes searched mine, like he was trying to read what I was thinking.

I was supposed to be reading *him*. Not the other way around. And I had no idea what to think. Because no matter what anyone said, I did always go back to one thing. The bomb was in *my* car. Not Miller's. It was in mine. Someone was trying to hurt *me*. The Locatelli thing made sense. A rival family trying to hurt my father.

I didn't know if I believed their story or not. It didn't matter, though. Because I wasn't a murderer. And I was so done with this family. "Thanks for meeting with me. But I think it's time Kennedy and I get going."

"Angel, wait," my father said. He grabbed my hand on the table, his cool touch sending a shiver down my spine. "I know we've had our ups and downs. But I truly am sorry about Miller. I've always just wanted you to find happiness."

Tears started to pool in the corners of my eyes. I knew it was stupid…but a piece of me actually believed him. A piece of me believed everything he said. I'd always just wanted him to love me. For real. I'd wanted a dad that loved me unconditionally. And wasn't that what he was saying when he said he always wanted me to find happiness?

"Like I've found with Matt," Poppy said.

What? I pulled my hand out of my father's.

"Matthew Caldwell," Poppy said. "That's what I was trying to tell you earlier. I completely forgot the two of you were an item a million years ago. I hope that there's no ill feelings. I really want you to be happy for us."

Matt was dating…Poppy? I just stared at her. I was over him. I had been for years. But if I hadn't been? This would have been the final nail in the coffin. I guess he did always have a thing for brunettes. The image of him fucking that brunette in his swimming pool swirled around in my head. "Yeah," I said. My voice betrayed me though, coming out all croaky and weird. I was over Matthew Caldwell. And I had no idea why my stomach suddenly felt upset. I quickly cleared my throat. "I'm happy for you, Poppy. For both of you."

For just a second Poppy looked surprised by my answer.

Was she trying to bait me? What happened to blood not hurting blood?

Her surprised expression quickly turned to a smile and I shook away my thought. I probably just imagined the look.

"Really," I said. "I'm happy for you. But I really should be going."

"What about lunch?" my father asked.

"I'm suddenly not hungry. I'm sorry." I didn't wait for anyone to say anything else. I slid out of the booth and hurried out of the restaurant.

Kennedy quickly caught up to me on the sidewalk. "Are you okay?"

I took a deep breath, the stale city air not quite filling up my lungs. "Yeah. I'm fine."

"I'm sorry. I was trying to tell you about Poppy and Matt before they arrived…"

"It's really okay."

"Your face isn't screaming *okay* right now."

I shrugged. "Really. It's fine. I just…" my voice trailed off. I just *what*? I'd seen a different side to Matt than he showed everyone else all those years ago. I felt like I'd seen the real him. But maybe all the rest of it had been real instead. I swallowed hard. "I just hoped he'd end up with someone...nicer."

Kennedy pressed her lips together.

"What?"

"Are you saying you'd be more okay with that?" she asked.

"I don't know. I always just wanted him to be happy. And I can't imagine him being happy with someone so...cold." I'd felt the same way when I heard about James marrying Isabella. It just felt wrong. "But I mean, it's his choice obviously. And it's none of my business. I got over him a long time ago."

Kennedy took a deep breath. "I need to tell you something. A lot of somethings actually. I'm just so worried you're going to hate me."

CHAPTER 9

Sunday

Matt

I heard laughter and turned around. Penny had her hip propped against the doorjamb and was wearing a huge smile.

"You really are a great dancer," she said.

"I know." I shimmied my shoulders and she laughed again. "Did you two enjoy your nap?"

She nodded. "We must have just passed out. Liam was up all night. You've calmed him down though."

Liam did seem perfectly content and happy in my arms.

James walked into the room with a big yawn. "Hey, Matt. What's up?"

I stopped dancing to the imaginary music, but I kept bouncing Liam on my hip because he was less fussy when he was moving. I was about to tell James why I'd stopped by, but he was looking around the room.

"Wait, how did you get in here, Matt?" His gaze paused on Scarlett.

"It wasn't me," she said.

"There's no one else here, pumpkin."

She pressed her lips together. "It was an accident."

"Accidents don't happen on purpose."

"This one did. Right, Uncle Matt?"

I did not want to be in the middle of this. But Scarlett really needed to stop opening the door. I would have thought she'd learned her lesson by now. "It's okay, we were just having a dance party," I said, hoping to change the subject.

"A dance party?" Penny asked and lifted Scarlett into her arms. "But where's the music?" She tickled Scarlett's side.

"We don't need music," Scarlett said through her giggles.

"Hmm." Penny twirled her daughter in a circle. "I guess we don't." She kept twirling her around.

I cleared my throat and turned to James. "I actually need your help with something."

James looked at Penny and then back at me. "Is this about Kennedy? Because I really think it's too soon. You're just going to freak her out."

Penny stopped spinning in circles. "Too soon for what?" she asked.

"He's going to propose to her."

Penny raised her eyebrows. "Matt, I know I said you were going to regret not living your life...but I didn't mean you should propose to someone you've known for two weeks."

"I've known her on and off for 16 years."

She kept her eyebrows raised as she placed Scarlett back down on the floor. "There's a pretty big gap in there between high school and right now."

I knew she was right. But she and James couldn't possible understand the situation. I knew Kennedy. I got her. And she got me. I had been struggling for so long and Kennedy made me feel lighter. She made me feel like I wasn't so broken.

None of my friends realized just how much I'd been struggling. And I didn't have to explain myself to them.

I knew proposing to Kennedy was the right choice. To show her how serious and committed I was to us. I just had to win her back first.

Which meant her not seeing what was sure to make its way into the tabloids tomorrow morning. And not just because she'd probably be pissed about people thinking I was going to be engaged to Poppy. The real problem was that I'd have to explain it. And ruin the surprise that I was at the jewelry store because I was going to propose to *her*. Which she probably wouldn't believe because I hadn't found a ring yet.

"I really appreciate the advice, but that's actually not what I'm here to talk about. I need James' help making sure some pictures of me don't make it online."

Liam started making those cute little noises he made when he was happy. I smiled down at him and he did it again.

"What kind of pictures?" Penny asked.

"One of the jewelry stores I visited today must have tipped off the paparazzi. They cornered me outside the last jewelry store I visited and with all that buzz about Poppy and me being in a relationship…"

"You're worried Kennedy will be pissed," James supplied.

"And my only explanation will be to tell her I was there for her. And it'll ruin all my plans."

James nodded. "Okay. I can help with that."

I breathed a sigh of relief. "Thank you, you're a life-saver."

"Here, let me take him so you two can get to work." Penny lifted Liam out of my arms. "Thank you for watching the kids."

"No problem. Next time you guys can just call me if you need some help."

Penny smiled. "I might just have to take you up on that."

I followed James down the hall and into his study.

***

I walked over the weird little moat to Tanner's apartment, doing my best to ignore the tarp shifting beneath me. Seriously…what was in that thing?

There was a splashing noise and I jumped. That moat gave me the willies. I quickly let myself in with my key.

I pulled out my phone as I walked down the hallway. Still nothing new from Kennedy. I was lucky I looked up at the last minute, because I almost ran right into the new chairs placed in the middle of the hallway. It was definitely a weird place for chairs. They were right in the way. Also from what I could see of the back of them, they looked like desk chairs with really high backs. Which made even less sense since there was no table. And why would there be any of that in a hallway? Luckily the hallways were quite wide or they would have completely blocked my path. I was about to sidestep them when they both spun around perfectly in sync.

Tanner was sitting in one and Nigel was in the other. And they both looked very stern. Actually, Nigel's sternness looked more sassy than anything.

"I'm very disappointed in you, young man," Tanner said.

"What?" I just stared at him. "Tanner, you're younger than me. How many times are we going to have this conversation?"

"Right, of course I am. But I act much older than you. Clearly."

Did he? Because this wasn't the first time he'd accosted me in a weird way in his apartment when he was "disappointed in me."

"How could you do this to us?!" Nigel screamed at the top of his lungs.

"Nigel, stop it, you're acting hysterical." Tanner turned back to me. "How could you do this to us?!"

I laughed. "I have no idea what the two of you are upset about but…"

"You're engaged?!" Tanner said as he glared at me.

For fuck's sake. How did they know about this? I should have known better than to ask for Rob's help. Now the whole world knew. Not that I wasn't planning on bringing Tanner into the loop. I just thought I'd get a chance to tell him myself. To avoid exactly this.

Nigel stood up before I could respond and kicked his chair. It rolled into the wall with a quiet thud. "Ow," he said and grabbed his foot, hopping awkwardly in his lederhosen.

"Are you okay?" I asked.

He collapsed back in the chair. "I'll never be okay again," he said with a heavy sigh. "And now my foot is broken to bits."

"You guys, I'm not engaged."

"You're not?" Nigel asked. He suddenly didn't seem at all concerned about his hurt foot.

"No." I sighed. "I was thinking about asking Kennedy to marry me. But I haven't asked her yet. And I was going to tell you. How did you even find out?"

"Young Robert called me to gloat," Tanner said. "Hours ago. Where have you been all morning and afternoon?"

"Where have you been all morning and afternoon?"

"I was here the whole time," he said.

"I thought Nigel said you were at church?"

Tanner laughed. But when he saw that I was serious he cleared his throat. "Yeah. That's where I was. I'm a religious man of worship. Of many gods," he added.

Why did Nigel and Tanner both talk so weirdly about church? And what was he talking about many gods for? Was he a big believer in Norse mythology or something? I shook my head. It wasn't important. "So yeah, guys, I'm sorry. I was going to tell you when I saw you next. But you weren't here."

"I was here," Nigel said and folded his arms in front of chest.

"Nigel, why are you here? Don't you have *things* to do?" I gave him a look which I hope he knew meant he was supposed to be finding dirt on Poppy. We had a deal. And that didn't involve him angrily staring at me.

"I'm on a break," Nigel said. "It's scheduled into my calendar. I'll show you if you'd like. It's very full. Do you have a problem with that?"

Yes, I did have a problem with that. Nigel and his stupid calendar. How many breaks did he get? His sassy response seemed to mean he didn't get my subtle hint about his *things* to do. I needed out of this mess. And I needed Nigel's help to do that. Which meant being angry with him wouldn't help anything. I took a deep breath. "Sorry, Nigel. I know you have scheduled breaks."

He smiled. "It's okay, Master Matthew. You've been forgiveth."

Tanner gave him a weird look.

Nigel cleared his throat. "I meant Mr. Caldwell."

I actually thought Tanner was looking at him strangely because Nigel had just said forgiveth. But yeah, the Master Matthew thing was weird too.

"So you're going to propose to Kennedy?" Tanner asked, quickly changing the subject. "And you went to Robert instead of me?" Normally he was joking around, but he looked a little hurt.

"I'm sorry. I would have told you first but you weren't here." That actually had been my plan.

"Right. I was with the gods." Tanner sighed. "But you're serious about this? You're in love with Kennedy?"

"Yeah." I nodded my head. "I love her."

"So that means the two of you must have slept together?"

Why did he always insist on knowing who I was currently sleeping with? I shrugged. "We hooked up in the elevator after leaving James' place."

Tanner nodded. "Nice. Elevator sex is always great. High-five!" He put up his hand.

I didn't bother correcting him. I just high-fived him instead. I hadn't actually had sex with Kennedy. We were trying to take things slow. And for some reason slow wasn't something Tanner understood. To him sex meant love or something. For a guy who was all about true love, it really made no sense.

"If you'll excuse me for one moment." Tanner spun back around in his chair so I couldn't see him.

"What are you doing?" I asked.

"Nothing," he said. But he didn't turn back around. "Glasses me," he said and put his hand out to Nigel.

Nigel pulled a pair of glasses out of the front pocket of his lederhosen and handed them to Tanner.

Tanner's hand disappeared behind the high back of the chair again.

"Tanner?"

He ignored me. I looked over at Nigel.

Nigel started whistling and looked up at the ceiling. What were they doing? I waited another minute, hoping they'd naturally stop being weird. But of course that didn't happen.

I took a step forward to see what was up, but Tanner poked his head out from the side of the chair to look at me. "Kennedy Alcaraz? With a Z at the end of her last name, right?"

"Mhm."

"You're sure it's not an S? Or maybe there's two Ls in there?"

"It's A-L-C-A-R-A-Z." I spelled it out for him and he just stared at me.

"Really?" he asked.

"Really."

"No tildes or accent marks anywhere?"

"No." Why was he suddenly so interested in the spelling of Kennedy's last name?

"You're 100% positive?"

"I've seen it spelled, yeah."

"Got it." He disappeared behind his chair again.

Seriously, what the hell was he doing behind that chair?

He whispered something at Nigel and Nigel looked very happy.

"Tanner?" I asked.

"He needs a minute," Nigel said. "Would you like me to draw you a bath while you wait?"

"No, I don't want a bath. I want to know what Tanner is doing."

"I can't confirm or deny what he's doing," Nigel said. He started whistling again.

"Tanner," I said firmly. "What the hell?" I walked up to the chair and tried to peer around it.

But Tanner spun it so I couldn't see.

I moved again and he spun his chair again, blocking me.

I tried to run around the chair, but he was faster. "Tanner!"

Tanner spun back around to finally face me. "I'm sorry, man," he said. He looked very serious all of a sudden.

"Oh." I knew what this was about. "Did Rob also tell you Kennedy dumped me last night? Because I don't really see it that way. She just needs some time to get used to this. I'll win her back."

"Oh, she already dumped you? Well, that's grand. Now you don't have to dump her. Phew. Case closed. Class dismissed. Finito."

"Um…what?"

"I was so worried to tell you…that's why I just quadruple checked. You and Kennedy aren't a good match, I was wrong. My bad."

"What are you talking about?"

"I'm very sorry that I brought her back into your life, but it's a no go. Abort mission."

I just stared at him.

"You're a bad match," he said. "You should just stay friends."

"But I love her," I said.

"Nah." Tanner shook his head. "You don't."

"How the hell do you know?"

Tanner lifted up his hands. "Don't shoot the messenger, man. I'm just telling you what I know."

"How would you know if we're a bad match or not?"

"I mean, it's not that you're a bad match per se. It's more that you're not a *perfect* match. It's not true love. We'll keep looking."

"I don't want to keep looking. I'm going to propose to her."

"No, you're not," Tanner said.

"Yes I am."

"You can't!" Nigel said. "You can't do it if it's not true love! You won't be happy! Kennedy isn't the love of your life. If she was Tanner would know it!"

"And let me guess, Nigel…you're the love of my life?"

Nigel's cheeks turned red. "You really think so?"

"Nigel, stop it," Tanner said.

Nigel kept staring at me.

"Cut it out," Tanner hissed when Nigel didn't stop.

"Yes, Master Tanner," Nigel said and winked at me.

For the love of God. "I don't know what the two of you are up to, but it's not funny." Sure, James and Penny thought proposing was a bad idea. Same with Rob and Mason. But only because it was too soon. They weren't making up shit about true love like I was an idiot. "I'm proposing to her," I said more firmly.

Tanner winced.

"Seriously, what the fuck, Tanner? You're supposed to be happy for me."

"I am happy for you to...be a good boy and not propose to Kennedy."

"Stop it," I said.

"You stop it."

"You're both being rude. I just told you I loved her. Why the fuck would you tell me we're a bad match?"

Tanner nodded. "I know this news is hard to take. I'm trying to be delicate here."

Was he really? Because I'm pretty sure he was acting like a complete asshole.

"You threw me off when you said she already dumped you. It made my delivery of the news all wrong." He cleared his throat. "Let's start over." He rubbed his hands together. "I've got it." He leaned forward in his chair. "Do you trust me, Matt?"

"Only some of the time."

He laughed. "Good eye."

What?

"I know for a fact that Kennedy Alcaraz with one L and a Z at the end with no tildes or accent marks is not the true love of your life."

I just stared at him.

"I thought she would be. I pushed you together for a reason. But I know now that I was wrong. I'm wrong sometimes. Not often. But I can admit when I am. I do sincerely apologize."

I opened my mouth and then closed it again. This was still coming off very rude. And I had no idea what to say to him. Also...what the fuck was he talking about? How could he know any of this for a fact?

"I know you're probably a little hesitant to trust me with your love life again. But I was close on this. Very close." He shook his head. "I think I must have just been a hair off really. So give me a few days to find your actual perfect match. I was close with Kennedy. It's just not quite perfect."

I just stared at him.

"Two days," he said. "That's all I'm asking. Give me two days to find you someone more suitable."

"I thought you liked Kennedy."

"I did but I just checked my…um…thingamajig." He coughed. "And now I know otherwise. I said I was sorry. But facts are facts."

His thingamajig? "Were you just masturbating behind your chair, Tanner?" And why did his dick have anything to do with Kennedy and I being a good couple?

"What? Behind this chair? No. It's leather, my boy. It wouldn't stand up." He patted the seat of it. "Besides, I would never do that out here. That would be extremely dangerous."

Nigel nodded.

"Um…yeah. I'm sure your trouser snake isn't that big."

Nigel laughed. "Sorry," he said and cleared his throat. "I like that term. Trouser snake. That means penis, yes? Trouser snake." He smiled.

"My trouser snake is very big," Tanner said, ignoring Nigel's question. "But that wasn't what I meant. Anyway…true love. Round two. I've got it this time, I'm sure of it. I should get to work." He clapped his hands together and stood up.

"Tanner?"

"Yeah?" he said.

"I thought you'd be happy for me." For all his talk about being my best friend over Rob…he wasn't acting like it. He was acting like a complete ass.

"Why would I be happy for you for choosing a lifetime of unhappiness with Kennedy? Sure, your life would be perfectly adequate with her. But nothing special."

"That's a really shitty thing to say."

"Is it?" Nigel asked. "Which part? Did he get a language thing wrong? Ha!" He pointed to Tanner. "You do it too! You're bad like I was bad with the fax machine! People don't use those anymore, Tanner. People no longer like automatically getting messages in their hand for some reason. Times change, huh?"

"Nigel," Tanner said. "Shut your whore mouth."

Nigel nodded.

I had no idea what was happening. But I was really pissed at both of them. "I'm going to my room."

"Good idea. Just stay in there for a few days until I find someone new. It shouldn't take long. And again, I really apologize for bringing Kennedy back in your life. Thank goodness you came to me before you popped the question. That would have been a disaster."

I shook my head and pushed past him. All my friends sucked today.

CHAPTER 10

Sunday

Brooklyn

I stared at Kennedy. How could she possibly think I could hate her? After all these years, I'd been worried *she* hated *me*. It was never the other way around. I'd lived with so much guilt. "I could never hate you, Kennedy. I'm the one that messed everything up back in high school. All of it. There were so many days where I wished I could apologize to you one more time."

Kennedy shook her head. "I wasn't mad at you." Tears started pooling in the corners of her eyes. "I was just so upset over the situation. And I've regretting my last words to you every single day." Her voice cracked.

"But they weren't your last words. I'm here right now."

She sniffed. "I know. And there's so much I need to tell you." She wiped the corners of her eyes with her fingertips. "First of all, there's nothing to be at all upset about because Matt and Poppy…"

"I really don't want to talk about Matt anymore," I said, cutting her off. I didn't know why everyone kept bringing him up, like I came back to New York because of him. Hell, it was the exact opposite. I'd vowed to never step foot in this city again because of him. I took a deep breath. "Come on. I need some fresh air." I grabbed her hand to pull her to the crosswalk. There was only one place I knew of in the city to get fresh air.

We crossed the street and went into one of the entrances to Central Park.

I wrapped my arms around myself as we walked in silence. Each step into the park made me feel colder. I'd made a mistake. This air wasn't fresh. It was claustrophobic, filled with memories of me with Matt. I stopped at a bench and sat down before we had a chance to turn the corner. Because I knew what was down that path. There was this cute little bridge that Matt had taken me to all those years ago. With a perfect view of our wedding venue.

It was so weird how much time changed things. I could never imagine being sad here back then. And now? I felt empty.

Kennedy sat down beside me, but she didn't say a word.

I looked up at the trees above us. The leaves were yellow, orange, red, and brown. I'd fallen in love with Matt during a fall just like this.

But now I just wanted everyone to stop talking about him and what could have been. Because it hadn't happened. And now fall meant so much more to me. I wrapped my arms tighter around myself. It meant raking leaves and jumping in them with my family. It meant long strolls around the lake, hand in hand with Miller, and watching Jacob stomp on the crunchy leaves.

"Brooklyn," Kennedy said, breaking the silence. "It's fine that you don't want to talk about Matt. And I wish you'd tell me why. But I'll drop it if that's what you really want."

I breathed a sigh of relief.

"But just because you don't want to talk about him with me…I really think you should go see him."

Why wasn't she letting this go? "I have nothing to say to him."

"How is that possible? Brooklyn, he thought you were dead for 16 years. You owe him an explanation."

"I don't owe him anything."

"But…"

I stood up. "Please, Kennedy. He's happy and that's the end of the story. I think it's better if he just keeps thinking I'm dead."

She scrunched her mouth to the side as she stared at me. "Better for him or for you?"

"For both of us."

"I don't think that's true. Brooklyn, it destroyed him when you left…"

"I didn't leave!" I didn't know why I was yelling at Kennedy. None of this was her fault. "I didn't leave," I said more quietly.

"I know. Your dad forced you to stay at that safe house. But… years of your life were missing from your note, Brooklyn. Why didn't you come back when you escaped? Why didn't you come home?"

"Home?" I took another deep breath. That word hit me like a punch in the gut. *Home.* I used to think Matt was my home. But I was wrong. About all of it. And now I was standing in the middle of Central Park desperately missing my actual home. The one I'd made with Miller. I tried to blink back my tears. What the fuck was I doing here? Tears started to stream down my cheeks.

Kennedy leapt to her feet and embraced me in a big hug. "I'm sorry. I'll drop it. I'm so sorry."

I hugged her back. "I'm sorry too." As far as I was concerned, those were the words I'd needed to say all these years. I owed them to her and no one else.

I never should have come back here. Jacob and I needed to go home.

***

There was no reason to stay on the run. My father said my name was clear. And I didn't want to go to Canada and start over. I loved my home. Miller had wanted to raise Jacob there. So that's what I was going to do. I was going to raise our son where Miller's memory would be all around us. That's what he would have wanted.

I crouched down in front of Jacob. He'd just woken up from his nap and I could tell he was still a little sleepy. "Hey, sweet boy," I whispered and ran my finger through his hair.

He closed his eyes again, like he was as upset to face the day as I was. But he'd be better once we were home. We both would be.

I looked over at Kennedy. She didn't need to say it. I could see it all over her face. She was disappointed that I was leaving. Or maybe she was just disappointed.

But she knew how hard loss was. She'd lost her father. She knew how twisted up my heart was. And I couldn't be here in this city where memories made me feel even sicker. I just needed time to heal. Maybe I'd be able to open up about everything to her in time. Just…not right now.

I ran my fingers through Jacob's hair again. "It's time to go home."

He finally opened up his eyes. "Nooooo," he said, in the adorable, drawn-out way I loved.

"It's time, Jacob."

"Noooo."

I wasn't expecting this response. I thought he'd be happy. "You'll get to sleep in your own bed."

"Noooo."

I pressed my lips together. Was he thinking about how hard it would be to walk through our front yard ever again? Because I was. I knew it would be hard. But we were strong. We'd get through it. We'd remember the good, not the bad. "You know, I was thinking, when we get home maybe we can get you a pet. Something snuggly."

"Noooo."

I thought for sure he'd be excited about that. He loved his stuffed animals. And I thought some extra noise in the house would do us both good. "Sweet boy, we have to go home."

"I want us to stay here with Aunt Kennedy and my abuela."

Abuela? I looked over at Mrs. Alcaraz. She pressed her lips together and quickly turned back to the stove. Had she asked him to call her that? It made my heart ache a little less. Jacob hadn't gotten to know my parents or Miller's. As far as I was concerned, my father would never meet him. Mrs. Alcaraz had always treated me like her own daughter. She was the closest thing Jacob would ever have to a grandmother. And it all just made me…want to curl up in a ball and cry.

God, this was all just making it harder to go.

"We can't stay here," I said. "We have to go home."

A spoon clattered in a pan and I looked up. Mrs. Alcaraz was staring at us. "No," she said firmly. She wiped her hands on her apron and walked over to us. "Mi amor." She put her hands on both sides of my face. "I mean yes. You both stay here. With us."

"I…we can't inconvenience you like that," I said.

"We're family. This is home." She patted my cheeks before letting go.

"But you don't have room for us…"

"I'm actually looking for a new place," Kennedy said, cutting me off. "So there will be an empty bed here soon anyway. Might as well not let it go cold." She smiled at me.

"See," Mrs. Alcaraz said. "No cold beds." And then she turned to Jacob. "You want to help roll out dough?"

"Yessie!" Jacob stood up on the couch and reached for her.

She scooped him up into her arms, balancing him on her hip. I was used to Jacob being shy. But he felt comfortable with Mrs. Alcaraz after just a few hours alone.

Abuela. I watched the two of them laughing in the kitchen. It had been a really long time since I'd heard him laugh like that. The same way he used to laugh running around our back yard, without a care in the world. He was happy here.

"Please stay," Kennedy said and put her arm around me. "Even just for a little longer."

I watched as Mrs. Alcaraz showed Jacob how to cut the dough. I could already smell the filling for the empanadas on the stove. The whole apartment felt warm and cozy. Just like it always had. Just like when I used to call this apartment home.

I dropped my head onto Kennedy's shoulder. How was I ever supposed to leave now?

CHAPTER 11

Sunday

Matt

I'd been good all day. But as soon as I made it to my room, I caved and called Kennedy.

It went straight to voicemail.

Fuck. I collapsed on my bed and looked up at the ceiling. I waited a few minutes and then called her again.

And again it went straight to voicemail.

She'd specifically asked me not to call her, and now I'd called her twice. I ran my hand down my face.

Perfect match my ass. I didn't believe in perfect matches. Or the one. I couldn't afford to. That's what I'd been doing the past 16 years, and all I'd accomplished was feeling like shit.

There was no true love. No such thing as a happily ever after. I knew that for a fact.

But I also knew that I loved how I felt around Kennedy. And that she made me laugh. She made me feel like myself again. I didn't realize how much of myself I'd lost over the years. But Kennedy knew me. The real me. The person I'd left behind. What was wrong with that?

I stared at the ceiling.

What was Tanner's problem? No, what was the problem with all my friends? I just needed one person to have my back. Instead I had four traitors. Five if you counted Nigel. And since when had I started counting Nigel?

There was a knock on the door.

"Go away," I mumbled. I hated how I'd been sent to my room and now I was acting like I did when I was a kid and my mom was mad with me.

Nigel popped his head in anyway. "Do you want me to draw you a bath?"

"Not right now, Nigel."

"Are you sure? There's a new massage feature I just installed."

I looked over at the bathroom door. I couldn't see the whole tub from here, but it looked exactly the same. "What massage feature?"

"An old-fashioned one." He lifted up his hands and wiggled his fingers.

Was he seriously saying that he wanted me to sit ass naked in the tub while he massaged me with his hands? What the ever living… "Nigel, aren't you busy?"

"Not in the slightest."

Seriously? "I thought we had an agreement. You're supposed to be talking to your connections amongst Poppy's staff."

"Yes, so that we'll have more time together."

Right. I just nodded. That was not at all the reason. "So…where are you with that?"

"Well, I'm on break."

This guy was always on a break. "I'll talk to you to-night then." I thought my tone was dismissive, but Nigel's head didn't move.

"But I thought we could hang out just us bros right now," Nigel said.

What about what just happened in the foyer made him think I wanted to hang out with him or Tanner right now? "I'm busy."

He just stared at me. "What if I supplied the dirt right now?"

I sat up in my bed. "You got something?"

"Oh, I've got *lots* of things."

Why did that sound so sexual? "Spill it."

He looked behind him and then back at me. "Not here," he whispered. "It's not secure."

Wow, he must have actually found something good. I climbed out of bed and opened up the door for him. He'd only stuck his head into my room. And now I realized it was because he was hiding the fact that he was wearing a floor-length trench coat over his lederhosen today.

"Here," he said and shoved a matching trench coat into my hands. "Put this on."

I unfolded the coat. "And why exactly do you want us to look like a pair of child molesters?"

"It's a covert operation." He slid on some sunglasses and handed me a matching pair. "Slip on your disguise and meet me at the docks."

Before I could ask him any questions, he hurried off. Why the hell were we meeting at the docks? I knew he preferred to do stuff like this in person. But why wasn't Tanner's apartment secure?

I sighed and looked down at the trench coat in my hands. I wanted to weigh the options, but there was really no decision here. If this is what Nigel wanted to do, I had to do it. I needed that dirt on Poppy in order to get out of this mess.

I slipped on the trench coat, put on the sunglasses, and walked down the hall.

Tanner was sitting in the formal dining room flipping through his binder full of women. "Good heavens, Matthew," he said with a laugh. "There's no reason to give up women and prey on young boys. I'll find you a suitable match."

I laughed. "Yeah, I know I look like a pedophile. Nigel made me wear it."

Tanner flipped a page of his binder. "It's best not to pander to him. Remember what I told you when you first moved in, just think of him as being one with the furniture."

I knew Tanner always said that. But I was pretty sure Nigel was his other best friend.

"I know it's hard because he's a very vocal piece of furniture. But if you give him a little leeway he'll go rogue. In the twenties, I gave him his first day off and look how that has escalated. He barely works an hour a day now."

"The twenties? So like...last year or something?"

"Hmm?" Tanner looked up from his binder. "Yes. The twenties. That's what I said. We're living in the twenties."

Okay. "Well, he does seem to have a lot of scheduled time off."

"See what I mean? The next thing you know you'll be pulled into all his shenanigans and forgetting the task at hand."

"And what's the task at hand?"

"Of that there are many." He sighed and rubbed his eyes. "Never ending, really. But I'm focusing on Kennedy's replacement right now. Quick question. Do you have any feelings for Kennedy's mother?"

"What? No."

He shook his head. "I just feel like I'm *so* close. I don't know what I'm missing. I think I might pay the Alcarazes a visit." He closed his binder.

"Please don't do that."

"I just want a quick look around."

"Would you stop interfering? Haven't you done enough?"

He rubbed his hands together. "Not until you've bedded the one. Now if you'll excuse me, I have work to do." He pushed himself away from the table. "And you have little boys to prey on."

I couldn't help but laugh.

Tanner tossed me a sharpie. "Just in case you want to add the signature pencil thin mustache."

Point made. I pulled off the jacket and sunglasses. It would be better if I just put them on right before I got to the docks. I didn't want to spend the night in jail.

***

The sun was just setting as I parked my car in the abandoned parking lot. The docks stretched for a mile. And Nigel hadn't said exactly where to meet him. Why hadn't we just driven together?

I stepped out of my car and pulled on my sunglasses and trench coat. Just like Nigel's, the fabric almost touched the ground. Why was it so long? Was it made for a giant or something?

I looked left and right, trying to search for one of Tanner's cars. Unless Nigel had taken a taxi. I smiled to myself at the thought of how the driver would have reacted to Nigel's outfit.

There was a clicking noise behind me. I spun around to see Nigel rolling out of my trunk. He grabbed a folder before slamming the trunk shut. And then he smoothed down his wrinkled trench coat. "It's time," he said.

"Were you in my trunk that whole time?"

"I didn't want anyone to see us together," he whispered, then looked both ways. "Hurry. This way." He lifted the collar of his jacket and walked toward one of the abandoned warehouses.

Seriously? Had he really been in my trunk during that whole drive? Why would he do that? I shook my head. Why did Nigel do anything he did? I quickly followed him.

"What did you find?" I asked.

"Things you wouldn't even believe," he said as he opened the door to the warehouse.

"Can't we just do it out here?" A few years ago, Tanner had transformed one of these warehouses into an invite only club. But it wasn't this one. And I didn't even want to know what diseased animals were scurrying about in there.

"Someone might have tailed us," Nigel said before disappearing through the door.

"Who would have tailed us?" I called after him. But he didn't reply. *Damn it.* I stepped into the warehouse and had to jump out of the way of a rat. *Gross.* I caught up with Nigel as I did my best not to get tetanus.

He pulled out a sheet of paper from his folder. "Last Tuesday at 0900, Poppy Cannavaro, known associate of Richard Pruitt, bought a ticket." He handed me the paper as we kept walking.

I scanned the sheet. "She bought a ticket to a Broadway show?"

"Yes. Does she seem like a theater enthusiast to you?"

"What does this have to do with anything?"

"Exactly. She's not a known aficionado of the theater. How utterly suspicious."

"I don't care what she's a fan of. I want to know what shady stuff she's up to."

"Very well. I'll cross Broadway shows off our to-do list."

"What to-do list?"

Nigel turned the corner as he pulled out another sheet of paper. "There's a new player in town. I saw her leaving Richard Pruitt's residence late last night at 2200."

"I'm not great with military time."

"But it's the best form of time."

"In what way?"

"You'd understand if you'd lived through the Great War."

"Which war was that?" I asked.

"The First World War."

"Well why didn't you just say World War I then?"

"Because it was the Great War!" Nigel stopped walking. "It's not important. What's important is this new player I think. And it was at 10 pm peasant time." He handed me the sheet of paper with his write up about what he saw. Apparently he'd been sitting in some bushes outside of Mr. Pruitt's apartment complex for two hours last night. And I had no idea why.

I didn't follow Nigel to the docks and enter a creepy warehouse to be called a peasant or to hear about stuff that didn't involve Poppy. "Nigel, I asked you to look into Poppy. Not Mr. Pruitt."

"One and the same, one and the same." He pulled out another sheet of paper. "Do you know what Poppy and Richard were doing this afternoon?"

I sighed. "No. What?"

He handed me a photo of the two of them arguing outside of some diner.

"Okay? So they're fighting about something. Did you happen to hear what about?"

"The new player," Nigel said. "It's all about the new player. I didn't get a name, but it got heated. Very heated."

That shouldn't have sounded sexual. Poppy was Mr. Pruitt's niece. "Nigel, did you find any dirt on Poppy specifically?"

He waved his thick folder in the air. "Oh, I'm just getting started, Master Matthew." He cleared his throat. "I mean Mr. Caldwell." He pulled out another sheet as he pushed through a creaky old wooden door.

Why were we going farther into this warehouse?

"Poppy likes pancakes over waffles." He handed me her grocery list from last week.

How was that helpful?

"And her daughter loves chickie nuggies."

Great. That was not useful at all. Each step into the warehouse grew darker and darker. I grabbed my sunglasses to pull them off.

"Keep the disguise on," Nigel said. "It's of the utmost importance to our covert operation. We should have a name for it, don't you think?"

"Operation grocery list?"

"I don't think that's what this is about," he said.

"Then why do you keep handing me grocery lists?"

"Patience, young one."

Well, now he was just talking like Tanner. I was older than Tanner and I was definitely older than Nigel. "I can't see anything with my sunglasses," I said.

"Don't worry, we'll be there soon."

"Where?"

He pulled out another sheet of paper and had no trouble reading it in the dark. "Poppy is a bad tipper. Sometimes only 5% at upscale restaurants." He handed me the paper even though I couldn't see it in the dark.

"That's a bad quality, but nothing illegal."

"It should be. I live off tips."

"Do you?" Shoot, I didn't know that. Should I have been tipping him for my baths?

"No. But they help me afford my third home."

"Wait, you have three homes?"

"Don't all houseboys?"

"I don't know any other houseboys," I said. But three houses seemed extreme. Hell, I only had one home.

"No? That's good. I'm all you need. You can say it if you want. That I'm all you need."

There was no way I was saying that.

He sighed and pushed through another squeaky door and hit a light switch.

I shielded my eyes. It was blinding even with my sunglasses on. I blinked until the white dots left my vision. "Nigel, why are we in an empty room?"

"A secure, empty-ish room." He pointed to a table in the center of the room with a sheet draped over it.

Okay...

He handed me another paper. "Poppy Cannavaro is a plagiarizer. Her sophomore year in college she almost got expelled because she didn't cite a quote correctly."

"That's great, but...how does it help me?"

"Plagiarism is punishable by guillotine, yes? We have her just where we want her."

"No, Nigel. It's not."

"Oh. It used to be, I think. It's been a few years, maybe." He pulled out another sheet of paper from his folder, which still looked very full. "Her daughter's father has joint custody. He sees her on Wednesdays and every other weekend."

"Nigel, do you have anything useful in that folder?"

"It's all useful. Poppy's ex-husband also believes in spanking. Of children. How naughty, right?"

What was he even talking about? "Can I please just see it?"

"Fine. Here." He handed me the whole folder.

I thumbed through a few pages. "Why are there so many grocery lists?"

"You asked me to talk to the help. Her chef was very unhelpful."

I kept scanning through the documents. Searching for money laundering. Racketeering. Any white-collar crimes or something much worse. But...half of the documents were about her food preferences. I looked up and Nigel. "You really didn't find anything?"

"I told you about the plagiarism. And the new player in town."

"Nigel..."

"Wait. Do you hear something?" He cupped his hand to his ear.

"I swear if we get murdered in this warehouse..."

"No, not a person. Me thinks me hears a wonderful machine." He pulled out a remote from his trench coat pocket and hit a button. Something whirred to life.

I turned to the table in the middle of the room with a sheet over it.

Nigel walked over to it and pulled off the sheet…revealing a printer that looked straight out of the 90s. It even had the little holes on the sides of the paper that needed to be ripped off.

"Oh, wait! Now what is this!?" Nigel said and clapped his hands. "Is that a…fax machine? Oh my, I know you don't like those. But wait!" He pulled out the sheet of paper that had just printed. "What's this? Evidence?"

I reached for it, but he pulled it back, almost tripping over his trench coat.

"But Master Mathew doesn't believe that fax machines are a good source of communication. So I guess he doesn't want what's on this paper. He'll have to make do with the trivial things in the folder I prepared."

"Give it to me, Nigel."

"Then say that fax machines are still on trend." He lowered his sunglasses to stare at me, like he really wanted to soak this in.

I just stared at him. "Nigel, they're really not."

"Very well." It looked like he was about to rip the sheet down the middle.

"Wait!"

He just stared at me. "Well then."

I sighed. "Fax machines are on trend."

"*And* a reliable and quick way to communicate."

I shook my head. "And a reliable and quick way to communicate." *But not as reliable and quick as freaking emails.* I put my hand out.

"*And* better than electronic texts," he said.

"Are you referring to normal texting or is that something else?"

"The usual kind I think. On the cellular devices."

I laughed, but he looked serious. I cleared my throat. "Fine. And better than electronic texts on cellular devices."

"More secure too," Nigel said. "So very secure."

I really didn't think that was true. Nigel said he didn't want a paper trail. And he'd literally printed out thousands of papers and set up a weird fax machine in the center of an abandoned warehouse to print out more of them. "Yup," I said. "More secure too. So very secure."

He handed me the sheet of paper that he'd just faxed himself.

There was an image of Poppy Cannavaro putting a car bomb under a car. Nigel had circled the spot and labeled it. And a newspaper clipping was photocopied at the bottom about a young man who'd died in a car explosion.

"She's a *murderer*," Nigel whispered.

I thought I'd be happy. This was exactly what I wanted. But I wasn't happy that an innocent man was dead. Or that Poppy's daughter would have to grow up without a mother. I kept scanning the article. *Wait, not an innocent man.* Apparently this guy was in the mafia too. Why had Poppy blown up another mafia member?

"Thank goodness for faxes," Nigel said. "Operation Murderer complete. I'd actually already named it, but I didn't want to ruin the big reveal."

This would get me out of my fake relationship with Poppy. It would keep Scarlett safe. But it would ruin another family in the process.

"I knew you'd be devastated when you found out fax machines are better than texts," Nigel said as he pushed his sunglasses back up the bridge of his nose. "It's okay. We'll all wrong sometimes. But we must be going. This warehouse has a rat infestation problem that gets significantly worse at dusk. Grab the fax machine for me, will you?"

"Sure." I folded up the sheet of paper and slid it into my pocket.

"Oh I love the old models," he said, tenderly caressing the machine. "They get all warm when they print. I'll put it with me in the trunk to keep me warm on the way back home."

"You can sit up front," I said.

"I prefer the trunk." He winked at me.

I had a lot of questions about that. But none of them mattered right now. I lifted up the overheated, bulky fax machine and followed Nigel out of the warehouse. The squeaking of rats growing louder with every step. If I got rabies, I was going to throw this thing at Nigel's head.

CHAPTER 12

Monday

Brooklyn

I wasn't thinking about where I was going as I ran through Central Park. But my feet seemed to remember the paths I'd walked years ago. And before I knew it, I was at the edge of a bridge. I leaned over to catch my breath instead of crossing it. I wanted to just turn around and run in the opposite direction. Instead, I found myself lifting my head and staring at the restaurant where I'd planned to marry Matt. I'd imagined us taking wedding pictures right here with all our friends. And I had no idea why my feet had led me here.

Despite what my father and Kennedy thought, I didn't come back to the city for Matt. Honestly, I didn't even know why I was here. But Jacob was happy. And his happiness made me feel some small semblance of normalcy. And I didn't know how to keep going without that.

I turned away from the restaurant. No, I had no idea why my feet had led me here. I started running in the opposite direction, pushing thoughts of Matt out of my head.

The farther I ran, the more out of breath I got, the better I felt. There was this doom pressing against my chest. And running made it lighter. Just like it had at the beach house all those years ago. I'd lost people before.

I'd loved and lost. And I'd always found a way to pick myself back up.

That wasn't true. I felt tears running down my cheeks as I ran faster. I'd always found someone to help me pick myself back up. Matt. I shook my head. No. Miller. Miller had always been there to help pick me back up. I'd been mourning the loss of my mother and my uncle when I'd stumbled into Miller's bed. He'd held me through the night. He'd held me when Matt wasn't there at the beginning. And he'd held me every night since I'd chosen him.

I wasn't strong.

And I didn't know how to lift myself back up from losing him.

I veered off the running path and into the grass. I let myself collapse and cry. How was I supposed to pick myself up without him?

I hugged my knees into my chest.

I hated how weak I felt. I hated being outside my safe bubble back at the lake house. I hated this fucking city and the fucking memories that plagued me. I wanted to scream at the top of my lungs like I'd started doing at the beach. Which I'd started doing again when I couldn't get pregnant with our second child. I just wanted to fucking scream out the pain.

But I was in the middle of a crowded park. I wasn't in the middle of nowhere. And I didn't know how to expel the sadness out of my body. I didn't know how to stop making my heart feel like it was burning. I just wanted my lungs to stop working.

It should have been me.
It should have been me.
It should have been me.

I didn't know how to be strong enough for our son. But Miller would have.

It should have been me that died.

***

I wasn't sure how long I sat there. But when the walking paths grew more crowded, I knew I needed to head back. Mrs. Alcaraz and Kennedy both had to go to work. Jacob needed me.

I took a deep breath and pushed myself up. I shouldn't have come to Central Park. I thought breathing the fresh air would help soothe my soul somehow. Make me feel closer to Miller. But it just made it worse. There was a hole in my chest. I wasn't even sure how I was still breathing.

My body felt heavy as I walked back toward the city streets. And even heavier as I got a taxi back to Kennedy's.

Miller wasn't coming back.

I forced my chin not to quiver and blinked more tears out of my eyes.

And I was all Jacob had.

No, I didn't feel strong right now. But I'd figure it out for him. I'd do anything for him.

The taxi got stuck in traffic a few blocks from Kennedy's. I climbed out and walked down the sidewalk.

I could do this.

I had to do this.

I passed by a newsstand and slowly exhaled. But then it felt like I was choking. Isabella's face was plastered on a tabloid staring back at me. With big bold letters: "WEDDING DATE SET FOR THIS WINTER."

I lifted up the tabloid. It wasn't Isabella. It was Poppy Cannavaro. I shook my head. God, she looked so much like Isabella. I swallowed down the lump in my throat and started to read the article. It was filled with direct quotes from Poppy:

"I knew the proposal was coming."

"The two of us were always destined to be together."

"Matthew has always been close to our family."

"I'm not sure either of us knew what true love was until we met."

"The venue was an obvious choice. It was where Matthew took me on our first date."

Each quote made me feel more and more sick to my stomach.

At the bottom of the article there was a picture of the two of them kissing at a restaurant. No, not just a restaurant. The restaurant where I was supposed to marry Matt. Was that where they were planning on getting married?

My dear cousin my ass. True love? Destiny? *My* wedding venue? *What a bitch.*

Matt wasn't quoted at all. But him making out with her in *our* restaurant was proof enough of his feelings. What had happened to him? How could he look at her the same way he used to look at me? I shook away the thought. I knew that wasn't fair. And yet…why *her*? Of all people.

At the bottom of the page it said that the rest of the article was on page 6. Was there seriously more? Maybe that's where some quotes from Matt would be. I started thumbing through the pages.

"Are you going to pay for that?" the cart vendor asked.

"Oh. Yeah, sorry." I reached for my wallet in my jacket pocket. I handed him a couple dollars and did my best not to crumple the tabloid in my fist.

I had no idea why I was so angry.

I was over Matthew Caldwell. I'm pretty sure I stopped loving him as soon as I saw his hands all over someone else. And I'd finally convinced my heart to stop loving him too. It had taken me years to quit him. But I had.

And seeing him suddenly staring back at me in a photo felt like a slap in the face. I hated how looking at him with another woman made my heart race and my palms feel sweaty. Like I was reliving that day I went to see him 16 years ago. I completely avoided thinking about him because he betrayed me. But also because I still wanted him to be happy. He was supposed to be happy.

And how could he be happy with Poppy? He was allowed to make his own mistakes. But Poppy? Seriously? She was practically Isabella's twin. And *our* wedding venue? Had I really meant so little to him?

I shook the thought away. I already knew the answer to that. He didn't give a shit about me.

"Excuse me, madame," a man said before I grabbed the handle to Kennedy's apartment building.

Madame? I turned to look up at the man. He was in a freshly pressed suit and his hair was perfectly pushed to the side. It looked like he'd stopped by on his way to work.

Basically he looked put together. The complete opposite of me. I was drenched in sweat and my face was surely puffy and red from crying.

"Do you happen to know a Kennedy Alcaraz? It's spelled A-L-C-A-R-A-Z, no tildes or anything unfortunately." He sighed, like he was truly devastated about the spelling of her name.

That was a very weird way to ask if I knew someone. "Yes…"

"Oh, thank goodness. I've been trying to buzz her." He pointed to the intercom. "But there's no answer. And I've called a few times too, but she hasn't responded. I really just need to talk to her for a moment. It's quite urgent, actually. Would you mind letting me up?"

"Oh…um…" I stared at him. I wondered if she was dating this guy. I had kind of been hoping that she and Felix had found their way back together. The cut of his suit and his expensive shoes screamed NYC elite. Which didn't really scream Kennedy to me. "I'm sorry, what did you say your name was?"

"Tanner." He put his hand out for me. "Tanner Rhodes."

I shook his hand. Kennedy hadn't mentioned a Tanner. But we really hadn't had a chance to catch up. "I'm sorry, Tanner, but if Kennedy isn't speaking to you, she probably has a reason."

A smile spread across his face. "I'm not a suitor, if that's what you're wondering."

"A suitor?" I laughed. I'd been living in a bubble, but I didn't think people had started talking like that again.

"We're friends," he quickly added. "Obviously no one uses the term suitor anymore. Quite a shame really." He cleared his throat. "What I meant is, she's actually dating my best friend. Bro code and all that modern stuff. So friends of friends is what we are. Exclusively platonic, but I really need to see her." He tilted his head to the side. "You look very familiar by the way. I'm trying to place it." He shook his head. "Have you ever posed for a painting? I feel like I've seen a whole gallery of just you."

I laughed. "No."

"Are you sure? I swear I've seen your face."

"Trust me, I'm not a model."

He shook his head. "But I've definitely seen you before. I'm sure of it. In the painted form. I feel like the artist's name is on the tip of my tongue. Don't you hate when that happens?"

I laughed. "Yeah."

"But I can't shake it. What did you say your name was?"

"Brooklyn."

For a second it looked like his face froze. But then he looked back at the intercom. "Wait. Don't tell me." He turned back to me. "No, do. Are you're *living* with the Alcaraz's?"

I nodded. "I mean, just until I..." Until I what? Found my own place? Convinced Jacob to go home? "I'm just a guest."

He clapped his hands together. "I knew it. And you're reading about Matthew Caldwell!" He sounded so excited as he pointed to the tabloid in my hand. But then he gasped and grabbed my hand. For a second I thought he was going to kiss it. But he was just staring at my ring. "You're married?" The joy from his voice was gone. He sounded more devastated by this than the spelling of Kennedy's last name.

"Yes. I mean…no." I had to stop lying to myself. Hiding from the truth was just a fairytale. And I learned a long time ago that my life was no fairytale. "He…passed away recently." I pulled my hand out of Tanner's.

"So you're single?"

Was he hitting on me right now? Hadn't he heard the *recently* part of that? This was one of the weirdest conversations of my life. "I wouldn't really say that." Even though Miller was gone, I was still married. I'd promised Miller forever. And I meant it.

"I could kiss you right now I'm so happy!" Tanner said.

Okay, I think this guy might be a crazy person.

"But that's been getting me in trouble as of late. And alas, I don't want to get my face smashed in."

"I do have a pretty good right hook," I said.

He laughed. "Not by you." He rubbed his hands together. "This is fantastic. Fated. Do tell me. Because I need to rectify a few things to set it all in motion. You knew Kennedy back in high school, yes?"

How did he know that? I nodded.

"Did she ever have a crush on anyone? Someone she might be more suited to?"

More suited to than who? But…there was someone I'd just been thinking of. "Felix Green."

"The art dealer?"

"Is that what he does?" I bit the inside of my lip. That's what his parents did. But they'd dealt more than art. And I wondered if Felix was back in the drug business. I really hoped not.

"This is really quite something," Tanner said. "I know *him*. I know *you*. I'm so good at this. Some days I doubt my talent, but not today!"

"Good at what exactly?"

"True love."

Okay, yeah, this guy was nuts. "I should really be getting up. My son's waiting for me."

"You have a son? How old? Ah, it doesn't even matter. This is perfect. He's great with kids."

"Who's great with kids?"

"Just you wait for it. I love a big reveal. It was lovely to meet you, Brooklyn Sanders." And with that, he walked away.

Had I told him my last name? I shook my head and opened the door. I must have. That was seriously the weirdest conversation of my life.

I let myself into Kennedy's apartment.

"Mommy! Yo hablo español!" Jacob called from the kitchen table.

I smiled down at him. He hadn't been the most talkative child. I was a little worried I was a bad teacher. But now he was picking up Spanish? "You speak Spanish now? Is that so?" I kissed the top of his head.

"Más o menos," Mrs. Alcaraz said. But she looked proud of him.

"Mi abuela," Jacob said and pointed to her.

"Mi amor." She patted his cheek. "The both of you," she added and smiled at me. "Now eat." She put an omelet down on the table. And I realized that Jacob was already eating one. I breathed a sigh of relief. How had she gotten him to eat anything besides cuppycakes? I set the tabloid down on the table and took a huge bite. Seriously, there was no better cook than Mrs. Alcaraz.

Kennedy hurried out of her room, hopping on one foot as she pulled on her boots. "I really need to set a backup alarm," she said with a laugh. She leaned down and gave Jacob a big hug. "Now you better eat all of that, or I'm going to steal it."

Jacob took another big bite of his omelet. Maybe Kennedy was the one I needed to thank for him eating normal food again.

"There was a guy outside looking for you. A Tanner Rhodes? Do you know him?"

"Oh. Yeah. I was just running late so I didn't have time to speak to him. I'll call him later."

"He's...odd."

Kennedy laughed. "He is a little odd, isn't he? But he's also incredibly nice. Did he um...happen to say anything to you about anything?"

That was vague. "Weirdly enough we talked for a while, but I honestly have no idea about what. I still don't even know what he wanted to speak to you about."

Kennedy laughed again. "That sounds about right. I promise I'll call him. But I have to get going..." her voice trailed off as she picked up the tabloid.

"Can you even believe it?" I asked. I knew Matt and Poppy were dating. But all that stuff in the article? It just felt like a big middle finger to me. I took a deep breath. No, it wasn't a middle finger to me. I'd been dead. Matt had just forgotten about me. I wasn't sure why I was so shaken about it. He'd forgotten about me ages ago.

"No," Kennedy said deadpan. "I can't." She shook her head. "I'm sorry, I really have to go. See you guys later," She ruffled Jacob's hair. "See you tonight, Mama." She kissed her mom's cheek and hurried out the door.

It was only after she left that I realized she'd taken the tabloid with her.

CHAPTER 13

Monday

Matt

I stared down at the sheet of paper again. I'd asked Nigel how he knew that the car Poppy blew up related to the newspaper clipping. But apparently Nigel had connections on the force. It seemed like he had connections everywhere. And the license plate number on the car that Poppy blew up belonged to the Locatelli family.

But the Locatellis were supposed to be friends with the Pruitts and Cannavaros. So...why had she done it?

For some reason, that question kept going around and around in my head.

I wanted to pick up the phone and call the police station. Let them know the truth. But I just kept staring at the picture. *Why had she done it?*

And was it even her choice? Surely Mr. Pruitt was actually behind the hit.

But...*why?*

My intercom buzzed. "Matthew, you have a visitor."

I ran my hand down my face. If I ignored it, my administrative assistant would send whoever it was away. I just needed a second alone to think. Nigel hadn't stopped talking about fax machines last night. I literally went to bed and he sat at the bottom talking about the miracles of communication via fax.

The intercom buzzed again. "It's urgent. No, wait!"

I looked up as the door flew open.

For a fleeting second, I figured it was Poppy here to off me. I put my hands out in front of me like that would stop the bullet from entering my skull.

But it did not prevent me from being hit on the side of the face with a magazine. *What the...* I shielded myself again, but lowered my hands when I noticed who it was. Although I didn't love the look of fury on her face. "Kennedy?"

She whacked the magazine against my chest. "Are you fucking serious?" She hit me with it again. "Puta mierda!"

I grabbed the magazine before she could hit me again. James had gotten rid of all the tabloid articles about me. But this one wasn't about me really. It was an article about Poppy, with direct quotes from her about our supposed engagement. What the fuck was she talking to the press for? *Damn it.* I thought I had this under control. But one of those paparazzi scumbags must had gone straight to Poppy.

"You're a dick, you know that?" Kennedy said.

"It's not true."

"Yes you are!"

"I meant the article isn't true. Do you see a picture of a ring on her finger?" I tried to skip to page 6 for the rest of the ridiculousness, but Kennedy snatched it out of my hand.

"I knew the proposal was coming," Kennedy quoted. "The two of us were always destined to be together." She glared at me.

"I didn't propose..."

"Matthew has always been close to our family," she continued. "I'm not sure either of us knew what true love was until we met." She hit me with the tabloid again.

"Would you stop it!"

"I feel like such an idiot. No, you're the idiot. I can't believe you. You proposed to her while we were dating?" There were tears in her eyes now.

And I knew I wasn't explaining any of this right. "Kennedy…"

She tried to slap me, but I caught her hand.

"I didn't propose to Poppy. It's just a dumb tabloid. I *adore* you, Kennedy. I love you."

"No you don't."

She tried to step away from me, but I caged her against my desk.

"What the hell do you want from me, Kennedy? You won't return any of my calls or texts. But you storm in here upset about this fake news about Poppy? And you freak out when I tell you I love you? Do you want me to be miserable?"

"No…"

"Just tell me what you want."

"I don't know!"

She might not know. Her heart might be confused. But mine wasn't. I wiped her tears away with my thumbs and I kissed her.

And she melted into me. I could taste her salty tears on my lips. And I felt the desire there. The same desire I had. I swear if it wasn't the middle of the morning I'd take her right here on my desk.

My fingers tangled into her hair as she moaned into my mouth.

I knew she felt this. I knew she wanted me. So why the hell did she keep pushing me away? I moved my hand to the back of her head, holding her to me. *Stop pushing me away.*

But she decided to do the exact opposite. She pulled back, knocking my coffee cup off my desk.

Shit.

And just like that, we parted. I grabbed Nigel's fax to save it from destruction. And Kennedy grabbed some tissues to blot the mess up.

"I have to go," she said without looking at me.

"Kennedy."

Something was tearing her up inside. And I just wanted her to let me in. "Are you coming to practice this afternoon?" The guys were counting on her. And the homecoming game was this weekend. Jefferson needed her help and encouragement to kick.

"I shouldn't. I shouldn't even be here…"

I was losing her. I knew that Rob said Kennedy and I had already broken up. But that wasn't true. Kennedy was struggling with something. And I wanted to be there for her. Because as far as I was concerned, we were a team now. "It was you."

"What?" She finally turned to look at me.

"The rumors about me proposing to someone." I knew this ruined the surprised, but I needed her to know just how much she meant to me. I walked over to her. "I was ring shopping. Some paparazzi found out about it. I thought I hushed the story, because I wanted this to be a surprise." And I was seriously going to kill the person who told Poppy I was proposing to her. The escalation of that article about us already being engaged was levels of insane I hadn't seen since Isabella. "Kennedy…" I was about to kneel.

"I swear if you get down on one knee right now, I will lose it."

I laughed. But I also stopped in my tracks.

And she finally smiled.

"I meant what I said. I adore you. I love you."

Her bottom lip started to tremble.

"And yeah, right now is not the right moment. I don't want you to lose it."

She wiped her own tears away this time.

"But I was ring shopping for you. I'm going to propose to you. I'll ask you at a better time. And you can tell me no a million times and I won't stop asking."

She exhaled slowly and looked up at the ceiling. "I have to go."

I laughed, but this time it was forced. "That's all you have to say?"

She shook her head, her teary eyes meeting mine again. "I think that some things were always meant to be. And I'm not the kind of person that stuff like that happens to."

I tried to process her words. That wasn't exactly a no...but it certainly wasn't a yes. "Maybe you're not the kind of person that stuff like that happens to. Because you were supposed to wait until this moment to get it. It's fate, Kennedy."

"Then fate is cruel and twisted. I'm sorry, Matt. I have to go." She walked out of my office as quickly as she'd come.

"Please just come to practice!" I called after her. "I promise I won't propose!"

She didn't respond.

I picked up the tabloid and stared at the picture of Poppy kissing me. Seriously, what the fuck? I thought she seemed a little better than Isabella. But this was just crazy. I shook my head. Why did I think someone who loved car bombs could possibly be sane? She needed to be locked up.

But then I started to think about her daughter again. Would she be worse or better off without her mom?

I was done debating this. I slid the evidence into my pocket and walked out of my office.

***

I had the whole drive over to the Cannavaro estate to come up with a better idea. Like going to the cops. But for some reason I'd decided on this. Everything I did seemed to backfire recently. Hopefully this would go a little better.

I'd try this first. And if it didn't work, I'd go to Mr. Pruitt.

The Cannavaro estate was on the outskirts of the city, luckily not that close to my parents' house. If I'd had to grow up with Poppy, I probably would have blown up my own car.

I parked my car in the large circular driveway. Why was she here on a Monday anyway? Didn't she have evil business to conduct in the city? I climbed out of my car. The place reminded me of the Pruitts' apartment. Only even larger and more ostentatious. Not that I could really talk. My parents lived in a house almost this big. And the only inviting part of that house growing up had been the kitchen. And now none of it was inviting. Because it was just filled with memories of ghosts.

Poppy opened the front door like she'd been expecting me. I looked back at my car, wondering if it was bugged or something.

"Darling!" she said and hurried down the stairs. "Where is it?" She put her hand out.

"Where is what?"

"My ring." She lifted her hand a little higher. "Don't worry about whatever speech you had planned or anything. But it better be at least 4 karats or I'm going to have to exchange it." She wiggled her fingers.

"I'm not proposing, Poppy."

"I've heard differently."

"Well, you've heard wrong."

She pouted. "But I've already gone public with the news."

"And why the hell would you do that?" *Oh right, you're freaking insane.*

"Because I trusted my source."

Ah. There it was. She had the tabloids wrapped around her fingers too. Because of course she did. She probably threatened them with death if they didn't leak stuff to her.

"I'm not here because of the article," I said.

"Well, have you at least signed the relationship agreement Uncle Richard sent over? We'll need a marriage amendment added, but we should start with the basics."

"I'm not marrying you. And I'm not signing anything." I pulled out the folded piece of paper from my jacket pocket. "And you're going leave Scarlett and all my friends and family alone. Or I'll go public with this." I handed her the paper.

She scanned it and smiled. "I don't know what this is. But if you're planning on spreading rumors about me killing someone with a car bomb, then that's slander, Matthew."

"Not if those rumors are true."

"Well, how do you know if it's true?"

"For starters, you're not denying it."

"Oh, right." She laughed and put her hand to her chest, feigning shock. "Oh my goodness! This isn't true!" she said with way too much hysteria. "I'm a mother! Not a mobster." She put the back of her hand to her forehead like she might faint. And then smiled at me. "Better?"

"No, not better. You killed someone, Poppy."

"You're welcome."

Seriously, I'd sat across from this woman at dinner and had a civil conversation with her. But it was like she'd snapped overnight. Why were all the women in my life losing it?

Poppy laughed. "Oh. I keep forgetting. You don't know."

"And what don't I know?"

She shrugged. "I'm enjoying the secret for now." She looked back down at the photo. "And this is a terrible angle of me. Couldn't you have taken a more flattering picture?"

"Stay away from my family and friends."

She shrugged.

"And this," I gestured back and forth between us. "Is done. Do you understand?"

She shrugged.

"I'm serious, Poppy. I need to hear you say it."

"Say what precisely?"

"That my family and friends are safe. And our fake relationship is finished."

"Because of this? Really?" She shook her head. "I swear, soon you'll be thanking me for taking care of the Locatellis. I did it for you."

How on earth had she done it for me? "Are we in agreement?"

"I'll consider it," she said with a wink, which made me think she wasn't really processing anything that I was saying. "By the way, I'm loving this new you. I knew you would be good at the financial side of the business, but now that you've shown you're willing to blackmail the love of your life? We're going to be unstoppable."

Brooklyn is the love of my life, not you. I swallowed hard. *I mean Kennedy.* Either way, Poppy was most certainly not the love of my life. She was an insane person. "If I go to the police, Gigi will grow up without a mother. Think of her."

She laughed. "I'm a Cannavaro. I'd never step foot in prison. Could you imagine? I don't even think they have a masseuse on location." She shook her head.

"And you're underestimating my family's resources."

"Oh, I don't think Daddy Caldwell would like you pulling his business back in with Uncle Richard's. Do you? Don't want to sully his name all over again."

As if on cue, my phone started ringing. It was my mom. *Shit.* She'd probably heard about the tabloid. She didn't read them, but people talked. Of course the news would have gotten back to her. I'd only just told her about Kennedy. She was probably equal parts confused and horrified. I ended the call, but my mom immediately started calling again.

"We'll both take some time to think it over, yes?" Poppy said and handed me the paper back.

"I don't need time to think it over."

"Now that I know my future hubby is capable of blackmail, I'll need a few days at least to get the wording of our marriage amendment just right."

"Poppy…"

"And remember, 4 karats." She pointed to her ring finger and then walked back into her family's mansion.

Well…that didn't go as planned. Crazy ran in her family. I knew that for a fact. But I still hadn't expected any of this. Blackmail was one thing. Although it was extra crazy blackmail since it involved possibly kidnapping Scarlett. But now murder? And a fake engagement? Or was it a real engagement to her? She seemed to be really turned on by my blackmail.

Poppy had been fairly normal just a few days ago during our fake dates. It was almost like something had set her off. Just like it had set Kennedy off. What the hell was going on?

CHAPTER 14

Monday

Brooklyn

It took me all of two hours to break my promise of not going back to Central Park. But I'd do anything for Jacob when he looked up at me with his big brown eyes. Miller's eyes. And Kennedy had told Jacob about the Central Park Zoo last night. Of course I couldn't say no.

It was easy to avoid spots that triggered memories on this side of Central Park though. I'd never really explored over here very much.

"Are we there yet?" Jacob asked.

I laughed and picked him up.

"Por favor," he said.

"Sweet boy, you're picking up Spanish very quickly."

"Sí. Are we there yet?"

I laughed and kissed his cheek. "Yes, we're almost at the zoo." Soon I wouldn't be able to understand a word he said. I needed to take lessons from Mrs. Alcaraz too if I was going to keep up.

Jacob had been so shy back home. But he was really coming out of his shell here. He loved Mrs. Alcaraz and Kennedy like they truly were related to him. I knew I'd been coddling him. Sheltering him from the real world. But he was stronger and braver than I even knew. And I couldn't help but feel a little guilty for letting my own fears hold him back.

He should have been in pre-school, socializing with kids his own age. I'd wanted to be enough for him. But…he deserved more than a life of fear. He deserved a real teacher. And friends. I'd been scared of taking any risks, and the worst had happened anyway. I kissed his cheek again. *I'm sorry, sweet boy. I'm sorry about all of it.*

Jacob pointed up ahead. "The zoo!"

I couldn't help but laugh at his excitement. He'd never been to the zoo. Or seen many animals other than the neighbor's cat or dog. And fish in our lake. This was a new adventure. I pressed my lips together. A first experience that Miller would miss.

"The zoo!" Jacob said again.

I hugged him a little tighter. *We've got this. Together.*

Jacob wiggled in my arms after we walked through the archway. I grabbed us a map and then set him down. He took off at record speed. I ran after him as he ducked and dodged between people on his way to the first exhibit.

He stood at the gates in awe, staring through the bars.

I crouched down next to him. "Those are sea lions."

"Lions go roar!" he said.

I laughed. "Mhm. But these are more like…seals." *Right?*

"Roar!" he said again.

I pictured Miller reading his favorite book about animals to him. The lions went roar. And the made-up bits about monsters going rawr. I pressed my lips together and looked down at the map.

"Okay, little dude. We have…penguins, monkeys, snow leopards. Oh and there's a tropical zone."

He looked up at me. "Tropical zone?"

"It's like snakes and bats and things."

His eyes grew round. "Yessie."

"Okay, let's head that way first." I slid my hand into his and we walked past the sea lion enclosure.

The tropical zone was inside. And the air hit me with a memory. But this one wasn't of Miller. Or Matt. I pictured holding my mom's hand, just like Jacob was holding mine as we'd explored the Longwood Gardens Conservatory. The air was hot and sticky and with the large trees it almost even smelled the same.

"Mommy," Jacob tugged on my hand.

I hadn't even realized I'd stopped walking.

"Sorry. Let's go see the snakes." We walked over toward the glass and Jacob peered in.

I saw one slither by and pointed.

His little nose hit the glass as he tried to get closer. He looked so happy. And it was so much easier to smile when he was smiling. I was pretty sure I'd just found his new favorite thing.

We spent the next hour exploring the rest of the tropical zone. And I was happy that Jacob seemed just as interested in the parrots as the snakes. I certainly preferred fluffier animals. Being in here made me feel like my mom was here with us. Or that I was at least getting one of her big hugs. But I could tell Jacob was antsy to go back outside.

"What do you want to see next?" I ruffled his hair. "Grizzly bears? Or…" I pulled the map out again.

"Monkeys," he said and pointed to a picture of monkeys on the map.

"Good choice."

We wandered outside and down the walking path. The monkeys were even better than the parrots. But I preferred Jacob's interpretation. He jumped around yelling "Eee! Eee! Eee!"

"I think there's some red pandas over there," I said and pointed down another path.

"Red…pandas?"

I laughed. "They look more like raccoons than bears. Do you want to see?"

"Yessie." He slid his hand back in mine and we walked toward the next exhibit. And as soon as the exhibit came into view he ran off again to get closer. But this time I held back. Because the little red headed girl next to him at the red panda enclosure had started talking to him. She was a little shorter than him, but they must have been close to the same age.

They laughed about something.

I swallowed hard. As hard as it was to believe, this was the first time Jacob had ever spoken to someone his own age. And he didn't have stranger danger at all. They both laughed again and started jumping around like monkeys together. I felt tears welling in my eyes.

"Is that sweet little boy yours?" a woman asked from beside me.

I nodded and looked over at her. She was pushing a stroller and her hair was the exact same shade of red as the little girl's. There was no doubt in my mind that she was her mom. "I guess everyone always knows you're her mother without having to ask?"

She laughed. "Yes. But if anyone looks closely, she actually looks much more like her father."

I doubted that. She was a spitting image of her mother, minus the fact that the little girl's eyes were brown and her mother's were blue.

"And she's certainly less shy than I was at her age. She gets that from her father too."

"Well, I thought Jacob was shy until about two minutes ago when he started talking to her."

"I've always loved the name Jacob. It was actually one of my top choices when we had this little guy." She gestured toward the sleeping baby in the stroller.

I bit the inside of my lip as I looked down at her baby. And for just a second, I wanted to cry at his adorably peaceful face. He reminded me of everything I'd lost. Everything I'd never have now. I bit my lip even harder and looked away. "And what name did you land on for him?"

"Liam."

I smiled, even though it was forced.

"And the hyper little redhead flirting with your son is Scarlett."

I laughed, and it wasn't forced at all now. Flirting was probably an exaggeration, but the two of them seemed to be having a blast.

"You know…you look so familiar," she said.

"I get that a lot. I must just have one of those faces." Why did complete strangers keep saying that to me? I had a feeling there was some woman with a similar face to mine who posed for paintings that was very popular right now or something.

"And I'm being incredibly rude. I didn't catch your name. I'm Penny." She put her hand out for me to shake, but at the exact same time her son started crying. "Oh, sorry. One second." She leaned down and lifted him out of the stroller, and in a couple minutes he'd fallen back asleep in her arms.

"The red pandas are Scarlett's favorite exhibit," she whispered. "She's convinced she's related to them."

I laughed and kept my eyes on my son. It seemed like anything could set me off these days. And I hadn't been expecting to be standing next to a baby. But I should have. We were at a zoo.

I would have wandered off, but the woman genuinely seemed nice. And it would be rude to run off when our kids were chatting.

"One of my friends told her that she could actually pet one." She rolled her eyes. "I could kill him for that. Now every time we come here, she runs straight to this exhibit and asks if she can pet them."

Scarlett turned to look at her mother.

"Oh no. Just wait for it. It'll probably happen in three, two, one…"

"Mommy, Mommy!" Scarlett yelled and ran up to her. "Can I pet one today?"

"Not today, sweetie."

"But Uncle Matt said I could."

I laughed, picturing the Matt I used to know telling this stranger's kid that. And it was weird. And stupid. But I could totally picture it. Even though there was no way Matt was this little girl's uncle. She didn't look anything like Mason. Her eyes were more intense. Actually, those eyes did look a little familiar... I quickly shook the thought aside. I did not know these people.

"So you can pet one when your Uncle Matt takes you." Penny shrugged at me.

Scarlett sighed. "But I told Jacob we could pet them. Isn't that right, Jacob?"

My son nodded.

Penny looked over to me for help.

"That's okay," I said. "Maybe next time. How about we go look at the snakes again instead?"

Scarlett gasped.

"She hates snakes," Penny said with a laugh. "And Scar, we've been here for hours already. It's getting late. We should head home for lunch."

"Peanut butter and jelly?" she asked.

Her mom nodded.

"Can Jacob come?" Scarlett looked up at me.

"Oh," I said. "Thank you so much for inviting us, but we were just going to grab some lunch here."

"But Ellie makes the best peanut butter and jelly. I was just telling Jacob. Puhleeeeease."

I didn't know who Ellie was. And I really didn't want to impose. I still wasn't sure Jacob and I were staying in the city. Letting him make friends was probably a mistake…

But my heart melted when Jacob looked up at me. "Please, Mommy. I want peanut butter and jelly."

I looked back at Penny. "I mean…if it's not too much trouble…"

"We'd love to have you," Penny said. "But…"

"It's fine," I quickly said. "We didn't want to inconvenience you anyway."

She laughed. "It's no inconvenience at all. Really. But I have a few errands to run today right after lunch. And I really need to get those errands done or I'll have to take tomorrow off too."

"Really, it's okay…"

"Could we maybe do Wednesday instead?" she asked before I could finish. "If you're free? That way the kids will have time to play."

I smiled. "That sounds great." I needed more to fill up my days. It was the quiet moments that killed me the most.

"We actually live really close to here. So hopefully it'll be easy to find." She was still balancing Liam on her hip as she pulled out a pen and paper. She jotted her address down on the paper. "Does Wednesday at noon work?" Apparently her writing disturbed Liam's slumber, because she handed me the paper just as he started crying again.

"That sounds great," I said over his cries.

"Fantastic. See you both on Wednesday!" she said as she wrassled a very protesting Scarlett into Liam's spot in the stroller so she could manage on getting the two of them out of the zoo.

Jacob smiled up at me. "This was the best day ever!"

"You like your new friend?"

"And the sea lions. And the little red pandas. And the snakes!"

"Well we still have time to see the grizzly bears. Race you there?"

He took off before I could even count to three. The little cheater. We were both laughing as we reached the next enclosure. I lifted him up so he could get a better view. Jacob had made a new friend. And I was pretty sure I just did too. Maybe staying here a little longer wouldn't be the worst thing.

CHAPTER 15

Monday

Matt

Kennedy didn't come by practice. And I knew I wasn't the only one feeling let down. Jefferson hadn't made a single kick all afternoon. It was like Kennedy alone held the power to help him do it. And the whole team's morale seemed down. I had to fix this before homecoming. The last thing we needed was a loss on their big day.

I walked over the moat and into Tanner's apartment. My stomach growled when I saw the feast that had been laid out on the dining room table.

Tanner was sitting there reading the newspaper. "Ah, you're here!" he said as he folded it up and set it aside.

"What's with the spread?"

"Nigel was in a spicy mood."

"Ew, what?"

Tanner pointed to the food. "It's all at least a 7 out of 10 on the Scoville scale. So watch out. Your unrefined palette may not be able to handle it."

"I can handle spicy food." It had taken me eating a lot of Mrs. Alcaraz' cooking back in high school, but I'd gotten used to it. She'd definitely had fun torturing me with that extra spicy omelet when I spent the night though. Hopefully this food wasn't as spicy as those death eggs.

"We'll see about that." Tanner poured me a glass of milk all the way to the brim. "Just in case."

"Very funny." I sat down and put some rice on my plate. "You know I can handle heat."

"I have no way of knowing that."

"I've eaten at Kennedy's house before." I took a bite of the white rice. I thought it was plain, but my mouth was already on fire. What the hell had Nigel done to this rice?

"Ah. Speaking of Kennedy, do you know a Felix Green?" Tanner asked.

"What?" I croaked, trying not to grab the glass of milk.

"He's an old friend of mine."

"An old friend of *yours*?" I put some chicken on my plate, hoping that would cool my mouth down. But a bite of that just made it worse.

"Indeed. Rumor has it that the two of you schooled together as youths."

"Um…we went to high school together." I started coughing.

"That's what I said."

I laughed, but I'm pretty sure it was more of a hiss because my mouth was literally on fire. "That's definitely not what you said."

"Well, regardless, is he a good chap?"

"You just said you know him." I cleared my throat and ate a green bean that might as well have been a chili pepper.

Tanner shrugged. "In the art scene, sure. But is he a good man?"

"Yeah. He's a good guy." I started choking again.

"Fantastic stamp of approval. He'll be in town later this week. And I'm thinking of inviting him out to dinner. Good heavens, you're sweating like a whore in church, young lad. Drink your milk."

I hated that he was right. But if I didn't drink something soon my head was going to explode. I took a huge gulp of milk.

Tanner looked very satisfied with Nigel's disgustingly spicy food. He took a bite of the same chicken I'd eaten and didn't look at all phased.

"So, just the two of you?" I asked when my throat finally calmed back down.

"Hm?" Tanner looked up from his food.

"Just you and Felix going to dinner?"

"Nonsense. My art collection barely fits as is." He gestured to one of the statues covered with a sheet.

"So…why are you having dinner with him?"

"I'm not. It'll just be Kennedy and him. Somewhere with a hotel upstairs so they can shag and we can tell if it's true love right away."

"What the hell?"

"I just got your blessing…"

"Telling you he's a good guy isn't a blessing for Kennedy to fuck another guy."

"Is it not?"

"No! What the hell is wrong with you? Kennedy had a crush on him in high school."

"Exactly. I'm thinking they might be a good match."

"What the hell is your game here?"

He smiled.

"Stop smiling."

Tanner's smile just grew. Like it did when he was up to no good.

"What's wrong with your face?"

"I'm quite happy. And you will be too soon enough."

I sighed and pushed away from the table. "Stop interfering with my life."

"Trust me, I'm helping."

"How is luring Kennedy to a dinner in the hopes that she'll bang her ex-crush helping me?"

"You're not thinking of the bigger picture," he said. "I promise, I have it all under control." He started smiling at me again.

I glared at him. "I'm going to bed."

"But you barely touched your food," Nigel said from behind me.

I jumped. I hadn't seen him. Today he was actually doing a good job at blending into the wall. "It's too spicy, man."

A smile crept across his face. "I love it spicy."

Okay. Nope. I'd had enough. "You're both acting extra weird today," I said.

"No we're not," they both said at the same time.

"Even that was weird. What the hell is going on? Everyone's lost it. First Kennedy. Then Poppy. And now you two."

"Maybe you need a bath…" Nigel started.

"I do not need a bath!" I exhaled slowly. They were both looking at me like I was insane. But they were being fucking nuts. "I'm going to make myself very clear here. Kennedy is not going out with Felix."

"But…" Tanner started.

"Period. And I like showers."

"But you're all sweaty…" Nigel started.

"Baths are for infants!" I yelled.

"That isn't true…"

"Fine. And women with a glass of wine and a book!"

"I'll bring you wine and a book then," Nigel said.

"I don't want wine and a book!"

"But you just said…"

"I don't want a bath!" I screamed.

"Matt, calm yourself," Tanner said. "You're acting hysterical."

"Hysterical? You're the ones who are hysterical!"

Nigel and Tanner calmly looked at each other.

Fuck. Fine, maybe they weren't acting hysterical right this second. But they were freaking crazy. I took a deep breath. "I just need a night alone," I said to Nigel. And then I turned to Tanner. "And I need you to tell me you're not setting the girl I love up with her high school crush."

"I can't promise that," Tanner said.

"What the fuck, Tanner!"

"A bath and some green juice will fix the hysteria," Nigel said calmy.

God, I wanted to yell so many obscenities. And flip the table. And shove a bunch of spicy food down Nigel's throat. But I was pretty sure he'd love that, so I stayed completely still. "I'll be in my room," I said. I gave them each one final hard stare and then walked away.

"I'll be by for your bath in just a moment!" Nigel called after me. "I just have to book that restaurant for Kennedy and Felix's sex date."

I was going to kill both of them. I wasn't sure I'd be able to stop myself.

***

My call to Kennedy went unanswered again.

I knew she kept pushing me away.

But she'd also kissed me back.

And wasn't that proof enough that she didn't want to end things?

Her words after I'd told her I was planning on proposing rattled around in my head. *"I think that some things were always meant to be. And I'm not the kind of person that stuff like that happens to."*

What did she mean by that? What things were always *meant to be* that didn't involve her and me? Because this felt *meant to be* to me.

There was a knock on my door.

I didn't bother to tell whoever was on the other side of the door to go away. Because it was either Tanner or Nigel, and both of them loved walking in uninvited.

Tanner opened up the door. Both he and Nigel strolled in. Tanner handed me one of the glasses of scotch he was holding.

"A peace offering?" I asked.

"Just a boys' chat."

I stared at him. "That's not a thing. I'm pretty sure it's a girls' chat."

"But we're men and we need to talk," Nigel said.

"Okay. I'm guessing this is about an apology?"

"You can apologize to us later," Tanner said. "But first…"

"I'm not apologizing to you. You should both be apologizing to me."

Nigel shook his head. "All I did was try to bathe you."

"That actually sounds worse than what it was," I said. "But that's not what you need to apologize for." Or maybe it was. I didn't even know anymore.

Tanner took a sip of his drink and then set it on my nightstand. "You're really angry that I'm trying to help you find true love?"

"You're trying to set Kennedy up with Felix. That's not true love."

He sat down on the edge of my bed with an exaggerated sigh. "Matt, you can't give your heart to Kennedy."

"I already did."

He shook his head. "It's impossible. Because I know for a fact that you're still in love with Brooklyn. And you can't love two women at the same time, despite what reality TV wants you to think."

"Brooklyn's dead."

"That doesn't mean those feelings just vanish."

"You think I don't know that? What the hell do you think I've been doing for the past 16 years? And I'm finally happy and you…"

"But are you finally happy?"

"Yes…"

"You can really get down on one knee and propose to Kennedy? Let her walk down the aisle and say 'I do' to her? Father her children? Have a whole life with someone when your heart still belongs to another?"

"I love Kennedy."

"Maybe on some level you do. But she isn't the love of your life. And saying that you love Kennedy doesn't answer my questions."

He didn't need to tell me that. His questions were stuck in my head now. Could I really get down on one knee? Marry her? Have children with her? When I still loved Brooklyn? I just stared at him.

A smile slowly stretched over his face. "You see…I'm the voice of reason," Tanner said.

"I don't think that's a phrase that suits you very well." But his words were tumbling around in my head. Not the voice of reason garbage. But all those promises I'd be making to Kennedy if I proposed. All the promises to Brooklyn I'd be breaking. I'd said goodbye to her at her gravestone. I thought getting the ring back would feel like a piece of my heart was back too. But…was it?

I'd been so sure a few days ago. But with Kennedy pushing me away and now Tanner's stupid words in my head… Earlier he said it wasn't true love. That it couldn't possibly be. I don't know why he thought he was an expert on any of this. He definitely was not.

But…was I actually over Brooklyn?

I took a sip of my drink.

Could I ever give someone else my whole heart?

I took another sip.

I thought I could. But sitting here with Nigel and Tanner staring at me after those questions? I felt like a liar. All that was left of Brooklyn in this world was the promises I'd made to her. The promises I'd kept. If I broke them…what would be left? I didn't want her to disappear completely.

I tried to shake the thought away, but it clung to my chest, wrapping around what little heart I had left.

I just wanted to be happy. But could I ever truly be happy knowing I broke those promises to Brooklyn?

"You still love Brooklyn," Tanner said, as if he could read my mind. "And you always will."

"So I'm doomed to a life of sorrow?"

"No," Nigel said. "You can hang out with me."

"Nigel!" Tanner said. "Can't you see this isn't the time or place? Matt needs to be alone to think about the fact that his heart still belongs to Brooklyn."

Honestly...I'd rather hang out with Nigel than think on that. But the questions kept spinning around in my head.

"Matt, I just want you to sit in this room for the rest of the week and ponder those questions," Tanner said. "Nigel will bring you food and anything else you require." He turned to go.

"I'm not staying in this room for the rest of the week. I have work, man."

"Can't you do it remotely?"

Yes. But I didn't want to. "No, I can't."

"I can bring a fax machine by that you can use. Since you love them," Nigel said.

"Faxes won't help."

Nigel looked horrified.

"I mean...I have a few meetings. And practice every afternoon. All of that has to be done in person."

"In person meetings are better," agreed Nigel. "Face to face."

Tanner glared at Nigel. "Fine. You may leave to go to your meetings. But I am making some plans for us, so try to keep your schedule as clear as possible."

"That was very vague," I said.

"I also may be out of town for a day. Two tops." He shook his head. "No, a day will do. Actually, what are your plans for this weekend?"

"It's the homecoming game."

He clapped his hands together. "Homecoming! Genius! Nigel, come with me. We have work to do!"

My phone buzzed and the two of them froze.

Kennedy had finally texted me back: "Dinner tomorrow?" I'd been waiting all day for this text. And now Tanner's stupid questions were rolling around in my head. I showed the text to Tanner.

He looked absolutely horrified. "Say no," he said.

"I'm not doing that."

"Say you have bath plans," Nigel offered.

He wishes. "I'm having dinner with her."

"You really shouldn't," Tanner said. "Just tell her you're busy."

"I'm not busy."

"But you will be soon."

I texted her back confirming before they could stop me. Nigel threw himself on the bed and tried to wrestle my cellphone out of my hands. And by try to, I mean he did it in three seconds flat.

"What the hell was that, Nigel?" I said. I didn't realize he was so quick. Or so weirdly strong. Why had he made me carry that fax machine?

Nigel stood up on my bed and stared down at the phone. "It's too late." He handed the phone to Tanner.

Tanner shook his head. "This will not do. What restaurant will you be dining at?"

"I'm not telling you that."

"Well, just make sure to let her down easily. Nigel, get off his bed."

Nigel reluctantly climbed off my bed.

I wasn't breaking up with Kennedy. I could picture saying yes to all of Tanner's questions. But then I pictured Brooklyn's face. And her voice echoed around in my head. *"Liar."*

CHAPTER 16

Monday

Brooklyn

Kennedy seemed distracted all night.

When I'd first seen her this weekend, I thought she looked happy.

But now?

She'd barely touched her food.

She kept looking at her phone.

And she kept avoiding eye contact with me.

If there was one thing I knew about my best friend…this all meant something was very wrong. So once Jacob had finally settled down from talking about our zoo adventure, I wandered into Kennedy's bedroom.

I didn't wait to be invited. I just climbed in her bed beside her. She was lying down, but I stayed up, just pulling the blanket over my legs. "Talk to me, Kennedy. I can tell something is wrong."

"I messed everything up." Tears pooled in the corners of her eyes. "And I didn't even realize I was doing it. I just want to rewind time and do it all differently."

I nodded. "I feel exactly the same way."

She sniffed. "What did you mess up?"

"My whole life?" I sighed. "I don't know. I keep wondering if there was possibly a way to undo all of it. To make different choices. For Miller to still be alive. But if I rewound too much and didn't choose him, then

I wouldn't have had 15 perfect years. I wouldn't have Jacob. I wouldn't be me. Rewinding time would just cause more heartache. And you'd never even know how much you missed out on."

"Yeah." Kennedy sighed and just stared at me.

"This is where you share your thing."

"I…can't. I can't say the words."

"Since when have you not been able to tell me stuff?"

"For 16 years Brooklyn."

That was fair.

"I missed you so freaking much," she quickly added.

"I missed you too."

"After I went to college, it was hard to visit my mom because everything here reminds me of you. Heck, we even shared this bed for a bit."

"I'm really sorry, Kennedy."

"Trust me, I'm not looking for an apology. Yeah, maybe there's a small piece of me that's furious with you. But a much bigger part is relieved. I'm so happy you're here. I wouldn't change that for the world. And I'm the one that needs to apologize to you."

I frowned. "What on earth do you have to apologize for? I'm the one that disappeared."

"Got kidnapped and then disappeared," Kennedy said. "That kidnapping thing is a very important detail."

Whatever she needed to tell me seemed bad. Or else she would have spilled it already. "Just rip the Band-Aid off," I said.

"I never meant for it to happen. And I'm trying hard to undo it, but I'm having a really hard time be-cause I…" her voice trailed off. She took a deep breath.

"I think I may have accidentally fallen in love with Matt."

"My Matt?"

She winced when I said it.

And I wasn't even sure why I said it. I just meant...the Matt I knew. Matthew Caldwell. I swallowed hard. "Sorry, just...Matt. You're in love with Matt?" I shook my head. It was stupid, that my heart was racing. Even stupider that the knife I'd felt in my chest so many years ago was back, twisting slowly. Matt wasn't mine. He could date whoever he wanted. And Kennedy could date whoever she wanted. "Okay," I said.

"Okay? That's all you have to say?"

What the hell did she want me to say? That I was fine with it? Because I wasn't sure I was fine. It felt like the knife in my chest twisted deeper. I exhaled slowly. I'd asked for this, hadn't I? By praying he found happiness too? "How long have you two been dating?"

"Not long at all. Like I said, it was hard for me to come back to the city. But I got this job opportunity I couldn't pass up and...I ran into Matt. Literally. When I was shooting some photos. And I swear we were just friends. And then it somehow kind of tumbled into more. And I...I don't know what happened."

"Okay," I said.

"Stop saying okay. It's not okay! I feel awful. And I told him to stop calling me. I told him we were done. But it's like he's crawled into my veins."

Yeah, I knew that feeling. Like you couldn't shake him. And I was embarrassed to admit that he still had a hold on me after all these years. Or else hearing all this wouldn't be making me feel like I'd just run five miles.

"As soon as you came back, I pushed him away. But when I saw that stupid tabloid this morning I got so mad and I stormed over to his office and I somehow kissed him and I'm sorry. It's still done. I just slipped once and it won't happen again." Tears were running down her cheeks now. "God, I'm such a monster."

And I wanted to hug her and tell her it was going to be okay. But my mind had just stopped. *The tabloid.* Matt wasn't dating Kennedy. Or if he was… "Kennedy. He's *engaged* to Poppy."

"He's not engaged to Poppy. They're dating publicly because Matt got into a little situation he's trying to get out of, but…"

"You're dating him in secret?" *Oh, Kennedy.* I wanted to cry for her. She'd gotten tangled up in him. Just like I had. And he'd break her too.

"I know that sounds bad…"

"Yeah, it does sound bad. You know how much it hurt me when he kept me a secret in high school." I shook my head. "Has he really learned nothing from his past?" God, that boy was such an idiot.

"He has. He…"

"No he hasn't, Kennedy. You're his dirty little secret just like I was. And you deserve better than an asshole like him."

"Whoa. He's not an asshole."

I just stared at her. I knew I was breathing hard. I knew my palms were sweaty. I didn't even know why I was so upset. Matt wasn't mine. I didn't love him anymore. I'd let him go.

"He's going to break up with her." Kennedy shook her head. "This is coming out wrong. They're not even really dating. It's just for the press."

"I bet it is."

"You don't understand," Kennedy said.

"I do. I understand exactly. Because he put me in the same position 16 years ago!"

"But he fixed it…"

"Fixed what? My life is a fucking mess because of him!"

"I don't think that's fair," Kennedy said. "You're the one that didn't come back when you escaped…"

"I did come back!"

"What?" She pushed herself up to face me. "When?"

I climbed out of her bed and started pacing. God, the last thing I wanted to do was relive this moment. I still remembered feeling like I couldn't breathe. Running to James and Rob's treehouse. It felt like my life was over. Like I'd lost my whole world.

I shook my head. No. It didn't compare to what I was feeling now. Because I actually had lost my whole world now. And this was worse.

I was just a kid back then. Matt betrayed me. He didn't feel sorry. And that was the end of our story. I was young and stupid, and this shouldn't still hurt so fucking much.

My feet finally stopped pacing and I turned to Kennedy. "When I escaped…I came back to him right away."

Kennedy shook her head. "That can't…but he still thinks you're dead, Brooklyn."

"We made all these promises to each other. He was the only thing that kept me going, really. Knowing he was out there missing me as much as I was missing him. My dad started bringing me photos. Showing him hanging out with other girls. Drinking, partying with his friends. But I fixated on his eyes." I tried to picture one of those old photos. "He looked as sad as me. My dad was just messing with my head. I was sure of it."

"He was sad," Kennedy said. "He was barely holding it together. You two must have been feeling exactly the same way."

I shook my head. "That's what I wanted to believe. I convinced myself it was true. That he needed me as much as I needed him. But it didn't look like he was missing me when I came to his house at the end of the next summer."

Kennedy just waited.

"He was banging some random brunette in his family's pool." Her face was permanently etched into my memory. Her laughing. Her hands on my man. And worse, his hands on her. His laugh. His smile. He was so happy.

"Brooklyn…"

"He broke me. And he promised not to do that. He promised me." I shook my head. He'd promised me a lot of things. And he'd broken all of them.

"He thought you were dead."

"Yeah. But he didn't even wait a year. I would have waited a lifetime for him." It was dumb and naïve. But it was still true. I'd loved him so much.

Kennedy opened her mouth and then closed it.

There wasn't really anything else to say. I got her point. Matt thought I was dead. So of course he was allowed to put his dick into whoever he wanted. Of course he was allowed to be happy. I just never expected him to move on so quickly. It made me feel worse than being his dirty little secret. It made me feel like I'd never meant anything at all.

And just thinking about that hurt made the knife in my chest ease. I'd made the right choice all those years ago. I wouldn't undo a second of it. I'd let Matt go. I repeated it over and over to myself until I exhaled slowly. I'd let him go.

"So you didn't speak to him when you visited?"

"He was a little busy." I sat down on the edge of her bed.

"I really think you should speak to him now."

"And say what, Kennedy? We were done 16 years ago."

She shook her head. "Whoever that girl was in his pool, it meant nothing, I'm sure of it. He was just trying to…"

"Fuck me out of his system?" I laughed. "No. It didn't look like that. It looked like…" my voice trailed off. "He was happy." I exhaled slowly. "And despite how much of jerk he was to me, I want that for him. Because for just a brief amount of time, he made me happy too, you know?" He'd fixed me just to ruin me all over again. The thing I was still most angry about was all those stupid tears I cried over him. All that time I wasted when I should have been with Miller. Because my time with Miller had been cut way too short.

Kennedy nodded. "I think the two of you could be happy together now."

I just stared at her. "He's dating you *and* Poppy. I think his hands are full."

Kennedy laughed, but it sounded forced. "I broke it off with him. Yes, I had a slip-up today, but…"

"Does he make you happy?"

"Yeah, but…"

"Like I said…I want him to be happy. And I definitely want you to be happy."

"I want you to be happy too," she said.

I nodded. "That'll never be with Matt though." I took a deep breath and slowly exhaled. "I hate him more than I ever loved him."

"Hate is a strong emotion. Almost as strong as love."

"I don't love Matthew Caldwell. And despite whatever he's told you, he doesn't love me either." I wasn't sure he ever had. "I shouldn't have said I hated him. I just…I'm done letting him hurt me. I'm over him. I've been over him for years. So if you want to date him, despite the fact that he's putting you second, that's your choice."

"You know I can't do that."

"Yes you can. Kennedy, it's been 16 years since I dated him. I don't even know him anymore. If you like him…that's okay with me." It had to be okay with me. But I also knew what them dating meant. That eventually I'd have to see him. Hang out with him. Coexist with him. I couldn't understand Matt with Poppy. But I could understand Matt with Kennedy.

Kennedy was kind and sweet. She had the biggest heart of anyone I knew. It was like I accidentally wished this upon myself when I said Matt should be with anyone but Poppy. I hadn't meant Kennedy. But this was going to be okay. It had to be.

"I think the years have twisted your memory of him," said Kennedy. "I swear he's still the same guy he was in high school."

No, he was the same *boy* he was in high school. Because he was dating the girl he had real feelings for in secret. He was exactly the same. And I couldn't believe that Kennedy couldn't see it. He was going to hurt her just like he hurt me. He'd promise her the world and take it away. And she knew all that. So there wasn't really anything I could say to stop her. It was her decision.

"You need to tell him that you're alive," she said. "I can't keep this secret for you. It's tearing me up inside."

"I…" my voice trailed off. God, I didn't know what I wanted to do. Stay? Go? Jacob loved it here. He loved Mrs. Alcaraz and Kennedy. And I wasn't ready to go home yet. I wasn't sure when I would be. Because it wasn't a home without Miller. I blinked fast to keep my tears at bay. I'd have to face Matt eventually. And it was better if I did it myself. "I'll tell him."

"I can give you his number if you want," Kennedy said.

I pulled out my cellphone and handed it to her. She typed in his number and handed it back to me.

She stared at me like I was going to call him right this second.

"Tomorrow," I said. Tomorrow seemed easier than today.

"Okay." She looked just as upset as when we started this conversation.

She'd been keeping her relationship with Matt a secret from me. Or, end of relationship. Or whatever it was. Because I told her I didn't want to talk about Matt. And she'd also been keeping my return a secret from Matt. I'd put her in a terrible position.

I didn't want her to feel bad. About any of it. "You really can keep dating him," I said. "It's fine with me." It had to be.

She shook her head.

"Really, Kennedy. I promise I don't have feelings for him anymore."

She eyed me skeptically.

"I knew him half a lifetime ago. I'm not the same person now. And even if I was? There are some things too big to get over."

Kennedy nodded. "Maybe."

"Definitely."

She puffed up her cheeks and then blew out an exhausted exhale. "I didn't mean to fall for him, you know?"

I nodded. Yeah, I knew exactly how she was feeling. I'd never meant to fall for Matt either. My staring at him at Empire High was what first got me in trouble with Isabella. And not keeping my hands to myself had resulted in her torturing me. Loving Matt had set all these catastrophic things in motion. So yeah, I knew what she meant.

"It's really okay," I said. I meant it when I said it. But as soon as the words fell from my mouth I bit the inside of my cheek. Why was my heart still racing so fast?

CHAPTER 17

Tuesday

Matt

Kennedy was supposed to meet me here fifteen minutes ago. I stared at the menu as Tanner's questions rolled around in my head.

Could I really propose to someone that wasn't Brooklyn?

Marry someone that wasn't Brooklyn?

Have a family with someone that wasn't Brooklyn?

Have a life without her?

I was still nursing the drink I'd grabbed from the bar. And it was like the wait staff knew not to approach me. They probably assumed I was in a terrible mood because I was being stood up.

They were right. I was in a terrible mood. But not because I'd been stood up. Even though this was Kennedy's idea, I only half expected her to show. I was in a bad mood because Tanner's questions had really gotten stuck in my head.

"Matt."

I stood up too fast, almost knocking over my drink. "Hey." I smiled at Kennedy and tried to give her a hug. She dodged a little but somehow still got captured in my arms. Her arms stayed firmly at her sides as we finished the world's most awkward hug.

But right before I pulled back, her arms finally wrapped around me. "I'm sorry, Matt. I'm so sorry."

I didn't reply. I just held her.

Yes, Tanner's questions were still stuck in my head. But this right here? I loved this. I loved having someone that relied on me. It had been a really long time since someone had needed me.

She took a step back and wiped beneath her eyes.

"You look beautiful tonight," I said. She did. She was wearing a tight black dress and thigh-high black boots. Like she was purposely trying to drive me insane.

"Thanks, Matt."

I pulled out her chair for her and she sat down.

I quickly sat down too. And then we just stared at each other.

"I'm really surprised you showed up," Kennedy said.

I laughed. "You're the one that was late."

"I know." She wrapped her arms around herself, as if she was literally holding herself together. "I just...I knew it was going to hurt when I walked in here and you were a no-show."

I just stared at her. "Kennedy, nothing would have made me miss this dinner."

She twisted her mouth to the side. "I just figured after that phone call..."

"What phone call?"

"Oh. After that text I guess..."

I shook my head. "I have no idea what you're talking about."

Her eyebrows raised. "You didn't hear from someone today?"

"Who exactly are we talking about?"

Her face fell. "I thought…" she pressed her lips together as she fiddled with the bracelets on her wrist. "Nothing. It was my mistake."

"Kennedy, please just tell me what's going on. Are you in some kind of trouble?"

"No." She gave me a tight lipped smiled. "Everything's fine."

I could be dense, but I knew enough to know that whenever a woman said everything was fine, it was anything but. "You gotta tell me what's going on here."

She looked down at the menu instead of responding.

"Kennedy." I reached across the table to grab her hand.

"Bonjour!" our waiter yelled.

I jumped and dropped her hand. Why was our waiter yelling at us? I looked over at him. "Nigel? What the hell?"

"Not Nigel! I'm Francois!"

I just stared at him. He was definitely Nigel. In a waiter uniform and a very fake looking mustache. He was also wearing glasses he didn't need. And his hair was all styled to one side and gelled down in a way that screamed French pervert.

"Do you know each other?" Kennedy asked me.

"I…"

"No," Nigel said cutting me off. "I have never seen this man in my life." He put his hand to his chest like he was shocked by the accusation. "I have a way with faces. I'm Francois."

Kennedy looked back and forth between us. How exactly was I supposed to explain to Kennedy that I was currently living with this psychopath? And why was Nigel's French accent so impeccable?

"Okay…" Kennedy said.

"Can I get the two of you some refreshments? I hear the wine list is fantastique here." He cleared his throat. "I mean I know it. Because I work here. I'm Francois!"

Why did he keep yelling his fake name? I didn't know whether to confront him again or just try to ignore it. My train of thought stopped when I caught sight of someone in a corner booth staring at our table over the top of his menu.

He had a big, bushy, fake looking mustache. His hair was also heavy on the gel, even though it was mostly hidden under a bright red beret. And he had rounded glasses…instead of his usual square ones. Yup, that was definitely Tanner. Dressed oddly similar to Nigel even though he was pretending to be a patron and not a fake waiter. What the hell were they doing here? This was completely insane.

And how had they known what restaurant I was going to? I'd only texted Kennedy about the place a couple hours ago. How had Nigel infiltrated the staff so quickly?

Tanner lifted his menu to hide his face when he realized I was staring at him.

Yeah, I was not going to engage in this. I'd just ignore them. They could spy all they wanted. It wasn't like they were going to ruin my night. "Just bring us a bottle of whatever," I said.

"Very well, Master. I mean, sir." Nigel hurried off.

"I have so many questions," Kennedy said. She was finally smiling. "Do you know him?"

"You wouldn't believe the story if I told you."

She laughed. "Well now I'm dying to hear it." She put her elbows on the table and leaned forward slightly.

"You know how I'm living with Tanner right now?"

"Yeah."

"Well don't look, but Tanner is dressed like an enthusiastic French diner over in the corner booth…"

She turned to look.

"I said don't look!" I said and grabbed her arm.

She started laughing.

"Bonjour!" Nigel yelled and put two more candles between us on the table, pushing my hand off of Kennedy's arm. "Candles for our best table!" He put several plates of oil down on the table even though there was no bread to dip it with. And did they even do that at French restaurants?

The candles were meant to scare me. To make me keep my hands on my side of the table. Those bastards knew candles and oil still freaked me out a little after Ash had accidentally set my dick on fire.

"Drinks!" Nigel yelled. "I'll be back with the drinks!" He ran away.

I shook my head. "And that is Nigel. Tanner's houseboy."

Kennedy laughed. "So all this is…"

"I have no idea."

She smiled. "I think we should try to trick him into admitting he's Nigel. Whoever can make him confess he's Nigel first wins."

"Wins what exactly?"

"Whatever the person wants."

I knew what I wanted. Her. "Deal. I'd shake on it, but I'm pretty sure he wants me to catch fire."

Kennedy laughed. "It does appear that way. Did you do something to upset Nigel or something? And did you say that he was Tanner's *houseboy*?"

I did not want to tell Kennedy about Tanner's bullshit true love thing. "It's been a long day. And I really don't want to get into it." A soon as I said the words, I realized I was doing exactly what she was doing. Keeping secrets. Not sharing. I wanted us to be a team. I shook my head. "Okay, the real story? And please don't take any offense to this at all. Because they're always doing weird things."

"I can tell." She'd finally snuck at glance at Tanner.

Tanner lifted up his menu again to hide.

"Tanner's convinced he's an expert on true love. A matchmaker of sorts. And seriously this means nothing. Because I've never seen that guy get any couples together. But he doesn't think we're a perfect fit."

Kennedy pulled her eyebrows together.

"It's all ridiculous. I know he likes you. I can't tell if it's like a jealousy thing or something? Obviously us spending time together means I have to spend less time with him. Rob used to make fun of me all the time when I was dating Brooklyn, but that was just because he missed me." I realized a second too late that I'd mentioned Brooklyn. I was trying really hard not to do that. But ever since I'd told Penny about her, it just felt normal to talk about Brooklyn again. And it was a problem, because I was pretty sure that was what kept getting me into messes.

Kennedy shifted in her chair. "So…we're not true love?"

I cleared my throat. "According to Tanner. But Tanner also presumably thinks that his disguise is working, so his judgement is clearly suspect."

She smiled.

"I'm pretty sure he lost his mind this weekend. Get this...he was actually planning on setting you up on a date this week."

Kennedy laughed.

"I seriously wish I was kidding."

"With who?"

I just shrugged. I knew he was setting her up with Felix. But I wasn't going to let that happen.

"I guess that's why he came to my apartment to talk to me yesterday."

"Wait, what? I specifically asked him not to do that." But of course he didn't listen. Why was Tanner being such a dick?

"I didn't let him up. I was...getting ready for work. But he keeps texting me with really vague messages about needing to speak with me urgently."

"That was probably about the surprise date."

"Wait," Kennedy said. "He didn't tell you about what he saw at my apartment?"

"No." I frowned. "I thought you said you didn't let him up."

"I didn't. I..." she looked over at Tanner. "I don't understand why he didn't tell you."

"Tell me what?"

"Wine!" Nigel yelled.

I looked up at him as he searched his apron for a corkscrew. But he sighed when his hands came up empty. Then reached behind himself and pulled out a sword.

Where the hell did he get a sword?! I scooted away from him as he raised it. Had Nigel finally snapped? I didn't even know what I meant by *finally* there. He was clearly just nuts all along.

But he wasn't threatening me with his sword. He slashed it across the neck of the bottle and perfectly cut off the top. The cork and a bit of glass fell to the ground and a little white wine spilled out over his hand. He slowly poured us each a glass.

"That was very impressive, Nigel," Kennedy said.

"Thank you. I mean, no! I'm Francois!" He slammed her glass down in front of her.

She burst out into laughter as he walked away. "I win."

I couldn't stop laughing either. "That was actually really awesome."

"Right?"

"But you didn't win. He has to actually confess that he's Nigel."

"He answered to his name though. That's a confession."

"Not technically."

She gaped at me. "No way. I won."

"No you didn't," I said with a laugh. "Just watch and learn." I tilted my head to the side and cracked my neck.

Kennedy rolled her eyes at me.

But she wouldn't be rolling her eyes when Nigel came back over and confessed his true identity.

"I didn't expect you to show up tonight," she said. "And I definitely didn't expect to be laughing so hard the entire time."

I smiled at her.

"It's a shame that we're not a perfect match," she said. "I pictured it, you know?"

"You're not seriously believing Tanner?"

"No. I'm not believing Tanner. I'm just…" she shrugged. "Technically I'm allowed to be here. I'm allowed to love you. But I can't help but think that maybe there is a perfect match for *you*, you know?"

"For me? What about you?"

"I think I'm kind of used to being alone. God," She rested her chin in her hands. "This whole thing is so messy. I can't undo any of it. And I don't want to. The damage is done."

"Because you love me," I said, flashing her my cockiest grin.

"Oh, shut up, Matt." She tossed her napkin at me.

And it was like I was having a flashback. It flew so close to the candles and I couldn't help it… A high-pitched scream filled the dining room. I knew it was me. But it still surprised me when I heard it.

Kennedy burst out laughing when the napkin didn't set on fire and hit me in the chest. "What was that?"

"You know what happened to me!"

She started laughing harder.

I tossed the napkin on the table and walked over to her. I grabbed her and pulled her to her feet, cradling her face in my hands.

"Maybe we're not a perfect match, Kennedy" I said. "Maybe we're an imperfect one. But it's the imperfect things in life that make it memorable, right?" I didn't wait for her to respond. I leaned down and kissed her.

And she didn't push me away this time. She kissed me back.

My nose brushed against hers as she slowly pulled back.

"Well, this night has certainly been memorable," she said.

Out of the corner of my eye, I saw Nigel pick up a bottle of champagne from a nearby table. But he didn't seem interested in the champagne, because he just tossed it over his shoulder and picked up the ice bucket that it had been in. *What is he doing?*

Kennedy must have seen me watching him, because she turned to look at him just as he tossed the ice right in our faces.

Yup, I was going to kill him.

But Kennedy was laughing so hard.

"Nigel, what the fuck?" I said, but I was laughing too. I wiped the water out of my eyes.

"I thought you were on fire. And the name is Francois!"

I started laughing harder. "Cut it out, Nigel." I reached out and tore his fake mustache off.

He screamed at the top of his lungs. "My mustache! What have you done?! You've ruined Francois' signature style!"

"The jig is up, Nigel," Tanner said and removed his beret. "We've been caught."

I just laughed because it was all I could do. "Is anyone else craving pizza?"

"Yeah, let's get out of here," Kennedy said through her laughter.

"Us too?" Nigel asked.

"Oh, the night has barely even begun," Kennedy said and grabbed the discarded bottle of champagne. It was a miracle that it hadn't shattered.

She wanted to hang out with all of us instead of eating in this stuffy restaurant with the terrible service. Even though she knew Tanner didn't believe in our relationship. And that Nigel was a crazy person. But it didn't matter, because they were my friends, and she got that.

Tanner sighed. "Why does she have to be so lovely?"

She really was. Kennedy fit in my life. And I wasn't letting her go.

CHAPTER 18

Wednesday

Brooklyn

Wow. The entryway to Penny's apartment building was insane. I looked back down at the handwritten note Penny had given me. This was definitely the right place. I felt like I was back in high school. In a world I knew I didn't belong in. I pressed my lips together. Well, maybe I'd belonged once. For a little bit.

It reminded me a lot of Felix's apartment. All clean lines and modern décor. I smiled to myself. I wondered how Felix was doing. I'd been thinking of him a lot ever since Kennedy's friend Tanner had asked me about him. Did Felix still live in the city, or had he moved somewhere new? There were a lot of people I'd love to catch up with. But…it was probably a bad idea. I still had no idea if I was staying.

I looked down at Jacob. He was staring at the place in awe. I squeezed his hand and he smiled up at me. Who was I kidding? I'd stay as long as he kept smiling. I just kept telling myself I might leave so I wouldn't have to call Matt. Or text him. Or…something.

I'd promised Kennedy I would. But I just didn't know what to say. I'd typed out a few texts, but I'd deleted them all before sending. I knew she thought it mattered. But I wasn't so sure. My dad had tried to reach out to him and he hadn't cared. I didn't know why

I was even worried about sending a text. It was unlikely that Matt would even bother to respond.

"Mommy," Jacob said and tugged on my hand.

God, I'd completely spaced out. I'd been doing that a lot recently.

Jacob held my hand as we walked across the stretch of marble floor up to the concierge desk.

"Hi," I said. "I'm supposed to be meeting Penny."

"Of course." The concierge said with a smile before he glanced down at his notepad. "Name?"

"I'm not sure what her last name is."

"Oh, sorry, I meant your name, ma'am."

"Oh." I laughed. "Brooklyn Miller?" I didn't know why it came out as a question.

"Brooklyn Miller." He looked back down at his notebook with a frown. And then he moved to look at his computer. "I'm so sorry, but you're not on the list. If you could give me one moment please." He lifted up his phone. "There's a Ms. Miller here to see you." He paused and stared at me. "Yes, she has blonde hair. And there is indeed a young boy with her." *Pause.* "Very well." He hung up the phone and smiled. "She's expecting you. It's the penthouse suite."

"Oh. Okay." I didn't know if I was supposed to go or wait for him to go with me. "Do I just…go up?"

"Yes, it's the top button, Ms. Miller."

"Thank you so much." Jacob and I hurried off to the elevators.

"Mommy," Jacob said.

"Yes?"

"Where *are* we?" When the elevators dinged open, he jumped back, dropping my hand.

And I realized he'd never been on an elevator before. He'd never even seen one. "We're visiting your friend from the zoo, remember?"

"Sí."

I smiled. He seemed to prefer Spanish these days. "This will take us up to see them."

"Noooo," he said.

"Jacob, I promise it's safe."

"Nunca." He took another step back.

How could I resist him when he said nunca in that cute little accent he'd somehow adopted from Mrs. Alcaraz? "Okay, sweet boy. We'll take the stairs." I lifted him into my arms and carried him into the stairwell.

The penthouse was a long way up. And I'd broken a sweat a long time before we finally exited onto what I hoped was the correct floor. There were only two doors. One labeled security and the other with no label at all.

So Penny lived in a penthouse in a luxury apartment building? With what appeared to be her own security. I'd definitely just accidentally been thrust back into the world of the elite. There was a little part of me that wanted to hightail it back down those stairs. But a much bigger part of me wanted a glass of water. And Penny had seemed so kind. Just because I'd never belong in her world, it didn't mean Jacob couldn't be friends with Scarlett. Maybe they could even go to the same school.

My stomach churned. God, I guess I really was planning on staying. I'd text Matt tonight. I'd just do it and get it over with and everyone could just keep on going with their lives.

I wiped a bead of sweat off my forehead and knocked on the door.

A few moments later it opened all by itself. I almost jumped back like Jacob had when he saw the elevator. But then I looked down at the cute little redheaded girl holding the doorknob.

"Hi!" said Scarlett with a huge smile.

Was she supposed to be opening the door? I looked behind me like maybe she was expecting someone else.

"Come on, Jacob, let's play Barbies," Scarlett said.

Jacob looked up at me.

He didn't know what elevators were. Or Barbies. He'd never known anyone his own age, and we'd mostly played outside together as a family. "They're dolls," I whispered to him.

He scrunched up his face. "Can we play soccer instead?" Jacob asked.

"Soccer?" Since when did he like soccer?

"Fútbol," he said in a Spanish accent.

I stifled a laugh. He'd gotten that all mixed up. Yes, soccer was called football in Mexico. But football wasn't soccer.

"I have a ball," Scarlett said. "Come with me." She took off running.

Jacob squirmed in my arms. I set him down and he ran after her, leaving me standing awkwardly in the doorway.

Penny appeared in Scarlett's place, almost a spitting image of her daughter. "Did Scarlett open the door?" She blew a strand of hair out of her face as she adjusted Liam on her hip. "We keep telling her not to do that."

I laughed. "I think she was just excited to play."

"Oh I know, she hasn't stopped talking about Jacob ever since they met at the zoo."

"Jacob was equally excited."

Penny smiled. "Well, come in, come in. Can I offer you something to drink or…"

"A glass of water would be amazing. Apparently Jacob is afraid of elevators. We took the stairs."

"All the way up?" She opened the fridge and pulled out a pitcher of water. She expertly balanced her son while somehow managing not to spill any water. "I've lived here for years and I've never taken the stairs. But in my defense…cardio is the worst."

I laughed. "I'm the exact opposite. I love running."

"Ugh, you and my husband both. He's always trying to get me to jog in Central Park with him."

The horror in her voice made me laugh again.

She handed me the glass of water.

I downed half of it in one gulp as she sat down at the kitchen island.

"Help yourself to more. And if you want, we can order takeout for lunch. But sometimes I like to indulge in the occasional peanut butter and jelly sandwich too."

"I'm totally down with peanut butter and jelly," I said as I poured myself another glass of water. Their fridge was immaculate. Everything was labeled and there wasn't a single spill on the glass shelves. And everything was organic. I was a little surprised that the person who owned this fridge ate peanut butter and jelly sandwiches.

Penny smiled as I turned around. "I knew I liked you. I know it's probably weird, but my husband has this thing about loving children's food." She shook her head and laughed. "Wow, that sounded so weird. I just meant food he never got to eat growing up. Peanut butter and jelly with juice boxes has become a lunchtime staple in our home."

What kind of monster parents did her husband have? "Not weird at all. For a few weeks there all my son would eat was cupcakes. Which he calls cuppycakes. So I'm thrilled that he's excited for PB&J."

"Cuppycakes?" Penny looked down at her son. He'd fallen asleep, his head resting against her chest. "Don't you just want to freeze time so they keep saying stuff like that forever?"

I wanted to freeze time for a lot of reasons. I'd go back a month and relive the same day over and over if I could. Instead of saying any of that, I just nodded and sat down next to her at the kitchen island. I cleared my throat. "So what do you do?"

"I'm an author." She laughed. "Well, not really. I don't know why I said that. But I'm writing a book. And I hope to get it published one day."

"What's it about?"

"It's about how I met my husband. A love story of sorts."

I plastered on a smile. I didn't really want to hear about a love story right now. But it felt a little rude not to ask. "And how did you meet?"

"Oh it was all very scandalous. He was my professor."

"Really?"

She laughed. "You don't have to pretend like you haven't heard all about it."

I shook my head. How would I possibly know about that? I didn't even know her last name. Were her and her husband frequently in the tabloids or something? I wouldn't put it past her because of where she lived. Paparazzi loved snapping photos of the rich and famous. But the more I learned about Penny the more confused I was. She was an unpublished author with a professor husband. Yet they could afford this apartment? Maybe her parents were wealthy? "I'm actually not from around here, so I know very little about the goings on of NYC."

"I wish I knew less. I swear I'm going to hit the next paparazzi who wakes Liam up with those ridiculous bright flashes."

I laughed. "Do you need to go put him down?"

She kissed the top of Liam's sleeping head. "No, he'll cry as soon as I put him in his crib. He prefers his naps like this."

I couldn't help but laugh again. I couldn't even count how many times I'd let Jacob nap just like that. I loved that my heartbeat soothed him to sleep. And how many times he'd crawled into me and Miller's bed once he was a toddler, insisting he needed to sleep in between us. Yeah, I definitely wanted to go back and freeze time.

"So if you're not from around here, where did you grow up?" Penny asked.

"Delaware."

"No way. I'm from Delaware!"

"Really? What are the odds?"

"I know. That's insane. But it's not the first time this has happened to me. I'm having serious déjà vu right now. This sounds completely crazy, but almost all my male friends married girls from Delaware even though they're all from New York. I swear it's fate. My husband and his friends basically all grew up together. And I just think there's something about people from Delaware that clicks with them."

That was so odd. Almost all of them married girls from Delaware? How did they even all meet girls from Delaware if they were here in the city?

"Did you go to the University of New Castle too?" Penny asked.

I shook my head.

"That's actually where I met my husband."

"And you were a student when you met him?"

"Yeah, but he's not that much older than me."

"Oh, I wasn't judging you at all. My husband is actually quite a bit older than me." *Was.* He *was.*

"And how did the two of you meet?"

He was my bodyguard. I fell in love with him in a cage. I tried desperately to push him away for a boy who'd forgotten I'd existed. But he waited for me. He'd waited. And our time was cut short. I missed him so much I could barely breathe. "It's a really long story."

"I have all afternoon," she said with a smile.

I reached down and touched the metal bands on my ring finger. I felt the tear trail down my cheek a second too late.

"Are you okay?" Penny asked. She reached out and grabbed my hand.

And just that tiny touch of warmth was like a dam breaking in my chest. A heavy sob fell from my mouth.

And then she hugged me. Even though we were practically strangers. She hugged me and she didn't care that my tears soaked her shirt. Or that I was probably a psychopath that she'd let into her home. She just hugged me. Like we were old friends.

Liam started to squirm. I could tell my sobbing was waking him up.

"I'm so sorry," I said and finally pulled back from her hug.

There were tears in her eyes too even though she didn't even know what was wrong.

"My husband passed away recently."

It was like she could feel my pain. Like she knew what it was like to lose someone. "What happened? I'm so sorry, don't answer that. We don't have to talk about it at all if you don't want to."

"No, it's okay. It was a…terrible accident." But it wasn't an accident. The only accident was that it wasn't me behind the wheel of that car. And I still wasn't sure I believed my father. Had it been a rival family? Or had it been him?

"I'm so sorry," Penny said.

"Say something to distract me," I said and forced a laugh.

"I almost lost my husband. And that seems so stupid to say because I didn't and you…" her lips trembled. "I'm so sorry. This isn't a very good distraction!"

"No, it's okay. Tell me that story." I said and wiped away my tears. This was probably the weirdest conversation ever had between two people that didn't know each other. But she was making me feel better.

She wiped away her remaining tears too. "Well, my husband was married to a psychopath before he met me."

I laughed. I'd had my fair share of psychos in my life. I was just glad Isabella was dead.

"She paid someone to shoot him on our wedding night."

"No."

"Three times. I didn't think he was going to make it."

God, I couldn't even imagine that pain. To be robbed of happiness so soon. I'd gotten 15 years with Miller. And it wasn't enough. But at least I'd had that. Fifteen years of happiness.

"And I found out I was pregnant with Scarlett while he was in a coma."

I put my hand to my chest.

"And then his ex showed up at the hospital and tried to finish the job herself. If we didn't have bodyguards, I don't know if either of us would be alive right now. Or my daughter." She looked down at Liam. "And I never would have gotten to have this little guy either."

If I hadn't had a bodyguard, I wouldn't be alive either. Miller had fixed my heart. He'd given me Jacob. He'd given me the whole world. I blinked fast so I wouldn't start crying again.

"If I hear the name Isabella, I still get all sweaty and panicky," Penny said.

"The psycho's name was Isabella?" I shook my head. "An Isabella ruined my life too."

"What?"

"Yeah. She was insane. Back in high school, my Isabella…" I shook my head. "Poor wording. I never ever want to call her my Isabella."

Penny laughed.

"But she tried to kill me. She had a whole plan and everything. She made it her sole purpose to ruin my life."

"What the hell? In high school?"

I nodded. "Isabellas, man," I said.

"The worst."

I laughed.

"Wait. So we're both from Delaware. We fell in love with older men. And were tortured by Isabellas." Penny shook her head. "It's like we're the same person."

I laughed. "I know, right?" It was good to be laughing again. And seriously…she was right. We were so similar.

"Penny, I'm home!" said a deep voice.

"In the kitchen!" Penny called back as she slid off her stole. She practically ran across the floor to greet her husband.

Just like I used to do when Miller came home.

He appeared in the doorway and I swear I stopped breathing.

He leaned down and kissed his wife, cradling her face in his hands. And then he leaned down farther to give his son a kiss on the forehead. He looked back up at his wife's face with all the adoration in the world.

I recognized the look.

I was pretty sure he'd given it to me once.

"I have a friend over," Penny said. "She's the mother of the little boy Scarlett met at the zoo." Penny turned around. "Oh, I'm so sorry, but I don't think I ever caught your name. James this is…"

She was waiting for me to fill in the blank.

But James' eyes met mine.

I'd still never met anyone that had stared as intensely as James Hunter.

My past collided with my present.

"Brooklyn," James said, filling in my name for me. "You're alive." He said it like he didn't truly believe the words coming out of his mouth.

"Brooklyn?" Penny asked. "Matt's Brooklyn?"

James didn't respond. He just walked over to me.

I was frozen.

"Brooklyn," he whispered. He put his hands on the side of my face just like he'd done with his wife. But not in adoration. It was like he was taking me in. Like he couldn't believe I was real. Like he had to touch me to know for sure. "You're alive," he said again.

"James." My voice cracked. I stood up and I hugged him.

And suddenly everything made sense. Why Scarlett's eyes looked familiar. The dark brown intense stare. Why Scarlett had someone in her life she called Uncle Matt. Why Penny's Isabella sounded just as crazy as my Isabella.

I did know this family.

I buried my face in James' chest.

Once upon a time, James had tortured me. And for just a short while, I think maybe he had feelings for me. I remembered him sitting with me in the shower as I cried. I remembered that stupid kiss during homecoming. I remembered him as a boy. All I'd known about his future was that he'd married Isabella. I'd been worried about him. Furious at him. But most of all I just missed him.

"This isn't real," he whispered. "You're dead. You died."

I was sobbing all over again as I pulled back and looked up at him. I shook my head. "You went to Delaware." I'd told him once that the people there were nicer. And he'd gone. Penny said most of the guys she knew married women from Delaware. Who was she referring to? Mason? Rob?

James took a step back from me. "Where the fuck have you been?"

His shock had turned to anger rather quickly. Just like the boy I used to know.

Well, I had questions too. "You married Isabella? How could you?" My voice cracked.

He lowered his eyebrows at me. "Because you died, Brooklyn."

I shook my head. That wasn't an answer. He didn't do that because of me.

Penny walked back over to us. She put a hand on James' shoulder.

He turned to her. "I don't understand."

"We ran into each other at the zoo," Penny said. "I thought...I knew she looked familiar." She turned back to me. "Matt showed me pictures of you. But I didn't...I hadn't caught her name. I just knew Scarlett liked her son and..."

"You have a kid?" James asked. He looked down at my hand. "You're married? Does Matt know?"

I shook my head.

He pulled his cellphone out of his pocket.

"James, please don't," I said.

"He deserves to know." He put his phone to his ear.

"I'm going to tell him. But not like this. Please, I have to do it myself."

James didn't put his phone down.

I looked over to Penny for help.

"James," Penny said and stepped between us. "I think maybe you should talk to Brooklyn first. Hear her story. I don't think anything is what you think it is."

He kept the phone to his ear.

"Please just let her explain," Penny said. "We'll call Matt later, okay? Right after. Please. And she just said she's going to talk to Matt. Right?" Penny asked and looked back over at me.

"Yes." I was. Just…not like this.

James slowly lowered the phone. "Brooklyn…" he shook his head. "You ruined his life."

I swallowed hard. "I don't think you have the right story there."

He stared at me.

"You have it all backwards. Matt broke my heart."

CHAPTER 19

Wednesday

Matt

I was just about to answer the call when James ended it. "I wonder what he wanted," I said.

Rob shrugged. "I don't know. I was actually just about to head over there for lunch. Want to come with me to find out?"

I stared at him as he ate a bite of his hotdog. "Is this not lunch?"

"No," he said as we walked away from the hotdog stand. "This is an appetizer. I want whatever Ellen's making for lunch."

I laughed. "Wait, do you always go over to their apartment on hot dog days?"

"I mean, I love hanging out with you. But my lunch break is longer than yours. And Ellen is a great cook."

"I can take longer lunch breaks," I said.

Rob laughed. "I don't think so. You see...I own Hunter Tech. So I set my own hours."

"You own half of Hunter Tech. The same stake I have in MAC International."

"Yeah, but I have to answer to James. Who doesn't care what I do. You have to have meetings with your dad."

True. Kind of. "James definitely cares what you do." I polished off the rest of my hot dog.

"Then why does he never ask why I'm at his house every hot dog day?"

"Probably because he doesn't want to have an awkward conversation about how his brother is running his business into the ground."

Rob laughed. "We're having our best year ever. I'm a great boss. Don't be jealous."

"Mhm." We started walking back toward our offices. Or I guess he was heading to James' place.

"So how's the breakup going?" Rob asked. "Do you need me to buy you a pint of ice cream for you to drown your feelings in while watching a romcom? I promised Daphne I'd watch one with her tonight anyway if you want to crash."

"Kennedy and I didn't break up."

Rob shook his head. "We've already had this conversation…"

"I know, but you were wrong. We've actually kissed twice since then."

"So like…sex with an ex thing? That's still being broken up."

"No, it was just kissing. And we're not broken up."

"Kiss with an ex doesn't have the same ring to it. And it's even less momentous than sex. You and Kennedy have definitely broken up."

"Then how do you explain the fact that we went on a date last night?"

"I'm guessing it was a dinner as friends."

"No it wasn't."

"So it was just the two of you?" he asked.

Technically Tanner and Nigel had crashed our dinner. But that didn't mean it was any less of a date…

"You paused. You weren't alone. That's not a date."

"Tanner's been acting weird," I said, changing the subject to something that would distract Rob.

"Well it's about time you've realized that! Did you see him with the man bun? Or was it the weird shoes?"

"Neither. But he keeps saying Kennedy isn't my soulmate."

Rob was quiet.

"What?"

"I really like Kennedy," Rob said. "I think she's great. But..."

"Not you too," I groaned.

"Do you think that maybe...just maybe...you like her because she reminds you of Brooklyn?"

"She's nothing like Brooklyn."

"I guess I mean that she reminds you of your time with Brooklyn."

I pushed my hands into my pockets and stopped outside my office building. "Trust me, if being with Kennedy made me think of Brooklyn, I'd be avoiding her. Not dating her. Kennedy reminds me of being young. Of a time when I wasn't hurting. She makes me feel 16 years younger. And it's because of her and only her."

Rob smiled. "So when are you going to propose?"

"When she stops pushing me away."

"I'll be the first one to congratulate you when it happens, you know that. I just needed to say my piece." He slapped me on the back. "I'm happy for you, man."

Finally, one of my friends wasn't being the worst. "You're officially my best friend."

"I know. Are you going to tell Tanner that?"

I laughed. "Nah, it's more fun this way."

"I'll record it next time to really piss him off."

"Actually, I'll say it again so you can record it now. Did you know he's trying to set Kennedy up with Felix because he thinks they might be a better match?"

Rob shrugged as he pulled out his phone.

"What was that shrug for?"

"I always thought they'd be good together. They were practically inseparable the last two years of high school. Minus whenever you'd literally sit between them at lunch and mope." He held up the phone to me. "Okay, say it nice and slow."

"I'm not saying it now."

"Why not?"

"Because you just said Kennedy and Felix would be good together."

"They would be."

"What the hell, man?"

"I didn't say they'd be better than the two of you. But I was always surprised they didn't hook up. Probably because of that douchebag Cupcake, don't you think? He really messed her up."

Yeah. He had. At first I thought what happened with him was why she was pushing me away. But we'd talked about that. I told her we could go slow.

Rob put his phone closer to my mouth. "Say it," he whispered.

Honestly, Tanner and him were both being terrible. But maybe this would get Tanner to focus on being a better friend instead of ruining my life. "Rob is my best friend. I like him the most of all my friends."

Rob smiled and stopped the recording. He put the phone back in his pocket. "Tanner is going to be so pissed."

"Are you not sending it now?"

"Nah, I'm going to send it at the perfect moment. Maybe whenever he gets hitched I'll text it to him while he's standing at the altar."

"Dick move."

Rob shimmied his shoulders. "You mean big dick energy. I've got it in spades."

"Yeah, that's not what I said. And would you stop saying that?"

"What was that? I didn't hear you." But he stopped shimmying. "I gotta go before they're all out of food. Sure you don't want to come?"

"Yeah, I really do have a meeting this afternoon. And I have to leave early because it's one of the last practices before homecoming. You're coming this weekend, right?"

"To the homecoming game? We wouldn't miss it. Pretty sure you're stuck with all of us coming now."

I didn't mind that. I felt like I'd faced all my demons head on. The past was in the past. And I was finally okay with that.

CHAPTER 20

Wednesday

Brooklyn

James didn't say a word as I filled him in on the past 16 years.

And he wasn't showing anything in his expression.

Penny had told us she'd leave us alone to catch up. But now as I stood here, staring at James, waiting for him to say something, I really wished she was here. I could use one of her hugs right now.

"Your father is a liar," James finally said and stood up. "You already knew that. And you should have known better."

"I should have known better? You married Isabella. After everything she did to me, how could you…"

"I was a fucking mess, Brooklyn! You knew me back then. You knew I didn't have control over my life or my choices. And then I…then I lost you."

I swallowed hard.

He shook his head. "Losing you made everything a thousand times worse."

"But…I saw the pictures. The four of you were so happy…"

"Matt was not happy. He was fucking broken. He was barely holding on. He was worse than me. And trust me, I can't even imagine what that was like. Because I was drowning every day. And you can't sit there and judge me for making shit decisions when you made one too."

"I made the right choice. I loved Miller. I'll always love him."

His eyes softened.

"He gave me 15 years of happiness." I shook my head. "More than that, really. I fell in love with him at the beach house. Even though I'd tried to stop it. I loved him for 16 years. And yes, maybe I should feel a little guilty. But I literally saw Matt's dick in someone else, so I'd call it even."

"That's not fair, Brooklyn. He thought you were dead."

"You don't think I know that? You don't think I tried to convince myself he still cared? But I was already so broken…" I stood up.

"We were too!" He ran his fingers through is hair and sighed. "We were broken too," he said more calmly.

"I never meant to hurt anyone."

"But you did. You made choices acting like you meant nothing to all of us. And I don't know how you could possibly think that's true. It's like you didn't think of any of us at all. And we never stopped thinking about you."

I tried to blink away the tears in my eyes. I couldn't stand here and tell him I never stopped thinking about him either. Because I had stopped. I'd forced myself to stop.

He shook his head. Like he was disappointed in me. But that wasn't fair. Because I was disappointed in his choices too.

I was done with this conversation. I'd told James everything. All of it. I hadn't left a word out. He'd listened, just like Penny had asked him to. But he didn't understand. And I didn't think I could make him understand. He hadn't been there. He didn't know how isolated I was at that beach house. How the only thing keeping me going was knowing Matt was missing me too. How badly I was relying on that one fact. And it wasn't true. I'd seen it with my own eyes.

"You need to go see Matt," James said.

Just the thought made me feel like I couldn't breathe. I picked up my cup of tea that Penny had brought in and walked over to one of the pictures on the living room wall. It was from James' wedding. James and Penny were wrapped up in each other. And the rest of the Untouchables were smiling in the picture. Rob. Mason. Matt. I stared at the smile on his face. How could James say he wasn't happy? He looked plenty happy to me.

"I stayed away because I thought everyone was happier that I was gone," I said. "My father made sure I thought that."

"I wasn't happier you were gone, Brooklyn." James walked up next to me. "None of us were."

I looked up at him. "Kennedy said that Matt hired a PI because he didn't believe I was dead. Is that true?"

"Yes. He tried to find you. He tried to find you for years. I think there's a part of him that still believes you're alive."

"I'm having a really hard time believing that's true." I stared back at Matt's smiling face in the picture. I told myself I stayed away because they were all happy. But it was only half true. I stayed away because I was happy too. And I refused to feel guilty for that. I refused to feel guilty for loving Miller. For breaking my promises to Matt. I used to tell myself that he broke his promises first. That helped ease the pain. And it was true, despite what James said.

"He still loves you," James said.

I shook my head. "He's engaged to Poppy and dating Kennedy. I don't think there's room for anyone else." I laughed but it came out forced.

"He's not engaged to Poppy. And he's only pretending to be with her because she threatened Scarlett."

I looked up at him. "What?" Kennedy had said that Matt was stuck in some kind of situation with Poppy.

"He's doing it to protect my daughter."

I just assumed it was something like what happened in high school. But he was doing it to protect Scarlett? How the hell did he get into that mess? I exhaled slowly. Did it really matter what the reason was? Maybe it really was different. I mean...in high school he'd always claimed he'd been trying to protect James. But that was nonsense. This, on the other hand, appeared to be legit.

"Matt's a good man. Yes, we were all dumb kids. Yes, we all made mistakes. But you're alive. And you can fix it."

"Fix what?"

"Matt."

I shook my head.

"Brooklyn, Kennedy is the first person he's ever dated since you."

I shook my head. "That can't possibly be true."

"I'm not saying he hasn't slept with anyone else. You know that from that summer. But it was just sex. You knew what he was like before you met him. He slept around. But he didn't love any of those girls. He never went out with any of them. He's always loved you."

"James, I really appreciate you sticking up for him. And I'm so happy you're all friends again. But…" my voice trailed off. "Too much has happened. Too much time has passed. I told Kennedy she could date him. And I meant it."

He shook his head. "I don't even know if Matt's capable of loving anyone else. He puts on a brave face, but he's…he's never been the same."

People's hearts were bigger than they realized. I knew that better than anyone else. "I think Kennedy and Matt could be really happy together." For some reason my bottom lip was trembling. I clenched my jaw to make it stop. And when that didn't work, I took another sip of tea and hoped that James couldn't tell. I didn't know why it was happening. I meant what I said. I hoped Kennedy and Matt would be happy together.

"Kennedy is wonderful," Penny said.

I turned to see her leaning against the doorjamb. "But I don't think…I just…" her voice trailed off. "God, this is all my fault."

"What?"

"I'm sorry, I was trying really hard not to eavesdrop." She walked into the room. "But there's a lot you missed out on, Brooklyn. Matt was so torn up about losing you, he made all of his friends promise to never even mention your name. I only found out about you several days ago by accident. Matt never wanted me to know because he didn't want me to look at him like he was broken." There were tears in her eyes. "And when he told me all about you, it was clear as day he still loves you. But I told him that you'd be upset with him for spending his whole life miserable, missing you. I encouraged him to go after Kennedy. It's my fault."

James walked over to her, wrapping his arms around her. "It's not your fault, baby."

"Yes it is. He waited for you for 16 years. Seriously, Brooklyn. He waited. He kept his promises to you. And he would have kept waiting if I hadn't told him you'd want him to live his life."

I pressed my lips together. Penny had given him the perfect advice. Matt should have known what I'd want for him. He knew how I felt about wasting time. So why had he wasted so much? He was supposed to be happy. I'd thought he was happy.

"It's not your fault," I said. "It's mine." I turned back to the pictures. "And his." I wanted to think it was mostly his. I'd told myself that for years. But what if I really did have all the information wrong? Despite what I'd seen?

I blinked back my tears as I walked over to the next picture. And there she was. The woman Matt had been banging in his pool 15 years ago.

I didn't even realize my teacup had fallen out of my hands until it smashed into a million tiny pieces on the floor.

"Are you okay?" Penny asked as she rushed over.

"Who is that?" I pointed toward the woman with dark hair in the picture. Matt's arm was slung around her shoulders. It was from James and Penny's wedding day. And the woman was clearly one of Penny's brides-maids. They were friends? I felt my heart pounding in my chest. Was Matt dating her too? James had just told me that Kennedy was the first woman that Matt had dated since me. It certainly looked like he was dating this woman.

"That's James' sister. Jen."

That's why she looked so familiar that day. She had the same dark eyes as her brother. The same sharp features.

"Do you know her?" Penny asked.

I looked over at James. "That's who Matt was having sex with. In the pool."

James groaned. "Ugh, please don't tell me that."

"You didn't know?"

"No, I knew they hooked up a few times. But I didn't ask for details."

Just a few times. Why was I relieved? My stomach twisted into knots. I wasn't allowed to be relieved. I wanted him to be happy. I did. Matt was allowed to date whoever he wanted. But my stomach just kept twisting.

"An emotionless brick wall," Penny said.

"What?" I asked.

"Jen said it was like having sex with an emotionless brick wall."

"Seriously, guys, stop," James said.

But a small part of me wanted Penny to keep going. So having sex with Matt was like having sex with an emotionless brick wall? That was definitely not how I remembered it.

"It's because he was still in love with you," Penny said. "He wasn't giving his heart to anyone else."

I nodded. I wasn't even sure why I was so emotional right now. It just suddenly felt like my whole life was a lie. There was a lump in my throat that wouldn't go away.

There were tears in Penny's eyes. James reached out for her and she wrapped her arms around him.

I hadn't meant to upset anyone. This was why I'd stayed gone. Part of the reason. A fear that I'd upset everyone. But I'd also been terrified that no one would care at all.

"This sandwich is top notch, Ellen," said a voice from the kitchen.

No, not just any voice. Oh my God.

Rob appeared in the doorway eating a PB&J sandwich. "This really hits the spot. Hey guys, what's up?" He popped the rest of the sandwich in his mouth. "Shit, Penny, are you okay?" He finally followed her gaze and his eyes landed on me.

He didn't look as shocked as James did. A huge smile instantly spread across his face. "Sanders? Is that you?"

I smiled. God, I'd missed the way he said my name. I nodded. I couldn't help the tears that leaked down my cheeks.

"Sanders!" He ran over to me and lifted me into his arms. He twirled me around and I couldn't help but laugh.

He finally set me down on my feet.

"I can't believe it." He looked back over at James and Penny. "Matt's going to freak. I was just with him for lunch. He almost came over. Wait." He looked back at me. "Sanders, what the fuck? How are you here? How are you? What the hell is even happening?"

Just then Jacob ran into the room followed quickly by Scarlett to chase the ball they'd just kicked in. And they were both butt naked.

Oh no.

"Well that's new," James said with a laugh.

"Who's that?" Rob asked.

"My son. Jacob."

"Damn. I mean, sorry. Shoot." He leaned down to give Jacob a high five. "What's up my man with the big dick energy?"

"Rob," Penny said.

"Sorry. I'm trying to work it into my vocabulary more because it makes Daphne laugh."

But Jacob high fived him instead of hiding.

"Okay, let me go find his clothes," I said. "I'm sorry, he really hates clothing."

"Totally understand," Rob said. "I do too. It's fine, they can run around naked. Cause I need to be caught up real quick. Ellen!" he yelled. "We need more sandwiches!"

I laughed.

"I really missed you, Sanders." He hooked his arm around my shoulders. "I'm telling you, everyone was a mess without you."

"Including you?"

"I mean…someone had to make these guys laugh."

I smiled at him. For that, I'd always be grateful. "I missed you, Rob."

"I know. So how are we planning on breaking this news to Matt? Because I only just had to stop keeping all the old stories about you a secret from my wife. And I'm not doing this whole thing again." They all turned to me.

"I'm going to tell him."

"When?" Rob asked.

"Soon…ish?"

He raised his eyebrows at me.

"I will, I promise."

"I'm not keeping this secret either," James said. "I won't. I know you've been through hell, but so has he."

"I'm going to tell him, guys."

They all nodded as Jacob and Scarlett continued streaking through the room.

"Okay, let's play ball," Rob said and tore his shirt off. "You next, Brooklyn."

"Rob," Penny said. "Excuse him…he…"

"Is an endless flirt? Yeah, I know," I said with a laugh.

"Ah, no running there," James said and lifted Scarlett up into his arms before she had a chance to run barefoot over the broken glass.

Rob started kicking the ball back and forth with Jacob and Liam woke up and started crying.

It was pure and utter chaos. And for the first time since I'd come back to New York, I truly felt a semblance of home. Of family.

These guys had been my family.

I thought that feeling would fade. But it hadn't at all.

And that scared me.

Because what if my feelings for Matt hadn't faded either? It was easy to see him in pictures. It was harder to hear stories of him over the years. And I couldn't imagine how I'd react when I finally saw him face to face.

"Heads up, Sanders!" Rob yelled and kicked the ball in my direction.

So much had changed, and yet it was somehow completely the same. The main difference was that I was no longer a Sanders, despite Rob's nickname for me. I was a Miller. And I'd always be a Miller.

CHAPTER 21

Thursday

Matt

"Where are you going?" I asked as Tanner rolled a suit-case through the dining room.

"I told you. I have a thing."

I just stared at him.

"An out-of-town thing. I mentioned it the other day."

"You're leaving me here with Nigel?" I asked.

"Well, I can't exactly take him with me. He'll scare her off."

"Scare who off?"

"No one." He started whistling as he untucked a fe-dora from under his arm, rolled it down his arm, and hit it up with his elbow. It landed perfectly on his head. "I love vacations. It's one of the only excuses to wear one of my old hats."

I didn't think his hat looked old, but it did look a lit-tle off. The brim was too wide. Or too long. Or something. "I didn't even realize you liked hats."

"I have a whole hat room," Tanner said.

"Where?"

He looked over his shoulder at the hallway. "Don't go poking around. It'll upset Nigel."

"Right…because I'll get burned?"

Tanner laughed. "Who said anything about you get-ting burned if you poked around?"

"Nigel. I'm pretty sure he said 'Snoopers get burned.'"

"I mean…that's an old phrase, isn't it? I recall now. It's nothing weird about the apartment. But…don't snoop. And now you're looking at me like you're going to snoop. Nigel!" he called.

Nigel ran into the dining room holding a tray of sausages. "Does Mr. Caldwell need some more sausage?"

"No, I'm good," I said. Nigel had been serving me sausages non-stop for days now. And I wasn't loving that for me.

"Nope, his plate is still full," Tanner said. "But I need you to keep your eyes on him while I'm away."

Nigel frowned. "I'm not coming with you? I packed my trunk already."

"I need you here," Tanner said and slapped his back. "So that Matt won't find that room with the surprise."

"You mean the room with all the pictures and the red string?"

Tanner laughed. "No. I don't have one of those rooms."

"But…"

"Shh!" he cleared his throat. "Just…don't let him get into anything he shouldn't." He leaned down and I definitely heard him whisper, "But yes, including the room with the pictures and red string."

Nigel nodded.

"Very well, I'm off!" Tanner tipped his hat at me as he rolled his suitcase.

"Wait, how long will you be gone?" I asked.

"If she falls asleep I'll be back tonight. Otherwise I'll be back tomorrow."

"What the hell does that mean? Are you going to bang her while she's..."

"Good heavens, no. But I'm known to drive too quickly and it scares people. I'll drive stupid and slow if she stays awake. Scratch all of that. I'll just put her to sleep. Nigel, get me the sleep aid, will you?"

Nigel nodded and went back into the kitchen.

"You're drugging this girl?"

"It's not a sex thing, Matt. I'm not even interested in her like that." He stood there for a moment. "I mean...she's hot, don't get me wrong. Beautiful, really. She has that girl next door vibe that I'm so fond of. Sorry what was I saying?" He snapped his fingers. "Right. She's not a match for me."

"Okay..."

"I promise everything is fine. I'm not drugging anyone for sex purposes, and you're not going to snoop. I'll be back this evening."

Nigel hurried in and handed Tanner a to-go cup.

"I'll need a sippy cup too," Tanner said. "I haven't seen the little one, but I'm thinking small."

Nigel ran back out of the room.

"The little one?" I asked.

"Well, it would be quite alarming if he was a teen. That would add in a whole new set of questions I'd have to get to the bottom of."

"Wait, how many people are on this road trip?"

"Aren't you full of questions this morning. Don't you have to get to work?"

"I thought you wanted me to stay in my room."

Tanner laughed. "Touché."

"But yeah, I do need to get to work." I left my sausage plate uneaten and stood up. "I'll walk down with you."

"Nope," Tanner said.

"Why?"

"Because I'm doing things. You wouldn't understand. Just…don't follow me."

"Well now I really want to follow you."

"No."

I just laughed. Because I had no idea what was going on. And he was acting stranger than usual.

Nigel rushed back in with a sippy cup.

And now I just had more questions than ever. Seriously…Tanner didn't have kids. So why the hell did he have that in his house?

"I'm off," Tanner said.

"Have a nice trip," I said. "And don't do anything illegal."

"I'm not going to promise anything. But I'll be on my best behavior with her. And you two behave while I'm off." He waved and then walked out of the room whistling. "Oh and Nigel," he said and popped just his head back into the room. "I'm taking the limo, so you'll have to run your errands with a different vehicle."

"But I like the limo," Nigel said.

"I know you like being extra at the grocery store. I swear I wouldn't take it if I didn't need all the space for boxes."

Boxes? Seriously, what the hell was Tanner doing?

Nigel sighed. "Fine."

"Bye," Tanner said and this time he really did leave. Because I heard the door close behind him.

Nigel was standing there staring at me. "What shall we do today while Master is away?"

"Um…I'm going to work."

"Great, I'll go change into my work outfit."

"Nigel, you don't…" but he was already walking away. Was he seriously going to follow me to work?

***

Nigel was sitting behind my desk when I got back from my meeting. Scrolling on my computer even though I hadn't given him my password.

"What are you doing?"

He jumped. "Internets."

I glared at him until he pushed back the chair and stood up. Every time I saw him today I was still somehow surprised by his choice of "work clothes." He was wearing coveralls like he thought he was going to be spending the day at a construction site. Even though he knew where I worked. None of it made any sense.

"Sorry," Nigel said. "I like the internets. It's fun. Did you know that there's a thing called Google that always tells the truth about anything you ask it?"

"That's definitely not how the internet works. And don't you have a computer at home?"

"Yes. I have a whole computer room at home."

"Like with games and stuff?"

"No, it's just a big computer that takes up a whole room. Almost as big as this office. And slow. Very, very slow. And no internets."

"It's just internet. No 's'."

"I don't think that's right," Nigel said.

"Wait, are you talking about one of the very first computers? Those huge old things? A mainframe?"

"Yes."

"Why don't you have a laptop?"

"I don't like little things. I like big things. The bigger the better."

Seriously, why did everything he say sound so sexual?

"What shall we do now?" Nigel asked. "Do you want me to staple more documents? Or to clean the coffee machine again? I can answer more phone calls. But it didn't seem like you liked when I did that. Or I can go pick up second lunch?"

Second lunch? We'd just eaten. And why did he eat two lunches? He'd been hovering all day. I'd been given him odd jobs around the office, but he always came back within minutes claiming he was done.

And that actually gave me an idea. "I need a contract."

"Oh. A sex one? I'll need more details, please."

"No, not a sex one." What was wrong with him? "You get everything done so fast. And I had this idea in my head for a contract with Poppy. The Pruitts and Cannavaros love contracts."

"So a love contract, then? You can add intercourse requirements to that. Or not. If you're not into that with Poppy…"

"No. Not a love contract."

"So you are into that with Poppy?"

"Nigel, you know I don't like Poppy."

He smiled to himself and grabbed a notepad. "Then what is the contract for?"

"Poppy knows that I know she killed someone. But I think me blackmailing her might have made her fall in love with me because she's a crazy person. So I'm not sure if my blackmail is going to deter her from doing anything, but she would never break a contract. The Cannavaros and Pruitts have some kind of obsession with them. So I need a contract for her to sign. That promises she won't hurt anyone I know or love."

"Thank you for protecting me," Nigel said.

Wow, this wasn't about him. But I guess it did include him. "You're welcome, Nigel."

He started writing down some notes.

"And in exchange for her signing the document I will promise not to go to the police. That needs to be very clear. No loopholes or anything."

He nodded and kept writing.

"Done." He handed it to me.

It was ten pages long. With clauses and everything. It took me longer to read it than it had for him to handwrite it. Seriously…how had he done that? Maybe I needed him to come to work with me more often… "This is excellent work, Nigel." Except for the clause at the end requiring Poppy to seal the deal by sending me a 72" freestanding tub made of rare Italian petrified wood. Although it did look pretty comfortable…

He smiled. "Can I use your computer to type it? I like typing."

"Of course."

He jumped back onto my chair and started typing at record speed. It only took a few minutes before he was printing it out. "Shall I fax it to her?"

"You know what, Nigel? I think that's the perfect way to deliver it." That would really fuck with her head. Getting a fax in the middle of the afternoon. I smiled to myself.

The faxing process actually took longer than the typing. But I didn't even care. Nigel looked so happy when he finally turned around.

"You know what? Let's go get that second lunch," I said.

He beamed at me. "Can we get jambon-beurre?"

"I have no idea what that is."

"It's Parisian street food. I used to eat it all the time when I was little. You'll like it. It's filled with meat."

I laughed. "Sure."

"I love break time," Nigel said. "Just two boys on the town."

In the middle of the workday. "You said you ate this all the time when you were little," I said as we made our way to the elevators. "Nigel, did you grow up in France?" Because he'd done a pretty great accent when he'd dressed up as Francois the other night.

"Oh…I've moved all over."

"That's what Tanner always says too."

"He has also moved all over. Staying in one place gets…boring after a while, you know?" He sighed and stared at the elevator.

"Am I boring you, Nigel?" I asked with a laugh.

"No, it's more like the place gets bored of us."

That was such a sad sentiment. "I don't think I could possibly get bored of you, Nigel."

He smiled.

"Really. We're friends." I put my hand on his shoulder. Despite all the weirdness, Nigel truly was my friend. And he'd helped me out of my situation with Poppy. I owed him a lot.

"Friends? You mean it?"

I nodded.

"Okay, I'll go through with my plan then."

"Um…what plan?"

"You'll see. Let's go get our meat on!" He hurried onto the elevator and slid his hand down the entire row of buttons.

"Nigel, why didn't you just hit the first floor?" I asked and stepped on beside him.

"Don't you have to give it directions?"

"Hitting the main floor button is the direction."

"But like…tell it the path?"

"Nigel, don't you take the elevator up to Tanner's penthouse?"

"No. I like the stairs."

Of course he did. We slowly descended, the doors sliding open at every floor. "You know what? I like the stairs too. Let's take them." Otherwise we'd be in this elevator all day. I felt sorry for the guy who got in as we were getting off.

"What the fuck?" he said under his breath as the doors closed shut.

Nigel and I both laughed.

"Will you be coming with me to practice today too?" I asked.

Nigel nodded.

This would actually be great. Kennedy agreed to come to practice too. And I was pretty sure that if Kennedy could win Nigel over, then Nigel could convince Tanner that she was good for me.

I'd get a signature from Poppy.

I'd propose to Kennedy.

And I'd finally get the family I always wanted.

HOMECOMING

But as soon as I thought it, I heard Tanner's words in my head. *"Can you really have a whole life with someone when your heart still belongs to another?"*

CHAPTER 22

Thursday

Brooklyn

I pushed Jacob's hair off his forehead. He was sleeping so peacefully. He'd made a new friend here. His first friend, really. Actually, he'd made several. We'd spent the rest of yesterday afternoon kicking the ball around with James, Rob, Penny, and Scarlett. All while I tried to ignore James' piercing gaze.

I knew what I had to do if I was going to stay.

And yet…I didn't know how.

Matt deserved to know the truth. Especially if a lot of my assumptions about him were dead wrong.

But every time I tried to give him the benefit of the doubt, I kept picturing him laughing in the pool with James' sister. *James' sister.* What kind of friend did that, anyway?

I looked down at my sleeping son. He wanted to stay in New York. And that meant I had to. I had to put him first.

But the thought of staying twisted my stomach into knots. I didn't know what staying entailed. Could I really just avoid my father in the city? He wanted me to take over his business. I had no desire to do that. I just…I didn't know what I wanted from my future anymore. I'd had it all laid out in front of me. Clear as day. But my future had been ripped away. Lazy days with Miller on the back porch or out on the dock. Jacob playing with a younger sibling. Tears stung my eyes and I tried my best to blink them away. That future would never happen now.

"I'm so sorry," I whispered to Jacob.

He slowly opened his eyes. "Por qué?"

I laughed. "Jacob, I don't know as much Spanish as you do."

He just blinked at me. "Why are you sorry, Mommy?"

"For everything that was taken from you."

"By Abuelo?"

I hadn't told him about my father's involvement in what had happened. But Mrs. Alcaraz talked to him almost exclusively in Spanish. And I had no idea what she'd been saying. "I'm going to figure that out, okay? I promise." I still didn't know what to believe. Poppy had corroborated my father's story. But I didn't trust either of them.

"Can I meet him?" Jacob asked. He sat up, suddenly full of energy.

I shook my head.

"But he's my abuelo."

"Do you know something I learned from your daddy?"

He shook his head.

"That real family isn't about blood. It's about looking out for each other. Loving each other unconditionally. You and your father are my family. Kennedy and Mrs. Alcaraz are our family." *James, Rob...* I stopped my train of thought before it led to dangerous territory. I'd been about to think of Mason. Who had really been the brother I'd never had. I remembered playing video games with him. Seeing him laugh and smile when he rarely did that at school. And thinking about Mason would lead me to thinking about Matt.

"But he's my abuelo," Jacob said.

"I know he is in name, sweetie. But he was never a dad to me. And if he wasn't a father to me, he's not a grandfather to you. Do you understand that?"

He nodded. "But I can I meet him?"

"Sweet boy, why do you even want to?"

"I need to tell him something."

"And what do you need to tell him?"

He shrugged his shoulders.

"I'll think about it, okay?" But I only said that to appease him. I needed more time to think. I needed to make sense of what had happened. But that was impossible. It was all senseless. Families fighting. Ruining lives. No, Jacob could not meet my father.

"Where's my abuela?"

"Mrs. Alcaraz had to leave early for work. But that means I get to make you…"

"Cuppycakes!"

I smiled. "Exactly." I booped him on the tip of his nose.

Kennedy hopped out of her room on one foot as she pulled on her boots. "Morning, guys," she said. "What are the two of you up to today?"

"We're going to see my abuelo," Jacob said.

"Jacob, I didn't say yes." I lifted him off the couch and into my arms. "We're going to bake and then maybe we can go play in Central Park."

"Can we go play with Scarlett again?" asked Jacob.

"Um…another day." I think I needed some time before we did that again. I couldn't stand that judgement on James' face. I knew he felt bad about what I'd been through. But I was pretty sure he also thought all of this was my fault. That I'd chosen to stay away. But it was more complicated than that. And he had no right to be upset with me. It certainly seemed like his life had turned out just fine. He had an amazing wife and two kids. It's not like he was still married to the troll.

Kennedy hadn't said much about me running into the Hunters. But her silence screamed volumes.

"Anything else you're going to do today?" Kennedy asked.

I knew what she wanted me to say. That I was going to text Matt. Or go see him. Or something. I'd promised her I would.

I was saved from replying when there was a knock on the door.

Kennedy frowned. "Did you buzz someone up?"

I shook my head. And then my heart started pounding. Was it Matt? He was an expert in sneaking into this building…

But when Kennedy opened the door, her friend Tanner was standing there. In a wide brimmed hat and a huge smile.

"Good morning, ladies."

"Hey, Tanner," Kennedy said. "Can I help you with something?"

"Not this morning. But answer your door tonight, yes?"

"Okay…" She looked so confused.

He walked into the apartment and looked around before his eyes settled on me. "We're going on a little road trip. We should be off. It's quite a long drive."

I looked over my shoulder like he must be talking to someone else. "Sorry…we?"

"Yes. You, me, and the little one."

"A road trip!" Jacob looked so excited.

"Mhm." Tanner leaned down to look him square in the eye. "And you should look outside at what we're driving in."

Jacob wiggled out of my grasp and ran over to the window. "Mommy, Mommy. His car is so long!"

"It's a limo," said Tanner.

"Um…" I looked over at Kennedy. What the hell was happening?

"We better hurry," Tanner said. "We want to beat traffic."

"I don't think a road trip is a good idea right now."

"But, Mommy, there's a limo!"

"Yeah, Mommy, there's a limo," Tanner said.

"I'm sorry, could I talk to Kennedy in private for a second?" I hooked my arm through hers and pulled her to the side. "What is he talking about? A trip?"

Kennedy shrugged. "I honestly have no idea. And what exactly am I answering my door to tonight?"

I laughed. "How should I know?"

"Well, you know what I do know?" Kennedy said. "That Jacob looks really excited about that limo."

I looked back at Jacob. God, he really did. How was I supposed to say no to that excited grin? And at least this would distract him from wanting to talk to his grandfather. "How well do you know this Tanner guy?" I asked.

"Me?"

"Yes, you. Aren't you guys friends?"

"He's actually Ma…"

"*My* best friend!" Tanner said way too loudly and looped his arm around Kennedy's shoulders. Apparently we hadn't been far enough away from him to hide our conversation. "She was going to say *I'm* her best friend. And she's mine. Isn't that right, Kennedy? We're each other's best friends?"

"Um…" Kennedy said.

"I'm quite honored, really. To be such good friends with someone so wonderful." Tanner slapped her on the back.

Kennedy laughed. "Thanks, Tanner."

I guess they were close then.

"We really should be going," Tanner said. "We don't want to hit traffic on our way to our top secret destination."

"Top secret?!" Jacob started jumping up and down.

"That's right, little man." Tanner walked over to him. "Is that what you're wearing?"

Jacob looked down at his wrinkled t-shirt. "For a little bit."

Tanner laughed. "I have no idea what that means. Let's go!"

"So I can trust him?" I asked Kennedy.

She nodded. "Absolutely. He's a good guy. Even if he is a little strange."

Honestly, a ride in a limo and a surprise road trip seemed perfect. Especially because it meant I could delay talking to Matt. "Okay," I said. "We're in."

Tanner opened the door for us and Jacob ran out.

"Where exactly are we going?" I asked.

"It's a surprise."

I wanted to ask more questions. But it was hard not to be caught up in Jacob's excitement. I ran after him down the stairs, out the front door, and right up to the limo.

"Wow," Jacob said. "It's so long!"

I ruffled his hair.

"Breakfast shake?" Tanner asked and handed me a to-go cup. He handed a sippy cup to Jacob filled with the same thing.

Had he been holding those a second ago?

Jacob took a big sip and his eyes grew round. "Chocolate!"

I smiled and took a sip too. "Thanks, Tanner. This is really nice of you."

"Anything for my best friend's friend," he said. "Drink up."

I took another sip. It was the most delicious breakfast shake I'd ever had. It really just tasted like a chocolate milkshake. Wait…was it a chocolate milkshake? I took another sip. It didn't really matter, it was just as healthy as a cupcake would have been for breakfast.

"After you, m'lady," Tanner said and opened the limo door.

We all climbed in and the limo pulled out onto the road.

Jacob started running around the inside of the limo examining everything.

"How old is the little one?" Tanner asked.

"He's four."

"That's probably a good age."

"For…what?"

"For everyone involved. Babies cry all the time. And toddlers can be a handful. But he's almost in kindergarten. He's practically an adult."

"Hardly. He's just a little boy."

Tanner laughed. "Oh I know. And thank goodness he's not a teen. What kind of things is he into?"

"He loves football."

"Does he now? Well, that's splendid. I couldn't think of anything better. And what about you? What kind of things are you into?"

"Um…I love baking."

He just stared at me. "That's it?"

"And running."

"Exercise is such a good stress reliever. Stress ages most people, so it's good to get ahead of it."

"Do you like exercising too?"

"Oh, no, I don't need it," he said. "Tell me more about yourself."

He just said that stress ages people. Did that mean he was never stressed out? Or that he just hated exercising?

"I should really be taking notes," he said and grabbed a clipboard from the seat next to him. "Sorry, what is the little one's name?"

"Jacob."

"Got it. Jacob. Four years old." He scribbled on the paper. "Football. Perfect. Go on."

"Um…"

He kept writing.

"Why are you writing all these things down?"

"Oh, I'm planning a…thing."

"What kind of thing?"

"Another surprise."

"This is already quite a nice surprise."

"This one isn't really for you. Well, I mean, it kind of is. But it's actually for my best friend."

"It's for Kennedy?"

"What?" Tanner looked up from his notes.

"You said it's for your best friend…which you said is Kennedy."

"Indeed I did say that."

"So what's the surprise? It's not her birthday or anything."

"Well, if I revealed it, it wouldn't exactly be a surprise, now would it? Ah look, we're out of the city."

I turned to look out the window. "Do you like her as more than a friend?" I asked. If he was going to all this trouble to win me over, there must be something else there.

"Who?" Tanner asked.

"Kennedy."

"Oh, we're still talking about her."

I laughed. "Who else would we be talking about?"

"I have no idea. I was hoping to be talking about you. I need more information. What makes you tick? What's your favorite pastime? What's the most romantic thing Matt ever did for you?"

I yawned. "I'm so sleepy. Wait…what?"

Tanner cleared his throat. "Nothing."

"Did you just ask about Matt?" I yawned again.

"I think you're just tired. The open road will do that to a person. Here," he said and pulled a blanket off the seat next to him. "Why don't you take a nap?"

Had that blanket been there a second ago?

He placed it on my lap. "Really, just rest. I'll let you know when we get there."

I looked over at Jacob, who was already fast asleep. We'd just woken up. But honestly, a nap sounded amazing. I guess the open road really did make me sleepy.

"I think I might just take you up on that." I yawned again as I pulled the blanket over myself.

"Good, good. You'll need all the rest you can get. Saturday is going to be a big day."

"What's Saturday?" I mumbled as my eyelids started to feel too heavy to keep open.

"The surprise of course."

"Right. For Kennedy."

"Sure."

And the last thing I remember was that I didn't see a driver through the glass partition. It looked like the car was driving itself. *God, I really am exhausted.*

CHAPTER 23

Thursday

Matt

I blew my whistle. "Jefferson, get out there and show them how it's done," I said.

Jefferson looked up at Kennedy instead of at me.

She whispered something to him. And then he smiled and ran out onto the field.

"Thanks for coming to practice the last two days," I said to her. "Everyone missed you. Including me."

She didn't look up at me, but her cheeks grew rosy. "No problem, Coach Caldwell. I can't let the Empire High Eagles lose their homecoming match. That would be the end of your illustrious coaching career."

I laughed.

"Go Henry!" Kennedy screamed at the top of her lungs.

I looked over to see Jefferson's kick go perfectly between the uprights. "You are a freaking amazing assistant coach. The perfect number two."

She didn't respond to that at all.

We'd had a really fun date on Tuesday. We'd stayed up till 2 am at some random pizza place talking the night away with Tanner and Nigel. But ever since then, she'd been hot and cold. One minute we'd be laughing. And the next she'd wrap her arms around herself, totally closing off.

I watched her as she did exactly that. She folded her arms and stared at the field.

"Did I say something wrong?" I asked.

"No."

"Kennedy…"

"You didn't. I actually love everything you say." She gave me a sad smile. "I'm just in a really bad headspace right now."

"Okay. But I'm here to talk about it."

"I know."

"So…"

She laughed and looked up at me. "Coach Caldwell, get your head in the game. We have a game to win this weekend." She grabbed my whistle from around my neck.

For a second I thought she was going to pull it down so that I'd kiss her.

Instead she leaned forward and blew into the whistle and turned to the field. "Enough chit chat, Smith! Let's run the next play!"

"Yes, ma'am," Smith said and gave her a little salute. She smiled.

"You like bossing them around, don't you?"

"I like making them win."

Jefferson ran off the field. He seemed less out of breath than usual.

"Water?" Nigel asked.

I turned around. Nigel had set up a little stand filled with cups of water. All within 10 minutes of us stepping out here. Where had he even gotten the water?

"Thanks," Jefferson said and grabbed the little cup Nigel handed him. But instead of drinking it, he just lifted up the glass to inspect it. "Is this crystal?"

"Only the best of the best for Master Matthew's team."

Wait, he was serving water in crystal glasses? "Nigel, that's a little fancy."

"Oh. Is it too fancy? Did I do a bad job? Maybe I need to be punished."

Everyone was very silent all of a sudden.

I cleared my throat. "No, Nigel it's perfect. But in the future, paper cups are fine."

"No, paper cups are for paupers and vagabonds."

What? "I don't think that's a thing."

"It is." He went back to filling up more of the crystal glasses. I guess we'd just be very fancy from now on. Wait…had I accidentally just asked Nigel to come back? I needed to stop doing stuff like that.

I watched as Jefferson sat down on the bench and some of the guys started talking to him right away.

"It's really working," I whispered to Kennedy. "I think we made him some friends."

"You mean *I* did that. Because *I* helped him learn how to kick."

"Is that so?" I looped my arms around her and pulled her in for a kiss. But before my lips met hers, Nigel chucked the water out of two glasses at us. And then he chucked the crystal glasses at my chest.

"Nigel, what the hell?"

"Sorry. They slipped." He shrugged. "Oops." That last word came out very sarcastic.

That was the second time this week he'd thrown water at me and Kennedy. What the hell was his problem? We'd been having such a nice day together.

HOMECOMING

But Kennedy was laughing, wiping the water from her eyes. And I found her laughter quite contagious. So I started laughing too.

Nigel shook his head and went back to his water boy position.

CHAPTER 24

Thursday

Brooklyn

"Brooklyn," Tanner whispered. He lightly touched my arm. "We're here."

I slowly opened my eyes.

Tanner was crouched in front of me in the limo. Jacob was still fast asleep behind him.

"Where are we?" And why did Tanner look so serious?

He put his hand on the side of my face before I could turn to look out the window. "I need you to know that I've done a lot of these. More than I ever dreamed I'd have to endure. But you have to face this head on. If you let the loss of someone close to you linger in your heart, it'll make you sick. Trust me. I've made that mistake. And I wouldn't wish that on anyone. You have to set the pain free with the wind. You have to."

I didn't need to look out the window. I knew where he'd taken me. I could already feel the tears welling in my eyes. "I'm not ready." My voice cracked.

"You'll never be ready. And it's not goodbye. It's just choosing to keep living. For your son. And for you." He let his hand fall from my cheek.

I looked out the window as the tears streamed down my cheeks. Our lake house didn't look the same. The grass was overgrown. Patches were burnt away. And the gravel driveway up ahead had a scorched mark in the middle. A piece of abandoned caution tape blew in the wind. But my car was gone. Miller was gone. I started sobbing harder.

"You have to keep living, Brooklyn."

"Tanner, I can't…"

"I know how vehemently you believe in not wasting time. That you never know when life can be cut short. And all of it is short. Life is so fleeting for the living. You can't afford to waste a second of it. Do you understand me?" It looked like he was holding back tears as he stared at me.

I thought about what he said about loss earlier. How he knew exactly what to say to me in this moment. "You've lost someone too?"

He nodded. "A great love. But my heart's still beating. I'm still breathing. Life has to be lived. You can't hide from the pain. It'll follow you until it breaks you. You have to let it go."

"But I love him so much."

"I know." He squeezed my hand. "And you don't have to do this alone. We're going to do this together, okay? You can hold my hand the whole time if you need to. I'm right here."

I didn't know how Kennedy met this man, but God was I so grateful for him in this moment. I wasn't sure I could have done this with someone who knew me better. I needed a stranger. A very knowing stranger.

"Are you ready?" he asked.

"No." But I nodded my head.

He smiled. "Do you want me to wake Jacob? I'll be honest, I'm not great with kids. But I didn't think you'd want to do this without him."

"Could you maybe carry him inside? I don't want him to see the front yard."

Tanner nodded. "Okay." He let go of my hand. And then he awkwardly lifted my son into his arms. He was somehow holding him away from him, yet holding him close at the same time.

I'd honestly never seen someone hold a child so strangely. But Jacob rested his head on Tanner's shoulder, still fast asleep.

I opened up the door and stepped out. I breathed in the fall air and smiled through my tears. It smelled like Miller. It smelled like home. But I knew better than anyone...home wasn't a place. Home was a feeling. A feeling you got when you were with the people you loved.

I felt so small standing there.

Tanner slipped his hand into mine. "I arranged for a few things inside," he said. "And I'll make some calls to find someone to cut the grass."

How had he arranged any of this? How had he known where I lived? But all the questions rolling around in my head were drowned out by the pain in my chest. It felt like I was dying inside. Like my heart was burning, turning into ash in my chest. Miller's truck was still sitting in the driveway. A few dings from flying metal on the back. But otherwise...it was untouched.

"It was supposed to be me," I said. "He was moving my car the morning of the explosion. My car was blocking his in. It should have been me."

"Your father pushed this whole thing under the rug. I had my own team out here earlier this week to check what exactly was under that rug."

Kennedy must have filled him in about what was going on. "And what did you find?"

He shifted Jacob in his arms. "I do believe it was supposed to be you. There's no bomb anywhere on Miller's truck. But, Brooklyn...you're here. And you can't afford to keep thinking like that."

How could I not? "What else did you find?"

"You want to know if your father did it?"

I nodded.

"I'm still working on that. You lost power that night, right? My team found all the security cameras. But they all went out for about two hours."

"Yeah, there was a storm."

"No one was seen on your property before or after the gap in footage. I don't think it was a storm that knocked your power out. It's too convenient. Someone was behind it. And until we look into your father's alibi, I'd keep my distance from him. Because if he was behind it...he was gunning for you, Brooklyn."

"Trust me, I'm keeping my distance from him regardless." And Poppy. A part of me wanted to believe my father wouldn't hurt me. But the more I learned about Poppy, the more it seemed like she didn't like me. "Could you also check out Poppy Cannavaro? I think she might have been involved too."

"I'm already on it."

"I can't believe you're doing all this for a friend of Kennedy's that you don't even know."

"Yup, anything for my best friend."

We both just stood there for a moment, staring at the house.

Even the air here smelled like Miller, and it was destroying me. Which meant walking into the house would probably be the death of me.

"I'm right here with you," Tanner said.

I just nodded. "How long did it take to get here? Shouldn't it be dark? It's a long drive to the city…but it's still daylight."

"You're procrastinating."

I was. But that didn't mean I wasn't curious about how fast we'd been driving.

"Come on," Tanner said. "I've got you."

I let him guide me up to the front door.

I remembered the first time I came here. The snow had been falling and I'd been worried sick that Miller had moved on. I'd chosen him. I'd finally decided to put him first. Why had I waited so long? I'd missed out on time with him.

Tanner slowly opened the door.

I was right.

Inside was worse.

Miller was everywhere.

And I wanted to cry with relief and heartache at the same time. He was here. It was like I could still feel him. Like I'd turn around and he'd be walking in behind me. Wrapping his arms around me and telling me everything would be okay. I felt like I might collapse without him holding me up. I couldn't breathe. I couldn't breathe this air. I couldn't keep going without Miller.

Tanner pulled me into a hug.

And I clung to him. He held me and Jacob until I stopped gasping for air. Until my tears subsided. Until I was completely numb and Jacob started to wake up.

Jacob looked up at Tanner.

"Hey there, little man."

Jacob just stared at him.

"We're here to pay tribute to your father," Tanner said. "To start letting your heart heal. We're not saying goodbye to him, we're just…"

"No hablo inglés," Jacob said.

I put my hand on his back. "Jacob…"

"No hablo inglés!" he screamed and jumped out of Tanner's arms. He ran away from us and pushed open the back door.

"Jacob!"

I ran after him, the screen door slamming shut behind me.

Jacob was running toward the dock.

"Jacob, stop!" I ran after him, catching up to him on his little legs. I grabbed him and pulled him into my arms.

"Nooooo!" Jacob said as he tried to fight his way out of my grip. But it wasn't just his normal elongated version of the word. It was filled with heartache as the tears started. "Noooo." He said again as the fight left him and the tears poured down his cheeks.

I pulled him to my chest. *No.* Yeah. He had that right. *No.* None of this was fair. None of this should have happened.

"Noooo," he sobbed.

I didn't know what to say to make it right. I didn't know how to make his heart stop hurting when mine was hurting too.

"Please don't leave me too," Jacob said as he looked up at me.

I'd been in his shoes before. I'd lost my mom and my uncle. And I'd felt that same thing. That they'd left me. But now that I was older…I saw it differently. They hadn't wanted to leave me all alone. They loved me. And Miller loved us. He hadn't left. He was taken. "Sweet boy, your father didn't choose to leave you. He'd never choose to leave us."

"But he's gone."

"No." I put my hands on both sides of his face. "Never." I made sure he was staring back at me. "Nunca."

"Nunca? You promise?" Jacob said. His bottom lip was still trembling.

"Jacob, your father will never be gone. Do you hear me? He'll be right here with us. In your heart."

"And in the stars," Jacob said, remembering what I'd told him.

"The brightest star."

Jacob nodded. "I want to go home."

"This is our home."

He shook his head, making my hands fall from his face. "I want my abuela. And to play with Scarlett."

"Is that really what you want? You want to stay in the city?"

"Yessie. He's okay too," Jacob said and pointed to Tanner.

I smiled. Yeah, Tanner was okay too.

Tanner cleared his throat and walked over to us. "I arranged for this to be here. I thought you might want to spread his ashes." He handed me an urn. "I wasn't sure if you'd want to keep it. Or maybe spread them here." He pulled off his hat and held it to his chest, paying his respects.

I looked down at the container in my hands. Miller's presence was so big. This didn't feel big enough. And I didn't know what to do with it. I looked back up at Tanner. "What did you do? When you lost the woman you loved?"

"Oh, I…" he looked out at the water. "I would have spread her ashes if that had been a choice."

"Why wasn't it?"

He cleared his throat. "It happened…abroad." He shook his head, like he was shaking away the memory. "I'm going to give you two a moment alone. Do you maybe want me to box a few things up for you?" Tanner asked.

"Um…" I looked back at Jacob.

Jacob nodded. "I want everything from my room."

"Jacob, we don't have a place to stay in the city. We can't take everything right now…"

"I actually think I have a solution for that," Tanner said. "I was just about to put a place up for sale, but the two of you could stay there."

"Tanner, that's so generous, but I can't…"

"I insist. The Alcaraz' apartment wasn't meant for four. Plus, this place has a yard for Young Jacob to play in."

"Can I still see my abuela?" Jacob asked.

"Of course," Tanner said. "It's not too far away."

Jacob looked up at me. "I'd like a yard, Mommy."

"Thank you, Tanner," I said. "Just for a bit until we find our own place."

"I'm sure that will happen faster than you think." He smiled and then walked back up to the house.

I didn't know what he meant by that. But I turned back to Jacob. "Come here, baby." I sat down on the edge of the dock, letting my legs hang off the side.

He sat down next to me.

"Where did you have the most fun with Daddy?"

Jacob pointed to the water.

"That's what I was thinking too." I looked out at the lake. "Your father will always be in the stars. But there's a piece of him in here." I tapped the side of the urn. "I think he'd like being in the water, don't you?"

"He'd really like that, Mommy."

"Yeah." I tried to blink my tears away. "Do you want to take the boat out to the middle?"

Jacob nodded.

I needed to move my body. Rowing the boat would help get rid of some of this nervous energy in my veins. Maybe bring me some semblance of peace, if only for a few minutes.

I untied the little rowboat and helped Jacob into it.

Miller loved this house.

We'd wanted to raise our family here.

And even though Jacob didn't want to live here right now, it didn't mean he wouldn't want to come back eventually. I'd never sell this house. We'd keep it.

No, Miller wasn't next to me anymore. But his memory was here. In this yard. In this lake. He was everywhere. I missed him more than life. But he'd keep living here. And we could visit whenever we wanted. Maybe when our hearts were beating normally again.

Miller would want his ashes here. I rowed the boat out to the center of the lake. Miller always used to row it. And the ache in my arms was a welcome distraction.

When we reached the middle of the lake, Jacob climbed into my lap and wrapped his arms around me.

I kissed his forehead and hugged him back.

Neither of us knew what to say. But as we sat there in silence, that felt okay. Because this wasn't goodbye.

I'd love Miller until the day I died. This would never be goodbye.

I let Jacob turn the urn upside down and dump the ashes into the lake.

"Now he's in the lake and the sky," Jacob said.

I nodded. "And right here." I put my hand on his chest. "Always right here."

CHAPTER 25

Thursday

Matt

Nigel was pretending to read the newspaper while I watched TV, but I could see him staring at me over the top of it. And he kept sighing heavily whenever he stole a peek.

"Okay, that's enough." I turned off the TV. "Just tell me what's going on, Nigel."

"Nothing is going on."

"Then why do you keep sighing heavily and staring at me?"

"I always stare at you and breathe heavily. It's just how I breathe."

"Nigel," I said firmly.

"Fine!" He threw the paper. "I have a secret."

I just waited, but he didn't go on. "What is it?"

"A good houseboy never shares his secretses."

"If you didn't want to tell me, you wouldn't have made it so obvious you had one."

He shook his head. "I can't tell you. Master Tanner would be very cross with me. And I'm looking to take some vacation days for a renovation I'm doing. I'll need a month off, so I must be on my best behavior."

What renovations? "Just spill it, Nigel."

"Which secret do you want?"

How many secrets did he have? "The one that has you sighing."

He pressed his lips together. "Okay, fine! But I'm only telling you because I like Kennedy very much after our pizza night and today. And sometimes Master Tanner is wrong. Rarely, but sometimes."

Every word out of his mouth twisted my stomach into knots. "What's going on with Kennedy?"

"Tanner's having someone pick her up and take her to a fancy dinner."

Oh no. I knew where this was going. And it wasn't a secret. Tanner had told me it was going to happen. And I'd completely forgotten about it.

"With Felix," Nigel said.

"Yeah, I got that." I stood up. "Where are they meeting?"

"Master Tanner's favorite Thai restaurant."

"The one he always says is so romantic?" God, why did I even know this information?

Nigel nodded.

Fuck. "Okay. I'm going." I stood up.

"You can't go!" Nigel said. "At least...not without...Francois!" He gave me a cheeky little smile.

"Okay, Francois. Let's go ruin their date."

"Yes! Just let me go get my Francois outfit."

"Hurry though." Felix was not stealing Kennedy from me. He'd done his best to steal Brooklyn away in high school. There was no way I was gonna let that happen again.

***

"The costume doesn't make any sense, though," I said for the fifth time. Not that it mattered now. We were already walking into the restaurant.

"But this is Francois' signature style," Nigel said.

"Whatever. How are you going to wait on Kennedy's table though?"

"Watch and learn." He strutted up to the hostess stand. "Hi, I'm Francois. And I'm handling table…" he grabbed the clipboard right out of her hands.

And for some reason she just let him.

"Table 27. That is mine."

"Of course. Table 27 is all yours, sir."

"Call me Francois."

"Yes, Francois."

"And don't let anyone disturb me as I work. It's very important that I'm not distracted from the task at hand."

"Very well, Francois," the hostess said.

Nigel walked back over to me. "It's done."

"That was the weirdest conversation ever," I said. "Why did she just agree to any of that?"

"Because I'm good with the ladies."

"You are not."

He looked shocked. "But I just…" he pointed over his shoulder. "It's a subtle art that I've been perfecting for decades."

"You mean like…two decades."

"No. Yes. I meant yes. I'm two decades old. I'm practically a child." He smiled at me.

Why is he smiling at me like that? "Nigel, just focus."

"That's Francois to you."

"Okay, Francois, focus. What's the game plan here?"

He pulled me over behind a fake plant. "Kennedy has already arrived at table 27." He spread the leaves so we could take a peek.

Kennedy was sitting all alone.

"You need to get in there before Felix arrives. And act like a proper suitor."

I stared at Kennedy. She was in a dress similar to the one she'd worn on our date. But this one was olive green and it made her tan skin pop. She looked beautiful. "Does she know?"

"Know what?"

"That this was going to be a date with Felix?" Why was she so dressed up?

"No. A driver was sent to her house with a note letting her know she was being escorted to a romantic dinner. The note wasn't signed because Master Tanner loves surprises and grand reveals. As all people do."

Do all people love that?

"Actually, she probably thinks it was from you."

"You really think so?" Because I really didn't love the idea of her dressing like that for someone else.

Nigel nodded and pushed the leaves of the plant back in place. "So the game plan is to pretend it was from you."

"You're sure it wasn't signed?"

"I'm positive. I'm the one that wrote it."

I breathed a sigh of relief. "Okay, I'm going in."

"I'll be by to take your drink order soon. Hut, hut," Nigel said and then slapped me on the butt.

I moved away from him. "Why did you just touch my butt?"

"I learned it earlier on the football field. That's what men do to each other after a game plan. And this was a game plan. And I did the hut hut."

I don't think he understands anything about football. "Well, don't do it again."

"But why?"

"Because I didn't enjoy it, Nigel."

"It's Francois. And I'm not sure you're supposed to enjoy it. It's more for the enjoyment of the one doing the spanking."

"Yeah…don't touch my butt."

"Okay, Master Matthew. Francois won't do it again."

God, that meant Nigel would. But I didn't have time to argue with him right now. The only thing that mattered was that Kennedy didn't have a romantic dinner with Felix.

"I'm going in," I said.

"Hut, hut," Nigel said and slapped my butt again.

"Francois, what the fuck?"

"That one was from Nigel."

I pressed my lips together to avoid yelling at him and drawing the attention of every person in this restaurant. "Don't throw water at us tonight."

"Nigel will not throw water at you tonight."

Okay. So that meant *Nigel* would keep touching my butt. And *Francois* was going to throw water at me. *Great.* I walked out of our hiding spot and right up to Kennedy's table.

"Hey."

She beamed up at me. "The car was a nice touch, Matt. But it wasn't necessary."

I leaned down and kissed her cheek. I loved that I didn't even really have to lie. It was just like Nigel had said. She assumed it was from me. "You look beautiful tonight."

"Thank you."

I sat down across from her. She was dressed to the nines. And I was wearing a pair of jeans and a t-shirt. It was actually just what I'd worn to practice today. I didn't exactly look like a guy who had planned a romantic dinner and sent a car. But...I really didn't think she cared how I dressed. I would have changed, but Nigel had changed into his Francois costume in record time and we didn't want to be late.

"So what's good here?" Kennedy asked.

"I don't know, I've never been here."

"The note said it was one of your favorite restaurants."

Damn it, Nigel! That was important information. "I actually had Nigel send you the note. It must be one of his favorites."

"You have Nigel running errands for you now?"

"No, but I had to take him to work with me today and I needed to give him something to do." That was partially true.

"Was it Take Your Nigel to Work Day or something?"

I laughed. "Well he did act like a kid. So...yeah, kinda. I think he's scared of elevators. And he hit *all* the buttons."

"Oh no." She laughed. "You're joking."

"I wish I was."

"Well that explains why he was at practice too. I thought you were replacing me as your assistant coach."

"Never."

She smiled and looked down at the menu. "So...you haven't gotten any calls or texts recently, have you?" She kept her eyes trained on her menu.

"I get calls and texts all the time."

"Right...but from someone unexpected?"

This was the second time she'd asked me this weird question. "If you're wondering if I've picked up faxing with Nigel, I promise I haven't."

She laughed.

"Kennedy?" someone said from behind us.

I turned to see Felix standing there. I wish I could say he looked terrible. But he didn't. He looked almost exactly the same as he had back in high school. His hair was still longish and pushed to the side. And I could easily picture a joint dangling out the corner of his mouth. But he was dressed a hell of a lot nicer than I currently was.

"Oh my God, Felix!" Kennedy stood up and practically threw herself into his arms.

I watched the way his hands slid down her waist. "It's been forever," he said.

"I can't believe you're here." She stared up at him.

I hoped I was just imagining the stars in her eyes. I stood up and cleared my throat.

Kennedy stepped back from him.

"Wow, Matt. Hey, man," Felix said. He went in for a hug and I slapped him on the back. Probably harder than I usually did.

"Good to see you, man," I said. It actually was good to see him. But not under these circumstances.

"Wait." Felix looked back and forth between us. "I'm so confused. I got a note saying a secret admirer wanted to take me to a romantic dinner."

Damn it, Nigel! Why had he not told me that tidbit of information?

Kennedy looked at me.

I avoided her gaze. "Surprise...I'm your secret admirer," I said to Felix with a laugh. And then I kept laughing while I tried to figure out how to make this less awkward. "Not really. I'm just messing with you. But I can't believe you got in the car. You could have been murdered."

"Wait you actually sent that note? Or not?" He looked more confused than ever.

"Yeah, but don't worry, I'm not your secret admirer. I was just hoping it would freak you out."

"So you didn't want me to come?"

"No, I did. Like I said...I was just messing with you." *Please stop asking questions.* I slapped him on the shoulder. Again, a little too hard. But it was like he didn't even feel it.

He just shrugged. "Okay then. So the three of us are having a romantic dinner." He laughed. "Kennedy, it really is great to see you." He smiled at her.

And I swore she blushed.

"Yup, surprise, Kennedy! I did this for you." What was I even saying? "A little Empire High reunion."

Kennedy's smile faltered. "Is this everyone? Or is someone else coming?"

"Who else would be coming?"

"Oh...um...never mind," she said.

"But you guys are at a table for two," Felix said.

"Yeah, someone must have fucked up. I got it." I grabbed a chair from the table next to us.

The man frowned at me. "Hey, we were waiting for another..."

I ignored the rest of what he was saying and put the chair down right next to Kennedy's. "Let's get to it then." I sat down.

They both sat down too. And I scooted my seat flush with Kennedy's.

"So…" Felix looked back and forth between us. "What's going on with you guys?"

Kennedy said, "Nothing," at the same time that I said, "We're dating."

Kennedy looked up at me.

I put my arm around her shoulders. "We're dating," I said.

Felix's eyebrows pulled together. "The two of you are dating?"

"Um…" Kennedy said. "Kind of. It's complicated."

"Yeah, I'd think so." Felix shook his head. "I mean…what about Brooklyn?"

"I think she'd be happy for us," I said.

He laughed. "That's what you think? That she'd be happy that her fiancé is dating her best friend? I think you might have it all backwards."

Damn it, Felix! The last thing me and Kennedy needed right now was more doubt. I should have never fake invited this guy to dinner with us.

CHAPTER 26

Thursday

Brooklyn

When I saw the pile of boxes in the living room I started to panic. I didn't want anything to change. It needed to stay exactly the same. "Tanner?"

He walked into the room carrying another box. "Yes?"

"I changed my mind. I don't want to move anything. I just…"

"You want it to look exactly the same. I figured. I get it."

Does he? Because it looked like he was packing everything up. "Then what are all these boxes?"

"I only packed up Jacob's things like he requested," Tanner said and patted my son on the head. "And some necessities for you."

But there were so many boxes. I peered around a stack of boxes and saw that the living room had been left completely untouched. And then I opened the lid of the box closest to me. It was filled to the brim with all my lingerie. I slammed it closed and stared at Tanner.

He shrugged. "You never know."

No, I did know. I wouldn't be needing any of that. I pushed it aside. "But what are all the other boxes?"

"Most of what's out here was just some stuff that was boxed up already. Some old things, I think. They were in the back room."

Oh. It was mostly stuff from high school. Stuff I hadn't look at in ages. "I don't need any of that either."

"You never know," he said again.

Jacob opened one of his boxes and pulled out a toy truck. He started zooming it across the floor.

"There is one more thing I arranged," Tanner said. "I met with Miller's lawyer and..."

"Miller didn't have a lawyer."

Tanner lifted an envelope off one of the boxes. "He did."

When had he met with a lawyer?

"He left you everything. No fine print or anything. It's all yours."

I nodded. "Okay." I stared at the envelope he was holding. "So...what is that?"

"He wrote you something. It was with the will." He handed me the envelope. "How about I play with Jacob and you can read it somewhere in private?" He didn't wait for a response. He turned to my son. "Trucks? Don't you have a limo in that box?"

Jacob laughed. "No. But you can use this truck if you want, Abuelo Tanner." He handed the truck he was playing with to Tanner. And then he went to the box to grab another.

"Abuelo?" Tanner asked.

"Yessie," Jacob said and sat down. "You're Mommy's family. So you're my abuelo. Or my...aunt? Like Aunt Kennedy?"

Tanner laughed.

"Jacob," I said. "Tanner isn't..."

"No, it's okay," Tanner said. "Abuelo Tanner works for me." He pulled off his hat and put it on Jacob's head. "I don't mind. I'm an old soul."

The hat slid down over Jacob's eyes. He pushed it back up. "I'm not allowed to talk to my other abuelo. Mommy won't let me."

"Why do you want to talk to him?" Tanner asked.

Jacob shrugged, just like he did when I asked that same question. And then the two of them started to play.

For a second I just stood there and watched them.

It was such a normal moment in our house. Jacob playing and laughing. But it all felt foreign to me.

I never got to say goodbye to Miller. I never got to tell him one last time how much I loved him. How grateful I was for him being patient with me. For giving me the life I always dreamed of. For loving me when I was a mess.

And I had a feeling that this was a goodbye from him.

I didn't want to read it.

I didn't want to say goodbye.

I just wanted to close my eyes and for this all to be a terrible nightmare.

But I wasn't waking up.

I wandered down the hall and opened up our bedroom door. The sheets were still pushed down from when we'd scrambled out of bed. We'd been running late. I hadn't been thinking about anything but work.

How I wished I would have just laughed and slept the day away wrapped up in Miller's arms. I'd do everything differently. I'd never let him go.

I sat down on the edge of the bed and opened up the envelope. It was only two pages. How could a goodbye be so short?

And my eyes started tearing up at the very first line.

Hey Kid,

I always meant what I said. That I'd never leave you. But I know that if you're reading this, something has happened to me. And I'm so sorry that I'm not there with you right now. If I could change it, you know I would. You know I'd be there to wipe away your tears.

And I'm going to clear up something real fast. Because I know what you're thinking. Brooklyn Miller, you are not bad luck. Whatever happened, it wasn't your fault. Do you hear me? Can you hear my voice? You are not bad luck.

How could you possibly be when you gave me the best years of my life? You were my good luck charm.

I know you're probably rethinking everything right now. Our time apart all those years ago. You turning down my proposal. I wish you could see me laughing as I write this. Because all those little hiccups brought us here. And I wouldn't have changed a second of it. Not a second.

Look at the life we built together. You gave me the best gift I could possibly ask for. You loved a guy like me back. You gave me the family I always dreamed of. You chose me back.

Please wipe your tears away. Please stop rethinking all of it. Because every second of it was perfect. And I want you to remember it just like that. The way it always was.

I'll always love you. And I know you loved me too. I know that. Don't ever doubt that. I knew.

But you have to do what your mom told you. You have to keep living. I've given this a lot of thought. And I you need to hear me say this. I know there was someone before me. I know you still think about him sometimes. I just want you to be happy. And safe. And I want the same for Jacob. This isn't easy for me to say, but I need you to know that I'm okay if you choose him now. Because I never want you to stop smiling.

But I'm so grateful you chose me all those years ago. I owe everything to you, Brooklyn.

If you think he could help raise our son. I believe you. I've always believed in you.

You're so smart.

You're so brave.

And you're stronger than you realize.

And you're going to keep going. For me. For our son. Because Jacob's going to need you. Can you hug him for me? Tell him I'll never stop loving him. Please make sure he knows that. Don't ever stop dancing with him in the kitchen. Or playing football on Sundays. Keep doing the things that made all of us so happy.

And when you miss me, just look up at the stars. Because we were always written in them.

Yes, we promised each other forever. But we both know forevers are sometimes cut short. So you need to forget about all those promises. The only thing I want you to do is keep living. Embrace life. Be happy. Be so blissfully happy every day that you have. Don't waste another second of your time on this earth. Will you promise me that? Do this one last thing for me?

Keep living, kid.

Love always,
-Miller

I could barely see the words on the page I was crying so hard. He knew everything that had been going through my head.

How badly I wanted to do things differently. How I wished I hadn't wasted so much time. He knew me. He knew what would be eating me up.

And he didn't want me to be sad. I tried to wipe my tears away, but they wouldn't stop falling.

I didn't want this to be goodbye. I didn't want to move on. I didn't want him to want me to. I wanted to love him forever.

I would always love Miller.

I didn't want another man to raise our son.

I'd do it alone. And that didn't mean I wasn't living. Jacob was all I needed. It was us against the world now.

I started crying harder. I hated that Matt was a part of Miller's goodbye note. I hated that he still plagued my relationship after all these years. And I felt guilty that Miller had to think about that when he was writing this note. I looked back down at his words. *I know you loved me too. I know that. Don't ever doubt that. I knew.*

I lay down on the bed and curled in a ball. He knew. He said he knew. I closed my eyes and breathed in his smell from the sheets. I didn't want to move. I didn't want to keep going. Why did he have to ask me to promise him the hardest thing?

"Brooklyn," Tanner said gently.

I slowly opened my eyes as he crouched down next to the bed.

"Is there anything I can get you? Anything at all. Just say the words."

"I want him back."

Tanner grabbed my hand. "If I could, I would."

I tried to wipe away the rest of my tears. "Then I want one of his sweatshirts."

"I can do that." Tanner walked over to Miller's dresser. He opened up a few drawers until he found what he was looking for. "Here you go." He handed it to me and I pulled it on.

For some reason, I felt a little stronger wearing it. Like Miller's strength had transferred to me.

"I know this is hard, Brooklyn. But if you smile…eventually it'll become a real one. Trust me."

I nodded and gave him what I figured was a pretty pathetic smile. "Does it ever stop hurting?"

He sat down on the bed next to me. "The pain gets less. I'll let you know if it ever goes away completely."

"Is your smile fake? Because you smile a lot."

He laughed, but it sounded sad. "Some days I don't even know anymore."

I put my head on his shoulder.

We both sat in silence, listening to Jacob making vroom noises with his toy trucks in the distance.

"Can I ask what the letter said?" Tanner finally asked, breaking the silence.

"Everything he thought I'd need to hear. He wants me to keep living my life."

"He's a smart man. I have the exact same philosophy."

I lifted my head off Tanner's shoulder. "It was actually mine. I lost my mom when I was young. And then my uncle shortly after. Miller knew how precious time was to me."

Tanner nodded. "I always knew we'd get along."

"Always?" I sniffled and then gave him a smile. "We just met, Tanner."

"Right. Of course. But same friends and all that. It make sense that we'd get along."

"Yeah, I guess so." I sighed and wiped my cheeks, but they were finally dry. "It's probably getting late. We should head back."

"Is there anything else you want to grab?"

I nodded. "A few things."

"Take your time, okay?"

But I didn't want to stay in this room. It was too painful. And I already knew what I wanted. A few more of Miller's sweatshirts so I could fall asleep pretending his arms were around me. The bowls and mugs with Miller's name on them. I wanted Jacob to have them. And I wanted the pictures from our mantel. The one of me and my mom. The one next to it of Miller, Jacob, and I covered in mud after a particularly rainy football game. The one Miller and I had shot on our spur of the moment wedding, the snowflakes falling all around us. And the one of Miller holding Jacob after he was first born.

I was used to walking past these pictures every day. And no matter where Jacob and I ended up...I was going to continue to walk by these same pictures every day for the rest of my life.

CHAPTER 27

Thursday

Matt

"I know it's messy," Kennedy said. "Really messy. But…I don't know." She leaned forward, removing her hand from my shoulders. "That's why it's complicated."

Felix ran his fingers through his hair as he just stared at us. "Actually, it kind of all makes sense now. I remember back in school, whenever Kennedy and I were together, you'd come plop yourself in the middle of us."

"I definitely didn't do that," I said.

Kennedy laughed. "You kind of did."

"What?" I asked.

"Yeah, but I didn't mind. You were grieving. And I knew you just needed a shoulder to cry on. I wanted to be there for you. Brooklyn would have wanted that."

"It's probably the reason why the two of us never got together," Felix said.

Kennedy laughed. "Well, I think a bigger reason for that was that you didn't like me, Felix."

He just stared at her. "What are you talking about? I always liked you, Kennedy."

She laughed again. "Yeah, right."

"I'm not joking," Felix said. "I started talking to you freshman year and then you totally blew me off."

What the fuck was happening right now? It was like they'd completely forgotten I was even here. And where was Francois when I needed him?

"You tried to sell me drugs," Kennedy said.

"I tried to sell everyone drugs." He smiled at her.

"Either way, you clearly just wanted to be friends. I mean, you liked Brooklyn."

He shrugged. "Yeah, but...I liked you first, Kennedy."

She opened her mouth and then closed it again. Kennedy was rarely speechless.

I didn't like this at all.

"Bonjour! I'm Francois!" Nigel yelled.

Thank God.

Kennedy laughed. "Nigel, what you doing here? And why are you dressed like a waiter from that French restaurant again?"

"I'm not Nigel, Kennedy. I'm Francois!"

"Then how did you know my name?"

"Francois knows all things! I'm Francois!" He pulled out a notepad. "Now you two lovebirds, tell me what you'd like me to serve you."

Kennedy turned to me.

"He wants to know our drink order," I said.

"That isn't what he said."

I laughed. "I know. But it's what he meant."

She turned back to Nigel. "Just bring us whatever wine you recommend."

"Whatever *I* recommend?" A big smile spread across his face, jostling his fake mustache. He grabbed the mustache to keep it on. "Very good, mademoiselle. Very good indeed." He made sure his mustache was staying in place before he turned to Felix. "And what will the random gentleman who is clearly the third wheel have?"

"Um…a scotch will be great, thanks."

"Basic choice." And with that Nigel turned on his heel and hurried off.

I smiled. Nigel had just brought the sick burns for me. Maybe I'd forgive him for not warning me I'd invited Felix on a romantic date tonight.

"I'm so confused," Felix said. "Do you guys know that rude waiter?"

"Yeah, he's a friend," Kennedy said.

"Francois is your friend?" Nigel asked.

Kennedy jumped.

How had he gotten our drink order so quickly?

"Yeah, *Francois*. I do believe you are."

He nodded. "Yes. We are friends. The best of friends. And I have brought my favorite from the wine selection. I hope it's to your liking, friend."

Kennedy smiled at him.

And then he pulled a machete out from behind his back and lopped the top off the bottle.

Where the hell did that come from?!

Kennedy clapped for him.

I didn't think I'd ever seen Nigel so happy. Well, that wasn't true. He looked like that whenever he talked about drawing me a bath. Or when he discussed fax machines. He finished pouring our drinks and turned to leave.

"Um…where's my drink?" Felix asked.

Nigel completely ignored him and walked away.

"I'm pretty sure your friend hates me," Felix said.

Kennedy laughed. "It just takes some time for him to warm up to people. He didn't like me at first either. He kept throwing water in my face."

"Are you serious?" Felix asked with a laugh.

"I swear it. And his opinion changes quite quickly. He did that to me just earlier today on the football field."

"The football field?"

"Yeah, Matt is the head coach at Empire High. And I'm his assistant coach. Oh my gosh, Felix, you should come to the homecoming game this weekend. Matt, are there any tickets left?"

"No," I said. "I think they're all sold out." They weren't.

"Are you sure?"

I nodded.

"That sucks," said Kennedy. "I was hoping to grab one for my mom too. She wanted to come see both of us in action. She hasn't been able to stop talking about it. I should have grabbed them earlier. I really need to stop leaving everything to the last minute. She's going to be so disappointed."

Fuck. I didn't want to not let her mom come.

"There aren't any strings you can pull?" she asked.

I cleared my throat. "I mean…yeah. I'll figure something out."

"For Felix too?"

"Right. I'll get two tickets." *Damn it.* The last thing I needed was for Felix to be schmoozing Kennedy's mom during the whole game. Really, the last thing I needed was for Felix and Kennedy to hang out again at all.

"Thanks, Matt." She smiled up at me.

I reached out and tucked a loose strand of hair behind her ear.

And this time she blushed for me. I took a deep breath. I was just overreacting. She didn't like Felix. Sure, maybe she had years ago. But time changed things.

"Can you really imagine marrying her when your heart still belongs to someone else?" Tanner's words popped into my head uninvited. Okay, fine. Maybe time didn't change everything.

And Felix was definitely looking at her like his feelings hadn't changed. Had I really gotten in their way all those years ago? I didn't even realize I'd been doing that. I just...needed to hang out with someone that understood my pain. I never meant to get in the way of Kennedy's happiness.

"Are you okay?" Kennedy asked. She put her hand on my thigh.

"What? Yeah, I'm fine."

"You sure? I think you might have spaced out for a minute there. Felix was just asking what you do. I told him you run MAC International. How all your dreams are coming true."

I remembered telling Brooklyn that running MAC International was my dream. That Brooklyn was my dream. I'd pictured it all with her.

"You look a little pale," Kennedy said. "Do you need some water? Where is Nigel?"

"If you'll excuse me for a moment," I said. "I actually forgot I have a quick business call I need to make." I pushed myself away from the table and I didn't even hear Kennedy's response. I just needed some air.

I needed someone to tell me that my sadness in high school hadn't ruined Kennedy's chance at happiness.

I needed someone to tell me that everything was going to be okay.

I went out the front doors and breathed in the cool autumn air. And then I called Tanner.

It took him forever to answer. Which was highly unusual.

"Hey," Tanner said when he finally picked up. "I'm a little busy, but I'll be home in like half an hour."

"Get out of my head."

"What?"

I sat down on the curb and put my face in my hands. "I can't stop thinking about what you said. About if I could marry someone else when my heart still belongs to Brooklyn."

"Trust me, everything is going to be fine."

"How could it be? Felix liked Kennedy all those years ago. And I was in their way."

"Are you spying on their date?"

"No, I'm *on* their date."

It sounded like he closed a door. And then his voice was suddenly a little louder. "So you're doing the same thing you did to them when you were back in high school?"

"But I…" I let my voice trail off. "I really like Kennedy."

"I thought you loved her?"

"Yeah. I do. I love her. But I can't stop thinking about what you said."

"I know," Tanner said.

"I just…if I messed it up for them once before, I don't want to be the one that messes it up again. But I can't turn off my feelings for her."

"I know."

"But he sat there and told her that he liked her first. And I can't ever tell Kennedy that. I'll never be able to."

"I know," Tanner said.

"Stop staying you know. You don't know."

"Matt, it's all going to be fine."

I didn't respond. I just stared at the taxis zooming by on the street.

"I promise," Tanner said. "You just need to trust me."

I didn't believe that Tanner was an expert on true love. But I still found myself asking: "You think Felix and Kennedy are a good match? Better than me and her?"

"There's no way for me to know for sure this soon. But I think there's a good chance. How did she respond to seeing him?"

"Her eyes lit up. Whereas when she first ran into me again, she kneed me in the balls."

Tanner laughed. "Very different circumstances."

"Yeah." I sighed. "But still." I turned to look through the window of the restaurant. Felix and Kennedy were laughing about something. Besides for the empty chair next to Kennedy, it looked like the two of them were on a date.

Had I really always put myself between them during high school?

I hadn't meant to do that.

I hadn't been thinking.

I just…I'd needed Kennedy.

I still needed her.

"And are you with Nigel? I need his help with something and I can't get a hold of him."

I smiled as I watched Francois walk over to our table and sit in my chair. They were all laughing now. "Yeah, he's here too. He dressed up like Francois again."

Tanner laughed. "Is he fooling anyone this time?"

"Not even a little bit." I looked through the window. Nigel had disappeared. But then I saw him walk back up to the table with another glass of scotch. He proceeded to throw it right in Felix's face.

Kennedy said something to Nigel and they both started laughing. And then Felix started laughing too.

"What's so funny?" Tanner asked.

I hadn't realized that I'd chuckled. *Serves Felix right.* "Nigel just threw a drink in Felix's face."

"Why would he do that? He's only supposed to be throwing drinks when you and Kennedy are misbehaving."

"Wait, what did you just say?"

"Nothing. You'd think Nigel would be able to pull Francois off better since he's a born Frenchman. But alas, his acting is subpar. I hope the four of you enjoy the rest of your evening."

"Watching Felix flirt with Kennedy right in front of me isn't very enjoyable."

"I know."

We were both quiet for a moment.

"But Matt?"

"Yeah?"

"It really is all going to be okay."

Maybe for everyone else. I could just walk away and let Kennedy and Felix be happy together. But then I'd be alone again.

HOMECOMING

The autumn wind blew and it was like I could smell Brooklyn in the air.

I'd fallen in love with her in the autumn.

And I'd lost her in the same season.

The smell of fall always made me miss her. It made me feel so much regret.

I stared at the three of them happily laughing through the window. I was pretty sure I'd always be on the outside of happiness looking in.

CHAPTER 28

Thursday

Brooklyn

"This is too much," I said as I stared at the townhouse with the "sold" sign out front.

"Oh, it's not that one," Tanner said. "It's actually this one." He pointed to the one next to it that looked almost the same from the outside. "I um…haven't put it on the market yet."

The one without the sign looked even nicer. I turned to Tanner. He was holding a sleeping Jacob in his arms.

"Mrs. Alcaraz doesn't mind if I stay with her a few more nights," I said.

"I know. But I want to do this. I promise it'll all make sense."

He kept saying weird stuff like that.

"If you don't like it, we can drive back to Mrs. Alcaraz's. But at least go inside and take a look around. See if it could work for you."

"Well, how much is the rent?"

"Zero dollars." He walked up the front steps and pulled out a key.

"Tanner, I'm serious."

"So am I." He opened the front door.

It looked like the house had been completely redone. Some of the original molding had definitely been restored. And the wood floors were immaculate. I walked through the entryway and it was like my heart stopped.

The kitchen was yellow.

Not a bright yellow like my mom's. But a really light yellow. I was pretty sure the average house buyer would just think it was one of many shades of off-white. But I could see the yellow hue. And I couldn't really explain it, but it felt like I'd just walked into my home.

"Are you okay?" Tanner asked.

"Yeah...I..." my voice trailed off. The kitchen was top of the line. When I bought the lake house 15 years ago, our kitchen had been brand new. But this looked like it was just installed yesterday. "Did you flip this house?"

"No. A friend of mine did though. He put a lot of love and care into this place. He slowly renovated it while he was living here for the past few years."

I turned around in a circle. "Why would he ever want to leave?" I ran my hand along the granite countertop.

"Well, it's a family home. And he's single."

I nodded. This place did seem big for one person. I wouldn't want it alone. I needed Jacob's laughter to fill it.

"All the furniture was just delivered today," Tanner said. "If you don't like something, just let me know and I'll replace it."

"Tanner, you didn't need..."

"I had to get it for the staging anyway."

"Oh. So you rented all this furniture?"

He shook his head. "I don't rent things."

"But you're renting this place to me."

"No. I'm letting you stay here for free."

I couldn't stay here for free. But...I really did want to stay. I wanted to dance with Jacob in this kitchen. It just felt right. "How much is it to buy?"

He just stared at me. "You want to buy it? Brooklyn, you haven't even seen the whole place yet."

"I don't know how to explain it." I shook my head. "This house feels...warm. I can feel the love put into all the details. It feels like a home. And I want to give Jacob a home here. I want to give this city a real try. That's what he wants."

Tanner nodded. "I'll have to look at some comps to determine the sale price. But for now...you can just stay." He handed me the keys. "I'll go take Jacob to his room and then bring the boxes in. How about you take a look around. Let me know if there's anything else you need."

"You've already done enough."

"I would do anything for my best friend's friend," he said.

It was weird that he kept saying that. Especially since every time I brought up Kennedy he seemed to have no idea who I was referring to. I was really getting the sense that the two of them weren't that close. Maybe Tanner just didn't have many friends. Which made my heart hurt for him. He was an odd man, but I didn't mind that. I felt a little out of place here too. It was nice to have a new friend. Especially one Jacob liked so much.

"We should get this little man to his bed chambers," he said.

Bed chambers? I just shook my head with a smile and lifted Tanner's hat off Jacob's head. My little guy had completely lost his stranger danger over the past few days. He'd had so much fun playing with Tanner today. And Tanner didn't even care when Jacob ran all over the limo butt naked wearing nothing but Tanner's borrowed hat.

"Goodnight, sweet boy," I whispered and kissed his forehead. "Here's your hat back," I said and handed it to Tanner.

"Oh, no, he should keep it." Tanner put it back on Jacob's head. "I think he looks like a proper gentleman, don't you?"

I laughed. Jacob was still naked, except for that hat. "He definitely looks like an old-fashioned gentleman."

Tanner nodded. "Indeed. I'll be back down in a minute. Finish taking a look around."

I nodded and watched the two of them go upstairs. I ran my hand along the granite countertops. Honestly I didn't need to see the rest of the house. But I was a little curious. The kitchen was open to the living room. And it seemed just as homey as the kitchen. I wandered down the hall and out the back door.

There was a small yard back here. With a patio, table, and grill. It was cute. Nothing like the huge open yard the lake house had. But bigger than one would expect to have in the city. I could picture Jacob playing out here for hours.

I wrapped my arms around myself. I was still wearing one of Miller's old sweatshirts. And his smell on the fabric made it feel like he was giving me a big hug. I looked up and my eyes started to water. I wasn't sure how easy it would be to see the stars in the city. But on this cloudless night, away from the high rises, I could make out a few. Especially the biggest, brightest one. "Is this okay?" I whispered.

I knew I was crazy. Talking to a dead person. But I wanted some kind of sign that he approved of this house.

The wind blew and a few leaves fell from the one tree in the small yard. The autumn air reminded me of him just as much as the detergent on his sweatshirt. And somehow that breeze felt like a response. Almost as if he was here with us.

I hugged myself tighter. "I'm going to keep living, Miller," I said and looked back up at the stars. "I promise." I'd create a home for me and Jacob here. With the yellow kitchen. We were going to be okay. We had to be.

The back door opened and Tanner walked out. "Everything is unpacked."

"What? How? It's only been a couple minutes."

"Are you sure? I think it was longer than that."

I laughed. I was pretty sure. But honestly, I could stare at the stars for hours thinking about Miller. I shivered when the wind blew again.

"Come on in, it's getting cold," Tanner said.

I walked back into the house and down the hall.

Tanner had started a fire in the fireplace. And even that reminded me of the lake house. But it was the fact that he'd put the pictures on the mantel in the exact right order that really felt like home. I walked over to it and put my hands out, warming them from the cold. I stared at the picture of Miller kissing me on our wedding night. How many times had Miller and I made love right in front of a roaring fire?

Tanner cleared his throat. "Do you want some wine?"

I turned around. He was sitting on the couch pouring us each a glass.

"Oh…um…" Now that it was just the two of us, a roaring fire, and wine, this suddenly felt like it was supposed to be some kind of date.

"Don't look at me like that," Tanner said with a laugh. "It's just wine."

I nodded and took the glass. "I wasn't looking at you in any way." I took a sip of the wine.

"You looked very alarmed, Brooklyn."

"Did I?" I sat down next to him.

"You did. Believe me - I know the look a girl gives when she isn't into it. I've seen it thousands of times."

"Wow, I'm so sorry. Don't give up on love, though. I'm sure there's a girl out there for you."

"Oh," said Tanner with a laugh. "I've rarely had that look directed at me. My clients, on the other hand…" He shook his head. "Poor guys. If only they had the confidence to wear tuxedos like mine."

"Like yours?"

"I don't believe in the boring black and navy. I tend to go more bold."

I laughed. "So…a white tux?"

"No. More like neon stripes. And all sorts of patterns."

"That is quite bold." I took another sip of wine.

"You gotta have fun every once in a while. Or life gets stale."

I laughed again. "Like a loaf of bread?"

"Exactly like a loaf of bread. Well…I think. I wouldn't know. I always order my bread by the slice."

Is that a thing mega rich people do? "Gotcha."

We were both quiet as we stared at the fire. I'd never felt so comfortable in silence with a stranger before. I wondered if he was thinking about the love that he'd lost as he stared at the flames.

I wasn't sure how long we sat there in silence. But eventually the bottle was empty and my eyelids were heavy.

"I should probably get going," Tanner said.

I yawned. "It is getting late."

Tanner slowly stood up. "I think the two of you are going to be alright," he said.

"A free house to live in certainly helps. I really can't thank you enough."

He smiled. "I actually have a way you could thank me. I'm going to a high school homecoming football game this weekend. Would you and Jacob like to accompany me?"

Did he just ask me out?

"Don't give me that look again."

"What look?"

"The one you gave me earlier when you thought the wine was a romantic gesture. The game isn't a date. I thought that having you and Jacob there would make it slightly less dull. Maybe Jacob can explain to me why on earth they need to take 40 seconds between plays."

Going to a football game would make Jacob feel close to Miller. I nodded. "What school did you graduate from?"

"Me? Oh, nowhere you would have heard of."

"Didn't you just say you were going to your homecoming game?"

"Oh, right." He laughed. "Yes. That makes sense. I went to Empire High."

I pressed my lips together. "I actually went there. For a few months. When did you graduate?"

"I want to say…1990?"

I just stared at him. "That can't be right. How old are you?"

"Oh I meant in the 2000s. I'm bad with dates." He cleared his throat. "Well, this will be fun then. We can hang out together on the old stomping grounds."

"Actually…I don't know if it's a good idea."

"Bad memories?"

I nodded. "Some good ones too. But yeah, a lot of bad ones."

"Same. We can face all our old high school demons together. What do you say?"

"I really don't know…"

"Come on. You have to face your demons from the past if you're going to move forward."

He kind of seemed like an expert on this stuff. And for some reason I found myself nodding. Even though my head was screaming *no*.

"Great. I'll pick you both up on Saturday, okay?"

"Sure." It was like the word tumbled out of my mouth without my permission. I reached up and touched my lips. I really didn't mean to say that.

"Goodnight, Brooklyn," he said and leaned down to hug me. "It was a pleasure." He pulled back. "Miller's truck should arrive by the morning. If you need anything at all before Saturday, I left my number on your fridge. And really, everything is going to be okay. I promise."

I wasn't sure why, but I believed his words. Once I closed the door behind him, I quickly got ready for bed, and then climbed into Jacob's bed. I pulled him in close.

It's going to be okay. I kissed the top of his head. *We're going to be okay.*

CHAPTER 29

Friday

Matt

I was trying to focus on the homecoming game tomorrow instead of what happened with Kennedy and Felix last night. I didn't know what I wanted to do about that situation. Luckily I had lunch with Mason today. Maybe he could give me some advice.

Hopefully he'd have better advice than Tanner did last night. He'd just told me he was willing to send the two of them on a date *alone* this time. And that really didn't help anything.

Seriously…what the hell was I supposed to do? Sure, Kennedy looked happy talking to Felix. But I made her happy too. It wasn't like Felix was an upgrade over me. *Fucking Felix.*

Just focus on the game. Besides, Kennedy would be with me on the field. While Felix was in the stands. I had the advantage here.

My administrative assistant called my cell phone just as I was walking into the office.

"Hey, Mary, I'm on my way up."

"Thank goodness. That woman is here again."

"What woman?" I asked. But I didn't need to. Because a second later I could hear Poppy screaming at Mary to give her the phone.

Great. This was the last thing I needed today. "I'll be right up," I said and ended the call. I guessed Poppy got the contract. I'd kind of been hoping this whole thing could be done over the phone. But maybe it would be better in person. So she could see how serious I was about this.

As I stepped onto the elevator, I was glad Nigel wasn't with me today. He would have hit all the buttons. And Mary was a fantastic assistant, but no one could handle Poppy's wrath for too long.

I got off on the top floor and walked toward my office.

"I told her not to go in," Mary said. "But she ignored everything I said."

That sounded like Poppy. "Thanks, Mary."

"Do you want me to call security?"

"No, I've got it from here." I walked into my office and closed the door behind me.

Poppy spun around and glared at me. But I was a little distracted by the fact that her daughter Gigi was playing with my glass paperweights again.

I grabbed one from her and put it on a higher shelf before she could smash it.

"Did you send a *fax* to me yesterday afternoon?" Poppy said and lifted up a stack of papers. She looked so pissed.

I tried to hide my smile. Nigel was right, faxes were awesome. "Yes, I did."

"Who sends faxes? It's so inefficient. It just sat there all of yesterday and my assistant only found it this morning."

I loved that. The wait seemed to make her even more pissed.

"And what the hell is this?" She lifted up the papers. "Why is there a clause about a designer bathtub?"

I thought I'd told Nigel to take that out. "Ignore that clause. But I'm dead serious about the rest of it."

"I don't understand...I thought we were on the same page."

"Poppy I went to your house earlier this week and showed you the evidence I had against you. We were never on the same page."

"Of course we're on the same page. Just because you're blackmailing me doesn't mean we can't be together. I respect this cutthroat side of you. And a contract? It's a sexy touch."

She'd completely lost it. "Poppy, if you don't sign those papers, I'll go to the police now."

She sighed and set the contract down on my desk. "You don't mean that, sugar tits."

"Yes, I do. And seriously, don't call me that."

She just stared at me, a smile slowly spreading across her face. "Oh. This is about Brooklyn, isn't it?"

When I had a problem, why did everyone always just assume it was because of Brooklyn? "No."

"So you're not still in love with her?"

I clenched my jaw. I didn't even know how to answer that anymore. "It's not about Brooklyn. She's dead."

Poppy raised her eyebrows. She looked genuinely shocked by my response. "Fascinating."

"What are you talking about, Poppy?"

"You're spending all this time protecting your friends and family. It's a little ironic. Since they don't seem to have your best interests in mind in the slightest."

What the hell was she talking about? My friends had my best interests in mind. She was growing more delusional by the day.

"Darling," she said. "I'm the only one that's going to put you first. Forever and always. As soon as we walk down the aisle that is."

I grabbed a pen from my desk and handed it to her. "Sign it."

She looked around. "I don't see a marriage certificate anywhere."

"Sign the contract I faxed you."

She pouted. "But there's a whole section about how it terminates our original arrangement. Signing this would mean we are no longer together. That'll have to be taken out."

"That's what the whole contract is for."

"Oh, is it?" She picked up the stack of papers again. "I thought it was to make sure I wouldn't blow up any of your friends, family, or acquaintances. Especially someone named Nigel who you hold near and dear to your heart?"

What? I grabbed the documents from her. She'd already highlighted a few sections. And I saw Nigel's name highlighted in bright yellow under a 'near and dear' clause. When had he added that in? I swear it hadn't been in the original he'd shown me.

"I think what we both want is that cute little redhead to remain safe. So let's forget about the contract and just move forward with an engagement."

"Poppy…"

"And speaking of our pending engagement…why haven't you signed the relationship contract that Uncle Richard sent over?"

"Because I don't want to be in a relationship. Hence *this* contract."

"Well, give me some more time to look it over. I'll need to make quite a few amendments. But in the meantime, go ahead and sign the relationship contract."

Did she think she was negotiating with a toddler? "I'm not signing another relationship contract," I said.

"What do you mean *another*?" Her confident smile finally faltered.

"Mr. Pruitt made me sign one when I was dating Brooklyn. I'm not signing another damned thing."

"You have one with Brooklyn?"

"Had. I *had* one with Brooklyn."

"Interesting," she said. "I think I need to have a talk with my uncle."

"He doesn't need to be involved in this."

"Apparently he does. Regardless, like I said, I need more time to look this over. I think some clauses might nullify other contract's clauses and things of that nature. It's a whole big thing. I'll need a while."

"Poppy, why are you dragging this out?"

"I'm not. I'm protecting myself."

"How is dating me protecting you?"

She stared at me for a moment. "I already told you. I want to take over the company. And Uncle Richard is delusional. He's not seeing reason right now. My position in the company is in jeopardy."

"I know you think you need my help with finances, but…"

"It's not really about that anymore. He thinks he found a more suitable heir. Which is preposterous." Her voice was growing louder by the second. "I've been here the whole time. I know how everything works. I'm the better choice. He has to pick me!"

I suddenly had a feeling that Poppy's delusions had nothing to do with me. Well, maybe a little to do with me. But it seemed like she was more upset by whatever was going on with Mr. Pruitt.

"How about this…sign those papers and I'll have a talk with Mr. Pruitt. About how you're the perfect fit to take over for him." I truly believed she was. She was as unhinged as her uncle. She'd run the mob just fine.

"Really?" She smiled. "Great! Have that talk and we'll see about the papers."

"No, sign the papers and then I'll talk to him."

"I like it my way better. Kisses." She stood on her tiptoes and tried to plant a kiss on my lips, but I dodged it at the last second.

"Poppy…"

But she ignored me. "You're so funny, lover. Gigi, come," she said.

Gigi put the picture frame she'd been looking at back on the shelf, dangerously close to the edge.

I quickly pushed it back. And looked down at Scarlett's smiling face in the picture. I took a deep breath. I was doing this all for her. To make sure she was safe. And I could swallow my pride for a minute in order to make sure that was possible. "Fine," I said. "I'll talk to Mr. Pruitt."

"Wonderful," Poppy said. "Isn't that wonderful, Gigi?"

Gigi nodded.

God, that little girl really creeped me out. She looked just like a doll that had come to life to murder everyone.

"And after I do, you'll sign that contract?"

"Right after my lawyers finish looking at it."

"Quickly, Poppy."

"Of course. Anything for you, darling. But it's practically the weekend. It'll have to wait until at least Monday. And then they'll need a few days. Ta ta!" Poppy yelled and they walked out of my office hand in hand.

Lover? At least Monday? I sighed and sat down. The last thing I wanted to do was see Mr. Pruitt. But I could do it another day.

I needed to get my head in the game. If we won homecoming, Jefferson would be a legend. I'd accomplish what I'd set out to do.

Kind of. Really it was Kennedy who was helping make Jefferson so popular.

Fuck, what am I going to do about Kennedy?

CHAPTER 30

Friday

Brooklyn

I shimmied my shoulders and Jacob mimicked me. I laughed as he moved his hips to the beat of the music.

He'd insisted on wearing Tanner's hat again this morning, and Tanner was right…he looked like quite the gentleman. Minus the nudity.

But as we laughed and danced around the kitchen while I made breakfast, it felt almost normal. Jacob already had his toys thrown all over the living room. And it was like I could feel the love in the air.

I turned up the music. For some reason I had this idea that the louder the music was, the less sad I could be. And so far this morning, it was working. Jacob kept jumping up and down to the beat as I opened the oven and pulled out the cupcake tin.

"Cuppycakes?"

"Kind of." I pulled an egg bite out of the cupcake tin and plopped it onto his plate. I'd added some extra spices. He seemed fond of Mrs. Alcaraz's cooking and I wanted him to keep eating something besides sweets. And then I lifted him up onto the stool.

Instead of sitting on it, he climbed onto the counter. He leaned down to inspect the eggs, frowned, and looked back up at me. "Where's the icing?"

"These cupcakes don't need icing."

"They're muffykins?"

Aw. It had been so long since I'd made him muffins that I'd forgotten his endearing name for them. "No, it's not a muffin either."

He pushed it away.

"Just try it."

"Nooooo."

I tried to hide my smile. As much as I loved how he drew out the word "no," I needed him to eat this. I slid the plate back in front of him. And I just stared at him until he finally picked up his fork and took a bite.

His eyes lit up at the punch of flavor. "Más, más!"

"More?"

He nodded his head as he ate another big forkful.

I put another egg bite on his plate and gave myself a mental high five.

"So I have some good news," I said as I sat down in front of him. "Tanner invited us to a football game tomorrow afternoon."

"Can I be the running back?"

"Not one we'll be playing in. Or one on the TV. A real one. In person."

"Wow." Jacob's smile took up his whole face. "I love Abuelo Tanner."

I laughed. "Yeah, he's really nice. So you're excited?"

"Yessie." He took another bite of eggs.

"And Mrs. Alcaraz is coming over to play with you for a few hours while I run some errands."

"Where are you going?"

"Just to see a few people." Since Jacob and I were staying, it was about time I finally faced Matt. And I needed to see my father too.

He pushed his plate aside. "I come with you, Mommy."

"I actually need you to stay here."

"Por qué?"

"Why? Well...I'm going to see some people that aren't really friends."

His eyes lit up like when he'd eaten the eggs. "You're seeing Abuelo!"

Shoot. "Jacob..."

"Please, Mommy! I need to see my abuelo!"

"I really don't think..."

"Por favor!"

"You're going to see Abuelo Tanner tomorrow."

"Nooooo. I need to see my abuelo. Por favor!"

God he was so cute when he asked for things in Spanish. And he had been good and eaten his eggs. I was going to be telling my father he couldn't be a part of our lives, even though we were staying. And if this was goodbye...maybe it was fair for Jacob to see him just this once.

"Please, Mommy."

"I really don't know why you want to see him so badly. But...how about I run my first errand. And then before I go to your grandfather's I'll come pick you up. And we can go together."

He nodded. "I get to see my abuelo. Can I see Scarlett too? And zoo?"

"That's a lot of things for one day. How about you hang out with Mrs. Alcaraz, see your grandfather, and then we order pizza?"

"And then Scarlett and zoo?"

"Those will have to wait until another day, sweet boy."

"Then pizza *and* cuppycakes for dinner." He stuck out his hand like he was making some kind of business deal.

Was that something Tanner had taught him yesterday? It was almost as cute as his broken Spanish. "Deal," I said and shook his hand. "Now go put some clothes on before Mrs. Alcaraz comes."

"No."

"Jacob…"

"I have hat." He pointed to his hat.

Well, I couldn't really argue with that.

"Mommy, why is one of the rooms upstairs locked?"

I stared at him. "Which room?"

"The one next to mine?"

"I don't know, sweet boy. Want to go explore?"

"Yessie!"

I picked him up off the counter and we wandered upstairs. I still hadn't looked at all the rooms in the house. And I'd even slept in Jacob's bed last night. I grabbed the handle of the door next to his. And just like he'd said…it was locked. *Son of a bitch.* I really hated locked rooms. I'd need to ask Tanner about that.

***

I hit Kennedy's name in my phone.

"Hey," Kennedy said. "How was your limo adventure yesterday?"

"Eventful," I said as I made my way down the sidewalk to Miller's truck. I'd texted her last night to let her know Tanner had found us a place to stay. Mrs. Alcaraz had brought our bags over today. We hadn't brought much. But our trip yesterday had taken care of that.

Jacob pretty much had a replica of his room back home here. "So…where does Matt work?"

"Are you going to see him?"

"Yeah. Jacob wants to stay in the city. And I don't want to put you in an awkward position any longer."

"Thank you," Kennedy said. "He works at his father's company."

"Does he?" I smiled to myself. That was what he'd always wanted.

"Well, technically he's the CEO."

"That's amazing," I said. I was happy for him. Maybe he'd gone after all his dreams after all. Maybe, despite what his friends seemed to think, Matt really was happy. Fulfilled. In love with my best friend. I shook away the thought. That last part was none of my business.

I cleared my throat. "Well, I guess I should get this over with."

"Good luck," Kennedy said. "Not that you need it, of course. But could you maybe call me after? To just…let me know what…happened?"

I laughed, even though it was forced. "Kennedy, I promise nothing weird is going to happen. I mean, the worst is that I'm going to slap him."

Kennedy didn't laugh. "Okay just…please call me."

"I will."

"Thanks," she said. "And no matter what, just know that I love you. Really, no matter what."

She was being so weird right now. What did she think I was going to do? Bang him on his desk? She was seriously way off base here. "I love you too." I hung up as I climbed into Miller's truck.

I took a deep breath of Miller's scent that still lingered. Yeah, Kennedy was definitely way off base.

HOMECOMING

I took another deep breath and pulled the truck away from the curb. It had been 16 years since I'd spoken to Matt. Fifteen years since the last time I'd seen him. This was probably going to be the most awkward conversation of my life. But I needed him to know the truth. I needed to clear the air. I'd told Kennedy, James, Rob, and Penny that I'd do this. And I wasn't a liar.

Matt was the liar.

I shook away the thought. Thinking about that wasn't the best way to start a conversation.

It didn't take me long to get to MAC International's high rise. The commute from the house I was staying in was pretty easy. Not that that tidbit of information mattered at all. This would be the first and only time I'd be visiting Matt at work. Or visiting him period.

Finding a parking space was a whole different problem though. I circled the block twice before a space right out front opened up. I quickly pulled into the spot and cut the engine.

My heart was racing and I willed it to calm down.

This would be easy.

In and out in just a few minutes. I'd just pop in and say, "Hi, sorry about 16 years ago. My father kidnapped me. But then I stayed away because you were an asshole." Easy peasy.

My stomach churned as I leaned forward to look at the high rise out of my front windshield. The building was intimidating. All metal and glass.

I so badly just wanted to drive away. Just like I had all those years ago.

But Kennedy was my best friend. And Scarlett was Jacob's new best friend. Which meant in order for Jacob to hang out with her, I needed to do this for James and Rob.

It was easier to think about doing this for other people's benefit. Because I really, really didn't want to do it for me. I was content with my decision to leave that day when I'd seen Matt in the pool. I'd made my peace with letting him think I was dead. And I truly thought it was in everyone's best interest.

Maybe I should say something more along those lines. Instead of the him-being-an-asshole thing.

I took another deep breath and climbed out of the truck. I slammed the door and walked up to the building.

And when I reached the doors, I immediately turned around and walked back to the truck.

For fuck's sake. I walked back to the front doors. Then back to the truck. Then back to the front doors. And then I turned around again and ran straight into someone. It felt like running into a brick wall. I fell backward, and he wouldn't have moved at all if it wasn't to reach out and steady me.

"Sorry," said a deep voice. "I wasn't looking where I was going."

I knew that voice. I looked up at Matt's brother.

Mason looked down at me. And blinked. And then he immediately let go of my arms and took a step back.

He looked almost exactly the same. Just a more grown-up version. More domineering, if that was even possible. And his similarities to Matt made my throat feel dry. The same chocolate brown eyes. The same dirty blonde hair. The wide shoulders. It was like I was standing in front of Matt instead of Mason. And my stupid heart started racing even faster. And I wanted to slap him even though he wasn't Matt. Or maybe my heart wasn't racing. Maybe it was breaking all over again. It wasn't even Matt and I could feel the tears coming to my eyes. I could hear him laughing in that pool all over again. Living happily without me. I felt like a stupid teenager staring at a boy who would never love me back.

"You look just like someone I used to know," Mason said. He shook his head. His face had grown pale. Like he was literally seeing a ghost. And I guess he kind of thought he was.

"It's me," I said.

He shook his head. Blinked again. "Brooklyn?"

I nodded.

"But you're...you..." his voice trailed off.

"Mason, I'm so sorry," I said.

And then he closed the distance between us and pulled me into his arms. He hugged me so tightly I could barely breathe. "Sis," he whispered.

I don't think I would have heard it if his lips weren't right next to my ear. I could feel tears welling in my eyes. I used to love when he called me that. But I didn't deserve that nickname now. I wasn't sure how long we stood in the middle of the sidewalk like that. But I didn't want to let go. Mason had been like the brother I never had. He'd always looked out for me. He'd had my back. And I'd missed him so much.

Mason finally pulled back. "How is this possible?"

"It's a really long story."

Mason looked toward the front doors of MAC International. "I'm guessing you're here to see Matt," he said. "I was just going up. You can tell us the story together. Or...maybe I should let you go alone. Matt and

I were going to have lunch. I'll call him and tell him I got held up."

"Wait, you don't work here?"

He shook his head. "No, this was always Matt's dream. Not mine."

"Yeah." It was. Mason being the heir to this company was one of the reasons my father wanted me to be with him rather than Matt. But my father was wrong about most things.

Mason pulled out his phone to call Matt.

"Stop. I can't," I said. My heart hadn't stopped pounding. I needed more time. I couldn't do this. Seeing Mason made me realize just how hard this was going to be. It wasn't a matter of slapping Matt and walking away. My mind was racing. I felt like I'd slap him and kiss him and slap him again. And then cry for hours and tell him to fuck off. I needed to calm down. I needed more time. And as soon as I thought it, I heard the clock ticking down in my head. Just like it always did when something bad was about to happen.

I took a step back from Mason. "I'm so sorry, I can't. I can't..." I'd promised everyone I'd do this. I had to do this. "I can't breathe." I hadn't had a panic attack in years back home. And now that I was back, it was like they were plaguing me all over again.

Mason grabbed my hand and pulled me into the restaurant next to Matt's building. He found us an empty booth, told a waitress to fuck off, and ran his hand up and down my back.

"Breathe," he said. He kept rubbing my back. "Just breathe."

I closed my eyes and imagined being back home. I pictured being on the lake with Miller. The sun shining on my face. It was like I could hear his laughter in my head. I hoped that never went away. I hoped I'd always be able to hear him.

Mason shot off a text. And I prayed that he wasn't telling Matt to come meet us here.

I pulled my knees into my chest and stared up at him. "I know I have to talk to him. I promised James and Rob…"

"James and Rob knew you were alive this whole time?"

"What? No." I shook my head. God, the last thing I needed was to cause a rift between the Hunters and Caldwells again. "My son ran into Scarlett on Monday at the zoo and…"

"You have a son?" He looked down at my hand. "You're married? How the fuck could you marry someone else?" He pulled his hand off my back.

"Mason…"

"Do you have any idea how much you've hurt him?"

I wiped the tears from beneath my eyes. "You don't understand."

"I think I understand completely. You were alive and you stayed away…"

"That's not the whole story."

He just stared at me.

So I told him. I told him all of it. And when I got to the part about Matt in the pool with James' sister I couldn't stop crying. Because I was talking to Mason. No one knew Matt better than he did. And he was staring at me like I was heartless.

IVY SMOAK

I heard Kennedy defend Matt. I heard James. I heard Penny and Rob. But seeing Mason's face? It was like I finally believed I'd gotten everything wrong.

But it didn't change anything. I couldn't change the past. And even if I could...I didn't want to. It had been a long time since I'd thought I was a monster. But I felt like one right now. I felt like a Pruitt.

"I'm going to tell him," I said. "I swear I am. I just need..."

"You've already robbed Matt of 16 years, Brooklyn. I'm not going to let you rob him of any more."

I clenched my jaw to make my bottom lip stop trembling.

"And you're out of time. If you don't talk to him now, you're going to miss your chance."

"Miss my chance at what?"

"The life the two of you always should have had."

I shook my head. "I don't want that life."

"Are you sure about that?"

I pressed my lips together.

"You better be damn sure. Because he's finally ready to move on. He's waited 16 years for you. And if you won't tell him to wait another day, I'm not going to tell him either. He deserves happiness too."

"You mean with Kennedy?"

Mason nodded.

"But that's what I want," I said. "I want them to be happy."

"I think we both know that isn't true. If you didn't have feelings for him, you'd already be up there telling him your story instead of telling it to me. You're avoiding him because you still love him."

I shook my head. That's what Miller had said in his letter. That a piece of me still loved Matt. I didn't want that to be true. I really, really didn't. But...what if it was? Why else would seeing Mason have affected me like this? Why was I panicking about seeing Matt? Why couldn't I make myself go up to his office right now?

"I think Kennedy really likes him," I said. "And I don't want to interfere."

"But what if you wait and don't interfere? What if they move forward and then you realize you do still love him? What then? Every second you wait this situation gets messier and messier. You have the power to fix everything."

I shook my head. "I don't. Even if I did still like Matt, which I'm not saying I do, that would devastate Kennedy. She's the only friend I..."

"Think twice before ending that sentence, sis."

I smiled at him. "You can't call me that anymore."

"I think I might still be able to."

I sighed. "I will always love my husband."

"If there's one thing I learned in the past few years...our hearts are bigger than we realize, Brooklyn."

I swallowed hard. *Not that big.* I'd had a great love. A once in a million kind of love. And it was enough for me. I'd carry that with me always.

Mason looked down at his phone. "I really hate to cut our time short, but I really do need to meet Matt for lunch. He seems to be having his own crisis that he needs my help with."

That didn't sound good. "Please don't tell him I'm back. I need to do it in person."

"I won't say a word, Brooklyn..."

"Thank you."

"You didn't let me finish," he said. "I'll keep your secret for the rest of the weekend. Matt's busy and he needs to focus. But if you haven't told him by Monday, then I'm going to."

I exhaled slowly. Today I'd talk to my dad. Tomorrow I had the football game. Which meant that Sunday I'd talk to Matt. I could do that. I had to do that. "Thank you, Mason."

"I'm really glad you're okay."

I wouldn't say I was okay. I was a mess. But I knew what he meant. He was glad that I was alive. I think I was still coming to terms with that myself. Because it wasn't me that should still be here. It was my husband.

CHAPTER 31

Friday

Matt

"Isn't it a little early to be drinking?" I said as I sat down to next to Mason at the bar.

"It's Friday afternoon."

Yeah...*afternoon.* I shrugged and grabbed the beer he'd gotten me. "Cheers," I said and tapped my glass against his.

He didn't respond. He just downed his whole glass and ordered another.

"Are you okay?"

"Yup," he said, but didn't look at me.

"Are you sure?"

"I'm great. Tell me about your emergency."

I didn't even know where to start. "I got dirt on Poppy like I wanted, and I still can't shake her. And Felix is back in town. I went to dinner with him and Kennedy last night. And he was hitting on her right in front of me. Can you believe that?"

Mason finally looked at me. "Well that's great news."

"What?"

"I mean, the two of them were into each other in high school, right? That makes everything a hell of a lot less messy."

"How does it make it less messy? I like her."

"Right." He cleared his throat. "Fuck."

"Exactly," I said.

He took another sip of his beer. "So…what else is up?"

"What do you mean what else is up? Poppy is still blackmailing me. And I'm pretty sure Kennedy has feelings for Felix."

"Man, what are the odds that Felix shows up again out of the blue too?"

"Too? What do you mean?"

"Nothing, it's just weird." Mason shook his head.

"I have Tanner to thank for that. For some crazy reason he thinks Kennedy and I aren't a good match. So he decided to set her up with Felix instead."

Mason shook his head. "Tanner must know too."

"Know what?"

"If you'll excuse me for one second," Mason said. "I need to take a piss."

"Okay…" Why was he acting so weird?

By the time he came back I was halfway through my second beer. "Is your stomach upset or something?"

"No. I was just making some phone calls."

I laughed.

"No, seriously," Mason said. "I wasn't taking a shit. I needed to talk to James. And Rob. And Tanner."

I shook my head. "Sure."

"This is all so fucked up."

"Is it a real mess in there? I kind of needed to go too."

"I'm not talking about the toilet," Mason said. And then he just stared at me.

"Seriously, what's wrong?"

He exhaled slowly. "I promised I wouldn't, but this is all crazy. And I'm not going to lie to you. I…"

"Hey, guys," Tanner said and sat down next to me. "What are the odds that I'd find you two here?"

"Because you just insisted I tell you where we were on the phone," Mason said.

Wait, Mason really had made a bunch of phone calls while he was taking a massive shit?

"Oh, right. I remember now. A word, Mason," Tanner said and stood back up.

"Tanner, I really think that Matt has the right to know…"

"No," Tanner said.

"But he…"

"Shut your whore mouth," Tanner said.

What the fuck? Why did he keep saying that to people?

"Matt," Mason said. "It's about…"

"Blah boink!" Tanner yelled at the top of his lungs.

"Tanner what are you doing?"

"Distracting you." He waved his hands in my face. "Is it working?"

"Yes?"

"Great." And then he grabbed Mason's arm and yanked him off his stool. "A word in private, Mason."

Mason sighed. "Okay fine." They started walking toward the bathroom.

A few seconds later Nigel sprinted into the bar and ran straight past me toward the restrooms.

"Nigel?" I called.

And for the first time ever, he ignored me. I'll be honest, I was a little hurt.

Eventually all three of them remerged. They'd been in there a solid ten minutes. And I didn't know whether to be worried or annoyed.

IVY SMOAK

"Seriously you guys, what is going on?" I asked.

"Food poisoning," Nigel said and slid onto the stool next to mine. "Do they have meat sandwiches here? I'm starving."

"But isn't your stomach upset?"

"Oh." He frowned and pushed the menu aside. "Yeah, I guess."

"Okay, I'm not an idiot," I said. "I know you're lying."

Tanner shook his head. "No, it's like Nigel said. We're all three quite ill. Right, Mason?"

"Yup." Mason scratched the back of his neck. Which was a sure tell that he was lying.

But I had no idea why all three of them were lying to me. Maybe I was wrong. They had been in the bathroom a long time. "Do you guys need to head home?"

"That's probably a good idea to leave you alone," Tanner said. "So no one says anything. Because of the germs involved in that. Nigel, will you pull the car around?"

"Should he be driving if he's that sick?" I asked.

"Right," Tanner said. "I'll call an Uber. Rest on your laurels, Nigel."

"I love resting on my laurels," Nigel said.

Okay. "Do you guys think you'll make it to the game tomorrow?"

"Yes," Nigel said. "I'm the water boy. I'm very important."

"We'll all be there," Tanner said. "It's going to be the best night of your young life, Matthew."

"I mean...if we win it'll be pretty great." But I didn't know about the best night of my life.

"Sure the game is important. But there's only one true way to win at life. And this is going to be epic. Right, Mason?" He turned to Mason.

"I have no idea how this is going to play out. But I wouldn't miss this for the world," Mason said.

"Thanks man," I said. It was so great that all of them would be there for the game. It meant a lot to me.

Nigel sighed.

We all turned to him.

He looked up at me. "I really like Kennedy."

What did that have to do with the game?

"Hush, child," Tanner said and put his finger against Nigel's lips. "You don't mean that."

"Yes I do," Nigel said. "I think she's very nice. She let me sit with her and the other boys at dinner last night."

That was a really weird way to put that.

"Nigel, you little traitor," Tanner said. "You go get in the Uber."

"No." Nigel folded his arms in front of his chest.

"Right now, houseboy," Tanner said and pointed to the door.

Nigel sighed again.

"If you don't go right now, I'll call your contractor and tell him you don't need him for your project."

Nigel's eyes grew round. "Okay, I'll go. I need my contractor."

"What are you building?" I asked.

"It's more of a renovation," Nigel said. "I told you about it yesterday. You said we were friends and that I should go forward with the project."

I did remember him saying something weird like that. But I still had no idea what he was talking about.

"I'll see you for the big game," Nigel said. "Hut, hut," he slapped my butt and ran off before I could yell at him.

"What the hell was that?" Mason asked.

Tanner shook his head. "He's been out of control recently. Matt's been a bad influence on him."

"You think I'm making him act like that?"

"He never acted like that before you moved in. I don't know what the two of you have been up to, but he barely works at all anymore."

"That is definitely not my fault," I said.

Tanner shrugged. "It's fine. It's nice for him to have another friend. Mason, we should be going. We don't want the Uber to be expensive for you.. Then he turned to me. "See you at home," he said and started walking toward the exit.

"See you tomorrow," Mason said. "Should be an exciting day." He slapped me on the back and hurried to catch up to Tanner. I could hear them arguing on the way out.

"Why am I paying for the Uber?" Mason asked. "You ordered it."

"Why would I pay? You made me rush all the way down here because you have a big mouth."

"Well maybe you should have fucking told me all this when you found out."

"I've been a little busy trying to fix everything," Tanner said.

And then the door closed behind them.

Okay, they definitely weren't sick. But they were up to no good. All three of them.

CHAPTER 32

Friday

Brooklyn

This felt like a bad idea. But Jacob was so persistent, and I didn't want to say no to him. If he really wanted to meet his grandfather, I'd let him.

But just this once.

We stopped outside my father's apartment door. I looked down at Jacob.

He squeezed my hand.

I didn't need him to reassure me right now. I wasn't nervous about this because of me. I was worried about him.

I crouched down to look at him. "Remember how I told you that I didn't want you to meet my father? Because he's not a good man?"

Jacob nodded.

"Well, I'm pretty sure he's going to act really nice while we visit. But you can't believe it. It's just a show."

"Like on the TV?"

"Exactly like that. You can't ever trust him, okay? You have to believe me."

"Sí."

"So why do you want to see him so badly?"

He shrugged.

Why did he always do that when I asked him about this? Why was this so important to him? I pressed my lips together. I remembered when I desperately wanted to know who my father was. Maybe it was like that. He'd lost a family member and was just looking for someone to hold on to. Anyone. I wished my father could be that person for him. But…he definitely wasn't. I'd already made that same mistake with him. And I'd never give my father the satisfaction of hurting my son like he'd hurt me.

"I'm here to tell him that I'm no longer going to see him. Do you understand that?"

"Sí."

Jacob was so calm about this. I thought maybe he didn't understand how bad my father was. How this really was a goodbye forever. What if he liked my dad and begged to keep seeing him? He'd been begging me for days to get to meet him.

"And you're okay with what I said? That this will be the only time you get to see him?"

"Yessie, Mommy."

"Okay." I stood back up and knocked.

The door opened immediately. But it wasn't my father who answered.

Donnelley was standing there. One of the bodyguards that had worked for my father when I'd lived here. The one that Isabella had threatened. Recognition flashed across his face too. And so did a huge smile.

"Brooklyn?"

I smiled too and nodded.

He pulled me into a huge bear hug. "I cried for days when I thought…" his voice trailed off. "Mr. Pruitt told me you were back this morning. But I didn't…I can't even believe it. For years I thought…" his voice trailed off. "I can't believe you're really here. It's just so good to see you."

I pulled back and smiled up at him. "It's good to see you too."

He shook his head. "Are you really here to take over the family business?"

I looked down at Jacob. "No. We're here to say goodbye."

"Goodbye? But you just got back." Donnelley looked down at my son. "Hey, little man. You look just like your father."

Jacob just stared at him. For a second I thought his stranger danger was back. But then he said, "You knew my daddy?"

"Yeah. We were friends."

"I'm Jacob." Jacob put out his hand for Donnelley to shake.

His hand completely disappeared into Donnelley's massive hand as they shook.

"We can be friends too then," Jacob said.

"I'd like that, kid," Donnelley said.

I blinked away the tears in my eyes. The word *kid* felt like a knife in my chest.

"Do you know my abuelo?" Jacob asked.

Donnelley smiled. "I sure do."

"I need to see him," Jacob said. "It's very important."

"Let me go get him. Make yourself at home," Donnelley said before walking off.

Make yourself at home? I shook my head. This apartment wasn't a home. But Jacob wandered off into the dining room. He looked up at the huge portrait on the wall. I was pretty sure it had gotten damaged during the Thanksgiving incident. But it had been restored. And somehow the restoration made all of their eyes look even creepier as they glared down at the dining room table. I stared at Isabella. The artist really had captured her cruel eyes perfectly. I looked up at Mrs. Pruitt's stern face. I wondered if she still looked the same. She'd certainly had enough Botox to freeze her face in time.

Jacob was staring at them. He didn't really know that people here had thought I was dead. He didn't know that Miller and I were in hiding. He didn't know about Isabella. Or Mrs. Pruitt. I'd tried my best to shelter him. But I felt like he should know all of this. He should know why he wasn't allowed to see his grandfather. Why he couldn't be part of this family.

"Why aren't you in the picture, Mommy?"

I ruffled his hair. "Because you and Daddy are my only family."

"That's true," a woman said from behind us.

I spun around to see Mrs. Pruitt standing there. And I was right. She looked *almost* the same. But her face looked even faker than it had before. Almost…swollen and plasticky looking. And her lips were definitely larger. Like she'd overdone it on the lip injections.

I stepped in front of Jacob. "Where is my father?"

"Busy," she said. And then she stared down at my son.

I pushed Jacob farther behind me. I'd been so happy to see Donnelley that I'd completely forgotten that there may be more surprise appearances. My father said his wife was residing in the Hamptons. But here she was. Was she back for good? I kind of thought my father had implied that they'd decided to live separately.

Mrs. Pruitt turned her gaze back to me. "You ruined his life, you know."

For a second I thought maybe she was talking about Miller. Because there was a piece of me that thought that. If I'd just kept my hands to myself…Miller would still be alive. But I couldn't make myself regret it. I couldn't.

"Although I guess it really started with your mother."

I swallowed hard. She wasn't talking about Miller. She was talking about my father. How had *I* ruined *his* life? How had my mother? We'd stayed away from him until he literally dragged me back. None of this was on me or my mom.

"That slut ruined everything. You followed her destructive path. And now my daughter is dead."

How was Isabella's death my fault? "Don't you dare talk about my mother that way."

"Do you prefer the word whore? Prostitute?"

I turned around to cover Jacob's ears. "Stop it."

"You're in my house. I'll call your whore of a mother whatever I want!"

"Enough," my father said as he walked into the dining room. "Patricia, our meeting is over. You may go."

I hated that I was relieved to see him. But I was. The only person that scared me more than him was his wife.

"That wasn't a meeting! You've lost your damned mind. She can't take over, Richard. She's not a Cannavaro. She's not blood."

"She's my blood," my father said calmly.

"My grandfather will roll in his grave. This is Isabella's legacy. You'll tarnish the family's good name…"

IVY SMOAK

"I will not ask you nicely again," my father said. "You can either leave right now, or I'll have you escorted out."

"Just because you don't want me here doesn't mean this isn't my home," Mrs. Pruitt said.

"Now, Patricia."

"Next you'll tell me you're going to give the little half-breed the Pruitt name."

I pressed down on Jacob's ears a little harder. She didn't mean...she couldn't possibly be talking about my son? Half-breed? With what? The help?

"Get out!" Mr. Pruitt said.

"You'll pay for this," she spat.

He grabbed her wrist before she could storm off. "Don't waste my time with idle threats."

She pulled her wrist out of his grasp. And with one last hard glare at me, she strutted off, her high-heels echoing. I closed my eyes at the noise. It sounded just like Isabella. When she'd walked down the hallways of Empire High.

I jumped when my father put his hand on my shoulder.

"I'm sorry," my father said. "She was out of line. I didn't realize you were coming or she wouldn't have been here."

I shook my head as my hands dropped from Jacob's ears. "This was a mistake. Come on, Jacob, we need to go."

But Jacob didn't move. He was staring intently at my father. So intently that his eyes were almost in slits.

"Jacob," I said and put my hand down for him to hold, but he didn't take it. He just kept staring.

"Please don't go," my father said. "Patricia was out of line. Your mother wasn't...she..." his voice trailed off. "Your mother was the best thing that ever happened to me. She gave me you."

Right, and I gave you a free kidney. He was really full of it. But it was the things he said like this that made me falter. Because when he spoke of my mother, I could hear the love in his voice. But love wasn't enough.

"And you can ignore anything Patricia says. The company is yours. It was always meant to be yours."

I shook my head. "I came here to tell you that I'm staying in New York. Because Jacob wants to stay." I looked down at my son who was still just staring at my father. "But staying doesn't mean you're going to be in our lives. There's nothing you can do that will make me believe you didn't have a hand in what happened with Miller. I don't want you or Poppy or anyone you're associated with anywhere near my son. Or me. And I want no part of your business."

"But, Angel, you were made for this. You're my daughter..."

"I'm not. And I'm not your angel. Or your princess. I'm Brooklyn Miller." My voice cracked on Miller's name. "As long as you're associated with the mob, I want nothing to do with you."

For once my father was silent.

"It's time to go, Jacob." I wasn't sure what he'd wanted to see my father for. But I hoped it was just to see him. Because Jacob hadn't said a word. I put my hand out for him, but again, he still didn't take.

"What happened to your face?" Jacob finally said as he stared at my father.

Mr. Pruitt touched his nose. His eyes were a little less black and blue today. "Your mother hit me. She has a great right hook."

Jacob looked up at me and smiled. "Daddy told you too?"

Told me what? Before I could ask, Jacob punched my father. Right in the nuts. Really freaking hard.

"Jacob!" I yelled.

My dad buckled over and groaned.

"Jacob, why did you hit him?!"

"Daddy told me to. He said if anything happened that I should punch your daddy."

Oh my God.

My father had fallen to his knees and his face was scrunched up in pain.

"That was for Daddy," Jacob said. "You're a bad abuelo!"

I couldn't have said it better myself.

My father didn't say a word. And I wasn't worried about leaving him. Because he had at least one great kidney to hold him together. I scooped up Jacob into my arms and ran out of the room, through the foyer, and out the door.

"You shouldn't hit people," I said, even though I was silently high-fiving him.

"You shouldn't hit people," he said back to me.

Touché.

"But...Daddy said it's okay to hit *bad* people," Jacob said.

"Your father was right about that."

"I know," Jacob said. And then he smiled up at me. "I did good?"

"You did great." I kissed the top of his head as we hurried down the stairs. I doubted my father was running after us. But I still wanted out of this building.

"What's a slut?" Jacob asked.

Oh no. "It's a bad word. Something mean that you should never repeat."

"What about whore?"

I'd covered his ears, how had he heard that? "Don't ever say that either."

"Prostitute?"

I walked through the lobby and out the front doors, hoping no one heard my son say that. "Sweet boy, promise me you'll never say those words again."

"Sí. If we go to the zoo."

"Are you bartering with me?"

"Abuelo Tanner says bartering is the key to succession."

"You mean success?"

Jacob shrugged.

I couldn't help but laugh. My son had just hit my father in the nuts. And it was actually kind of hilarious now that we were far away from him. A last parting gift from Miller. Jacob had done everything Miller had told him to. And that deserved a special treat. "Okay, let's go to the zoo."

"Huzzah!"

I was pretty sure Rob had yelled that the other night when he made a family-room-soccer goal. Jacob was picking up everything.

CHAPTER 33

Saturday

Matt

"Where are you going?" I asked as Tanner walked through the dining room whistling. "The game is today, aren't you coming with us?"

"I'll be taking a second carriage today."

"Carriage?"

"It's a common term for a vehicle, old chap."

I just stared at him.

Tanner laughed. "I'm joking. What kind of weirdo would call a car a carriage?"

"Not Master Tanner," Nigel said. "Because he's a modern day boy."

Right.

And then they both started whistling.

"Seriously you guys, what's going on?"

"Nothing," they both said at the same time and then looked at each other.

"Then why aren't you riding with me and Kennedy to the game?" I asked.

"Because I don't wish to see Kennedy right now," Tanner said. "I talked to Felix last night and the two of them still haven't had sex and I'm very upset with her."

"She hasn't had sex with him because she's dating me."

"*Was* dating. Past tense. I should be off. Nigel, keep an eye on things for me, yes?"

"I have eyes on the target," Nigel said and stared right at me.

"What the hell am I the target for?" I asked.

"Nothing," they both said at the same time.

"Oh." Tanner turned back around. "I have a better answer to your previous question. I'm taking a second car because you and your water boy will have to stay late to clean up and I have things I must do later."

"You can't just change your answer. You were already rude about Kennedy. *Again*."

Nigel nodded. "You were rude to Kennedy. And that wasn't nice."

Tanner stared back at Nigel. "Are you seriously doubting me on this right now? We're already pretty deep into this."

Nigel shrugged.

"Let's just see how it plays out, shall we? It's already all arranged."

"Very well," Nigel said. "Let's proceed as planned."

They'd had an entire very weird conversation right in front of me and I still had no idea what was happening. "Seriously, what the fuck are you two up to?"

"Nothing," they both said at the same time again. Even though they'd literally just talked about a plan right in front of me like I was invisible.

"Is this about the room with the red yarn connecting pictures?"

"That is not a room that exists," Tanner said. "On another note, Nigel please check all the locks on the doors before departing for the homecoming game."

"Yes, Master," Nigel said and pulled out a huge keyring from his lederhosen. It had to have at least 50 keys on it. Where the hell did all those keys lead?

"I'll see you both there," Tanner said. And with that, he was gone. And so was Nigel with his ginormous keychain.

***

Kennedy was quiet on the way to the game. And she kept texting someone on her phone.

Each time she did it, I gripped the steering wheel a little tighter. I had a feeling I knew who she was talking to. *Fucking Felix.*

I looked in my rearview mirror at the back seat. Mrs. Alcaraz was awfully quiet too. But she seemed a little scared of Nigel back there. And I couldn't blame her. It wasn't every day someone wore bright orange lederhosen with nothing underneath and a blue hat. He insisted he wanted to dress in Empire High's colors. But he refused to wear the t-shirt I'd given him. Apparently the tag bothered him. Which was odd. Because I would have thought painted leather wouldn't feel comfortable either.

Kennedy checked her phone for the twentieth time.

I cleared my throat. "What's up?" I asked her.

"Hmm?" She immediately flipped her phone over.

"Have you heard from Felix again? I sent over the ticket for him."

"No, I haven't heard from him," she said.

She was either lying right to my face or she was texting someone else. But she looked so guilty. My stomach churned. I shouldn't have sat outside for so long at the restaurant. I'd basically let this happen. And now I regretted it. I wasn't going to step aside without a fight.

"Oh," I said, trying to sound as nonchalant as possible. "I know you guys are friends. And he's only in town for a bit."

"Right," Kennedy said. "Which is why he's coming to the game today. Eyes on the road, buddy."

I hadn't realized I was just staring at her. And I'd almost missed the turn into the school.

I didn't mention Felix again as we climbed out of the car. I went to grab the equipment bag, but Nigel was already carrying it. I swear it was almost as big as him, but he didn't seem phased at all.

"Can we talk for a second?" I whispered to Kennedy.

"Yeah, what's up?"

"In private."

She pressed her lips together. I thought she was going to say no. But she turned to her mom. "We'll catch up with you in a minute, Mama."

I watched as Mrs. Alcaraz kept her distance from Nigel on the way to the stadium.

Kennedy tucked a loose strand of hair behind her ear. "We don't want to be late," she said.

She was doing that thing again. Pulling away from me. So instead I stepped behind the car and pulled her to me.

"You look beautiful today," I said.

She laughed. "So you decided to hide me behind a car?"

"No, I pulled you back here to do this." I leaned down to kiss her, but her phone buzzed in her pocket.

She grabbed it and read the text instead of kissing me. And then she sighed.

"Everything alright?" I tried to ask as calmly as possible. Seriously, who the fuck was she texting? It had to be Felix. It just had to be.

"Yeah, I just…I'm waiting to hear from someone. But they're not texting me back."

"Is everything okay?"

"Mhm," she said. But I could tell that it wasn't. "We should really get into the stadium. The boys are counting on you, Coach."

"And you."

She smiled up at me. "I am a pretty kickass assistant coach, aren't I?"

"The best in the business. I actually have something for you."

"We're going to be late," she said.

I opened the trunk and pulled out an Empire High jersey with my old number on it. "I thought you might want to wear it."

She didn't take it. She just stared at the fabric. "You want me to wear your number?"

I thought she'd be excited. But by the look on her face, I'd played this all wrong. "Sorry, it was dumb. We're not in high school anymore. I think I was feeling weirdly nostalgic about homecoming…" my voice trailed off. I could hear Tanner's voice in the back of my head: *Can you really imagine marrying her when your heart still belongs to someone else?"*

I looked over at the school. Homecoming reminded me of Brooklyn, not Kennedy. What the hell was I doing? This was a really fucking dumb idea. I didn't know what I'd been thinking. And clearly she was thinking the same thing. That this was crossing some kind of line. My heart started racing. Would I always be tiptoeing around my past? Would I ever be able to make this feel right to Kennedy? Because it all felt right to me.

I cleared my throat. "Forget it. I really like the shirt you already have on." She was wearing a long-sleeved t-shirt that looked like it was from her days at Empire High. It was way more her. And I liked her exactly the way she was. I went to toss the jersey back in the trunk, but she grabbed my arm.

"No, I want it."

"Yeah?"

"Yeah, I was just surprised."

"Why would it surprise you that I wanted you to wear my number?"

"Because it's…" her voice trailed off. "It seems very official."

"Not as official as proposing to you…which I would have already done if you hadn't told me not to yet."

"I know, I just…" she pressed her lips together instead of saying anything else.

"Kennedy, seriously, what's going on?"

"I want it. I really want it."

"Okay." I handed her the jersey and she pulled it on. She couldn't even try to hide her smile now. She looked back up at me. "I need to tell you something. After the game."

"Or you could just tell me now."

She shook her head. "After."

"Or now."

She laughed. "I know I've been acting weird this past week. And I…I need to tell you something. Because I really like you. But I'm not supposed to tell you.

I've been put in an impossible situation and I keep waiting. And I…I just need to tell you. After the game."

"Seriously? Just tell me now."

"After."

"You're going to be the death of me," I said and put my arm around her shoulders.

She melted into my side. It didn't matter what she told me. As long as it wasn't about her being in love with Felix, we'd be good.

But I had a nagging feeling that Felix wasn't the only thing from our past that could ruin us. I knew better than anyone that young love didn't just fade away. I looked up into the stands like I always did when I entered the stadium. Like I was searching for Brooklyn in the crowd. A reflex that I needed to stop if I ever wanted to move forward. Thinking about her would do nothing but get me in trouble.

CHAPTER 34

Saturday

Brooklyn

I rummaged through a few boxes, trying to find something to wear to the Empire High homecoming football game. Tanner had done what I'd asked and left most of my things at the lake house, so there weren't many options. But I hoped I'd find something that worked.

I smiled when I found my old beat up Keds. It had been forever since I'd worn them. Over the years they'd gotten more and more run down. There was practically a hole in both soles. But I was feeling sentimental today. And they didn't just remind me of my mom now. They reminded me of my uncle too, when he'd fixed them for me. It felt like putting on armor as I laced them up.

For a second I just sat there staring at the shoes.

They didn't just remind me of my mom and uncle.

They reminded me of Matt. He'd told me he liked them. Even when I'd worn them with a dress.

I was about to unlace them, but then I froze. Because they also reminded me of Miller. My feet sinking in the snow as I walked up to him on Christmas morning at the lake house. After finally finding my way back to him.

And not just that…but he'd gone out of his way to find my Keds after Isabella had made me strip in the middle of nowhere to try to get rid of me. The night of homecoming 16 years ago.

The good was mixed with the bad.

I'd had a lot of memories in these shoes.

And I felt different wearing them. Stronger somehow. And I needed that today.

But I didn't come in here for shoes. I needed one of my old Empire High t-shirts. I doubted anyone I knew would be going to the homecoming game today. If I'd graduated there it would be….what? My 14th reunion? A nice non-round number that no one would bother celebrating. And based on the things James and Mason had told me, it didn't seem like any of them felt a pull to the school. They'd wanted to leave it all behind them. Just like I did.

Some people said that high school was the best years of their lives. I wasn't one of those people. Isabella had made sure of it.

I opened another box and stopped when I felt the leather sleeve. I slowly picked up Matt's old varsity jacket. I stared at the big E on the front. I was pretty sure I'd lived in this thing for weeks when Matt and I were dating.

I couldn't believe I still had it. And I don't know why, but I just kept staring at it. And staring. Until I eventually lifted the jacket to my nose and took a deep breath, wondering if I could still smell him. Or rather, smell that fall.

But it just smelled like the cardboard box it had been sitting in for the past 16 years. I sighed and put the varsity jacket back in the box. I didn't even remember what he smelled like anyway. And I wasn't sure why I was even thinking about what he smelled like. I wasn't going to get close enough to smell him tomorrow when

I talked to him. I was just going to…tell him what happened.

I kept staring at the jacket.

And maybe apologize. Because if what James and Mason had told me was true…Matt hadn't forgotten about me at all.

No. He'd forgotten me. I'd seen him. He hadn't looked broken to me. He looked…happy. He looked joyful. Living his life completely content without me.

And he was happy now with Kennedy. And I was happy for them. I wasn't going to mess up anyone's life any more than I already had.

I'd found a new home here. I couldn't explain it, but this house just felt right. Jacob loved the little yard. We'd been dancing when we cooked every day. We were going to be okay.

I closed the lid of the box just as another text came in.

I looked down at the message from Kennedy. She'd asked me to call her as soon as I talked to Matt yesterday. But I'd chickened out. And now I didn't know what to say.

She texted again: "I can't keep doing this. I can't eat. Or sleep. I feel physically sick. I have to tell him."

I knew that feeling. I'd cooked lots with Jacob and danced around the kitchen. But I barely touched my food. And I couldn't sleep at all unless I climbed into his small bed at night. Kennedy was sick to her stomach over someone that was alive. I was sick with grief. I loved her. But our pain wasn't the same. And maybe it was selfish, or maybe I was just a shitty friend…because I had a really hard time feeling bad about this. If I made her wait one more day for her happily ever after with Matt, she'd still get a whole lifetime of it.

I'd only ever have those 15 years with Miller. That's all I'd ever get. My happily ever after had been cut short. So Kennedy could wait another day for me to find the courage to face my past. And today was a big step. I was going back to Empire High. I'd be facing some of my old demons head on. If anything could give me the strength to confront Matt, it was this. I'd get through today. And then I'd get through tomorrow. And Jacob and I could keep going. Together.

"I'll tell him," I texted back.

"When? Please, Brooklyn."

I put my phone down. I'd do it tomorrow. And I'd text her right after. After all, I didn't have a choice now. Mason had given me an ultimatum. I needed to talk to Matt before the weekend was over.

But today? I was going to wear a plain blue shirt without the Empire High logo and have fun with my son. "Jacob!" I called. "Are you ready to go?"

He ran into the room. "Sí."

I smiled at him. We were both wearing jeans and blue shirts. I always thought he looked like a mini-Miller. But today I saw myself in him. Minus the hat. He was still wearing Tanner's hat. And it was officially the cutest thing ever.

"And you're going to keep your clothes on during the game?" I asked.

"Sí," he said and tipped his hat at me, like he'd seen Tanner do the other day.

I laughed and booped him on the nose. "Are you excited for the game?"

"Yessie, Mommy! Can we go now? It's football day!"

"Tanner should be here any minute. Race you to the door?"

He took off running before I even finished my sentence. That little cheater. He squealed when I lifted him up before he could reach the door. I turned backwards and held him out in front of me so I'd reach the door first.

"Nooooooo," Jacob said.

He was a cheater and he used his adorableness against me. I turned at the last second so that he could tag the door.

He smiled up at me. "I win. Now I get to go to the zoo tomorrow."

"Jacob, we just went to the zoo yesterday." I set him down.

"Then we can play with Scarlett?"

I'd get through today. I'd get through tomorrow. And then I'd start the rest of my life here. It probably would have been easier to just avoid all the untouchables. But…I didn't really want to do that. James, Rob, and Mason had been nothing but wonderful. And Jacob was allowed to be friends with whoever he wanted. Right now Scarlett was his only friend. Well, maybe Tanner too. Jacob had definitely taken a liking to him.

"I'll give her mom a call and see when they're free again, okay?"

Jacob nodded. "Abuelo's here!"

Oh, God, what? I looked out the narrow window by the front door. But it wasn't my father walking up to the house. It was just Tanner. Was Jacob referring to Tanner as just *Abuelo* now that he'd met his real grandfather and disapproved of him?

Jacob opened the door.

"Hey, little man," said Tanner. "Nice hat."

Jacob tipped the hat at him and Tanner's smile grew.

"I see you don't have any old shirts lying around either," I said.

"What?" Tanner asked.

"From Empire High."

"Oh." He looked down at the button down he was wearing. "Yeah. Even if I did none of them would have lasted that long anyway."

What the hell was he doing to his shirts? Washing them constantly on hot instead of cold or something? Or maybe he just dry cleaned everything. Even t-shirts. For some reason I couldn't imagine Tanner doing laundry.

"Ready for the best day of your life?" Tanner asked.

The best day of Jacob's life? I knew Jacob was excited about seeing a live game, but that was stretching it a little. But when I looked up, Tanner was staring at me instead of at Jacob.

"Best day ever!" Jacob yelled.

"Yup," Tanner said and winked at me.

It wasn't the first time that I'd suddenly felt like I'd walked into a date with Tanner without realizing it.

"Are you sure you don't need a jacket?" Tanner asked me.

"Yeah, I'm good." The leaves had started to change and the night air was crisp. But there wasn't a cloud in the sky.

"You sure? Maybe an old Empire High one or something? There were a lot of things in those old boxes."

I laughed. "I'm sure." I was a little relieved that this didn't feel like a date anymore. Wouldn't he want me to be cold so he could put his arm around me or something if it were?

"I thought I saw an Empire High jacket though?"

Oh. He'd just stumbled upon it in the boxes. "Yeah, that isn't even mine."

"No? Whose is it?"

I felt Jacob staring up at me too. "Just an old friend's," I said.

"An old friend's? Interesting."

"Yeah." I looked down at my Keds as words from Miller's letter starting swirling around in my head. *"I know there was someone before me. I know you still think about him sometimes."* I shook the thought away. "I had all my old stuff in storage. I never went through it. I really need to get rid of some things."

"I don't know," Tanner said. "Sometimes holding on to sentimental items makes you feel closer to the ones you've lost."

I nodded. He probably thought it was Miller's jacket. But it wasn't. And I wasn't sure why we were even talking about a stupid old jacket. The fact that I'd kept it didn't mean anything. I really had just never gone through the old boxes.

"Come on, we don't want to be late." He put his hand out. But it wasn't for me. It was for my son. Jacob jumped along beside Tanner as they walked over to a futuristic looking car.

The car doors rose up instead of out when he hit a button.

"Cool!" Jacob yelled as he climbed into the back seat.

"Only the best for my best friend's friend," Tanner said.

I laughed. "Do you drive Kennedy around in this thing too?"

"Who?" Tanner asked.

"Kennedy. Your best friend."

"Right. No. No I do not."

I just stared at him.

"Sorry," he quickly added. "Kennedy and I are feuding at the moment, so it's difficult for me to think of her as my best friend."

"Yeah? Why?"

"She's been making terrible decisions recently. I have her best interests in mind, but she's being stubborn."

I laughed. "That sounds like Kennedy."

"I'll be honest," he said. "I'm used to getting my way. It's not very often that I'm told no."

I was getting that vibe from him. Hell, he was practically a stranger to me and I'd gone on a road trip with him. And I'd let him give me a home to live in. I'd tried to tell him no to all of it...but he'd gotten his way. *Huh.* I'd thought I was a little stubborn too, but Tanner was very convincing. And kind. I'd never met anyone more generous.

"After you m'lady," Tanner said.

I laughed and climbed into the car. My father was wealthy. And I'd been surrounded by wealthy teenagers at Empire High. But I still don't think I'd ever sat in such an expensive car.

Tanner sped off.

"Are you a little nervous to be going back to our old school?" I asked.

"Empire High?"

What other school would I be talking about? "Yeah."

"Nope. It's going to be an amazing day. Just you wait for it."

"Right. The best day of Jacob's life?"

"No," Tanner said. "The best day of *your* life."

I was so confused. This wasn't a date. I'd made that perfectly clear to him the other night. So…what was happening today? And why was he so confident about it? "You're a super positive person, aren't you?"

Tanner laughed. "Yes. Like I said…I'm used to getting my way."

"And what exactly are you trying to accomplish today?"

"It's a surprise."

Okay. "Were you popular in high school?"

"A lot of the times yes. A few times not so much. One time not at all. That was a mess. Fashion changes quite a bit, especially in different parts of the world, but I've really gotten the hang of it now."

Did he get new friends every week or something? And in new countries? "You do dress really well." He did. He looked like someone who'd graduated from Empire High. Instead of wearing a t-shirt he was wearing a button-down shirt with the sleeves rolled up. And his expensive watch glinted in the sun shining through the windshield.

He flashed me a smile. "Are you hitting on me, Brooklyn?"

"What? No. I…"

"I'm just messing with you. We're going to be good friends, you and me."

I believed him. Because I already felt like we were.

I looked out the window. It was weird being back in the city. How it felt like home and so foreign at the same time. Speaking of homes…I turned back to Tanner. "What's in that room upstairs?"

"Which room? The master bedroom?"

"No, the one with the locked door."

"Locked door? Oh! Oh. That's just stuff that the guy who flipped the house left behind."

"So like…paint and stuff?"

"Exactly! Paint and stuff. You nailed it."

Okay.

He pulled into the small parking lot outside Empire High. Even though we weren't early, there was still an empty spot. I couldn't believe our luck. I'd figured we'd have to do street parking and walk two miles.

I stared at the school through the windshield. It looked almost exactly the same. Preserved in its tradition of old wealth. I remembered standing on those front steps, staring at a boy who I wished would love me back. I remembered kissing him there too. I remembered promising him forever.

I shook the thought away as I opened the door.

Jacob looked so excited, it was easy to focus on him instead of the school. I picked him up into my arms. Everything was easier when I was holding him close.

"Look, Mommy!" He pointed to the very top row of bleachers.

"It's big, huh?"

"Sí. Do they have cuppycakes?"

I laughed. He'd just eaten breakfast. A normal one, thank goodness. But he was used to being my little taste tester back at home. Which meant sampling goodies pretty much every day. "They might," I said. "We can check out the concession stand." I turned to go toward it, but Tanner stepped in front of me.

"We should probably find a seat first," he said.

"I'm sure we'll be able to find something. It'll only take a minute." I tried to sidestep him, but he got in my way again.

I laughed. "I'll go left, you go right." But we both went in the same direction. "Your left, not mine," I said and finally stepped past him and almost ran straight into someone.

Oh my God.

It felt like my heart had jumped into my throat.

I wanted to cry. I wanted to laugh. I just wanted to hug him. I hadn't forgotten about him either.

He'd promised to wait a lifetime for me. And a piece of me believed him. Even though I'd told him not to wait.

It felt like I was back in time. Sitting in the bleachers laughing about jogging during gym class. Mostly him making me laugh.

He'd always made me smile. And I was always so grateful that he could.

"Felix?"

CHAPTER 35

Saturday

Brooklyn

Felix looked almost exactly the same. Except he wasn't smiling at me. He used to always smile at me. He just looked shaken. And I got it. I wasn't supposed to be standing here.

"Felix?" I said again.

His eyes searched mine, but he still didn't say a word.

"It's me. Brooklyn."

He reached out and touched the side of my face. "Newb?"

I smiled and nodded. I'd forgotten how much I loved when he called me that.

I heard Tanner curse under his breath.

"Newb," Felix said again as he just stared at me, his hand still pressed against my cheek. And then he looked at my son.

"Hola, I'm Jacob," Jacob said and put out his hand for Felix to shake.

Felix looked like he was in a daze as he shook my son's hand. "And...this is your mom?" he asked my son.

"Yessie, this is Mommy."

He dropped my son's hand and then rubbed his forehead. "But..." his voice trailed off. "You're...you..." he shook his head again. "Brooklyn."

He finally smiled. "I can't believe you're okay. I'm so happy you're okay." And then he hugged me. Even though I was still holding Jacob. He hugged both of us. Like he could tell how badly we needed it.

And it was weird. Because I couldn't remember what Matt smelled like. I closed my eyes. But I remembered Felix. He smelled like grass and sunshine. He smelled like a summer's day. He smelled like happiness.

Jacob wiggled out of my arms. Apparently he did not appreciate the familiar hug as much as I did. Out of the corner of my eye, I saw him grab Tanner's hand. He was staring up at Felix.

And I realized I'd been hugging him a beat too long. I stepped back. "I know I have a lot of explaining to do. We were just about to hit the concession stand and then maybe we can all grab a seat together?"

"That's probably not possible," Tanner said. "The stands are pretty crowded. It's better if we split up. Right, Felix? Good chap." He slapped him on the back.

"Hey, Tanner," Felix said. Then he looked back and forth between us. "Wait, are you two friends?"

"Ummm…" Tanner started.

"Are you two?" I asked.

"He sells me art," Tanner said. "And he really should be going. There's probably a seat for one up there somewhere for you, Felix."

"Tanner, don't be ridiculous. Felix is an old friend. And I…I really need to catch him up."

Felix's eyes had wandered down to my hand. Or more specifically, he was staring at the wedding band on my ring finger.

"Maybe another day would be better though?" Tanner asked. "We're a little busy."

"Wait, are you two…?" Felix looked back and forth between Tanner and me.

"No," Tanner and I both said at the same time.

Although I understood why he thought so. Tanner was being weirdly possessive. And Jacob was holding his hand.

I cleared my throat. "Just um…we'll be right back," I said. "Jacob wanted a cupcake." I needed a second away from Felix. I needed just a second alone to take a deep breath. I didn't know why I hadn't expected to see anyone here. Of course I'd see a familiar face at homecoming. It was called homecoming for a reason. And yet…I really hadn't expected to see Felix. He hadn't exactly been high on school pride when we went here. But he'd been here for two years without me…

"I'm okay, Mommy," said Jacob. He looked up at Felix. "Who are you?"

"He's an art dealer, and we really should be going," Tanner said.

Why was Tanner trying to get rid of Felix? Maybe Tanner had hated the art Felix sold him or something? And by art I really hoped they meant art. And not drugs. But Felix didn't look like a drug dealer. He looked successful. Composed. Happy, even if a little shocked right now.

Felix cleared his throat. "Yes, I do that. But I'm also an old friend of Brooklyn's. Of your mom's," Felix quickly corrected.

"Like my abuelo?"

"Who?"

"My abuelo." Jacob looked up at Tanner.

Tanner laughed.

"Wait, Tanner is your grandfather? How is that even possible?" Felix said.

Yeah, that definitely wasn't possible, because I was pretty sure Tanner was about the same age as us. Maybe even a little younger.

"It's a nickname because we're bros," Tanner said.

"Abuelo," Jacob said. "It's football time!"

"Yeah it is," Tanner said and picked him up. "Let's go find a seat for the three of us." They started walking. Wow, Tanner really seemed to hate Felix.

"You really can sit with us," I said. "I don't know why Tanner is being so weird." Although...he was always a little weird. "Does he not like you for some reason?"

"We've always gotten along," Felix said. "But I barely know him."

Huh.

"I can't believe you're really here."

I smiled up at him. "It's really good to see you."

"You too. But I'm really surprised to see you here of all places."

"Yeah." I sighed. "Coming back to Empire High wasn't my idea. But Jacob wanted to see the game."

"I have a lot of questions about Jacob. And who his father is. And where that father is. And where you've been. But first...I didn't mean coming to the school. I meant because of...wait...does Kennedy know?"

"I just got back to town and she was the first person I saw."

"Are you serious?" He looked over my head at the field. The game was probably about to start.

"Yeah. Come on, let's go get to our seats."

Tanner was waving us over.

I grabbed Felix's arms to pull him up the stands.

"Kennedy knows you're alive?" Felix asked as we climbed the stairs. "She knows you're here?"

I nodded. "I mean, she doesn't know where I am right this second," I said with a laugh. "I probably should have asked her to come, but I doubt she'd want to come to a football game here. You remember how awful everyone was to her here."

"Um…"

"I mean, I know it got better when we started hanging out with you. And then with Matt and the rest of the untouchables." But still. I couldn't see Kennedy wanting to come back and reminisce. She couldn't wait to go to college and get away from this school. She'd been an outcast just like me. Neither of us belonged in this world.

"Ummm…." Felix said.

I laughed. "Really, you befriending us made everything better."

He smiled at me, but it quickly faltered. "I really need to tell you something."

"What is it?" I asked as we reached our seats. There was just this tiny slice of space left on the bleacher. Presumably for me. Although if Tanner would just put his legs down and sit like a normal person there would have been plenty of room for all of us…

"Scoot over," I said.

"This is just how I sit," Tanner said.

Jacob looked over at Tanner and mimicked his pose, taking up more room too.

I laughed.

"Hey, Brooklyn! Hey, Tanner!" Penny said from behind us.

My heart starting hammering against my ribcage. Seriously, why were so many people I knew here? If Penny was here that meant James was probably here too. And if James was here then that might mean…

"This area is a little crowded," she said. "How about you join us up there?" She pointed up the bleachers to a spot where all the untouchables were seated. Except for Matt. I breathed a sigh of relief. Seeing Felix was enough today. I'd catch him up on everything. And I couldn't wait to hear about how he'd been doing.

"Hi, I'm Penny Hunter," she said and stuck out her hand for Felix.

"Felix," he said and shook her hand. "Wait, are you married to James or Rob?"

She laughed. "James. I'm guessing you guys went to school here together? I need to hear all the stories. Come on, there's plenty of room with us."

"It might be better if we stay here," Tanner said. "I guess we can squeeze Felix in."

Penny laughed. "Come on Tanner. And Jacob, Scarlett is here…"

"Scarlett!" Jacob yelled and climbed off the bench.

"So I guess you've talked to Matt?" Penny said. "We haven't heard from him. Is he…how did he take it?"

"Oh, I haven't talked to him yet. Today I just want to have a fun day with my son. I'll see Matt tomorrow."

"Umm…" Penny said. She looked out at the field and then back at me. "So you haven't spoken to him yet? Or seen him at all?"

"No, I'll see him tomorrow." I'd just said that…

"Brooklyn, I think…"

"The game's about to start!" Tanner practically shouted as he stood up. "We'll sit with you guys, just everyone stop talking. I…uh…have a splitting headache." And then he added, "This is a mess," under his breath.

I picked up Jacob so he couldn't run off without me. "Do you need some Tylenol or something, Tanner?" I asked. "I'm sure the concession stand…"

"I'm good. I just…the reveal is going to be messy now." He picked Jacob up out of my arms to carry him.

"What reveal?"

"Come with me." Tanner grabbed my hand and pulled me up the bleachers.

James and Rob looked surprised to see me. But Mason just smiled. I assumed the blonde and brunette already seated were Mason and Rob's wives. I wondered if they knew about me. I was about to say hi, but James beat me to it.

"So you've told Matt?" James asked.

"Oh…um…no, not yet."

"Mason," Tanner said. "Haven't you been talking to the guys about *things*? Like I asked you to on the drive home the other day?"

"Oh, I didn't tell them anything," Mason said. "We're just here for the homecoming game. I heard it's going to be quite entertaining."

Tanner cursed under his breath.

"Wait, are you two dating now?" Rob asked. "Brooklyn, you can do a hell of a lot better than this clown."

"No…we're not…" I started, but Rob cut me off.

"Felix is that you?" Rob walked out into the aisle to give Felix a big hug. And then he glared at Tanner.

How did Rob and Tanner know each other?

"Let's all sit down," Penny said. "The game is about to start."

"I really don't think this is a good idea," James said and locked eyes with me. "Until you talk to Matt, I think you should go."

It felt like he'd slapped me. Honestly, it felt like high school all over again. Like I wasn't good enough to sit with them. Yeah, it felt exactly like that. I started blinking fast, because I was not in high school anymore. And I wasn't going to cry just because an untouchable was being mean to me.

"You're right. Tanner and I had a seat down there. So we'll just go back…"

"I mean you shouldn't be here at all Brooklyn," James said.

Wow. Okay. I'd thought he'd changed. But who ever really changed? James was an asshole. And he'd always been an asshole. "You know, just because I couldn't pay to attend this school doesn't make me less of a student than you."

"Brooklyn that's not what I meant," James said. "I'm asking you to leave because of Matt."

"Oh, I know, I got it. You're not friends with me. None of you ever were." It was crystal clear. I just didn't know why he'd acted so happy to see me a couple days ago. He was so full of shit.

"That's not what I'm saying," James said. He stood up and I took a step back.

"Mommy, I want to sit with Scarlett." Jacob was still in Tanner's arms.

I'd move heaven and earth for my son. I'd give him anything he wanted. Just not this one thing. I didn't know what I'd been thinking. These people were toxic.

And we weren't like them. My son would not be part of this world.

"Tanner, can we please just go home?"

"But…" Tanner said.

James was making his way into the aisle. And I didn't want to hear any more insults thrown my way.

"Jacob, come here, we're leaving."

But he clung harder to Tanner's side.

Sweet boy, please.

"Brooklyn," James said and put his hand on my shoulder.

"Don't touch me."

He lifted his hand off my shoulder.

I really hated when people touched me without permission. "Jacob, come to Mommy."

He ducked under Tanner's arm.

James put his hand on my shoulder again. "Brooklyn, I just meant that Matt…"

"She asked you not to touch her, man," Felix said.

I'd forgotten how good of a friend Felix had been. He'd always had my back. Always.

James glared at him. "I'm just trying to explain that Matt…"

"I know," I said. "I get it. He's one of your best friends. I'm leaving, okay? I'll keep my distance from you and your friends. I just need a second and I won't bother you again. Tanner, please," I begged.

"That's not what I'm saying," said James. "But you're going to ruin today if you stay."

"James, you're about two seconds away from getting punched in the face," Felix said.

"Well that's definitely not going to happen," Rob said.

"Everyone calm down," Tanner said. "Before I have to subdue all of you."

Rob laughed. "Not a chance, asshole."

Mason sighed and stood up. "This honestly feels a lot like homecoming."

I didn't want anyone to fight. And Felix looked like he was serious about being two seconds away from punching James.

"She doesn't know!" Tanner yelled. "Everyone stop! She doesn't know."

The crowd started cheering. I was pretty sure the football team had started running onto the field.

"She's not here to antagonize him," Tanner said. "She doesn't know."

Know what?

"Is this going how you planned, Tanner?" Mason asked.

"You know it's not."

Mason laughed and turned to me. "So you haven't talked to Matt yet?"

I shook my head.

"I'm pretty sure James was just asking you to leave because you haven't spoken to Matt yet. He wasn't trying to be rude. But this is an important game. And Matt's the coach."

"What?" *No. Matt's here?* Oh God, James was just trying to protect his friend. He wasn't being *that* much of an asshole.

"Are you kidding me?" James asked Tanner. "Why wouldn't you tell her that?"

"Surprise," Tanner said.

But I was barely paying attention. I turned around. And there he was.

I didn't know whether to smile or cry as I watched Matt jog out onto the field after his players. He was far away. But he looked the same. Maybe his shoulders were a little wider. And his hair was cut a little shorter. I just stared. The same way I'd stared at him for so long before he'd noticed me all those years ago.

I didn't want to be in my head about what happened back in high school. But I clearly was. I'd tried so hard to shut that door. The distance made that easy. But standing here right now staring at him?

I didn't expect to feel so…hurt.

Or happy?

Maybe I was happy that he looked so happy? Sometimes happiness made your heart beat weirdly, right?

He was coaching the Empire High team. That was good. That meant he wasn't as haunted by the memories here as his friends seemed to think. He spent afternoons and weekends here. He was fine.

And I was fine.

But my heart was pounding so hard, it was all I could hear over the roar of the crowd. And my palms were all sweaty.

I took a step forward instinctively. Like I was being drawn to him.

But my foot froze on the step when I saw Kennedy run up to him. In an Empire High jersey with Matt's old number on it. Matt wrapped his arm around her shoulders as they talked to the team.

I stared at his number on her back. I stared at her smiling at him. They were a couple. Matt and Kennedy. It sounded strange in my head. Because we'd always been Matt and Brooklyn.

No, not always been. Just for a short while. So long ago, it barely even felt real. But Matt and Kennedy? That was real. I could see it.

"She's the assistant coach," Felix said. "I was trying to tell you earlier."

I nodded.

"Are you okay?" he asked.

I was fine.

Because I had to be.

I'd told Kennedy it was okay. I was happy for them. I truly was. But my heart wasn't listening to my head. It ached. It physically hurt staring at them. I was happy for them. But I don't think I wanted to see it.

I watched him turn his head and stare down at her.

She tilted her gaze up.

No, I definitely didn't want to see it. I turned away to avoid watching them kiss.

The rest of the untouchables were staring at me. Waiting to see what I'd do.

But I was fine.

Just a little cold. I probably should have grabbed a jacket like Tanner had suggested.

But I was fine.

It felt a little like I'd gotten punched in the stomach. And stabbed in the heart.

But I was definitely fine.

I felt the tear slide down my cheek a second too late.

This time I didn't flinch when James put his hand on my shoulder. He leaned down to get face to face with me. "I'm sorry. I was just worried if he saw you and didn't know you were alive...I...I was just worried."

Everyone was still staring at me.

"But I never meant you shouldn't sit with us because you didn't belong. You've always belonged beside us. And you should sit with us. I want you to sit with us. Because you are our friend. You've always been, Brooklyn. No matter what happens. We'll all always be friends."

I looked up at him and wiped the tears from my eyes.

He smiled down at me.

"Thanks, James. But I think you're right. I should probably go." I turned to get Jacob, but he was no longer in Tanner's arms. He was sitting with Scarlett and they were giggling about something. He looked so happy.

"Really," James said. "Stay."

"Come on, sis," Mason said. "We're way up here. He probably won't even see you. He's busy."

Yeah, he definitely looked busy with Kennedy. I wasn't really worried about Matt seeing me. Right now I was just worried about my heart exploding.

"You knew," I said to Tanner. "You knew and you brought me here anyway."

"Surprise," he said again. "I have a confession. Kennedy's not my best friend. Matt is."

"Yeah, I kind of figured that." I shook my head. He'd set me up. He'd planned all of this. "What is wrong with you?"

"A lot of things are wrong with him," Rob said. "But the game is starting. And not to sound rude like my brother, but it might be good if you stay a little low. Just until you talk to Matt."

I nodded and sat down behind the tallest person I could.

But they didn't really block my view.

People started cheering, but I wasn't paying attention to the game. I couldn't keep my eyes off Matt. Matt and Kennedy.

They looked happy.

They really did.

I looked down at my lap.

And as badly as I wanted to be happy for them…I wasn't. I really wasn't.

I was a hypocrite.

I was a bad friend.

But it felt like they were rubbing their happiness in my face. When I was already drowning. And it was ironic because Matt used to be the one to take away my pain. And now the sight of him just made it worse.

I swallowed down the lump in my throat.

No. I was happy for them. I was. I forced myself to smile even though it hurt. This was what I wanted. For him to be happy. That was always all I'd ever wanted.

I held my breath and counted to ten.

This was for the best.

Kennedy deserved happiness. Matt deserved happiness. And Kennedy was amazing. He couldn't find someone better.

"Mommy," Jacob said. He'd left Scarlett and climbed into my lap. "Are you okay?"

"I'm okay."

"Snuggies?"

I smiled and hugged him, peppering his face in kisses. He always knew how to cheer me up. "Look, Empire High has the ball," I said.

He turned in my lap and didn't seem to mind that I kept my arms around him. I focused on the game and not the sidelines.

Miller would have been so excited to take Jacob to his first game. And obviously, he wouldn't have chosen this particular one. But I was going to be the parent that Jacob needed me to be. I'd promised Miller to keep doing things that would have made all three of us happy.

The receiver caught the ball and ran past the bench. Kennedy threw her arms around Matt as they cheered. I heard laughter in the seats around me. Jacob was cheering too. I closed my eyes and hugged my son tight. If I closed my eyes hard enough I could pretend that Miller was beside us. That we were still happy too.

CHAPTER 36

Saturday

Brooklyn

The game dragged on. Not that it was boring. It just felt like my heart was in my throat. The Empire High Eagles were winning by three touchdowns. The game was in the bag. But I doubted I'd get Jacob to agree to leave. It wasn't even halftime yet. And he was sitting next to Scarlett laughing again.

I'd been polite. I'd met Rob's wife, Daphne. And Mason's wife, Bee. I'd put on a fake smile. I'd talked about the weather. And I'd filled Felix in on what happened.

Now I just wanted to go home.

Not home to my new house in the city. But home home. I wanted to curl up in a ball in the bed I'd shared with Miller and cry myself to sleep.

And I couldn't stop hearing his words in my head. *"I know there was someone before me. I know you still think about him sometimes."*

I looked back down at my lap. I didn't want it to be true. It couldn't be true.

I was over Matt.

I'd been over him for years.

I'd had an amazing life with Miller. I loved him so much that I physically ached. My whole body hurt. And yet...I couldn't look at Matt on the field without tears welling in the corners of my eyes. Why?

"I need you to know that I'm okay if you choose him now. Because I never want you to stop smiling."

I fiddled with my wedding band.

"Don't waste another second of your time on this earth. Will you promise me that? Do this one last thing for me?"

I wanted to be able to promise Miller I'd follow his letter. I lifted my gaze back to the field. Matt was looking up at the stands. Like he was searching for someone. Probably his friends. I ducked my head down.

Being with Matt wasn't the answer. It couldn't be.

I'd learn how to smile again on my own. Jacob and I were going to be okay. I wasn't a kid anymore. I didn't need to rely on someone to take away my pain like I had in high school. I'd needed Matt back then. He really had helped me after my uncle died. But I didn't need him now.

"I was just trying to help," Tanner said.

I purposely hadn't sat next to him. But he must have switched with someone. I honestly didn't even know who I'd been sitting next to. I was so distracted. "Trying to help how? By lying to my face?"

"It was a tiny fib."

"So do you fib a lot?"

"Not by choice." He shook his head. "We're getting sidetracked. Brooklyn, I really am sorry. I thought it would just be the two of us sitting together. And Jacob of course. And that I could explain everything as soon as we sat down."

"Explain what exactly? What are you trying to do?"

"Get you back together with your fiancé."

It felt like he'd punched me in the gut. "Matt isn't my fiancé."

"Well, technically he is. He thought you died. You never actually broke up."

I scoffed. "I'm pretty sure he feels differently."

"What on earth do you mean?"

"Are you kidding me? He's currently dating two women. One of which is a monster. And the other is *my* best friend." I gestured to the field where Matt and Kennedy were standing side by side. She was wearing his freaking jersey for goodness sakes. And yeah, we weren't in high school anymore. But that still meant something.

Tanner waved his hand through the air. "I have a fix for all that. We're already making progress."

Progress? My stomach churned. "Did you take me back to my house to try and give me some semblance of closure with my husband? Just so that I could move on with someone who isn't even available anymore? Who I no longer even know?"

He pressed his lips together.

"Seriously, what are you trying to accomplish by interfering with my mourning?"

"I believe in true love. And I think Matt..."

"I can't do this." I stood up. I needed to get Jacob.

"Brooklyn, please," he grabbed my hand.

I pulled it out of his. "If you understood true love then you'd know that Miller was mine." I could feel everyone staring and I didn't care.

"I was just trying to help you move on..."

"He *just* died. I *just* lost him." I collapsed back down on the bench. "I just lost him."

"It's been weeks, Brooklyn."

"Weeks! Not months. Not years. I mourned the loss of Matt forgetting about me for years." My voice cracked. "And I will mourn losing Miller for the rest of my fucking life."

"I know. I wasn't saying you didn't love him. I wasn't telling you not to mourn him. Or saying that you'd ever forget about your love with him. I just wanted you to have an open mind..."

"For what? To be the third girl Matt is currently dating?"

"He doesn't love them."

"Then that kills me. Because Kennedy deserves someone that loves her. She deserves the whole world."

"So do you."

"I already had it. I had it and I lost it."

"You had it twice. You're one of the lucky ones. And yes, you lost it. But only once. Matt never forgot about you, Brooklyn."

"That isn't true."

"Once a month he gets shitfaced drunk and cries himself to sleep over you."

I shook my head.

"As his best friend I know that."

"Oh, give me a break," Rob said. He leaned forward to see me. "*I'm* Matt's best friend. And we all know it. Isn't this guy the worst, Brooklyn?"

I laughed, but it came out forced. I didn't think Tanner was the worst. But I did think he was wrong about this. "Matt wasn't crying over me. He was screwing everyone he possibly could."

"People mourn in different ways. I understand the way you mourn. Matt mourned a different way. A destructive way..."

"That isn't mourning!"

"Yes it is. He was broken. He's still broken. And I think you can fix him. And he can help heal your heart."

I shook my head.

"If you didn't still have feelings for him…you'd be able to look at the field. I know you're mourning. But it's a hell of a lot easier to keep going when you're surrounded by love. Trust me. I know."

"Tanner's the worst," Rob said between coughs.

I didn't trust Tanner. Not in the slightest. But I did believe that he knew. I believed that he'd lost someone. I could see it in his eyes. He looked…haunted. It was the same way I looked when I stared at my reflection in the mirror.

"I'm not ready to move on. And I can't move on with him. He's dating…"

"Someone that isn't you. And the kind of love Matt had for you isn't replaceable. You're not replaceable, Brooklyn."

Honestly, that was one of the sweetest things anyone had ever said to me. I wanted to be mad at him. But…how could I be? He was in pain too. He was looking out for his friend. He was a good person. I just…I couldn't do this.

"I'm not feeling well," I said. It was the truth. I felt sick to my stomach. And I hated that I felt sick to my stomach. "I think Jacob and I are going to head out early."

"Just wait until halftime. And then I'll take you home. I promise."

I nodded and looked back at the field. Instead of staring at Matt and Kennedy, I focused on the weird little man handing out water on the field. I didn't understand the lederhosen. Or how it had anything to do with being an Empire High Eagle. But I was guessing he was somehow the new mascot? It was a weird choice. But he was definitely a good distraction. He'd just thrown water in a player's face.

And this small part of me wished he'd just thrown it on Kennedy instead.

CHAPTER 37

Saturday

Matt

Kennedy started screaming at the top of her lungs when Jefferson made his second field goal.

And I cheered too. But I was a little distracted. Something felt off as soon as I'd walked onto the field. I looked back in the crowd for what felt like the hundredth time.

"That was amazing!" Kennedy said and hugged Jefferson as he ran onto the sidelines.

He tore off his helmet and beamed at her.

I looked back at the stands. It was packed today. And those were the worst days. Where I'd see a flash of blonde hair and think I'd seen Brooklyn. I wasn't sure her ghost would ever stop haunting me.

I loved Kennedy. I knew I did. I knew it was okay to move on. But Tanner's stupid words were in my head. And talking about Brooklyn more openly recently...it was like she was becoming less of a ghost.

It didn't make any sense.

I was probably losing my mind.

But whenever I turned back to the field, I felt the little hairs on the back of my neck rise. It was like I could feel her. Like she was up there cheering for me.

And if I closed my eyes, I could picture our homecoming. When I made a fool of myself during the parade and sang to her. I could feel her all around me.

"Did you see that?" Kennedy asked.

I opened my eyes. "Sorry, see what?"

"That epic field goal! It was like 50 yards. I think that's a school record!"

I smiled. "It was pretty epic." We were freaking killing the other team. And normally I'd be excited. But again...I just felt...off.

"Eyes on the ball!" Nigel yelled from his spot next to the water cooler. "Defense! That'll move the chains!"

None of it made any sense, but I knew he'd been studying the game. And the players seemed to be very entertained by him.

"Blitz!" Nigel screamed. "Hut, hut, hut!"

Jefferson laughed.

I wished I found Nigel as distracting as everyone else. But all I could think about was what Kennedy needed to tell me.

"Do you know if Felix came?" I asked. Seriously...why had I just mentioned him?

"Um...no, I haven't heard from him since dinner on Thursday. I told you that on the way over."

"Right."

"Are you feeling okay?" she asked.

"Yeah, I just...need to use the bathroom I think."

"You think? Do you need to go now? It's almost halftime. I can handle things."

"No, it's not like an emergency or anything."

She laughed. "I never said it was."

I looked back at the stands. Maybe someone was watching me? I knew Mr. Pruitt claimed there were no hitmen or hitwomen. But Poppy said the opposite. I continued to stare into the stands. It didn't feel like someone watching me though. I closed my eyes for a second. It felt like it had the night I went to Kennedy's and she wouldn't let me up to her apartment. Like something had shifted around me. And standing here was giving me major déjà vu again.

When I opened my eyes, I almost expected to see Brooklyn staring back at me. I felt her more than ever. I knew it was just the fall air and the game messing with my head. I tried to dismiss the thought, but I couldn't shake it.

"Tight end! Lateral!" Nigel screamed.

I ignored him as my eyes scanned the crowd.

"Touchback! Ice the kicker!"

"You always do that," Kennedy said.

"We rarely ice the other team's kicker," I said.

Kennedy laughed. "I'm talking about staring at the stands. Are you looking for someone?"

"No." I wasn't. I just liked seeing Brooklyn's ghost sometimes. I think I liked that thoughts of her still haunted me. As much as I wanted to move on. I felt closest to her here. "I was looking for Tanner. He usually stops by before the game."

"All your friends were coming, right?" She looked behind her.

"Yeah, they're near the top left." But that wasn't why I'd been looking in the stands. I think homecoming would always be the hardest game for me.

"Oh, well, Tanner is sitting with them," Kennedy said. "So you don't have anything to worry about…" her voice trailed off and then she immediately turned back around. Her face had grown pale.

"What's wrong?"

She covered her mouth like something was about to spill out. And then she shook her head. "Um…nothing.

I…think I have whatever you have. I need to go to the bathroom."

"Can it wait?"

She looked back at the stands and then covered her mouth.

"Kennedy, is your stomach alright?"

"Yeah. I just…"

"Is this about what you want to tell me after the game? Just tell me now."

"I…I…" there were tears in her eyes.

"Just tell me." I grabbed both her shoulders so that she'd really look at me. "Please, Kennedy. Just tell me the truth." I knew she liked Felix. I could tell. And I'd survive if she chose to be with him. I was used to being alone for the past sixteen years. I just wanted her to fucking tell me the truth.

"Fumble!" Nigel yelled. "Muff!"

I looked over at him. He was staring right at me. Yeah, I'd felt like I'd muffed all this up too.

CHAPTER 38

Saturday

Brooklyn

It looked like Matt was about to kiss Kennedy again. But he just stared down at her. I remembered him staring at me.

I'd wanted to forget.

I'd tried to forget.

But it was hard when Matt was right in front of me. Looking at someone else the way he used to look at me.

My heart was already broken. How could it keep breaking any more?

I tried to smile. When I was a teenager I'd gotten good at smiling through the pain.

But it was like Tanner could tell it was fake. He grabbed my hand and squeezed it.

"It's going to be okay," he said.

He didn't know that. And I was almost positive he was wrong.

"I shouldn't have come back here," I said. Being at Empire High somehow made me feel like no time had passed. I felt like a teenager all over again in this stadium. I felt...small. Invisible.

The ref blew the whistle for halftime.

"Ready to go?" I asked.

Tanner nodded. "Right after the halftime show. But I'm going to apologize in advance. I...um...did something."

"What did you do?"

He exhaled slowly. "It's a surprise."

"I swear to God, Tanner."

He smiled. "Matt told me a lot about you, you know. About how when you two first met it wasn't easy. But that all changed at homecoming. And I was hoping maybe I could jump start your feelings if…"

His voice trailed off as the homecoming parade started. The first float appeared and music blared through the speakers. My Dirty Little Secret by You're An American Reject.

If my feelings hadn't already been all twisted up, this definitely would have done it. I remembered Matt singing for me with some of his teammates. Confessing his love for me. Promising to never keep me a secret again.

But he was standing on the field with Kennedy.

And I was still in love with Miller.

And all of this was so fucked up.

Especially my heart. My heart was really fucked up.

A few of the players had jumped up on the float and had started dancing. The same weird hip thrusting moves that Matt had done 16 years ago.

Tanner had recreated it.

Except…it wasn't a declaration from Matt. I stared at him on the field. He looked just as bewildered as I felt.

He didn't want this.

Miller's note had gotten in my head a bit.

And so had Tanner's words.

But Matt didn't want me. And I was too broken to want him.

"I need some air," I said.

"We're outside," Tanner said.

"I meant I need to use the bathroom. Can you please just watch Jacob for a second?" I needed to get out of this stadium. I just needed to be as far away from these memories as possible. Because they still hurt. They still hurt so fucking much.

Sixteen years ago, this song had meant the world to me. Matt had meant the world to me.

I got up and started running down the bleachers. A part of me wanted to run toward Matt. But I knew that would be a mistake. We were both in love with different people. And we weren't in high school anymore.

CHAPTER 39

Saturday

Matt

The ref blew the whistle for halftime. Normally we went back to the locker room to make adjustments, but we were winning by a landslide. So I let the players stay out to watch the parade.

I was still staring down at Kennedy when the music started blaring through the speakers. No, not just any music. My Dirty Little Secret by You're An American Reject.

My hands were still on Kennedy's arms as I turned to look at the float. But instead I caught a glimpse of a ghost.

But it wasn't like the other ghosts I saw.

I didn't just imagine Brooklyn's face for a second.

It wasn't just a flash of blonde hair that disappeared as quickly as it had come.

She was there.

Racing down the steps of the bleachers.

"Matt," Kennedy said.

But I didn't hear her. My eyes were glued on Brooklyn. But it couldn't be her. My heart started racing.

"I'm so sorry," Kennedy said. "I wanted to tell you she was back. I swear I wanted to."

I let go of her arms. A part of me didn't believe my eyes. But that confirmed it. The blonde in the crowd wasn't a ghost. It was her. It was Brooklyn.

"You knew." I took a step away from Kennedy. "You knew she was alive this whole time and you let me..." *What the fuck?*

"No, not this whole time. She showed up last week..."

But I wasn't listening.

"Matt." She put her hand on my arm but I shook it off. "I'm sorry, she asked me not to say anything. I..."

I still wasn't listening. The song was blaring through the speakers. And it was like I'd been transported back in time.

Staring at the girl I loved. But she wasn't staring at me.

I started pushing through the crowd.

"Matt!" Kennedy yelled.

I could see Brooklyn up ahead. She was heading to the school. The crowd was all around me. I couldn't get through. "Brooklyn!" I screamed at the top of my lungs. "Brooklyn!"

But she didn't hear me.

I saw her run into the doors of Empire High.

CHAPTER 40

Saturday

Brooklyn

I thought about going to the restrooms, but the line was a mile long. So I kept running. And running. Until I reached the doors of Empire High.

I flung one open and ran inside.

And I was hit with more memories.

Everything was almost exactly the same.

I felt this fear in my chest about Isabella.

I remembered my uncle's smile.

I remembered laughing with Kennedy and Felix.

I remembered holding Matt's hand. Kissing him. Loving him. God, I'd loved that boy so much.

I kept running.

And I had no idea why, but I ran into the auditorium. The door closed behind me with a thud and darkness surrounded me.

Matt had kissed me here. He'd stolen my first kiss. The same way he'd stolen my heart.

And I'd tried to forget about him. I'd tried so fucking hard. And for a while I had. I thought I was over him. But as soon as I'd seen him, it had felt like a knife was in my chest. Like he'd just forgotten about me all over again.

I'd fallen in love with him when I was broken. I'd just lost my mom. And then I lost Uncle Jim too. I'd been so lost.

And in this stupid way I thought he'd saved me.

And I didn't understand how I could still feel this way.

Because I'd loved Miller. I'd loved him with my whole heart.

Miller told me I was strong.

But I didn't feel strong. I felt like a fucking mess. I was standing in an empty auditorium crying my eyes out over two men. Tanner's words echoed around me. *"You had it twice. You're one of the lucky ones. And yes, you lost it. But only once. Matt never forgot about you, Brooklyn."*

I was the only one who recounted things differently with Matt. Did that mean I was wrong? Really wrong about everything that happened?

What if he had been unhappy?

What if he had waited for me for 16 years?

What if he did still love me?

I just want you to be happy. And safe. And I want the same for Jacob. This isn't easy for me to say, but I need you to know that I'm okay if you choose him now. Because I never want you to stop smiling.

How was I supposed to keep smiling when I was drowning? I didn't know how to keep going. I wasn't strong enough.

The auditorium door swung open, leaving a trail of light for one moment.

Matt was standing there. For just one second our eyes locked. Before the door closed and there was only darkness.

CHAPTER 41

Saturday

Matt

"Matt?"

A part of me still felt like I was chasing a ghost. But that was her voice. Brooklyn's voice. I never thought I'd ever hear her voice again.

"Matt?" she said again, and this time there was a little fear in her voice. It reminded me of the first time I'd met her in here. I hadn't meant to scare her back then. I'd just…wanted her alone. I'd wanted her all to myself. I'd wanted to know that I wasn't too late to have her first kiss.

I felt the tears sliding down my cheeks.

This wasn't real.

This couldn't be real.

It was like I was back in time when I reached out and my fingers touched her skin.

Her exhale was sharp.

She felt it too, right? That it felt like a million years had passed, yet no time at all? There was the same electricity between us. And I was suddenly that same boy I was in high school. Standing in the darkness with the girl I was completely infatuated with. And there were thoughts running through my head, but I couldn't focus on any of them. The only thing that mattered was that she was here. She was breathing. Brooklyn was alive. And nothing had changed. Because she was still mine.

"Matt," her voice cracked.

How many times had she said my name just like that? With that same pain? I knew there'd be tears on her cheeks before I even touched the wetness with my fingertips. It had been 16 years, but I still knew her. I knew when she needed me. I'd really fucking needed her too.

CHAPTER 42

Saturday

Brooklyn

Matt's face had grown blurry to me over the years. I couldn't remember his laughter. And I'd forgotten how he smelled. But I remembered as soon as the doors closed.

He smelled like cinnamon.

The same aroma I'd surrounded myself with for years when I took up baking. I hadn't even realized it.

He'd been with me this whole time.

Baking had made me feel close to him.

Because I still fucking loved him.

And I hated myself for it. I hated that he still held a piece of my heart. I hated that Miller had known. I hated that Miller had to put it in a fucking goodbye letter.

"This isn't easy for me to say, but I need you to know that I'm okay if you choose him now."

The guilt was heavy on my chest.

But when Matt touched the side of my face?

When he wiped away my tears?

Everything subsided. Like his touch took away my pain.

It was like no time had passed. Like it was still me and him against the world. He'd always been able to make me feel better.

And I knew how to smile again. I knew how, if even just for a moment. I just needed to feel like I wasn't drowning anymore.

I stood on my tiptoes and kissed him.

And time stood still.

His lips were salty and I wasn't sure if it was from my tears or if he was crying too.

But then he kissed me back. And suddenly nothing else mattered.

I just wanted him closer.

I wanted more.

Take away my pain. Please just make it stop.

It was like he could read my mind. His hands slid to my ass as he hoisted my legs around his waist. My back slammed against the wall.

Each frantic kiss made me feel less. Yet somehow more.

More. I buried my fingers in his hair and breathed him in. *More. Please help me.*

I wasn't drowning anymore. I was just drowning in him. I couldn't help the moan that escaped my lips. I could feel his hardness pressing against me. And I remembered how good that felt. There was nothing in the world plaguing my thoughts when he was deep inside of me.

"More." I hadn't even realized I'd said the words out loud.

But he reached for the button on my jeans and I didn't stop him. I just kissed him harder. It only took me a second to unwrap my legs from around his waist and discard my jeans. His lips never parted from mine. He lifted me back up.

I had a million questions for him as he slammed my back against the wall again.

I was sure he had a million more for me.

But right now nothing else mattered.

I heard his pants unzip.

It was all wrong.

But it was also perfect.

I didn't care if someone could walk in and see us. For just one fucking second I needed to stop feeling like my life had stopped. Like it should have been me in that car.

He groaned as he thrust inside me.

It felt like my heart was ripping out of my chest.

Yet it felt like coming home. I held him tighter. It felt so much like coming home.

And I just needed more.

I gripped the back of his neck harder as he slammed into me again. And again.

Please don't stop. Please don't ever stop.

I'd only meant to kiss him. But this was a hell of a lot better to numb the pain.

All I could focus on was the building pleasure. And if I closed my eyes tight, I could just pretend we were back in high school. And he'd pulled me into the auditorium because he loved me. Just as much as I loved him.

How could I feel so numb, yet feel everything all at once?

Please don't stop.

Matt's hands wandered all over my body. My breasts. My ass. His fingers dug into my waist as he slammed into me harder.

I wrapped my legs tighter around his waist. And I didn't even realized I'd bit his lip until I tasted the blood. I wanted to touch him everywhere. And nowhere at all. But my hands were more willing than my head. I ran my fingers up underneath his shirt. It had been a lifetime since I'd touched him. Since I was wrapped up in him. His abs were more defined. The muscles on his back larger. All of him just felt bigger and more power-ful. Like he was more capable of carrying all my pain for me.

A moan fell from my lips as he thrust even harder inside of me. God, I'd missed this feeling. Of being his.

I was glad the lights were off. It was easier to push away the feelings of love. Or whatever the fuck we had. And focus on the feeling of him inside of me. Of his fingers on my skin. His tongue swirling against mine.

I felt drunk. Drunk on him. Numb to the pain in my chest.

CHAPTER 43

Saturday

Matt

I pushed her bra up, exposing her breasts to me.

She was here.

I broke our kiss for the first time to pull her nipple into my mouth.

She was mine.

I was in fucking heaven. And I was seconds away from exploding inside of her. Seconds away from losing control.

But who was I kidding? I'd lost control as soon as I saw her in the crowd.

I slammed into her harder as my tongue swirled around her other nipple.

I hadn't spoken a single word to her. But it didn't matter. She was alive. She was here. And she was seconds away from coming around my cock.

How many nights had I dreamt of this?

How many nights had I prayed she was still alive?

That she'd come back to me?

I tangled my fingers in her hair as I kissed the side of her neck.

This didn't feel real. I kept waiting to wake up. To reach out and feel the empty sheets beside me.

Her fingers dug into the back of my neck, drawing me back to the present. And I felt her pulsing around me. I heard her moaning my name. Practically a whisper. Like a distant memory.

Her pussy clenched around me. She felt the same. We felt the same. God, that felt so fucking good.

I slammed into her once more before I lost control. I was holding her so tightly that I was probably hurting her. But she didn't tell me to stop. I groaned as I came inside of her. Again. And again.

My chest rose and fell as her frantic kisses stopped.

The silence stretched between us as I untangled my fingers from her hair. And suddenly it didn't feel like a dream. The silence felt heavy. And the longer she didn't say anything, the heavier it got.

Where the fuck had she been for 16 years?

Why had she shown up here?

Why had she run to the auditorium?

Why was she crying?

Why did she kiss me instead of saying anything at all?

As I pulled out of her, I felt the metal pressed against my back for the first time. A metal band on her left hand. How had I not felt it before?

I took a step away from her.

Suddenly everything made sense.

What the fuck had I just done? I was dating Kennedy. I...I didn't know the woman in front of me. She sounded the same. She felt the same. But this wasn't the girl I'd fallen in love with. The girl I'd fallen in love with wouldn't have disappeared for 16 years. And she certainly wouldn't be wearing a wedding ring. She'd promised me all her firsts.

"What the fuck, Brooklyn?" They were the first words I'd spoken to her in 16 years. I'd regretted my last words to her back in high school. But I couldn't seem to find any better words right this second. *What the fuck?!*

"Matt…"

I took another step away from her. What had I just done? What the fuck had I just done? "You're married?"

"Matt, I…" her voice broke.

"I have no idea who the fuck you are. But you're definitely not the girl I knew." I pushed out of the doors of the auditorium. Hating my words. Hating myself. I turned around to go back in, but I took a step back instead. And another.

She was married.

I'd fucking kept my promises to her.

And she'd ruined my fucking life.

CHAPTER 44

Saturday

Brooklyn

Are you kidding me?

I'm not the girl he knew?

That was all he had to say to me? After all these years?

He didn't even give me a chance to explain. I just needed a few minutes to tell him what had happened. To have a conversation.

But he just walked away, like I meant nothing. And hadn't I known that all along? That I never meant anything to him?

I felt my tears falling as my back slid down against the wall. My butt hit the ground and I pulled my knees into my chest as I cried.

I'd done what Miller said.

I'd tried.

I'm sorry, Miller.

My sobs echoed in the empty auditorium.

I hated that Miller was right. That I still had feelings for Matt. That after all these years, he'd still had a piece of my heart.

And it was all so…dumb. Matt no longer loved me. I knew that. And I'd clung to him anyway.

I buried my face in my hands.

How could a broken heart break again? How was that possible? Weren't the broken unbreakable?

I cried harder, hugging my knees tighter to my chest.

I never should have kissed Matt. I never should have asked him for more. Because I didn't want it. I'd made a mistake. I wanted nothing from him. Ever again.

No.

Never.

Nunca.

Fuck you, Matthew Caldwell.

WHAT'S NEXT?

Matt and Brooklyn finally met back up!

But they still have a lot to talk about. Like the fact that
Brooklyn has a son. How is Matt going to react to Ja-
cob?
Find out soon in Book 7!

While you wait, see what Matt was thinking when he
first met Brooklyn back in high school.

To get your free copy of Matt's point-of-view, go to:

www.ivysmoak.com/ehh-pb

A NOTE FROM IVY

Thank you all for trusting me to tell this story straight from my heart. And for going on this crazy Empire High journey with me.

If there's one thing I know, it's that grief takes time. And a Miller sized hole in your heart? That's a lot of grief. I know you were probably hoping that Brooklyn bumped into Matt right away. But Brooklyn needed time. And I just needed more time too.

I hope you laughed just as much as you cried. I hope you wanted to throw your book a few times. And scream at the characters. But most of all…I hope you're excited to see what happens next.

Because The End is coming. It's going to be so hard to write those words for these characters. But there is one very important question that needs answers:

Who will Matt choose?

- Poppy?
- Kennedy?
- Or Brooklyn?

It's finally time for a happily ever after in the next book!

Ivy Smoak

Ivy Smoak
Wilmington, DE
www.ivysmoak.com

ABOUT THE AUTHOR

Ivy Smoak is the USA Today and Wall Street Journal bestselling author of *The Hunted Series*. Her books have sold over 3 million copies worldwide.

When she's not writing, you can find Ivy binge watching too many TV shows, taking long walks, playing outside, and generally refusing to act like an adult. She lives with her husband in Delaware.

Facebook: IvySmoakAuthor
Instagram: @IvySmoakAuthor
Goodreads: IvySmoak

Recommend *Homecoming* for your next book club!

Book club questions available at:
www.ivysmoak.com/bookclub